THE RED TIDE

Further Titles by Christopher Nicole from Severn House

Black Majesty Series

BOOK ONE: BLACK MAJESTY
BOOK TWO: WILD HARVEST

The Dawson Family Saga

BOOK ONE: DAYS OF WINE AND ROSES?
BOOK TWO: THE TITANS
BOOK THREE: RESUMPTION
BOOK FOUR: THE LAST BATTLE

The McGann Family Saga

BOOK ONE: OLD GLORY
BOOK TWO: THE SEA AND THE SAND
BOOK THREE:IRON SHIPS, IRON MEN
BOOK FOUR: WIND OF DESTINY
BOOK FIVE:RAGING SUN, SEARING SKY
BOOK SIX: THE PASSION AND THE GLORY

BLOODY SUNRISE
CARIBEE
THE FRIDAY SPAY
HEROES
QUEEN OF PARIS
SHIP WITH NO NAME
THE SUN AND THE DRAGON
THE SUN ON FIRE

The Russian Quartet

BOOK ONE: THE SEEDS OF POWER
BOOK TWO: THE MASTERS
BOOK THREE:THE RED TIDE

THE RED TIDE

Christopher Nicole

This first world edition published in Great Britain 1995 by
SEVERN HOUSE PUBLISHERS LTD of
9–15 High Street, Sutton, Surrey SM1 1DF.
First published in the USA 1996 by
SEVERN HOUSE PUBLISHERS INC of
595 Madison Avenue, New York, NY 10022.

British Library Cataloguing in Publication Data
Nicole, Christopher
  The Red Tide
  I. Title
  823.914 [F]

  ISBN 0-7278-4850-X

Typeset by Hewer Text Composition Services, Edinburgh.
Printed and bound in Great Britain by
T. J. Press (Padstow) Ltd, Padstow, Cornwall.

CONTENTS

'The call of the running tide
Is a wild call and a clear call that may not be denied.'
John Masefield

Part One

Twilight of the Gods

'But came the tide, and made my pains his prey.'
Edmund Spenser

THE BOLUGAYEVSKI FAMILY

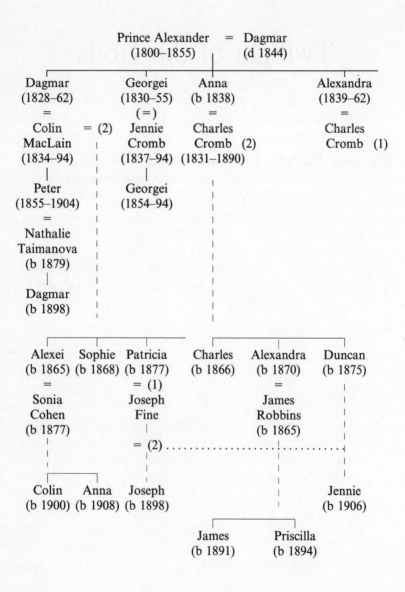

Prince Alexander = Dagmar
(1800–1855)   (d 1844)

Dagmar
(1828–62)
=
Colin = (2)
MacLain
(1834–94)
|
Peter
(1855–1904)
=
Nathalie
Taimanova
(b 1879)
|
Dagmar
(b 1898)

Georgei
(1830–55)
(=)
Jennie
Cromb
(1837–94)
|
Georgei
(1854–94)

Anna
(b 1838)
=
Charles
Cromb (2)
(1831–1890)

Alexandra
(1839–62)
=
Charles
Cromb (1)

Alexei   Sophie   Patricia
(b 1865) (b 1868) (b 1877)
=   = (1)
Sonia   Joseph
Cohen   Fine
(b 1877) |
                    = (2) . . . .

Charles   Alexandra   Duncan
(b 1866)   (b 1870)   (b 1875)
           =
           James
           Robbins
           (b 1865)

Colin   Anna   Joseph
(b 1900) (b 1908) (b 1898)

Jennie
(b 1906)

James   Priscilla
(b 1891)   (b 1894)

Chapter One

Death of a Strong Man

"Please inform the ladies," said Prince Alexei Bolugayevski, "that there is every possibility we shall be late." But he smiled as he spoke, and ruffled his son's thick black hair. Forty-six years old, Alexei Bolugayevski was in the prime of life. He stood six feet two inches in his socks, and if over the years he had put on a good deal of weight, he was still a fine figure of a man, especially when, as tonight, he was wearing the white full dress uniform of a general in the Russian Army. His complexion was fair as was his graying hair; his features were big and handsome; he exuded both confidence and forcefulness. No one would have supposed he was not Russian at all, but born of English parents.

His son, eleven years old in this autumn of 1911, did not in the least look like his father.

He had been named Colin after his famous grandfather, the first English Prince Bolugayevski. This Colin had the small features and dark hair of his mother. Alexei did not love him any the less for that, as even after twelve years of marriage he still adored his wife. He foresaw problems ahead, of course. Count Colin Bolugayevski was the undoubted heir to the Bolugayevski title and estates. But he was also half-Jewish. No one had yet raised this potentially prickly point. Russia was in a state

3

of such turmoil that Tsar Nicholas II needed all the loyal boyars he could find to sustain him, and nowadays Prince Bolugayevski was counted amongst those props of the throne. Tonight would see the final act of reconciliation between himself and the Tsar. He faced the door as the ladies emerged; they were staying in an hotel as the Bolugayevskis did not maintain a palace in Kiev; they seldom visited the capital of the Ukraine. On this occasion they had been commanded to do so.

The Princess Sonia came first. She would have deferred to her aunt-in-law, but Anna Bolugayevska was always a stickler for protocol, and a princess had to have precedence over a countess. Alexei's eyes shone as he gazed at his wife. Much of Sonia Bolugayevska's background still remained a mystery to him. He had no wish to know whether she had ever actually indulged in any of the acts of terrorism of which she had been accused, found guilty, and sentenced to exile in Siberia. Neither did he wish to know in detail what she had suffered, either at the hands of the Okhrana, the Tsar's secret police, or at the hands of her guards and fellow inmates in Irkutsk. That part of her life had officially been forgotten. That she *had* suffered, dreadfully, was apparent by her slight limp, for she had lost two toes on her left foot to frostbite during her escape from exile into a Siberian winter. But her beauty was undiminished. Sonia was thirty-four years old. She was tall, but although twice a mother – their three-year-old daughter Anna had been left on the family estate of Bolugayen in the care of her nurse – she remained slightly built; for this state occasion she wore her magnificent curling black hair in a somewhat tight pompadour. Her features were exquisitely carved, and dominated by her huge black eyes, which conveyed the essential animation of her character. Her gown was deep red, and her jewellery mainly rubies and diamonds.

But even Sonia's perfection was subdued by the presence of the woman who followed her. Anna Bolugayevska

4

was seventy-two years old. In her youth she had been the greatest beauty in Russia, and her sexual adventures, and misadventures, had become legends. In Boston she was still known as Mrs Charles Cromb, widow of the millionaire shipowner. But she preferred to live in Russia, where she had been born and bred, and to pay occasional visits to the United States to be with her son and daughter and grandchildren.

Equally, she travelled once a year to England to be with her other son and his wife, and their children.

Duncan Cromb's wife was also a Bolugayevska, and indeed, Anna's niece. But the Bolugayevskis had never paid much attention to small matters such as incest.

Nowadays, Anna constantly reminded everyone that her adventuring was done; it had come to an end during her shattering experiences in Port Arthur in 1904, when the Manchurian seaport had fallen to the Japanese. But she moved as vigorously as ever. Her hair, always a pale yellow, so that the fact that it was now entirely white was hardly noticeable, was worn in a huge, loose pompadour; her figure, maturely voluptuous, was sheathed in her blue gown, and she wore matching sapphires and diamonds. She glittered, in a way no other woman Alexei had ever known had quite equalled. Now she snorted as she watched her nephew pacing up and down. "*Tsar Sultan*," she remarked disparagingly. "One simply must be late for Rimski-Korsakov."

"We are attending the Tsar, Aunt Anna," Alexei reminded her. "Not Rimski-Korsakov."

"Is it true Sophie will be there?" Sonia asked, having kissed Colin and sent him off to bed with the nurse.

"I'm afraid she probably will," Alexei said.

"With her friend, of course," Anna remarked.

"That too. Kiev is their back yard. Now, are we ready?"

It was a mid-September evening, and still warm in the

south; the Bolugayevskis drove to the opera house in an open carriage. Alexei actually owned an automobile, because of his interest in all things new, but that too was on Bolugayen: one did not, in any event, ride to the opera in an automobile. The ladies wore fur jackets, but mainly to conceal their *décolletages* from the crowds which were always present to watch the aristocracy at play. The distance was not great, and then there were even more crowds. But these were controlled by almost as many policemen. Russia was still seething with unhappiness and discontent. The nation's morale had been shattered by their defeat, six years previously at the hands of Japan. No one was quite sure how such a catastrophe had happened. Those, like Alexei, who had been in the front line in Manchuria, remembered the frightening shortages of shells and bullets which had negated their every attempt at an offensive. Even he suspected that there had been corruption at home, causing those shortages. The peasantry which made up the vast bulk of the Russian population had no doubt of it.

The trauma of the peace, with Russia totally defeated for the first time in three hundred years, had been accentuated a year later by the great famine. A very cold winter had been followed by a very wet spring, and almost everywhere the harvest had failed. It had been estimated that more than ten million people had died of starvation. Alexei, with his carefully controlled reserves of stored grain, had been able to avoid such a catastrophe on the family estate of Bolugayen, but he had had to employ a lot of men, and use some forcefully unpleasant methods, to keep Bolugayen from being overrun by hordes of people in search of food.

And the famine had been followed, inevitably, by one of the worst outbreaks of cholera ever recorded, which had swept through the country and caused more than another million deaths. It had been at its peak here in the Ukraine, only the previous year, and the Tsar's decision to attend the opening of the Kiev Opera House was intended to show the people that the royal family was not afraid of the plague in its determination to do its duty. But it was a sobering reflection that there could not be a single person in the watching throng who had not, in the last couple of years, lost at least one close relative to either starvation or disease.

Like all the Russian aristocracy, Alexei searched his mind for a solution to the unending ills of his adopted country. He was becoming increasingly aware that the Tsar, so handsome and apparently debonair and determined, was in reality the weakest of men, who changed his mind from one meeting with his ministers to the next, and who, worse, was nowadays over-preoccupied with the health of the Tsarevich. No one knew precisely what was the matter with the seven-year-old heir to the throne. It was a closely-guarded secret, but it was rumoured that he suffered from some congenital illness which might place the very existence of the dynasty in peril: he had only sisters. But since the great famine, Nicholas II had taken at least one very important step: he had at last chosen a talented prime minister. Alexei caught sight of Peter Stolypin, greeting the rich and famous who were attending this opening night of the Kiev Opera House.

Stolypin wore the conventional beard and moustache, and a smiling, confident face. He knew his measures, which involved allotting a great deal of land owned by the boyars to the peasants while at the same time dealing rigorously with any disidents or would-be terrorists, were working, even if they had brought him much hatred and the assassination of his favourite daughter by a bomb intended for him. But he felt he could count on the support of the liberal-minded Prince Bolugayevski.

Bolugayen had itself been called upon to sacrifice several million acres, yet he considered the Prince his friend, even if, like all upper-class Russians, he could not approve of Alexei's choice of a wife. He clasped Alexei's hand. "It is good of you to come. I know his majesty will be pleased."

The two men made a considerable contrast, as Alexei remained clean-shaven. But now the Prime Minister was bowing over Sonia's hand. "Your Highness." And then smiling at Anna. "Your Excellency."

Anna sniffed. She did not like Peter Stolypin, simply because she refused to like any man, or woman, who attempted to interfere with the family or the family's wealth. "Is all well?" Alexei asked, quietly.

"How can it be otherwise?" Stolypin replied. "I do believe there are more policemen in that crowd than spectators. But come inside." He escorted them into the crowded foyer, and drew Alexei aside as the ladies were divested of their coats by anxious flunkies. "No, Prince Alexei. All is not well. Tell me, have you ever heard the name Rasputin?"

"Oh, indeed. He is the wild holy man from deepest Siberia, who is currently the social lion of St Petersburg. When we were there in the spring, it seemed no one was speaking of anything else."

"What did they tell you of him?"

"I really wasn't very interested, Peter Arkedevich. I gather he holds meetings, or seances, or whatever, which are attended by half the titled ladies in Russia."

"Do you have any idea what goes on at these meetings?"

"Should I?"

"I can tell you, Alexei Colinovich, that as far as I can gather from the Okhrana, there is a good deal of indecency. Trouble is, not even the Okhrana can actually get an agent into his apartment. They have tried, but he seems able to sniff them out and send them packing."

Alexei was frowning. "What sort of indecency?"

"Most of it is unmentionable. There is a rumour, for

8

instance, that one of this 'holy man's' pleasures is to be bathed, by his guests."

"Are you serious? We are talking of titled ladies, from what I have heard. I cannot believe that."

"Neither can I. But some people do. However, that is not the point. If the noble ladies of Russia choose to debase themselves to this monk, that is their business. What is serious is that this fellow has managed to worm his way into the royal family."

Alexei glanced at where Anna and Sonia were waiting, Anna somewhat impatiently, while the other people in the foyer were all clearly interested in the tête-à-tête between the Prime Minister and the prince.

None of them could go up to their boxes or take their seats until the arrival of the Tsar. And Stolypin wanted to confide. "It seems," he went on, "that Rasputin is the only man who can alleviate the attacks of severe pain which from time to time afflict the Tsarevich."

"What exactly is the matter with the boy?"

Stolypin sighed. "What I will tell you must be in the strictest confidence."

"Then why tell me at all?"

"Because I have an idea you may be able to help."

"Me?"

"Listen! The Tsarevich suffers from haemophilia." Alexei stared at him with his mouth open. "You know what that is?" Stolypin asked.

"His blood will not clot."

"Quite. It is an hereditary disease, apparently, which is transmitted in the female line, usually skipping a generation, but is only suffered by males. Thus her majesty has transmitted it to her son, although she does not suffer it herself. Presumably she inherited it from Victoria of England, her grandmother."

"But if that is true . . ." Alexei said slowly.

"Quite. If he bleeds, often internally, every time he is bruised, there is almost no possibility of the Tsarevich

9

surviving to grow to manhood. Certainly without the greatest care. This is where Rasputin comes in. He can alleviate the pain, even end the attacks."

"Well," Alexei said. "I suppose there is some good in all of us."

"There is no good in this charlatan," Stolypin said.

"But if he can cure pain . . ."

"I suspect he uses some form of mesmerism. From all acounts he has a dominating personality. The important thing is that he spends a good deal of time, either at the Winter Palace or in Tsarskoye Selo, with the royal family. He is allowed the most unlimited access, not only to the Tsarevich, but to the Tsaritsa and the grand duchesses. People are beginning to talk. And do more than talk. Look at this." He took a postcard from his inside breast pocket. "Don't flash it about, for God's sake."

Cautiously, Alexei took the piece of cardboard, gazed at a crude drawing, of a full-bearded man, wearing a monk's habit, seated, with a woman on his lap. The woman was naked from the waist up, her breasts carefully accentuated . . . and she wore a crown. "Surely this is treason?"

"Of course it is. But these are circulating throughout Petersburg and Moscow. Oh, we have located a couple of the presses and closed them down, but others spring up like mushrooms."

"Has the Tsar seen this?"

"I have shown it to him. He was appalled. But he will not take the simple solution: get rid of Rasputin."

"But if this fellow can really cure the Tsarevich . . ."

"Of course he cannot cure the Tsarevich. As I have said, he is a charlatan, relying as much on hypnosis as any knowledge of medicine. I have this on the authority of Dr Botkin, the Tsarevich's personal physician. Listen, Prince Alexei: have a talk with the Tsar."

"Me? I have been virtually in disgrace these past few years."

"I know that. But as he asked for you to come here

tonight he is obviously seeking a public reconciliation. I know he trusts you, understands that your . . . what shall I say? . . . misbehaviour? That it was purely to save your sister. Now he wants you on his side. And you are not one of the Petersburg crowd of sycophants and hangers-on. He knows your judgement is unbiased."

"What do you want me to do?"

"I want you to persuade him to get rid of Rasputin. For the sake of us all."

"Well . . ."

"Alexei!" Anna said severely, coming up to them. "You simply cannot talk politics at the opera. It is most rude. In any event, Sophie is here. Aren't you going to greet her?"

Alexei gave the Prime Minister a quick smile, and followed his aunt to the other side of the foyer, where two women were discarding their coats. The Countess Sophie Bolugayevska was his sister, and thus, like him, purely English in blood, the daughter of Prince Colin and Jennie Cromb. But in many ways she had become the most Russian of the entire family. Three years younger than himself, at forty-three she had allowed her good looks to dissipate into heaviness, and wore her yellow hair loose, as if she were a girl and a virgin. As perhaps she still was, so far as Alexei knew. She had long ago turned her back on the plans her family had had for her, both in terms of marriage and socially and had asserted her independence and her sexual preferences by living openly with the Countess Grabowska on her Ukraine estate. Janine Grabrowska was with her now; the two women were inseparable. Janine, at fifty, was as elegant as ever. She greeted Alexei with a warm smile. Sophie's was more tentative. "I had heard you were coming to Kiev for this occasion, Your Highness," Janine said, and gave a brief bow to Sonia. "Your Highness." She had not previously met the Princess. Now she smiled at

11

Anna. "Your Excellency, how good to see you looking so well."

Anna ignored her to address Sophie. "You are not taking enough exercise."

"Well, really, aunt," Sophie said. "I live a very active life." She stared at her sister-in-law; like Janine, she had never met Sonia. "I am charmed, Your Highness."

"It is my pleasure, Countess," Sonia said. "We should be delighted were you to pay us a visit." She glanced at Janine Grabowska. "Oh, you as well, Countess."

"Well," Janine said. "I think that would be very nice. Perhaps next spring. I . . ." She paused. There was a fanfare from the trumpeters who had been lined up on the pavement; the noise precluded any further conversation.

Everyone faced the doors, the men insensibly standing to attention whether they were in uniform or not, the women bracing themselves. Stolypin hurried forward to be the first to greet the Tsar as he entered. Alexei was always surprised by how small a man the Autocrat of All the Russias was; Nicholas II was not much over five feet tall. But he carried himself well, and was magnificently dressed in red tunic and dark blue breeches, a pale blue ribbon across his tunic, his left breast a smother of medals. He greeted his Prime Minister warmly, and then entered the foyer, while Stolypin in turn greeted the ladies who followed, principally the two grand duchesses, Olga and Marie, who were accompanying their father. But not their mother or their sisters, Alexei noticed, which lent substance to Stolypin's story of how ill the Tsarevich actually was . . . or indicated that the Empress and her two other daughters had no intention of exposing themselves to plague germs, even to please the people.

As for what he could possibly say to the Tsar . . . who, having greeted various other dignitaries, was now standing before him. Alexei bowed. "How good to see you again, Alexei Colinovich," Tsar Nicholas said.

"It is an honour to be here, sire." The two men gazed at

each other. As Colin MacLain's son, Alexei had been automatically commissioned into the Preobraschenski Guards when still a boy, as had his older half-brother Peter. But when the entire family had been plunged into disgrace by the involvement of their sister Patricia in terrorism and anarchy, both had been forced to resign. Yet Nicholas could never have doubted that they were two of his most loyal supporters. Prince Peter Bolugayevski had indeed given his life for Tsar and Motherland in the battle for Port Arthur. And Alexei, as Governor of Moscow, had put down the revolt of 1905 with ruthless determination, even if he had again been forced to help his sister escape the Okhrana. The Tsar had received him after the rising had been crushed, agreed as his reward to exile Patricia out of the country rather than return her to Siberia, and then sent him back to his estate of Bolugayen. They had not met since, and Alexei had not been offered employment. But Nicholas had commanded him to attend the state opening of the Kiev Opera House. "My wife, sire," Alexei said, and Sonia curtseyed.

"I am charmed, Princess," Nicholas said. He knew all about her, of course, and like everyone else in the court circle heartily disapproved of Prince Bolugayevski's marriage, not merely because she was a Jewess, but a Jewess who had dabbled in terrorism, or so it was said. But he needed her husband.

"You and the Princess must dine with me, Prince Bolugayevski," he said. "After the performance. There is much we need to discuss."

Alexei bowed again. "I shall be honoured, sire."

Nicholas smiled at Anna. "Countess, meeting you is always the greatest pleasure a man can experience."

"You flatter me, sire," Anna said; she was almost old enough to be his grandmother.

"You also will come to supper, I trust."

"It will be *my* great pleasure, sire."

13

The Tsar passed on, and Alexei and Sonia were introduced to the two grand duchesses, extremely pretty and attractively unaffected girls. Then they followed their father up the stairs to the royal box, while the band played the national anthem. Stolypin hurried up. "Do what you can," he said, and went into the body of the house; his seat was at the front of the orchestra stalls.

Alexei had naturally taken a box, and he escorted Sonia and Anna to their seats, stood behind them as the anthem was played, and then sat behind them. Anna was inspecting the people below her through her opera glasses. "Oh, there is Countess Carnovska. I hadn't expected to see her here. I must have a word with her during the interval."

"I'm surprised Nathalie isn't here," Sonia remarked. She too was looking at the faces beneath them.

"I doubt she'd travel this far from Petersburg even for an occasion like this," Alexei said. Nathalie Bolugayevska was his sister-in-law, the widow of his half-brother Peter. As such, she called herself, correctly, the Princess Dowager Bolugayevska. But Nathalie felt strongly that her daughter should have inherited Bolugayen, and was inclined to be difficult – especially when she had been drinking, which was usually the case. He was very glad she was not here.

Alexei allowed his gage a sweep of the auditorium, and he frowned. Standing behind the seats of the dress circle were quite a few young men. All were impeccably dressed in full evening wear, and most were joking and chatting as they waited for the curtain to go up; clearly they were the sons of Kievan society, attending this sumptuous occasion. But one of the men stood to one side, neither smiling nor speaking to the others, gazing down the aisle which led to the orchestra pit and the stage. Presumably he was someone who had been commanded to attend, whether he liked Rimski-Korsakov or not, Alexei decided, and at that moment the lights were lowered and the curtain went up.

14

Throughout the first Act his mind remained on the young man; he wondered if he would still be there at the first interval, or if he would have sneaked off somewhere to enjoy himself. Or drown his sorrows; he looked as if he had a few already. The music and singing ceased, and the safety curtain came down. The auditorium glowed, and a waiter came into the box with a tray of champagne and glasses. "I must go down and have a word with Elizabeth Carpowska," Anna said.

"I will come with you, at least as far as the cloakroom," Sonia said.

Alexei stood up and saw them out of the box. He sat down in Sonia's chair, close to the balustrade, a glass of champagne in his hand, looking down on the animated scene beneath him as people rose and moved about, chattered to their friends. He smiled; Peter Stolypin was entirely surrounded, mostly, he suspected, by people eager to be seen speaking with the Prime Minister rather than actually having anything to say. He picked out his aunt, emerging on to the lower floor, and smiling as only Anna Bolugayevska could smile at the people who hastily got out of her way as she made her way towards Countess Carpowska, who was seated some rows back from Stolypin. Then he frowned as he again saw the lone young man. He had not moved, but remained standing by the door to the foyer, continuing to gaze down the aisle. If he has remained like that throughout the first Act then he must be as stiff as a board, Alexei thought. The door to the box opened, and Sonia returned. He poured her a glass of champagne, and she sat in Anna's seat. "Enjoying it?"

"I think Rimski-Korsakov improves as he goes on," she said. "But I am enjoying being with you. Are we really going to have supper with the Tsar, afterwards?"

"Does that thought frighten you?"

"Yes," she said candidly. He could understand that. Simply because she was a Jewess, she had every cause to hate this man, because of the constant, savage,

15

pogroms against her people launched in his name. Equally, she could never forget that were she not the Princess Bolugayevska, she could be one of those hunted down and destroyed in the most brutal fashion by the 'Black Hundreds', as the irregular troops employed by the government for that purpose were called. Sonia's entire family had been hounded out of existence, so far as she was aware. And now she was being required to break bread with a man who could be called a murderer, even if Nicholas, personally, had never harmed a soul in his life. But she would do so, because the Tsar's favour safeguarded the future of her son.

The warning bell sounded, and the lights began to go down. Alexei looked into the auditorium, seeking the return of his aunt, and saw the lone young man at last move from his position against the wall. He frowned again as he watched the man walk steadily down the aisle, to join the throng of men still around the Prime Minister; they were just beginning to break up to return to their seats. The young man got right up to Stolypin, and spoke to him. Alexei, of course, could not hear what he was saying, both because he was too far away and because the auditorium was a huge buzz of sound as people returned to their seats, but it appeared as if the man was introducing himself, and was being acknowledged by the Prime Minister, for Stolypin was holding out his hand. The young man extended his hand as well. His back was turned to the other men, and they could not see his hand. But Alexei, looking down from above, could, and he saw that it held a revolver.

It seemed that no one heard the sound of the explosion, either, nor was there any immediate reaction to the sight of the Prime Minister sitting down rather abruptly. It was only when the young man stepped away, and hurried back up the aisle to the doors, that it could be seen that blood was pouring over Stolypin's white waistcoat. There was an immediate upsurge of noise. The women nearest to

16

Stolypin screamed, the men shouted, and began tearing at the Prime Minister's clothes in a vain attempt to reach the wound and staunch the bleeding. Alexei could not resist a glance to his right, to the royal box, where Nicholas was on his feet, staring at the scene beneath him as if paralysed; the grand duchesses appeared to be fainting with horror. Then he looked back down at the auditorium. "There!" he shouted, pointing at the young man, who was at the doors. "There!"

But it seemed no one could hear him; everyone was concentrating on the stricken minister. "Alexei!" Sonia gasped.

"Look after Aunt Anna," Alexei snapped, and burst out of the box, running along the corridor to the stairs.

Sonia gathered her skirts and ran behind him. Her injury did not prevent her moving as quickly as anyone; it simply made her somewhat awkward. Now she found herself in the midst of a huge throng of people who were shouting, screaming, rushing to and fro. She attempted to push her way through the mass, and was thrust hard against a chair set to one side. She sat down heavily, losing her breath and one earring, panting more with anger than alarm at being so treated, and found a man stooping beside her to retrieve the earring. "Allow me to assist you, Your Highness."

She looked up. He wore the blue full dress uniform of an officer in the Actirski Hussars, his cape draped over his left shoulder, his chest a mass of gold braid. His hair was black and thick, his features surprisingly small, for he was a big, tall man. Certainly he was handsome enough, and, she realised, disconcertingly young. "Captain Paul Korsakov, at your service, Your Highness." He held out the earring.

Sonia got her breath back and took the jewellery. "You know who I am?"

"Of course, Your Highness. Does not every man in Russia know the most beautiful princess in the land? I

17

saw Prince Bolugayevski joining the chase of the assassin. Allow me to escort you to safety."

Sonia stood up, trying to regain her composure, more from what he had just said than from being jostled. "Should *you* not also be chasing the assassin?"

"I have no idea what he looks like," Korsakov confessed. "Besides, there is already a sufficiently large hunting party. I would rather be of service to you, Your Highness."

Of all the effrontery, Sonia thought. He certainly knows I am married. I wonder what else he knows about me? But he had paid her an enormous compliment, and she could certainly use an escort, as the pandemonium was growing.

"The person you need to assist, is my aunt," she said. "She is in the auditorium. Help me find her."

"We should hurry," Korsakov suggested, and held her arm. She did not object, although when he said hurry he meant just that, and she received several more jolts and buffets as he pushed his way through the throng and down the stairs. The confusion in the auditorium was even greater than upstairs, the agitation of the members of the audience being heightened by the appearance of large numbers of policemen, trying to stop people from moving about, no doubt under the impression that the assassin might still be in the building. Meanwhile men were attempting to carry the Prime Minister up the aisle, not very successfully, because of the crush. Other people were screaming that they were hurt, or someone close to them had been . . . and Sonia's heart lurched as she realised she could not see Anna. "What does your aunt look like?" Korsakov shouted above the din. He was now virtually holding her in his arms as he sought to protect her from the people jostling to either side.

"She is very small and old," Sonia shouted back, her lips almost against his cheek. "And very beautiful."

"Of course, the famous Anna Bolugayevska," he

remarked, for the first time understanding who she was talking about. "Come."

He began to push his way forward again, to find a policemen standing in front him. "No one is allowed in, Your Honour."

"Listen," Korsakov said, "Let us through or I will break your arm."

The man gulped, and stepped aside. I have certainly accumulated a forceful escort, Sonia thought. But now people were parting to either side, and a few moments later they were facing Irina Carpowska, who was kneeling on the floor beside Anna. "My God!" Sonia cried. "Is she . . .?"

"She was knocked down when she tried to leave," the Countess said. "People trampled on her. Who are you?"

"Sonia Bolugayevska," Sonia told her, herself kneeling beside Anna. Anna's eyes were closed, and her face was twisted with pain, but she was breathing.

"I think she has fainted," Korsakov said. "We must get her out of here. Is your carriage nearby, Your Highness?"

"It was. But I don't know what is happening out there."

"Will you permit me, Your Highness?"

"Yes, please."

Korsakov thrust one arm under Anna's knees, put the other round her shoulders and stood up, lifting her as if she were a babe. He carried her towards the doorway, and the policeman, who had followed them into the auditorium, cleared a way for them. Anna sighed, and opened her eyes. "Why, young man," she said. "Whatever are you doing?"

"Making myself the envy of every man in Russia, Your Excellency," Korsakov assured her.

"Ahem," Morgan said. Patricia Cromb looked up from the letter she was writing. "There is a telegram, madam," Morgan told her, holding out the silver salver.

19

Harold Morgan had had an interesting life. A Welshman, he had as a youth of eighteen served with the 24th Welsh Fusiliers, and had been present at the immortal Battle of Rorke's Drift. Surviving that ordeal, during which just over a hundred British soldiers had resisted repeated attacks by well over three thousand battle-hardened Zulu warriors, had encouraged him to seek a quieter career, and he had become a gentleman's gentleman. When he had begun work for Mr Duncan Cromb, the American shipowner based in London, he had assumed that his every ambition had been realised. Duncan Cromb, the younger brother in a very wealthy family, had chosen to base himself in the London office, and seemed a totally settled young man. At that time, Morgan had had no idea that Mr Cromb had a Russian mother, much less that in her youth she had been one of the most famous female roués in history. Even less had he suspected that his quiet and refined employer was in the middle of a passionate and incestuous relationship with his second cousin, Patricia Bolugayevska. And even *less* had he suspected that his skills as a traveller and a soldier were going to be called into play to rescue the Countess Patricia from the depths of the revolutionary activity in Moscow in which she had involved herself.

Morgan had regretted not a moment of that wild adventure. He adored the Countess Patricia, and would willingly lay down his life for her, even if his hair was now grey and his moustache drooping. There had been no change in the Countess over the dozen years he had known her. He watched her slit the envelope with the silver paperknife he had thoughtfully laid on the tray. Her magnificent straight auburn hair contained the same strands of gray that it had on the day he had first met her; her body was still slender, though not emaciated as it had been according to Giselle, Patricia's maid, after her years in Irkutsk. It had been his pleasure to watch it fill out into the full maturity of a wife and a mother. She was

20

now a beautiful woman and at thirty-four had reached perhaps her apogee. As for what went on behind that splendid mask, Morgan reckoned that no man, including her husband, could truly tell. Did she still dwell on the floggings and rapings she had undergone as a prisoner of the Okhrana with the hatred he had heard her express? She gave no sign of it.

Was her heart still involved with those strange, anarchic, uncouth friends of hers, people like Vladimir Ulianov, who now called himself Nicolai Lenin, and his wife Olga Krupskaya, who had helped her escape from Siberian exile and had later called on her for help in launching their abortive and totally unsuccessful revolution? She certainly no longer corresponded with them. But she did correspond with her sister-in-law and closest friend, the Princess Sonia Bolugayevska. They had shared exile together, with all of its horrors, and it had been Patricia's decision, after escaping, to seek refuge on her family estate Bolugayen. It had been this move that had first allowed the Jewess into the orbit of Patricia's brother Alexei, and had caused him to fall in love. But did Patricia not still dream of her home, Morgan wondered, and the wealth and status that had gone with being the Countess Bolugayevska, an omnipotent existence she had handed on to her friend?

Morgan hoped not. Here in London madam had everything she desired. Duncan Cromb might be a younger son, but he was still a wealthy man, by most standards, if perhaps not that of the Bolugayevskis. This flat was one of the most expensive and elegant, and expensively and elegantly furnished, in London, even if it would have fitted into a single large reception room at Bolugayen. Patricia bought her clothes in Paris. And she was the mother of two splendid children. Surely she could ask for nothing more. Save . . . he frowned as he watched her also frown as she gazed at the words on the paper. "My God!" she said. "Aunt Anna!"

"She's not dead, I trust, madam?" Morgan was by

21

no means sure that would not be a good thing. He had only a brief acquaintance with the famous Anna Bolugayevska, when they had all gathered at Bolugayen following her return from Port Arthur and their escape from Moscow. No man could meet Anna Bolugayevska without regretting he had not known her in her youth, but Morgan, who had never found the time to marry, had formed the opinion that she was not really a good influence on the family.

"She's badly hurt," Patricia said. "Trampled in some panic at the Kiev Opera. What on earth was she, doing at the Kiev Opera? The family never goes to Kiev. I suppose Sophie had something to do with it," she grumbled. "But . . ." she looked up, her face suddenly animated. "Alexei wants Duncan to go to her. And he says I can come too!"

"But, madam, you are barred from Russia, by order of the Tsar."

"It is the Tsar who has given the permission for me to return, for this visit, Harold. Would you not like to visit Russia again?"

"Well, madam, in all the circumstances . . ."

"Listen, get me Mr Duncan on the phone." Patricia was on her feet now, prowling to and fro as the excitement took hold of her mind. "The children! They must come too. They have never been to Russia. Perkins? Perkins! Come in here a moment, please."

"I have Mr Cromb, madam." Morgan was standing by the wall telephone.

"Oh, thank you, Harold." Patricia waved at the nurse, who had just appeared in the inner doorway, and took the receiver from Morgan's hand. "Duncan! Duncan, darling."

"I was about to call you," Duncan said. "There's been the most frightful news from Russia."

"Oh!" Patricia was disappointed at having her thunder stolen. "How did you find out?"

"It came in on the wire."

"Aunt Anna is that famous?"

"Aunt Anna? Mom? Whatever are you talking about, my dear?"

Patricia raised her eyebrows to Morgan. "Whatever are *you* talking about, Duncan?"

"Why the attempt on Prime Minister Stolypin's life, of course. How did Mom get involved?"

"There has been an attempt on Stolypin's life? Where? How?"

"At the opening of the Kiev Opera House, last week. Someone walked up to him in the middle of the performance and shot him. He was badly wounded."

"The Kiev Opera House! My God, Duncan, Aunt Anna was there. And she was trampled on in the panic and is now seriously ill."

"Mom? Trampled upon?" Duncan sounded thunderstruck.

"There was a telegram from Alexei, just now."

"You mean she's been hurt? How badly?"

"Alexei doesn't say. But he wants you to go to her, Duncan. And he says I can go too. The Tsar has given permission. I'm starting to pack now."

Alexei was on the dock in Sevastopol to meet them. Duncan, having exchanged a succession of wires with his brother and sister in Boston, had taken a Cromb Lines' ship as far as Naples, where he had changed to a vessel of the Crimean Shipping Company, owned by his cousins. Now he escorted the entourage down the gangplank, while the seamen and stevedores stood respectfully to attention; Alexei was their ultimate employer.

The Prince wore the white uniform with the red collar and facings of a general officer, but no black arm band, Duncan observed with relief. He had been in a state of agitation ever since Patricia's phone call. It really was not possible to imagine anything happening to Mom. Anna

23

Bolugayevska had overridden so many extraordinary crises: as a young woman she had been mistress – as well as sister-in-law – of the famous Colin MacLain Bolugayevski, the founder of the English part of the family, and with him had fought her sister for possession of Bolugayen; as the wife of the American shipowner Charles Cromb she had had to adapt her wild Russian ways to the staid requirements of Boston society; as the mistress in turn, after Charles Cromb's death, of her own nephew, Alexei's older half-brother Peter, she had shared exile for Patricia's misbehaviour; and finally, she had fought for survival beneath the Japanese guns in Port Arthur, only seven years ago. To think of her now succumbing to a panic-stricken mob . . .

"How is she?" he asked, squeezing Alexei's hands.

"She has broken two ribs, and at her age this is a serious business. But Dr Geller says she will mend, if she is careful and behaves sensibly."

"Thank God for that."

Alexei was embracing his sister. Their greeting was a trifle hesitant, on both sides. If the last generation of Bolugayevskis had had to contend with the foibles of Aunt Anna, at least she had never been arrested for treason. And Patricia, if she had expressed her gratitude to her brother often enough for saving her life, had never once expressed any regret for being an anarchist. Not even Duncan knew if those tumultuous emotions still lurked in her heart and mind. "It is so good to be home," Patricia said.

"I am sure you will find that nothing has changed," Alexei promised her. "And these are the children?"

Patricia beckoned them forward. "This is Joe," she said.

The boy was thirteen, and extended his hand gravely, although his eyes were shining, both at the sight of the uniform – Alexei carried his huge plumed helmet under his left arm – and of the man himself, of whom he had heard so

24

much. Alexei shook hands with equal gravity. He knew all about little Joe, naturally. He knew that the boy was not Duncan's natural son, although Duncan had adopted him, but had been born out of wedlock in the wilds of Siberia, to a Jewish exile who had shared Patricia's fate but had died in the escape. But the father had been a friend of Sonia's even before he had met Patricia, and Alexei was therefore prepared to welcome his son, although since the shooting of Peter Stolypin the future, certainly as regards Russian Jews, had become ever more uncertain.

Joe's sister, Jennifer, named after Alexei and Patricia's mother, was entirely the child of Duncan and Patricia. At five years old she was already strongly built and fair-haired, in the strongest contrast to her slight, dark half-brother. Nor was she the least shy of her uncle, held up her arms to be lifted into his for a hug. "I like you," she confided.

"As I like you, little Jennie," he assured her.

There was no time to explore Sevastopol, although Joseph, steeped in history from an early age, wanted to hear all about the siege of sixty-five years before, and was disappointed that they were not able to ride out to Balaklava and see the famous Valley of Death that had been immortalised by Tennyson following the Charge of the Light Brigade. Colin MacLain had ridden in that charge, been wounded, and taken prisoner. But for that charge, and his father's adoption by the Bolugayevskis, Alexei reflected, none of them would be standing here now.

The train was waiting, because in Sevastopol the train always waited for the Bolugayevskis. As was the family custom, Alexei had reserved an entire carriage for his party and their servants. "Are you glad to be back in Russia, Morgan?" he asked. He remembered the valet from the last adventure.

"I am, sir," Morgan said. "Although I trust this journey will be less eventful than the last."

25

"We must hope so." Alexei nodded to the waiting conductor, and the train moved out of the station. "First stop Kharkov, as usual. I'm afraid our railways have not improved."

He sat with Duncan and Patricia in his own compartment, the men drinking brandies and soda and smoking cigars as the city fell away and they rumbled through open country towards the isthmus. "Tell us what happened," Patricia said.

Alexei told them about that evening. "It really was a panic. It is amazing how well-bred genteel people can turn into a pack of wild animals when they are made afraid. Aunt Anna had apparently stepped into the aisle, hoping to rejoin us upstairs, just before the shot was fired, and she was bowled over and knocked to the floor, whereupon several people actually stepped on her in their anxiety to get out. A woman of seventy-three! It really makes you despair of the human race."

"What about the man who shot Stolypin?"

"Oh, they got him quickly enough. A Jewish fellow, named Mordka Bogrov." He could not resist a glance at Patricia.

"I have never heard of him," she said. "Was he acting alone?"

"He is being interrogated by the Okhrana now. I have no doubt they will find out."

Patricia shivered. "Will he be executed?" Duncan asked.

"I would imagine so. Especially if Stolypin dies." Patricia shivered again.

The news was waiting for them when they arrived in Kharkov. The Prime Minister was dead.

Chapter Two

The Holy Man

"Here is the report you asked for, Your Honour." Captain Klinski placed the folder on the desk, and stood to attention.

"At ease, Feodor," Colonel Alexis Michaelin said, opening the cardboard cover. "A Jew. Another Jew. If I had my way I would stamp them out, eradicate them, rid Russia entirely of this pestilence."

"Yes, Your Honour," Feodor Klinski said, patiently. He reflected that his superior's capacity for hatred was probably the main reason he had been demoted to the command of the Okhrana in this remote town of Ekaterinburg, just beyond the Ural Mountains. As far as Klinski was concerned, the place was beyond the pale of civilised human society also, certainly with winter approaching.

As commander of the Petersburg office, seven years ago Alexis Michaelin had had the world at his feet, metaphorically as well as literally: he was a huge bull of a man who stood well over six feet and had a physique to match. His monocle, always shining brightly in the middle of his great bland face, was the sole suggestion of any weakness in his physical or mental persona, and Klinski knew that it was actually an affectation, and not worn because the eye was weak.

In St Petersburg, Michaelin had been able to arrest

27

and interrogate, torture and flog, and even condemn, those he had considered enemies of the State, without question. But his decision to allow Father Gabon to lead that infamous march on the Winter Palace in January 1905 had been his downfall. Gabon and his workers with their wives and children had appeared to wish only to present a petition to the Tsar. Michaelin, with his network of spies, could easily have stopped the march at its start; he knew the names of all the organisers and could have had them arrested. But he had chosen to let it proceed, in the full knowledge that the Tsar and Tsaritsa were not even in the Winter Palace, and could therefore be in no danger, because Gabon had been in his pay, an *agent provocateur* bound to do the bidding of his Okhrana employers. Michaelin had wanted the opportunity for a show of force to quell any incipient rebellion that might have been simmering following the Russian defeats by the Japanese, thus he had sent a message to the guard commander at the palace to be watchful, because the mob was very probably armed. The result had been a massacre, as the troops had opened fire on the entirely *un*armed crowd of people. Hundreds had been killed, in the name of the Tsar. The Tsar had been furious, and had sought a scapegoat; Michaelin had been removed from his post and sent to Ekaterinburg.

But he had never forgotten either his demotion or those he considered his enemies, high amongst whom were the Bolugayevskis. They hated him because he had arrested the Countess Patricia, had forced her to submit to rape and torture, and eventually, exile in Siberia, along with her friend and accomplice, Sonia Cohen, who now called herself the Princess Bolugayevska. But he hated them equally and was determined one day to bring them down, even from a provincial backwater like Ekaterinburg. And there it was. "Amongst those attending the opera on the fateful night were the Prince and Princess of Bolugayen," he read, his tone savouring every word. "Together with Countess

28

Anna Bolugayevska. The Countess was badly injured in the stampede following the shooting of the Prime Minister. Now, what do you think of that, Feodor?"

Klinski scratched his head. "Is it important, Your Honour?"

"They were there, Feodor."

"But so were several hundred other people, Your Honour."

"I am not interested in other people," Michaelin said. "The Prince Bolugayevski attends the opening of the State Opera House in Kiev. Why? To my knowledge he has never set foot in Kiev in his life before. He is accompanied by his wife, who is both Jewish and a known terrorist."

"Ahem," Klinski ventured. Michaelin glared at him. "She was once arrested for terrorism, Your Honour. A long time ago. Before she married the Prince. Since then . . ."

"Leopards do not change their spots," Michaelin said. "They were there, Feodor. And on the night they are in Kiev to attend the opera, for the first time ever, remember, the Prime Minister is mortally wounded, by a Jew." Another glare. "You do not see what I am driving at?"

"I do, Your Honour. But . . . I would say it is almost certainly a coincidence that the Bolugayevskis were there on the night the Prime Minister was killed."

"I do not believe in coincidences," Michaelin declared.

"Well, then, Your Honour, should we not report your . . . ah, our, suspicions, to the Petersburg Office?"

"Under no circumstances. This business could take me back to where I belong, *in* the Petersburg Office. But not if someone else gets the credit. Now listen to me, and I will tell you what we are going to do."

"Wow!" Joe Cromb commented, standing in the great hall of the Bolugayevski Palace in Poltava and looking around him. "This must be bigger than Buckingham

29

Palace!" Jennie couldn't speak, just held her brother's hand.

"It probably is," Duncan agreed. "I've never been inside Buckingham Palace."

Alexei had been giving instructions to the servants to have the windows draped in black. "But I think we should get out to Bolugayen as quickly as possible," he told Duncan and Patricia over lunch. "We'll leave in the morning."

"Do you think there'll be trouble?" Duncan asked.

"There will certainly be repercussions. A lot will depend on what this man Bogrov confesses, on who he names." Again he could not prevent himself from looking at his sister.

"I told you, I have never even heard of this man," Patricia said. "As for Stolypin, I never met him either."

"And we have the Tsar's permission for Patricia to return to Russia," Duncan pointed out.

"Oh, quite. I am not disputing that, as I obtained it for you. But we don't want any trouble with officious police officers; things aren't quite what they were in my father's day, when he told the police what to do rather than the other way around."

"What about Stolypin's death?" Duncan asked.

Alexei's shoulders hunched. "It is a catastrophe. He is the one man who might have saved Russia."

"Oh, come now. Saved Russia? Isn't that pitching things a bit strong?"

"You don't know the truth of it, Duncan. At the end of the day, you know, the Tsar, even the Tsar, only rules by the consent of his people, and that means the trust and support of his people. Nicholas lost that in the war with Japan because of his constant indecision, his summoning of a parliament, the duma, and then his dismissal of it because it opposed his concept of autocracy. Peter Stolypin was working to recreate that essential empathy between Tsar and people. And he was succeeding. Until

30

some maverick anarchist went wild. Forgive me, Trisha, but it was a dreadful crime."

"I agree with you," Patricia said.

"Now," Alexei went on. "There is no one to take his place."

"You're not going to tell me that Stolypin was the only worthwhile minister in Russia," Duncan declared. "What about that fellow Witte?"

"Witte is a very sound man. But he cannot stand up to the Tsar, much less the Tsaritsa. He is too steeped in the mystique of the throne, the determination that the throne speaks with the mouth of God, and is therefore infallible." He gave a twisted smile. "You realise I am speaking treason."

"Not to us. But there must be someone else. What about the aristocracy? What about *you*?!"

Alexei's smile was more twisted yet. "I am the brother of an anarchist." He looked at Patricia. "Don't take offence. It happens to be the simple truth, in the eyes of the powers that be. Anyway, I don't think I'd be very good at the job."

"I think you'd be very good at the job," Patricia said fiercely. "Oh, if you could know how much I regret those things I said. And even more, did."

Alexei squeezed her hand. "Does that mean, that if people like Lenin and his friends ever again raised the red flag in Russia, you would disown them?"

"Yes," Patricia said. "I would."

"I am so terribly sorry," Sonia said.

"I think we always knew he was going to die." Alexei sat behind his desk and began to open the mail that had accumulated during his brief absence; they had arrived on Bolugayen an hour earlier, and this was the first opportunity Sonia had had to be alone with her husband. "He was shot at point-blank range."

She sat in one of the chairs in front of the desk. "In a

31

way, I feel so guilty . . . because it was one of my people
. . ." She paused, waiting for Alexei to reasure her, as he
always did. But Alexei was reading a letter, with a frown.
"Not bad news?" she asked.

His head jerked. "Bad news? Good lord, no." He
grinned at her. "Old Witte. Keeping in touch, I suppose.
Not bad news." It was odd, Sonia thought, how men never
seemed able to realise that their wives always knew when
they were being lied to.

"Mom," Duncan said, sitting beside Anna's bed. "Oh,
Mom!"

Never had he seen his mother looking so frail. But as
always, there was nothing frail about her spirit. "I'm not
going to die, you silly boy," she said. "What are a couple
of broken ribs?"

He kissed her. "Alix and Charlie send their love."

"But they are not here. They have written me off."

"That's not true," Duncan protested. "I was closest.
But Alix is planning to come. She's probably already on
her way."

"I shall be glad to see her." Anna looked past her son
at Patricia, and held out her hand. "My dear, it is so good
to see you, here, in Russia."

"It is so very good to be here, Aunt Anna," Patricia
said. "But I am sorry you are not well."

The two women had had a stormy relationship. As a
girl, Patricia had had but a single dream, to be like her
famous aunt in all things. But when Anna had attempted
to come between her and Duncan they had quarrelled.
The fact that Anna had been justifiably opposed to second
cousins marrying, and that Patricia had yet won in the end,
had done nothing to bring about a reconciliation, especially
when Patricia had attempted to involve Duncan in her
revolutionary activities. But as that was all behind them
now, and as Patricia was the mother of Jennie – Anna
had never really recognised little Joseph – she allowed

32

her daughter-in-law a kiss. "I shall be up again in no time at all," she asserted. "Come and give me a kiss, Jennie. Not a hug. Hugs are not allowed, according to Geller."

"Say hello to Grandmama, Joseph," Patricia insisted.

Anna gazed at the boy. "You are all but a man," she remarked. "Be sure you always behave like one."

"Her bark is much worse than her bite," Sonia said. "And we should remember that she is in some pain, all the time." The two women sat together in the Princess's sewing room. The maids had been dismissed, and the children sent off to play. Sonia and Patricia wanted to be alone together, for the first time in a very long time.

Now they gazed at each other for some moments. They were both thirty-four, both beautiful, both wealthy . . . and they had shared so much. Too much, perhaps, ever to be remembered aloud. And in the strangest fashion they had changed places. This was Patricia's home, the house where she had been born and the estate in which she had grown up, certain always of her share in it, before her wayward ideas and her ability to sympathise with those less well-off than herself had led her to throw it all away. Sonia had been born into genteel poverty, and social ostracism, as the daughter of a Jew. She had not joined the revolutionary movement; she had been bred into it. She could have had no expectations beyond a lifetime of waiting for the dreaded knock on the door, even before her arrest and sentence to exile. Now she was Princess of Bolugayen. In all Russia, only the Tsaritsa and the Grand Duchesses would take precedence before her.

But even omnipotence can have its terrors. "Have you ever heard anything of your family?" Patricia asked.

"No," Sonia said. It had been in Jonathan Cohen's house that they had been arrested, sixteen years before.

"I am so terribly sorry about that," Patricia said.

Sonia stitched industriously. The tears for her parents and brother had all been shed. She no longer even felt

33

guilt for the religion she had had to abandon in order to become Princess Bolugayevska – or she pretended she no longer felt guilt. "Do you ever hear from Vladimir?"

"I hear *of* him," Patricia said. "But he calls himself Nicolai Lenin now. As if everyone does not know who he really is. But I do not suppose the Okhrana are at all interested in him, skulking in Switzerland." She gave a brief smile. "The ultimate revolutionary, conducting his revolution at a safe distance from the country he seeks to overturn."

"It is difficult to know what is going to happen," Sonia said. "Under Stolypin there have been three years of relative peace, apart from that dreadful cholera epidemic two years ago. Now . . . you know that his murderer was a Jew?"

"Alexei told me. Do you think he was sent by Lenin?"

"Heaven knows. Alexei doesn't think so. He thinks it happened because the government has been particularly hard on the Jews in the Ukraine, and in Kiev most of all. But the Communists are still active, in Russia as well as outside, whether they call themselves Bolsheviks or Mensheviks. Did you ever hear of a man calling himself Trotsky? I believe his real name was Bronstein."

"I met him, in Moscow, in 1904," Patricia said.

"Well, he was recently arrested and sent to Siberia, for handing out seditious literature. Communist literature." She shuddered. "It is better not to think about these things. Trishka, I have a problem."

"Tell me."

"I have told no one, up till now. It really must remain a secret."

"It will."

Sonia licked her lips. "On the night Stolypin was shot, and Aunt Anna knocked down, well, Alexei of course went chasing off after the assassin. I was left alone, in the middle of that mob, and I can tell you that though they may have been the upper crust they very rapidly degenerated into a mob. I was trying to reach Aunt Anna, but it was very difficult, until I was assisted by a man." She glanced at Patricia, her ears pink.

"What sort of man?"

"His name is Korsakov, and he is a captain in the Actirski Hussars."

"Why, that was Uncle Georgei's old regiment! He was serving with them when he was killed outside Sevastopol."

"I know. That's not really relevant. The fact is, well . . . this Captain Korsakov really rescued Aunt Anna, took her out to our carriage, and rode with us to the hotel. He stayed for some time, until Alexei came back. He flirted with Anna, and she, although she was in great pain, flirted back. Well, you know Aunt Anna. Then the doctor came, and Paul had to leave the room."

"Paul?" Patricia's eyebrows were arched.

The glow spread from Sonia's ears to her neck. "He spent the rest of the night, as I say, sitting with me. Alexei didn't get home until past three. So . . . we got on to first names."

"He is a fast worker, this hussar," Patricia remarked. "Is he handsome?"

"Very handsome."

"Age?"

"Oh . . . late twenties, I suppose."

"You mean he is younger than you?"

Now the glow had reached Sonia's cheeks. "Well . . . yes."

"So you have had a flirtation, in a cradle," Patricia said. "What's big about that?"

"Well . . . perhaps I was foolish, but I felt obliged to write him, once we knew Aunt Anna was going to be all right, and thank him for all his help. His reply arrived the day before yesterday."

"Let me see it." Sonia hesitated a moment, then got up, went to her escritoire, and took out the letter. Patricia perused it. "Undying love? Desires nothing more than your smile?"

"Yes." Sonia sat down again.

"Must see you again," she read. "Will die if I do not . . ."

"I hope you did not reply to this?"

"Finish it," Sonia recommended.

Patricia read to the end. "Coming here?"

"To visit Aunt Anna, and make sure she is well," Sonia pointed out. "That's what he says. But . . ."

"He is really coming to see you." Patricia raised her head. "You're sure you haven't given him any encouragement?"

"Well . . ." Sonia bit her lip. "He is awfully nice."

"And you are awfully married. To my brother!"

"I know. Believe me, I know. But we do owe this man a great deal. Perhaps even Aunt Anna's life. And he . . . well!"

"He is very handsome and you find a husband twelve years your senior a trifle boring."

"Now that is quite untrue and unfair," Sonia protested. "I love Alexei. I always have and I always will. But I cannot deny that he is a little . . . avuncular from time to time. Or that he remembers always that he saved my life. Well, I do not forget that either."

"You also are the Princess Bolugayevska."

"I know. Although . . ." Sonia shot her a glance. "I cannot think of a past Princess Bolugayevska who was utterly faithful to her husband. Don't misunderstand me, Trishka. I have no intention of betraying Alexei. But you cannot blame me for having a little dream, of other worlds, perhaps other men, from time to time. You'll not pretend you do not have such dreams."

Patricia was reading the letter again, in preference to answering. "He says he will pay you a visit before Christmas. Well, the solution is very simple. You will go to Petersburg. Come to think of it, I will accompany you. I so want to see Petersburg again."

"You mean . . . go now?"

"It is October. Everyone will be in Petersburg for the

36

start of the season. We shall take the children. I so want Joe and Jennie to see the city. But we shall tell no one we are going, so your gallant captain will not know."

"But if he comes here, and I am not here, without a word, he will be deeply offended."

"Is that not a desirable objective?"

Sonia considered. "Can we leave Aunt Anna?"

"She is telling everyone she is on the mend. I am sure she will not object. And she is the one this Korsakov says he is coming to visit. Well, she will be here to receive him."

"And Alexei and Duncan?"

"Whether or not they come with us is up to them. As I say, we shall certainly take the children. Oh, I am so excited, Sonia."

"Yes," Sonia agreed, somewhat soberly. She knew how easily Patricia became excited. But she had other things on her mind. "You do realise that Nathalie is using the Peterburg house as her own. We will have to take an hotel suite."

"We will do nothing of the kind," Patricia declared. "As I have just reminded you, my dear sister-in-law, *you* are the Princess Bolugayevska. Nathalie is only the Princess Dowager. Therefore the house is yours, and that you permit her to live in it is your decision. She will have to put up with us, if we decide to stay there. Or she can move out to an hotel herself."

"This is some spread," Joseph Cromb said, clinging rather precariously to the reins as the two boys topped a rise above the village. He rode regularly in London, but Rotten Row was nothing compared to this cross-country gallop past endless fields of harvested grain. "How far to the boundary of the property?"

Colin Bolugayevski gave him a contemptuous glance; although a year younger than his cousin, he had spent several hours every day in the saddle ever since he could remember. "A hundred miles," he said, in good English; he had been taught to use his father's and grandparents' language since he had been born.

"A hundred . . . you're having me on."

"Bolugayen is a hundred miles across," Colin asserted. "Has Aunt Patricia not told you this?"

"Mom doesn't talk too much about Bolugayen," Joe confessed. "You mean your dad owns all the land for a hundred miles?"

"Well . . ." Colin flushed. "We have had to sell some of it to the muzhiks. But the main part is still ours, yes. One day it'll be mine."

"Gee!" Joe commented.

"Don't your parents own a lot of land?" Colin asked.

"No. I don't think we do. Certainly not in England. My Uncle Charlie owns some in Boston, I guess. What does it feel like to know that one day you'll own all of this? That you'll be Prince of Bolugayen?"

"I have never thought about it," Colin said. He saw that Joe had regained his breath, and kicked his horse forward again. "What will you be when you grow up?"

"Plain Joe Cromb, I guess. I'll be an executive in the family shipping company. Sounds a bit of a bore. I'd like to join the army."

"Which army?"

"The American army, of course."

"Does America have an army?" Colin asked, ingenuously.

"Sure it does. Maybe it's not very big . . ."

"Russia has a standing army of a million men," Colin said. "With another three million reservists."

"That sure sounds like you were planning to take on the Japanese again," Joe agreed. "You ever thought of joining up?"

Colin smiled. "When I am thirteen I become an officer cadet, and when I am seventeen, I will be commissioned into the Preobraschenski Guards. Then in the course of time I will become a general, like Papa."

"Just like that? Heck. When I'm thirteen, I'm going to a public school." Colin gazed at him in amazement. "It's actually a private school," Joseph explained, "but in England they're called public schools. Very exclusive. It's called Winchester." He was anxious to get off a subject which Colin clearly could not understand.

"Won't you have to pass exams, prove yourself worthy of being an officer?"

"Of course not. I am Count Bolugayevski."

"And who do you really want to fight?"

"Anyone the Tsar tells me to. Now we had better go home. I believe we are to leave for St Petersburg tomorrow."

"That's a big city, huh? You reckon it's as big as London?"

"St Petersburg is the greatest city in the world," Colin said, so reverently that Joseph almost believed him.

"Why is it so important that you go to St Petersburg now?" Duncan asked. "Or at all, for that matter?"

He would never be able to forget that it had been in St Petersburg that Patricia had first become involved in anarchism.

"I cannot tell you," Patricia said. "You must just accept my word that it *is* important." She kissed him. "I also give you my absolute sacred word that it has nothing to do with anyone I might have known before. I have turned my back on all of that. You know that."

"Well . . ." She had turned her back on revolution after escaping from Irkutsk, and had yet allowed herself to be sucked back into those dark depths in 1904.

"Darling," she said, "I'm taking the children. And of course I'd love it if you'd come too."

"I don't feel I can. Not right now. I came here to be with Mom, and I think I should stay with her. I know she

39

claims to be on the mend, but she really is terribly weak, and with winter coming on . . . if she were to catch a cold it might be disastrous. Anyway, Alix is supposed to be coming over. I really should be here when she arrives."

"Of course. I quite understand. You can join us the moment you feel Aunt Anna really is well again. In any event, I'll expect you for Christmas."

"I think you should come back here for Christmas. It's the thought of you running into that thug Michaelin that bothers me."

"Michaelin is a disgraced man. It is he who is exiled to Siberia, now. Well, to the wrong side of the Urals, anyway."

"He could still happen to be in Petersburg while you are there."

"If I meet Colonel Michaelin on the street, I will simply stick out my tongue at him. He cannot arrest me for that. He cannot arrest me for anything: I have the Tsar's safe-conduct."

"Just so long as you remember only to stick out your tongue."

"Oh, I would like to kill him. I certainly hope to see him die," Patricia said, with just a hint of the old fire in her voice.

"I wish you wouldn't talk like that. By the way, is Alexei going?"

"I don't think so. He doesn't like Petersburg."

"Do you know," Patricia said to Sonia as the train pulled out of Poltava Station. "I feel just as if we were two schoolgirls, leaving our convent for the holidays."

"Some schoolgirls," Sonia commented, glancing at the four children, the two nurses and two maids who were sharing the double compartment with them; the servants would of course sleep in second-class.

"Oh, you know what I mean."

In fact, Sonia did know what she meant. She wasn't

sure whether or not she had been wise to confide in her oldest friend, especially as Patricia also happened to be her sister-in-law, but she had had to confide in someone, and there was no one else. Her personal maid was a very old family retainer named Grishka, old in the sense that she had been part of the Bolugayevski staff since her teens; she was still not yet forty. But she had been with the family on both their sojourns in Port Arthur, and at one time she had been Patricia's maid. She worshipped the ground Prince Alexei walked on . . . but did *she*, his wife not also worship that ground, Sonia asked herself.

What had driven her to flirt with Paul Korsakov? Most people would have said that she had had enough adventures for any woman's lifetime. But perhaps those adventures, which had included having to prostitute herself to live during her escape from Irkutsk, had had more of a destabilising effect on her character than she had realised. When she had first come to Bolugayen, it had been like re-entering the womb. There had been such an aura of safety about the place as to overwhelm the personality of someone who had never known such security at any time in her life, and had in addition just escaped in the most terrible circumstances from the most horrible existence it was possible to imagine. Alexei Bolugayevski had stood at the centre of that womb, the man who could end all of her nightmares, and had offered to do so. It was natural that she would have fallen in love with someone so gallant, handsome and dominant.

Alexei had remained all of those things. Of course, from the first she had recognised that he had a very serious side to his character, and that, for all the eccentricities of his sisters and his aunt, which had caused him so much trouble, he remained utterly devoted to the Tsar, to the very concept of tsardom. She had even understood that he might become more serious-minded as he grew older, without being able to evaluate what that might mean. Certainly, she knew he wanted to get back into the mainstream of Russian political and military life, and dreamed of an army command commensurate with his rank. Now that ambition had again been forced into the background. She had no idea what it was the Tsar had wanted to discuss with him at supper after the opera, because that supper had never taken place. And Alexei had not seen the Tsar since. The plain fact of the matter was that Peter Stolypin had been murdered by a Jew, and that Alexei was married to a Jewess. There was, of course, no suggestion that she or anyone known to her had had anything to do with the assassination plot. But there it was. Were Alexei to turn up in St Petersburg with his wife it would cause a closing of the ranks of polite society, and be a grave embarrassment to the royal family. But she was going anyway. Very quietly. And in any event the Princess of Bolugayen could not be prevented from travelling where and when she chose. Nor had Alexei raised the slightest objection to her visit to the capital, even as he had declined to accompany her.

What *had* possessed her to flirt with Korsakov? Patricia had been right. Running away was the only thing she could do. Patricia had been looking out of the window at the fields rushing by, long stripped of their grain and lying black and fallow as they awaited the first snow. Now she smiled at her sister-in-law. "Does Nathalie know we are coming?"

"No," Sonia said. "I thought we'd surprise her."

"Wow!" was Joseph's comment as they drove through the streets of St Petersburg in the hired carriage; he was bemused by the canals, by the Neva itself, and as they debouched on to the Nevski Prospect, by the immensity of the water opening before them.

"It's beautiful!" Jennie exclaimed. Colin looked supercilious, and Anna nestled in Grishka's arms.

Sonia looked apprehensive, but Patricia's eyes glowed as she looked across the inner water at the grim bulk of the

Peter and Paul Prison. She had been in that prison, and there experienced some of the worst moments of her life. But that had to be behind her now. She had meant what she had told Duncan, that she would like to see Michaelin dead. But she no longer wished to kill him personally, even if he had tormented her and humiliated her. That was history, and she had soared beyond his reach. As for the people she had met in the backstreets of this city, and who had become her friends and indeed her intimates, but who were now scattered to the ends of the earth, the Lenins in Switzerland, Trotsky in Siberia, Stalin . . . she had no idea where Stalin was, but he had the gift of survival, so he was probably somewhere safe, she wanted to forget them too. Only Sonia remained from those days, because Sonia had also made the transition from anarchist to aristocrat. And Sonia had almost been prepared to throw it all away like some stargazing teenager! She could have no doubt what Alexei's reaction would be were he ever to see that letter.

But Sonia! Sonia had always been the most private, conservative of women.

Her religion and background had made her so, but she had preserved that armour-like shroud over her personality, even when being mishandled by the secret police. Even during their trek across Siberia when they had been forced to offer themselves time and again just to live, where Patricia had gone to the men with a defiant but almost enthusiastic acceptance of her fate, Sonia, the more beautiful woman, had merely submitted, her mind clearly closed. But perhaps even then she had been dreaming of a handsome face, and a man her own age or even younger! How little, Patricia thought, do we actually ever know about anyone, no matter how intimate a friend?

"Wow!" Joseph said again, as the carriage turned into the drive and stopped. "Is this where we are going to stay?"

43

"This is our house, darling," Patricia said. "Well, Aunt Sonia's house."

Even Colin was gaping now, not at the house, which was very similar to the one in Poltava, although considerably smaller than that at Bolugayen, but at the automobile which stood outside the portico: there were not many cars in the south. "That's a Mercedes-Benz," Joseph asserted. "They build them in Germany."

"It's very big," Colin remarked.

The door of the house was opened by Dmitri the butler himself; he had overseen the arrivals from a window. "Your Highness," he said. "If we had but known you were coming . . ."

"It was a spur of the moment decision, Dmitri," Sonia told him. "You remember Countess Patricia? Mrs Cromb?"

"Your Excellency." Dmitri bowed. "Welcome back to St Petersburg."

"I am delighted to be here, Dmitri," Patricia said. Although he was sixteen years older than the last time she had seen him, he did not seem to have aged a bit – and what memories the sight of him brought flooding back. But then she had experienced the same emotions when again meeting Gleb, the butler on Bolugayen. Gleb was an even more faithful retainer than Dmitri, but his brother had betrayed the family, and herself, and died for it. She wondered if Gleb had any idea that it was his own master, the Prince, who had executed Rurik Bondarevski? All memories. But that secret belonged to Duncan and Morgan, and Alexei and herself. She did not even know if Sonia knew of it. And there were so many other memories. She could not prevent herself gulping as a woman emerged from the back of the hall and came towards her.

"Madame Rykova, our housekeeper," Sonia explained.

"Welcome to St Petersburg, Your Highness," Madame Rykova said. "Your Excellency." She gave a brief curtsey to Patricia.

"We have never met," Patricia said.

"No, Your Excellency."

"Yet you knew who I am."

"With respect, Your Excellency, you are a Bolugayevska. No one could have any doubts about that. I will prepare your apartments. And for the children." She bent a somewhat severe stare on the youngsters; clearly she saw in them disrupters of her orderly household.

"You really mustn't be so suspicious," Sonia whispered, as they went into one of the downstairs reception rooms.

"When I think of that woman Popova . . . you never met her."

"No. But I know she was an Okhrana spy. Alexei got rid of her. This woman comes with the highest references."

"So did Madame Popova." She looked at the door as Dmitri came in, bearing a tray with cups of tea. He was followed by a girl in her early teens, handsome in a heavy manner, of both feature and figure, with thick golden hair.

"Hello, Dagmar," Sonia said. "This is your Aunt Patricia."

Dagmar Bolugayevska stared at Patricia. "You were sent to Siberia," she announced.

Sonia gulped, but Patricia merely gave a cold smile. "That is true. Have you never been sent to Siberia?"

The girl looked bewildered. "Is your Mama at home?" Sonia asked.

"We've just come in," Dagmar said. "You never told us you were coming."

"No, I did not," Sonia agreed.

They all looked at the doorway, where Dmitri was bowing to the Princess Dowager Nathalie Bolugayevska. Patricia was quite taken aback. She had never met her late half-brother's widow, but she had heard all about Nathalie's drinking and her appalling lifestyle. Yet she had not expected to see quite such a huge woman. Nathalie was above medium height and could hardly

45

weigh less than a hundred and seventy English pounds; only the fact that she wore her thick golden hair in the fashionable pompadour prevented the suggestion that she had walked straight out of a Wagnerian opera. The truly remarkable thing was that she was more than a year younger than either Sonia or Patricia herself. "Sonia?" she enquired, her voice a low rumble. "What are you doing here?"

"I am visiting Petersburg, Nathalie."

"Ha! I would have supposed you would have been arrested by now."

"They're not arresting princesses this season," Sonia said sweetly.

"Ha!" Nathalie remarked, and left the room again.

"Mama doesn't like you, Aunt Sonia," Dagmar said. "I've heard her say so."

"Well, my dear, I don't like your Mama," Sonia said. "Now you can tell her you heard me say that." Dagmar followed her mother. "I did warn you," Sonia said. "That we would not be welcomed."

"And as I said, if they don't like us being here they can always leave." Patricia drank her tea.

In fact they saw very little of the Princess Dowager for the next few days.

Following their arrival, Nathalie decided to take her meals in her apartment. Dagmar was always about, watching the children play in the garden with a somewhat supercilious air. She did attempt to join in the boys' games on one occasion but Colin shooed her away. The girls were too small to interest her.

Sonia and Patricia, equally, kept to themselves, and let no one know they were in town, although they could not doubt that their presence was being talked about, at least by the servants, while Nathalie had a telephone in her apartment. But they only wanted to be ignored, went shopping together, reminisced together and played with

46

their children together. "It is splendid to see the way Colin and Joe get on," Sonia said.

"Well, they should," Patricia remarked, and flushed as she glanced at her friend.

"Do you ever regret, well . . . Joseph Fine?" Sonia asked.

"Of course I do not. Anyway, little Joe is as much Duncan's son as mine. Duncan has insisted upon that."

"You must love Duncan very much," Sonia suggested.

"I do. Oh, I will admit I didn't at first. I mean, I gave him my virginity, quite outrageously, when we were in Port Arthur together. My God, the things I did as a girl! If Jennie were ever to do anything like that . . . well, I don't know what I'd say, or do."

"You would sympathise and understand," Sonia suggested.

"I'm afraid I'm not a very sympathetic or understanding woman," Patricia confessed.

"But you did manage to fall in love with Duncan."

"I did, yes. He is such a . . . well, I suppose you'd have to say, noble person."

"That is just the word I would use about Alexei. So, you have never had any desire to . . . stray?"

"Of course. What woman doesn't? But like you, I have managed to resist the temptation, until now, anyway. Now you tell me, how do you get on having Aunt Anna in the house?"

"We get on very well. I think she has mellowed a great deal."

"You mean she no longer sleeps with every man who takes her fancy!"

Sonia smiled. "I think it is a case that the spirit may be willing but the flesh is weak." She looked up as the door was thrown open. That could only be one person.

"There is someone who wishes to meet you," Nathalie announced.

47

"We are incognito," Sonia said. "We do not wish to meet anyone."

"You are not incognito, as everyone knows you are in Petersburg," Nathalie pointed out. "And this is not an invitation you should refuse. It is from someone to whom even the Okhrana bows its head. To offend this person is to take a serious risk. Especially where one is already vulnerable."

Patricia raised her eyebrows. "You mean the Tsaritsa wishes to receive us?"

Nathalie tossed her head. "This person is far more important than the Tsaritsa. I am speaking of the staretz, Gregory Rasputin."

"Who?" Patricia asked.

"Have you not heard of Father Gregory?" Nathalie was astounded, and looked at Sonia.

"I have heard of him," Sonia said. "I have heard that he is a charlatan."

"Well," Nathalie said. "I would not say that too loudly if I were you. Or you may well find yourself back in Siberia. This 'charlatan' has the ear of the Tsaritsa. You are invited to take tea with him, this afternoon. Shall I tell him you refuse?"

Sonia looked at Patricia, who shrugged. "It sounds as if it might be a giggle."

To the surprise of Patricia and Sonia, Dagmar accompanied them.

"Father Gregory is very fond of Dagmar," Nathalie said, enigmatically.

They drove to Rasputin's house in Nathalie's Mercedes-Benz, with much tooting of the horn by the chauffeur.

"Tell me about this man," Patricia said.

"He is a holy man of great powers," Nathalie said reverently. "He can heal illnesses. He heals the Tsarevich when he is ill, which is often enough. But more than that, he can relieve sins."

48

"Surely any priest can do that," Patricia said.

"Not like Father Gregory. We are not speaking of an ordinary confessional." She glanced at her other sister-in-law. "He can even relieve your sins, Sonia."

"He will find that difficult," Sonia retorted. "As I am not going to confess any. We do not go in for that sort of thing."

"He will know," Nathalie said.

"Where does he come from?" Patricia asked.

"From a remote Siberian village."

"How did he learn to be a staretz in a remote Siberian village?"

"Silly girl," Nathalie said scornfully. "One doesn't learn to be a staretz. One is visited by voices, and one *knows*. We have arrived."

The Mercedes had turned into a driveway off the street, and come to a stop. Patricia looked out of the window at the large house. "I had no idea being a holy man was such a remunerative profession."

"Or such a busy one," Sonia remarked, for the driveway was entirely blocked with cars and carriages, and lounging chauffeurs and postilions, who gave the new arrivals no more than a glance.

"He is the very hub of Petersburg society," Nathalie assured them. They stepped down, and made their way through the waiting men, not one of whom was the least respectful. Indeed, Sonia heard one chauffeur say to another, "Here are some more plump chickens to be picked." She had no idea what he meant, but held her hat on her head and began to regret that she had allowed Patricia to talk her into this adventure.

But Nathalie did not seem the least concerned as she led them up an outside staircase and opened the door at the top. This gave access to a large reception room, which was absolutely crowded with people, all women, save for a supercilious looking major-domo standing by an inner doorway. The women turned to stare at the new arrivals,

49

and Sonia realised that all the glances were hostile, and that some of them must have been here for some time; the air was heavy with the scent of stale perfume. But the major-domo had recognised Nathalie, and hurried across the room, pushing women to either side with total familiarity and lack of manners. "Your highness. How good to see you."

"Is Father Gregory free, Anton?" Nathalie asked imperiously.

"At the moment no. But I will tell him you are here." Anton bowed and hurried across the room to open the inner door. Instantly there was a kind of surge towards it, by everyone present, checked when the door was firmly shut in their faces.

Sonia looked around the room. Presumably they would have to wait for some time, and there were no chairs left. One or two of the women, indeed, very well dressed, were actually sitting on the floor. But that was not something the Princess Bolugayevska could contemplate. "Perhaps we should come back another day," she whispered to Nathalie. "When he is not quite so busy."

"Another day," snorted the woman standing close by, who had overheard the suggestion. "I have been here every day this week, and I have not yet seen the staretz."

Sonia looked at Patricia, who winked. Patricia, with that streak of wildness inherited from some long-dead English ancestor, was enjoying herself thoroughly. While she was feeling more and more embarrassed. "It is true," Nathalie said. "He is always this busy. But he will not keep *us* waiting."

To Sonia's astonishment, only five minutes later Anton was back, standing in front of the closed door and beckoning Nathalie and her companions towards him. Just as if we were serving girls, Sonia thought. The other women were incensed. There were several hisses, and some uncomplimentary remarks. "Ignore them," Nathalie recommended. "They are just jealous."

50

Sonia glanced at Dagmar to see how the girl was taking it all, and was astonished to see that her niece-in-law was apparently totally oblivious of the people around her, but was staring at the door with enormous, shining eyes.

Anton opened the door for them, then immediately moved behind them, to restrain the other women and to close the door firmly as soon as they were through. We are being pushed into the lion's den, Sonia thought. Then gazed in consternation at the scene in front of her. A woman, from her clothes and jewellery very wealthy, was hastily restoring those clothes and jewellery to some semblance of decency. It was obvious that only a few seconds previously she had been naked, at least from the waist up. Her hat was on the floor, her hair had come down, and she was breathing heavily as she fastened her bodice, while her cheeks were flushed. But the most amazing thing about her was that these signs of excessive emotion were not caused by any embarrassment at being discovered in such *déshabillé* by four other women, but were, actually, just excessive emotion. "Why, Aimee," Nathalie remarked. "How nice to see you." And then ignored her. "Father Gregory! You see I always keep my word."

Sonia found herself gazing at the man standing beside the table, which, apart from the settee and four chairs, was the only furniture in the room; there were no paintings on the walls, not even a cross or an ikon, although there was an expensive carpet on the floor. The drapes over the two windows were also of expensive material. But the man! Or was it a monster? Rasputin stood some inches over six feet, and was built to match. His head looked bigger than it was because of the amount of hair; this flowed in black profusion past his ears and there joined his beard, also black, which stretched to the centre of his chest. He was not dressed like a priest, but more like a servant, wearing a white blouse outside of his pants, which were black, with his feet thrust into black boots. Sonia realised

51

that the blouse was silk, but so were the blouses of the servants on Bolugayen. He was in the act of filling a glass from a decanter of Madeira, but this he now put down as he came towards them. "You promised me the two most beautiful woman in Russia, and I never doubted it for a moment, Nathalie Alexandrovna," he said.

Sonia gulped, less at the deeply resonant voice than at the total familiarity with which he addressed a Russian princess. "Will you not introduce me?" Rasputin asked. As he did so he ran his fingers into Dagmar's hair, dislodging her hat so that it fell to the floor, and then sliding beneath her pigtails to caress the nape of her neck, almost as if he had been her father.

"This is Mrs Duncan Cromb, Father Gregory," Nathalie was saying. "Before her marriage she was the Countess Patricia Bolugayevska. She is my late husband's half-sister."

Rasputin released Dagmar to take Patricia's hand. Again Sonia could only stare in consternation as he drew off Patricia's glove to caress her fingers and the palm of her hand. Patricia was also staring at him, lips slightly parted, with that defiant but acquiescent expression Sonia remembered so well. "I have heard much about you, Countess," Rasputin said. "But the tales have not done your beauty credit." He released Patricia's hand to take the hat from her head and throw it on the floor, which he apparently regarded as the proper place for hats, and then used both hands to pull the pins from her hair, allowing it to cascade past her shoulders in auburn splendour. Again Sonia could only stare at such indecent familiarity, unthinkable with any woman he had just met, but with a countess and a Bolugayevska . . . "Such hair should never be confined," he said. "It makes me think of a stormy sunset." Patricia licked her lips.

"And the Princess Sonia Bolugayevska," Nathalie said.

Rasputin stood before Sonia. She gazed at his face, which was large-featured and surprisingly bland, although

52

the line of the mouth, even half-concealed by the beard and drooping moustache, was hard. But she found herself caught by his gaze, for his eyes had a magnetic quality she had never encountered before. Even as she realised how Patricia had been unable to make any response to his insolent compliment, she equally realised that her own brain was being emptied of coherent thought, as he stared into her eyes in turn. "She walks in beauty like the night," he said. "Of cloudless climes and starry skies; and all that's best of dark and bright meet in her aspect and her eyes."

Sonia's head jerked. If she had a copy of Byron's works in her library on Bolugayen, she had never expected to hear even his most famous lines quoted by a staretz from the steppes of Russia. She was surprised to hear herself speak. "You are a flatterer, Father Gregory."

"I speak the truth, Your Highness. Always the truth. Beauty such as yours is an experience, not a vision."

Nathalie gave a little snort. Patricia gazed at her with arched eyebrows; she was not used to being placed second.

"I will leave now, Father Gregory," the woman Aimee said. "May I come again?"

Rasputin continued to stare into Sonia's eyes. "Please do," he said. "When next I can be of service."

Aimee gazed at his back for some seconds, then past him at Sonia, then turned and went through an inner doorway, obviously seeking a private way out of the house rather than face the mob in the waiting room. "What had you just done to her?" Sonia asked, desperately attempting to resist the hypnotic quality of his gaze.

"I was granting her dearest wish," Rasputin said. And smiled as she raised her eyebrows. "A commission for her son."

"For which she had to pay a forfeit."

"For which favour she wished to reward me," Rasputin

corrected. "Will you take a glass of Madeira? You may pour, Nathalie." Once again he smiled at the astonishment on Sonia's face that he should address a princess as if she were a servant. "We do not use titles in this room, Sonia," he said.

"Very democratic. But I do not think I will have a glass of wine," Sonia said. "You see, Father Gregory, as I have no favour to ask of you, I can therefore have no desire to reward you. It is very good of you to receive us, but I think we will now leave."

"Come and sit down," Rasputin said, taking her hand for the first time. She looked at Patricia, who raised her eyebrows. Obviously she was not leaving until she had experienced . . . whatever there was to be experienced. Sonia allowed herself to be drawn across the room to the settee, where she was seated, with Rasputin between Patricia and herself. When the staretz moved, close to her, she became aware of a powerful odour. Part of it was from the fact that she estimated that he had not bathed for several days, but there was more to the stench than stale sweat. My God, she thought: we have really descended into an animal's lair. And he is on heat! Nathalie stood before them with the tray, and five glasses, for Dagmar, seated on Patricia's other side, was also taking a drink. "Now tell me of this sin from which you desire me to absolve you," Rasputin said.

Sonia's head jerked so hard that she almost spilled her wine. She looked past the staretz at Patricia, but Patricia was looking bewildered. Anyway, Patricia would never have betrayed her to Nathalie. "Sin?" she asked.

"Of course. We all sin, Sonia. And we know it, however hard we try to conceal it. But God in His wisdom also knows it, and He conveys His knowledge to His chosen one. So now, confess it to me."

Sonia licked her lips. But he could not possibly know. Anyway . . . "I have not sinned," she said.

54

"Not even in your mind?" Sonia's nostrils dilated as she stared at him. Rasputin smiled, and drew off her glove as he had done with Patricia. His fingers coursed over hers, and then stroked her palm. They were coarse fingers, and she had no doubt that were she to look at them she would find them repulsive, but their touch was almost as hypnotic as his eyes. "You are afraid," he said gently. "Is it of confession itself, or of the anger of God? Be reassured, little Princess. God loves sinners, as long as they repent and seek forgiveness. Indeed, He loves sinners more than those upright prigs who swear they have never sinned. To be loved by God, one *must* first sin. The greater the sin, the better. Take Nathalie here. She sins constantly, so that she may be forgiven by God, and draw closer to Him. Is that not so, Nathalie?"

"That is so, Father Gregory."

"So, Nathalie, illustrate my point to your sisters-in-law. Commit a sin." Nathalie trembled. She took the tray to the table, placed it there, and returned to stand before the staretz. Both Patricia and Sonia gazed at her, uncertain what they were about to see. But Sonia observed that Dagmar was smiling, a secret, knowledgeable smile, quite out of place on the face of a thirteen-year-old girl. Nathalie took off her own hat and threw it on the floor to join the others, then she knelt before the staretz, raised his white blouse, and unbuckled his belt. Sonia thought she was going to choke as the Princess Dowager of Bolugayen then unbuttoned Rasputin's breeches and lowered her head. She tried to rise, and found that Rasputin's grip had suddenly become very strong, holding her hand and pressing down so firmly she could not move without hurting herself. She looked at Patricia, but Patricia apparently did not need restraining, just sat there, her lips parted. This freed Rasputin's left hand, with which he stroked Nathalie's hair, causing that too to come down in thick yellow strands, and then moving down her neck to release the buttons, and slide inside to caress her back, inside the material, and to one side, to stroke the side of her breast.

The only sound in the room was their breathing. Then Rasputin said, "Enough, for the moment, Nathalie." Nathalie raised her head, and knelt straight. Her face was crimson, and she did not look at either of the other woman. "Nathalie has sinned," Rasputin said. "She has committed a great sin. Now, you see, I forgive her." He laid his hands on Nathalie's head and muttered a few prayers. "You saw those ladies outside," he went on. "Most of them have come here *to* sin, like Nathalie, that they may be granted absolution, and thus draw nearer to God."

"And you assist them," Sonia whispered. "My God! That is the foulest blasphemy I have ever heard."

"Sonia!" Nathalie was on her feet. "How dare you address the staretz in such terms."

Sonia also stood up. "Because he is everything I have been told of him. And worse."

Nathalie looked at Rasputin in terror, but he merely smiled. "When you are so vehement, your beauty is redoubled, Princess. Come back and sit down."

"I am leaving, now," Sonia said.

"But you have not yet sinned, and been absolved. If you do not wish to sin by touching me, I will touch you. Permitting me to do so, as you are a wife and a mother and a princess, will equally be a sin. Come to me, little Princess, that I may comfort you."

"If you touch me," Sonia said. "I will kill you."

Rasputin gave a shout of laughter. "Kill me? How may a child like you kill me, little Princess? I am God's instrument. I am indestructible. But I will not force you. If you wish to live in sin, then go. You will come back, when your burden is insupportable."

Sonia glared at him, then turned to Patricia, who had remained seated. "Are you not coming with me?"

56

"I . . . I would like to speak further with the staretz," Patricia said.

"Are you out of your mind?" Sonia shouted. "If you stay here . . ."

"She will be a much happier person," Rasputin said.

Sonia·gave him another glare, then turned to the door.

"I would not go out that way," Nathalie said.

"I will go out whichever way I choose," Sonia snapped.

The women almost bayed at her as she passed through them to gain the outer staircase. But they also jeered at her, as they could tell that she had not responded to the staretz. She stumbled down the stairs, commanded Nathalie's driver to take her home, and there called for champagne. Aunt Anna's recipe for everything, she thought. Well, it had kept Aunt Anna going for a very long time, and through some fairly murky experiences. But surely never one as murky as this. What would Aunt Anna have done? Probably enjoyed it, as she seemed to have enjoyed everything that she had experienced throughout her life. But then, Aunt Anna was unique. But Patricia was not unique.

She took another glass of champagne, walked up and down. It was past five and already the October evening was drawing in. Where *was* Patricia?

Deep inside her a voice was asking, over and over again, why didn't you stay? If only to observe? But if she had stayed, she wouldn't have been allowed merely to observe. Rasputin wanted her, for whatever foul purpose most interested him. Never had she seen so much desire in a man's eyes. Not even Korsakov's. She had come here to escape from Korsakov, and instead nearly stumbled into a far deeper pit. She went downstairs to be with the children.

"Where did you go this afternoon, Mama?" Colin asked.

"We went to take tea with someone, darling."

"Madame Rykova said you went to see a holy man," Joseph said.

Sonia glanced at him, "Why, yes, so we did."

"Do holy men drink tea, Aunt Sonia?" Jennie asked.

"Yes," Sonia said, listening to the growl of the car engine in the drive. She ran to the window, but she could not see the front porch from the nursery window. Nor was she going to receive them on the grand staircase. She had to present a front of total indifference to their disgusting behaviour. She took another glass of champagne, and realised the bottle was all but empty. Had she drunk a whole bottle, all by herself? She sat down, then got up again and picked up the book from her bedside table. Poor old Tolstoy had just died, unhappy and bitter, estranged from the wife to whom, in a fit of absurd renunciation of worldly things, he had given all his wealth. Thus the greatest of Russian writers had died a pauper. Now there was a sad business.

The door opened; neither Patricia nor Nathalie had ever adopted the uncharacteristic habit of knocking. But thankfully, Patricia was alone. If this was Patricia. She was hatless, her hair a tangled auburn mess, her cheeks pink. Her clothes were also disordered. Oh, my God! Sonia thought. But she kept her seat. "Did you have a good time, with the staretz?" she asked.

Patricia walked across the room to the wall mirror, peered at herself for several seconds. Then she turned, and picked up the champagne bottle. "I'm afraid it is empty," Sonia said. Patricia gazed at her. "Well," Sonia said. "I was worried about you." She pulled the bell rope. Patricia sat down. "Do you wish to tell me about it?" Sonia asked. There was a knock on the door. "Dmitri," Sonia said. "Bring another bottle of champagne and some fresh glasses." She had never been able to get into the family habit of smashing a glass as she had drained it, but she felt she might be able to do so tonight.

"I wish you had stayed," Patricia said.

"I wish you had left with me," Sonia countered. "We came here to stay out of that kind of trouble, not jump into it with both feet." Patricia humped her shoulders. "Will you tell me what happened?"

Patricia shrugged. "I sinned. And was absolved."

"You didn't . . ." Sonia bit her lip as Dmitri knocked again before entering with the tray of glasses and the bottle. He filled two. "Leave it," Sonia commanded. Dmitri bowed and withdrew, carefully closing the door.

"No, I did not," Patricia said. "It seems there are two kinds of sin, active and passive. Of course, Father Gregory prefers active sin from his acolytes."

"Father Gregory!"

"That is his name," Patricia said. "But he is quite happy with passive sin. I suppose he feels the one will inevitably lead to the other."

"And what was your passive sin?"

Patricia licked her lips. "I . . . he fondled me."

Sonia could not believe her ears. "You let him touch you? You didn't undress?" She looked at Patricia's clothes. Of course she had undressed.

Patricia drank some champagne, and hurled the glass at the fireplace. "It was what he wanted. Only from the waist up." She got up, filled another glass. "One is really quite safe with him, you know. Nathalie has told me. He never sleeps with any of his admirers. He is a holy man."

"But he can do anything else. Oh, Trishka! How could you?"

"It just sort of happened." Patricia faced her. "And I'm glad it happened. It was an experience. To be touched by such a man . . ." She gave a little shudder.

"Will you tell Duncan?"

Patricia shot her a glance. "Of course not. And neither must you."

"And Nathalie?"

"Well, she said she would not."

"And the servants?"

"The servants know nothing of it."

"Don't be absurd. The chauffeur drove us to Rasputin's

59

house. Do you not suppose he will tell the others? And did you not see the way Dmitri looked at you just now? He could tell you had undressed some time recently."

Patricia stood in front of the mirror again. "He will not dare speak of it. No one will."

"I hope you are right," Sonia said. "I hope to God you are right."

Chapter Three

The Husband

"You lovely boy," Anna said, smiling at the handsome young captain seated beside her bed. "To travel all this way, with winter coming on, just to see me."

"I regard your health as of great importance, your excellency," Korsakov said.

"You say the sweetest things. That fool Geller says I must take no exercise until the bones are entirely knit. But do you know, I am inclined to disregard him."

"I really think it would be unwise for you to move around, Your Excellency. Even getting out of bed . . ."

"I am not contemplating getting out of bed," Anna pointed out, toying with the buttons of her peignoir. "But that does not rule out moving about, if you were to get in here with me."

Korsakov gulped. "I really think that would be unwise, Your Excellency."

"Meaning that you have no desire for a seventy-three year-old-woman?"

"Your Excellency, you are still the most beautiful woman in Russia."

"From the waist down, at least," Anna agreed. "Do not fret, Captain, I am not going to rape you . . . today, at any rate. But you must stay awhile. Now, tell me about your name, are you related to that ratbag composer?"

"I am not aware of it, Your Excellency."

"Anna. I would rather have you call me Anna. Do you know my brother served in your regiment? He was killed defending Sevastopol. My God, that was fifty-six years ago."

"I wish I had been alive then."

She raised her eyebrows. "To defend Sevastopol?"

"To have known you when you were seventeen, Anna."

She squeezed his hand. "You must stay a long while, Paul."

"Thank you. I am told the Princess is not in residence."

"She has gone off to Petersburg, with her sister-in-law Patricia. Have you met my son, Duncan?"

"I look forward to it. He is presently out, I was told by your butler. And that both ladies are away. May I ask when they are returning?" Anna raised her eyebrows. Korsakov flushed. "I would like to meet the Princess again. And your niece."

"You are a rogue and a wretch," Anna told him. "The Princess is very beautiful, is she not?"

"Very," Korsakov said, without thinking.

"She is also totally chaste," Anna said. "She is a Jewess, and their moral standards are somewhat different to ours. She is also very much in love, with her husband."

"I but wished to renew our acquaintance," Korsakov protested.

"Well, you will have to renew your acquaintance with the Prince, instead."

"Captain Korsakov! How good to see you." Alexei shook Paul's hand. "I would have you meet my brother-in-law, Mr Duncan Cromb."

Duncan also shook hands. "The Countess Anna is my mother, Captain. You have my eternal gratitude for your help."

"You'll forgive my not being here when you arrived,

62

but I had no idea you were coming to visit," Alexei said, escorting Korsakov into one of the downstairs parlours, followed by Duncan and Gleb the butler with a tray of champagne.

Korsakov had already worked out why Sonia had hurried off to Petersburg; he had pressed too hard too soon. "I happened to be in Poltava, your Highness, and I thought I should come out here to see the Countess Anna."

"Of course, as you so gallantly rescued her. You must stay awhile."

"I'm afraid my duties require that I leave tomorrow, Your Highness."

"Oh, that is a shame," Alexei said. "I know the Princess will be sorry to have missed you. She is in Petersburg, Christmas shopping."

"I am sorry to have missed her as well, Your Highness. She is a very lovely and gracious lady. But with your permission, I will call again when next I am in this district."

"The wretch," Anna remarked.

Alexei sat by her bed. "Well, Aunt Anna, I think it was very gallant of him to ride all this way to see you."

"To see me," Anna said contemptuously. "He came here to see Sonia."

Alexei frowned. "Why should he wish to do that?"

"Because he would like to make her his mistress."

Alexei's frown deepened, and then cleared. "Anna, you are returning to the fantasies of your youth. Sonia? She is my wife."

"So?"

"Well . . . the whole idea is preposterous. She is not like that."

"Like me, you mean," Anna remarked. "I would have you know that I never once cheated on my husband,

63

whatever I may have done before I met him, or since his death. We were in love."

"As Sonia is in love with me."

"It pleases every man to suppose that of his wife."

Alexei glared at her, and got up. "You are an extremely wicked old woman."

Anna smiled. "Everyone knows that, Alexei. I was an extremely wicked *young* woman, too."

"And you glory in that." Alexei went to the door, but he hesitated with his hand on the knob.

"Alexei," Anna said. "I said that Korsakov would like to make Sonia his mistress. I did not say she would accept that. I do not believe she would. I think you are quite right in assuming that she is in love with you."

Alexei went outside. Anna was trying to mend fences while the horses were still galloping. "She is an extremely lovely and gracious lady," Korsakov had said. "And with your permission I will visit you again." But that simply could not be. Sonia *did* love him, and her children, too much ever to betray them. Besides, she owed him too much. Her very life! Still, it was not a situation he could ignore, certainly after Witte's letter!

He sat in his study, took the letter from his drawer, read it again, as he had read it a dozen times.

'*Feeling is very strong*, Witte had written. *I am afraid this is a natural reaction to Stolypin's death. I have even heard the opinion expressed that it would be best for Russia if the Jews were entirely expelled. Or destroyed. Of course we could never let matters go so far, but on a more personal note, there are those who are now recalling that the Princess Bolugayevska is not only Jewish but was once convicted of terrorism, was fortunate to escape hanging, through the generosity, or, as some would have it, the weakness of the Tsar, and that, again through that weakness, as some would have it, was pardoned and allowed to marry you. I am not for a moment suggesting that His Majesty would ever renege on his word. But I am bound to advise you that there can be no hope for the appointment you seek, either military or political, while the Princess Sonia is your wife. Believe me, my old friend, it grieves me to write like this . . .'*

Alexei laid down the letter. There was damnation, the price of falling in love with exquisite beauty without pausing to count the possible cost. When one is young, he reflected, one never does count the possible cost. But would it not be even more damnation to allow a letter like this to influence his life? And hers. And that of their children? On the other hand, if from Sonia's point of view their marriage was already over . . . what had Jesus said in the garden? Get thee behind me, Satan. But Satan would always be there, in his case.

"When do you expect your sister?" Alexei asked Duncan at lunch.

"She should be here in another couple of weeks. I know she left Boston a fortnight ago."

"Your mother is recovering very well, wouldn't you say?"

"She's the toughest old bird I have ever known."

"That must be a great joy to you," Alexei said. "I was wondering if we should not join the girls in Petersburg, as quickly as possible."

Duncan raised his eyebrows. "Is something the matter?"

"No, no, nothing is the matter. It is just that I find myself missing Sonia and the children."

"Well, of course I miss Trish and the kids as well," Duncan said. "But I really wouldn't like to leave Mom alone. Surely another couple of weeks can't be that important? Our being there isn't going to stop them buying up the city."

"I suppose not." Alexei looked up as Gleb bowed beside his chair.

"Post, Your Highness."

"I thought I heard the horn." Alexei sifted through the letters. "One for you, from London."

65

Duncan made a face. "Telling me what's gone wrong with the business since I left. Nothing from Trisha?"

"No. Nor from Sonia. But there is one for me from Petersburg. I do not recognise the writing." He picked up the silver paperknife and slit the envelope. Duncan saw that there was a single sheet of paper, folded in two, which Alexei now studied, a deep frown slowly gathering. When he was finished he remained staring at the paper for several seconds. Then he abruptly stood up, before the footman behind him had the time to hold his chair. "Mr Cromb and I will be leaving for St Petersburg first thing in the morning, Gleb," Alexei said. "Have the automobile prepared to drive us into Poltava, and inform Rotislav." Rotislav was his valet.

"Now say . . ." Duncan began.

"I think we should go into the office," Alexei said, and led the way past the waiting footmen. "Close the door," he said when Duncan joined him.

Duncan obeyed. "What's happened?"

Alexei held out the sheet of paper for Duncan to read. Duncan did this slowly, for although he had learned to speak fluent Russian, he was not so accustomed to the written word. "This is scurrilous nonsense," he remarked, when he was finished.

"You think so?" Alexei went to the sideboard and himself poured two glasses of brandy.

"Well, it's just an insinuation. Anyway, supposing Patricia and Sonia did visit this character, why should that cause us to . . ." he glanced at the paper again. "Look to our marriages? Sounds to me like someone stirring shit."

"You *have* heard of this man?"

"Well, yes. In a manner of speaking. He claims to be able to cure all sorts of illnesses. In the States, we'd call him a quack."

"Yes," Alexei said grimly. "But in the United States you do not have the sense of mysticism that affects the Russians, of all classes."

66

"We have our revivalist preachers, from time to time."

"Rasputin is not a revivalist preacher, Duncan. He is a vicious animal."

"Oh, come now. Is he not a personal friend of the Tsaritsa?"

"Yes." Alexei opened the drawer of his desk and took out the postcard Stolypin had given him on the night of the opera; he had pocketed it when his conversation with Stolypin had been interrupted, and had only found it later.

Duncan looked at it in consternation. "Of all the obscene lampoons . . ."

"Oh, it is obscene all right. But is it a lampoon? I was to discuss the situation with his majesty that very night. But of course, the murder, by a Jew, put the lid on that. I have not seen the Tsar since. Stolypin certainly felt that it was too close to the truth for comfort. Besides, Her Majesty apart, he had some information on this fellow's habits, when in the company of his acolytes, who seem to include every titled lady in Petersburg. One of his principal pleasures, it seems, is being bathed by these same titled ladies."

Duncan sat up. "You're not suggesting Trisha and Sonia . . ."

"This letter indicates that they have visited the staretz."

"An anonymous scrawl . . ."

"Does that mean it cannot be true?"

Duncan stared at him, then drank his brandy, got up, and refilled his glass from the decanter.

"Why don't your famed secret police do something about such a man?"

"Simply because he has the ear of the Tsaritsa. And through her, of the Tsar."

"And the Tsar permits such carryings-on?"

"He simply refuses to believe they can possibly be true. I am afraid this Tsar of ours is very much of a simpleton. There, I have spoken treason."

"Not to me. I happen to agree with you."

"Certain it is that he is entirely under the thumb of his wife. And of course, there is no one with the guts openly to denounce this thug. Well, that is going to change. I am not afraid to denounce him."

"On the basis of this letter?"

"On the basis of what I find in Petersburg. What *we* find, Duncan. It is your wife who is accused as well. Who also happens to be my sister."

"Yeah," Duncan said. "That's what bothers me. If we go stomping up there and call Rasputin out, or whatever it is you Russians do in matters of honour, we are going to plaster our wives' names all over the newspapers, and create one hell of a scandal."

"If they have really allowed themselves to be sucked into this monster's orbit, does that concern us?"

"Well, if you don't mind, old son, I would rather find out, from them, just what the truth of the matter is, before I go jumping off the deep end. Anyway . . ." he frowned. "Suppose it's true. What would you do?"

"What will *you* do?"

"You think it is true, don't you? Well, shit, Trisha had had a few adventures before we got married. As did Sonia."

"But they are both now married."

"Yeah. I guess the best thing I could do would be to get her out of Russia, fast. This place is no good for her. Never has been."

"You mean, you would forgive her, and carry on your life as if nothing had happened?"

"Well . . . what else could I do?"

"I'm afraid such a . . . what shall I say? . . . passive course of action is not open to the Prince of Bolugayen. Certainly not where the Princess is involved. I cannot merely take her out of Russia. We belong here. Therefore the matter must be settled here, once and for all."

"You mean you'd end the marriage? You can't be serious! I thought you loved her."

Alexei sighed. "I do. But I have my duty to the Tsar, to the country, to my family, to consider."

"Sounds to me like you have a slide rule of standards, old son," Duncan said. Alexei glared at him, and Duncan grinned. "So we're on opposite sides. We have been before, remember? But you came down on our side with a thump when you shot that Okhrana agent, Rurik Bondarevski, to save Trisha's life."

"That was instinct," Alexei said. "It is not something I am proud of. And it is only known to Trisha, you, and that man of yours, Morgan. You swore it would remain a secret."

"As it will," Duncan assured him. "I was just pointing out that there are occasions when blood must be thicker than politics or social standing."

"Blood," Alexei said. "One forgives things in a sister one could not accept in a wife."

"I'm afraid I must disagree with you."

"That is because you do not know the whole of the matter. I took a grave risk in marrying Sonia."

"Which you now regret, is that it?"

"I do not wish to regret it. But the facts are there. In addition to being an escaped criminal, Sonia is a Jewess. These facts are all well known in Petersburg, and to the Tsar. They may well be raked up again when the time comes for Colin to succeed me. If at that time his detractors can also rake up a scandal about his mother . . ."

"So if you were to get rid of her, you could then marry a true-blue Russian aristocrat and resume your proper place in society, is that it? Do you know, I used to be proud to call you my brother-in-law?"

Alexei did not take immediate offence. "You can adopt such attitudes, because, as I say, you do not know the whole of the matter."

"I thought you had just told me that?"

"I told you some of it. Suppose I also told you that Sonia is having an affair?"

"Now that I would refuse to believe. Who is she supposed to be having an affair with?"

"You saw him. That fellow Korsakov."

Duncan frowned. "I can't accept that."

"Why do you think he came here? It was to see her. Aunt Anna spotted that right away."

"Mom always did have an overwrought imagination. It doesn't make sense, Alexei. If Korsakov came here to see Sonia, then she must have known he was coming. So instead of waiting for him, she runs off to St Petersburg, several hundred miles away? That is hardly the act of a mistress."

Alexei drank some brandy. "I have thought about that. There are two possible answers to that question. One is that it is part of a great subterfuge. Sonia goes off to Petersburg a couple of weeks before Korsakov arrives here. How do we know they did not meet during that fortnight, following which he arrives here and says, oh, what a pity, I missed the Princess. Or again, having come here, and been apparently surprised and disappointed at missing her, he has now gone off again. How do we know he is not now on his way to Petersburg?"

"You really are quite paranoid about your wife, Alexei. Which I suppose is a form of love. But that theory won't work, because Sonia has Patricia with her. I'm not saying Trisha hasn't got a streak of wildness in her, but I do not think that she'd ever let Sonia compromise her marriage, if only for the sake of the family."

"Which brings us to the second possible answer," Alexei said. "That Sonia invited Korsakov here, then confided in Trisha – after all, they are the oldest and most intimate of friends – with the result that Trisha forbade her to go ahead with the liaison, and to prevent it, carried her off to Petersburg."

"To the arms of Rasputin, you say. Or at least the bathtub."

"I do not think this is a matter for joking, Duncan."

"I can see that it is not. However, we have a belief, both in England and in the States, that a man is innocent until he is proven guilty. Or a woman. I think you're adopting quite the opposite point if view."

"I am leaving for Petersburg tomorrow morning," Alexei said. "To find out. Are you coming with me?"

"Here is a note from Madame Xenia," Sonia said, sitting at the breakfast table with Patricia. As it was a fine November day, the children were already outside. "She says that Captain Korsakov visited Bolugayen for one night, and then left again."

Patricia ate toast. "That must have put Aunt Anna's nose out of joint." Then she frowned. "You haven't confided in Xenia?"

"Of course not. I merely told her to expect Korsakov, and to let me know when he had been and gone. So, I think it is now perfectly safe to return home. We shall leave tomorrow."

"Oh, don't be silly," Patricia protested. "Why should we do that? The boys clearly haven't missed us yet; there has not been a single letter from Duncan. Have you had anything from Alexei?"

"No. That bothers me too. I think we should go home."

"Well, I don't. Anyway, not tomorrow, Sonia. Don't be a spoil sport."

"What is so special about tomorrow?"

Patricia flushed. "I have promised Nathalie . . ."

"You mean you are going back to Rasputin's." Patricia, she knew, had been to see the holy man three times since that first occasion. She always went with Nathalie and Dagmar, and Sonia, who always refused to accompany them, had never asked what they did there, but she had no doubt at all it was something revolting.

That was another reason for her wanting to get Patricia out of the city as quickly as possible. If her sister-in-law

71

was merely following Petersburg fashion, as it appeared, the situation was still fraught with danger. Quite apart from the moral angle. But remonstrating with Trishka was a waste of time. She quite obviously was of the opinion that after all she had suffered, including having to act the prostitute just to live, she was entitled to sample everything life had to offer. That was a difficult point of view to argue against, especially when Sonia had herself shared all of that suffering. But Trishka, having married her own cousin, had side-stepped morality in any event, as well as having side-stepped the responsibility of being a Bolugayevska. And now she seemed unable to appreciate any other point of view. "Why, yes, I am going back," Patricia said. "On Friday."

"I would have supposed, with your entrée, you could go whenever you please. Why do you not go this afternoon, if you must, and let us get out of here tomorrow?"

"I am going on Friday because that is when the staretz wishes to see me. He knows as well as anyone that he cannot let any one woman monopolise his time. That would cause discord amongst the others. He does not want any scandals. Do you know, there are always people sneaking up to the Tsar and muttering that Rasputin must be sent back to Siberia. Fortunately, the Empress remains his friend. She needs him. But he still doesn't want any scandal about his private life."

"My God! Don't you suppose everyone in Petersburg knows about it anyway? As for you . . . you are married to a fine man who adores you, and yet you want another man to play with your breasts? That is absolutely obscene."

"You really don't understand," Patricia said dreamily. "Don't you ever want someone apart from your husband to play with your breasts? Or put his hand between your legs?"

Sonia stared at her in horror. "You haven't let him do that?"

Patricia's flush deepened. "I let him do whatever he

wants. I have told you, he will never bed me, because he is a holy man."

"Because he is a devil."

"You haven't answered my question. Didn't you dream, perhaps you still do, of Korsakov putting his hand inside your blouse? Of course you did. Do. But you couldn't risk the possible scandal, the possibility of a continuing affair with him making all manner of extravagant declarations of love and perhaps doing something stupid. Not to mention the fact that you would have been committing both a sin and a crime. So you ran away. But with Rasputin, don't you see, there is no possibility of an affair, of repercussions. While as for sinning, one goes to him, commits a sin, and is absolved. You can have the best of all possible worlds."

"With a man who is grotesquely ugly, who stinks like a peasant, because he is a peasant, and who blasphemes every time he opens his mouth?"

"So he repels you. You are in a minority. And he is still very anxious to get to know you. Will you not come with me, at least to say goodbye?"

"Get to know me!" Sonia shuddered. "Under no circumstances will I come with you. And I wish you would not go either."

"You are a prude and a spoilsport," Patricia said angrily. "Well, you go on back to Bolugayen. I am staying here until next week." She flounced from the room.

God, Sonia thought, what a mess one can make of things, through trying to do the right thing. She brooded on the situation for the next few days, taking her meals in her apartment with Colin and Anna, who understood that their mother had had a difference of opinion with their aunt but did not understand why. By Friday, however, she had made up her mind to leave, the more so as Patricia had refused another of her pleas to accompany her. She therefore told Grishka to pack for herself and the children. Perkins looked surprised; Patricia and Nathalie had already gone out.

"You are staying another week," Sonia told her. Perkins pursed her lips. There could be no doubt at all that below stairs knew all about their mistresses' visits to the staretz – or about what went on there.

Sonia went into the garden, where Joseph was endeavouring to teach Colin the intricacies of baseball, a game of which he had become fond during his last visit to Boston. The two little girls were being employed as fieldswomen, and seemed happy just to be allowed to play with their big brothers. Dagmar had, of course, gone to Rasputin's with her mother and aunt. She was clearly being turned into a sexual monster. But then, knowing her mother, Sonia supposed that might have happened anyway. She sat on a bench to watch them, enjoying the sunshine, the last of the sunshine, she supposed – the snow was in any event late – and was disturbed by the appearance of Dmitri. "His Highness is here, Your Highness."

Sonia's head jerked, and she stood up. "His . . .?" she looked past the butler at Alexei, and gulped: Duncan was behind him. "Alexei!" She hurried forward to embrace him, and to her consternation he held her arms to keep her away from him, and kissed her on the forehead. "Why didn't you let us know you were coming?"

"We wished to surprise you," Alexei said, and released her, stepping past her to embrace his children, who abandoned their game to greet their father.

Sonia looked at Duncan, who did take her in his arms for a kiss. "Sorry to turn up like this," he said. "But am I glad to see you. *Here*." She frowned at him, uncertain what he meant. "Trish around?" he asked.

My God, Trish! she thought. But she couldn't let her oldest friend down. "She's out at the moment. She'll soon be back."

"Oh. Right." It was his turn to be surrounded by children.

74

Alexei came towards them. "Shall we go inside? You chaps carry on with your game." He led the way. "You are having unseasonably fine weather," he said over his shoulder.

"It is pleasant, isn't it," Sonia agreed, following him, Duncan behind her. He knows, she thought. He knows *something*. Oh, my God! What to do? Keep calm, for a beginning.

Alexei went into the winter parlour, where a fire glowed in the grate. Dmitri was pouring champagne. "It is snowing further south, would you believe it?" Alexei asked. "The train was held up while they cleared the tracks. Thank you, Dmitri, that will be all."

"I will inform Madame Rykova of your arrival, Your Highness."

"Yes. She can make me up a bed in one of the guest apartments. Show Rotislav which one it is, will you. Duncan?"

Dmitri was looking to one and the other in consternation, while Sonia could feel the blood draining from her face; she had to sit down before she fainted. "Oh, tell Morgan to put me in with Mrs Cromb," Duncan said. Dmitri hurried from the room.

Sonia opened her mouth to demand an explanation, then closed it again. She just could not speak. Certainly not in front of Duncan, whom she hardly knew.

"May I ask where Patricia is?" Alexei inquired.

Sonia drew a long breath. "She's out." She looked at Duncan.

"And Nathalie?"

"She's out, too. With Patricia. They're out together."

Alexei handed her a glass of champagne. She certainly needed it. "Are they shopping?"

"Ah . . . yes. I think so. We were going to leave tomorrow, to come home. I was, anyway."

"Were you?" Alexei sat down, opposite her, throwing the tails of his coat across his thighs. Duncan remained

75

standing, awkwardly. "Korsakov has come, and gone," Alexei said.

"Korsakov? Oh!"

"You did not know he intended to visit Bolugayen?"

"I . . ." but she dared not lie; she had no idea what Korsakov might have told him. "He did write to say he would like to visit, to see Aunt Anna, but he didn't specify a date. I did not think it concerned me."

"Obviously it did not, as he wished to see Aunt Anna. May I see his letter?"

Sonia's head came up. "I do not read your correspondence."

"As I do not correspond with unattached women, there is no reason for you to do so."

Sonia felt her cheeks burning. "I say, old man," Duncan muttered.

"You may leave, if you wish," Alexei said.

"Well . . ." Duncan looked at Sonia. He too was flushing.

"I would like you to stay, Duncan," Sonia said.

"Oh. Ah . . ." He refilled his glass, and sat down, well to one side.

"The letter?" Alexei asked.

"I burned it."

He raised his eyebrows. "Do you burn all your correspondence?"

"I burn correspondence for which I cannot see any future use, yes." Sonia had regained her nerves. Things were obviously far worse than she had feared, but she was not a coward. She decided that the best, the only defence, was attack. "May I ask why you are interrogating me as if I have committed some crime?"

"I am trying to find out just what you have committed," Alexei said.

"That is an insulting remark," Sonia snapped, beginning to get angry.

"It is addressed to my wife. Will you answer me a

76

straight question? Have you had an affair with Captain Korsakov?"

"That is also an insulting question," Sonia said. "No, I have not." But she could feel herself blushing.

"I see. Well, then, will you answer another question?"

"First tell me that you believe me."

"I will tell you that when you have answered my second question." Sonia glared at him. "Have you visited this staretz, Rasputin, here in Petersburg?" Sonia bit her lip. If only she could stop flushing. "I can, of course, inquire of the servants, and others," Alexei said. "I should not like to have to do that."

Sonia sighed. "Yes. I have been to Rasputin's house." She gave a little shrug. "I was taken there, by Nathalie. She appears to be a great friend of the staretz."

"I am sure she is. You may, of course, remain in this house until I have made all necessary arrangements."

"You . . ." she could not believe her ears.

"I say, old man," Duncan protested. "I think you're jumping the gun. Did Patricia go with you, Sonia?"

Sonia bowed her head. "Yes. I think I am entitled to be asked what happened there."

"What happens when women visit Rasputin is too well known, and too obscene, to be inquired about," Alexei said.

"*Nothing* happened," Sonia said. "I will swear it, if you wish. We were introduced to the staretz, and we did not like him. I did not like him, anyway. So I . . . we, left and came home." She was short of breath.

"Well . . ." Duncan began.

"Say that you believe me," Sonia said to Alexei.

"It is a matter to be considered. I shall . . ." He turned as the door was flung open.

Nathalie was as dishevelled as ever, but she was smiling in total triumph. "Alexei! How nice of you to visit Petersburg." She looked at Duncan, frowning.

"Duncan Cromb, Your Highness," Duncan ventured. "We met in Port Arthur, twelve years ago."

"Of course. Anna's son. And you now are Patricia's husband. Patricia!" she called over her shoulder. "Your husband is here."

"Duncan?" Patricia hurried into the room, and Sonia saw that she too was somewhat dishevelled. "Duncan!" Patricia said again. "You know I hate surprises."

"Yeah. Well . . ." he looked at Alexei.

"It was my idea," Alexei said. "May I ask where you have been?"

Patricia looked at Nathalie, who continued to smile. "We have been to the staretz." She turned her smile on Sonia. "He asked why you did not come with us, this time, my dear." Sonia could think of nothing to say. She wanted to hit the woman.

"You've been to this character?" Duncan asked his wife. "Why?"

Patricia pouted. "He's exciting. And life is so dull."

Duncan was clearly at a loss for words.

"May I ask what happens when you visit this man?" Alexei asked, his voice deceptively quiet. He was apparently unaware that he was contradicting his earlier attitude.

"He is a holy man," Nathalie said. "We go there to be absolved from our sins."

"What sins?"

"Well, if we have no sins, he allows us to commit some, and then he absolves us."

Alexei joined the ranks of the speechless, but only for a moment. "You mean you commit a sin with this man to allow him to absolve you."

"That is what I mean, yes."

Duncan stared at Patricia with his mouth open. Alexei looked at Sonia. "Rasputin has never touched any part of me but my hand," Sonia said in a low voice.

"Ha!" Nathalie commented.

78

Sonia stood up. "And if you claim otherwise you are a liar," she said.

"Well, really! I am the Princess Dowager of Bolugayen. How dare you speak to me like that."

Alexei felt in his inside breast pocket and produced the folded sheet of paper. "Did you send this?"

Nathalie glanced at it. "Certainly not." But there were pink spots in her cheeks.

"Patricia," Duncan ventured.

"Oh, really, Duncan, it was just a giggle."

Duncan licked his lips. "I would like to speak with you, alone." He went to the door and opened it. Patricia hesitated, then shrugged and went through it. Duncan followed, closing the door behind him.

"I wonder if he will beat her?" Nathalie enquired.

"I would like you to go to your apartment, and wait for me there, Sonia," Alexei said.

Just as if he were her father, Sonia thought. But she could not have a scene in front of Nathalie. She went to the door and opened it.

"Are you going to beat *her*?" Nathalie asked.

"I am going to get to the bottom of this matter, and deal with that scoundrel," Alexei declared.

Sonia caught his arm as Alexei strode out of the parlour. "Alexei, please. What are you going to do?"

"Deal with that rogue, for a start."

"You cannot. Alexei, he has the ear of the Tsaritsa!"

"Is that supposed to concern me?"

"Alexei, you cannot call out a staretz!"

"I would not waste the time. But I am entitled to horsewhip any man who has debauched my wife." He shrugged her hand away.

"Alexei, he has never touched me. Do you wish me to go down on my knees to swear that?"

"The servants are listening, and watching," Alexei told her. "We will discuss what you will do, when I return." He strode towards the porch, where Dmitri, having overheard the conversation, was waiting with both coat and whip.

"Alexei!" Sonia shouted, "I am begging you. Horsewhip *me*, if you must. But do not go there." Alexei went out of the door.

"Well?" Duncan demanded.

Patricia went across the sitting room, opened the bedroom door, and threw herself across the bed, rolling on her back. "Are you going to beat me?" she asked.

"Oh, good lord, Trisha." Duncan sat beside her. "Do try to grow up. Did you sleep with this lout?"

Patricia stretched. "How vulgar you are. One does not sleep with a staretz, Duncan: it is against his vows."

"But not against yours."

She had closed her eyes. Now she opened them again. "It would not have been an act of love."

"Am I that unsatisfactory?"

"Darling?" She held his hand. "You were not here. It began as an adventure. Everyone goes to Rasputin. How was I to keep away? Especially when Nathalie had told him of me. Well, of us." She sat up. "I think it is Sonia he really wants to get his hands on."

"Get his hands on! My God, the things you say."

"The truth! Are you so afraid of the truth? He wanted to, well . . . feel me up."

"And you let him?"

"It was an act of admiration. And stimulation as well. And it could not be a crime."

"Because he absolved you. An utter rogue and charlatan."

"He is a staretz."

"The sort of fellow who puts one off religion. Oh, Trisha, how could you?"

"Oh, dearest heart . . ." she put both arms round him and kissed him, used her strength to push him flat, and rolled on top of him.

80

"Trisha," he protested. "Suppose someone came in?"

"No one has any business coming in," she said. "Duncan, I did not mean to . . . well, have anything to do with Father Gregory."

"Father Gregory!"

"That is his name, you know. I went, and Sonia went, because Nathalie wanted us to. As I said, she had apparently boasted of having the two most beautiful women in Russia both under her roof. So he wanted to meet us. Well, I was flattered. I expected nothing more than a meeting."

"You did not know of his reputation?"

"Rumours. There are always rumours. Perhaps that made it more exciting. But I was quite sure I could cope with any holy man from the steppes."

"Only you couldn't." He rolled her off him, but remained in her arms, as she was now in his.

"His eyes," she said dreamily. "I do believe I was hypnotised."

"You? Hypnotised?"

"When he stares into your eyes, anyone's eyes, believe me, you lose all will-power. You wish only to please him. And you believe him, that whatever you do, whatever he makes you do, he will absolve you of the guilt." Her eyes had been half shut. Now she opened them wide. "That is a very difficult proposition to resist."

"So what exactly did he make you do?"

"He made me do nothing. He . . . well, as I said, he unfastened my blouse and put his hand inside. And he felt my bottom."

"My God!"

Patricia squeezed the front of his trousers. "But the thought excites you. Do you know what he made Nathalie do? He made her, well . . . perform fellatio."

Duncan sat up. "And Sonia?"

"Oh, Sonia would have nothing to do with him. When he tried to touch her, she walked out."

"Thank God for that. Now listen." He turned on his knees beside her. "You must tell Alexei that. You must make him believe that."

"He won't."

"Why not?"

"Because I think he is beginning to regret ever marrying her."

"You can say that, about your own brother, and your best friend?"

"Sometimes it is necessary to face facts. And then there is the Korsakov business."

"You're not going to tell me Sonia actually did have an affair with that fellow?"

"No. She did not."

"Well, that is something else of which you have to convince Alexei."

"But she wanted to," Patricia said. Why do you think I brought her to Petersburg? So she couldn't go through with it."

"And landed her in deeper trouble than ever. God, what a mess. As for you . . ."

"Aren't you going to punish me? She fluttered her eyelids.

"Yes, I am going to punish you," he said. "We are leaving for Bolugayen tomorrow. And once Alexandra gets there to be with Mom, we are leaving Russia and going back to England. This place is no good for you." Patricia pouted, briefly. "But before we go," Duncan said, "you have got to sort out Alexei and Sonia. Only you can do it. You have got to make them believe in each other again."

"I've told you, I don't think even I can do that."

"You must try."

Another quick pout, then she smiled, and held his hands, and drew him to her. "Let's worry about them later. Duncan, I've learned so much, these past few weeks. Duncan, would you like me to show what I have learned?

82

We've never done that. Don't look so shocked. You would like me to, wouldn't you? And I do want to."

"Is it always as crowded as this?" Alexei asked the chauffeur, as the Mercedes edged its way into Rasputin's drive.

"Always, Your Highness." The chauffeur cleared his throat. "Have I Your Highness's permission to speak?"

"Yes. What is it?"

"May I recommend . . . well, Your Highness, this man is really very powerful."

"He is a staretz from the steppes," Alexei said. "And I am the Prince of Bolugayen. Wait for me here." The chauffeur bowed his head, and Alexei stepped down. The waiting drivers and chauffeurs looked at him with interest. As he was not a regular visitor to St Petersburg none of them recognised him, but they could tell at a glance that he was an aristocrat, and instinctively stepped out of his path. He marched up to the front door and banged the ornate knocker.

"You won't get in that way, Your Honour," ventured one of the watching men. "That door is only opened for the Tsaritsa."

Alexei was so taken aback he actually asked a question of an inferior. "The Tsaritsa comes here?"

"So they say, Your Honour. But if you wish to get in to see the staretz, you must use the side stairs."

Alexei stepped past the men and looked at the side stairs. Then he went up, the riding crop tucked up against his arm. At the top he threw open the door and stepped into the antechamber, again paused in consternation, at the sight of all the women.

They were equally surprised, and several stood up, no doubt fearing he might be their husband, Alexei deduced. But several recognised him. "It is Prince Bolugayevski!" The whisper ran round the room.

Anton the major-domo advanced. "May I inquire your

business, Your Honour?" He refused to concede a higher rank than that to an intruder.

"My business is with the monk Rasputin," Alexei said.

"Indeed, Your Honour? Is it a petition?"

"It is not a petition." Alexei stepped forward, and Anton hastily barred his way.

"You must wait your turn, Your Honour."

"I am the Prince Bolugayevski," Alexei announced. "And I wait for no man save the Tsar and the Grand Duke. And I find you exceedingly insolent. Stand aside."

"I will have to see if Father Gregory can receive you, Your Highness," Anton said.

For reply, Alexei pushed him to one side. Anton made to grab his arm, and Alexei turned, picked up Anton by belt and shirt front, and threw him several feet. The women screamed, and now all were on their feet, retreating against the wall as Anton struck a chair and went over with it, hitting the floor with a reverberating thud. Alexei opened the inner door and went in, leaving the door ajar. And for a third time in a few minutes checked in consternation, while the women, crowding into the opened doorway behind him, gasped.

Rasputin sat on the settee facing the door, a naked woman on his knees, while he caressed her stomach and between her legs. At the interruption, the woman gave a squeal of terror, and slid off his lap to kneel on the floor, hastily gathering her discarded clothing. "Jutta Svenkarska!" The whisper ran through the watching women and back to those unable to get a view.

"She has nothing on!" The whisper grew.

Rasputin stood up. He looked more irritated than concerned at the intrusion. "Do you have business with me?" he enquired.

"Yes," Alexei said.

"Then kindly close the door. Madam, you may dress in the inner room." Jutta Svenkarska scooped the last of her clothes into her arms, then scuttled for the inner room, buttocks gleaming. Alexei pushed the gaping women back into the antechamber and closed the door. "How did you get in here?" Rasputin enquired. "Did not Anton stop you?"

"He tried," Alexei said, and uncoiled the whip.

"I see." Rasputin went to the table and poured himself a glass of wine. "You?"

"I did not come here to drink with you," Alexei said.

"You came here to avenge the so-called honour of your wife. Or your mistress." Rasputin filled a second glass. "That is no reason why we should not have a drink, first." He held out the glass.

"You are an obscene swine," Alexei said.

"What is your name?" Rasputin asked.

"I am Prince Bolugayevski."

"Ah! The husband of the very beautiful Sonia."

"You admit that she came here?"

"Who am I to deny it?" Rasputin himself drank the second glass of Madeira.

"Then you admit you debauched her."

Rasputin considered, while refilling his glass. "I endeavoured to entertain her."

"You bastard!" Alexei snapped the whip.

"If you touch me, you are disgraced forever," Rasputin warned.

"As are those *you* touch. But you assume too much power to yourself, priest. Not that I intend to touch you. This will do." He snapped the whip again, and sent it curling through the air. Rasputin jerked straight, but the leather had already slashed across his shoulders. He gave a roar of anger and hurled the full glass of wine at his assailant, but Alexei comfortably side-stepped the flying glass and struck again with the whip.

This time Rasputin caught the thong, giving a little grimace as it wrapped itself round his hand, but pulling as hard as he could. As Alexei did not let go, the two men were dragged towards each other. Rasputin hissed, and bared his teeth, and brought up his left hand; they were roughly the same size. But Alexei, although the older, was also the fitter, and he was the first to swing his fist, catching Rasputin on the side of the face and sending him staggering across the room, releasing the whip as he did so. Alexei stepped back to swing the whip again, but as he did so, the roof seemed to fall on his head.

Chapter Four

The Scandal

"This will not do," the Tsar said. "This simply will not do, Prince Bolugayevski. I can tell you that Her Majesty is extremely displeased." Listening to the polite words, Alexei could not help but wonder what this man's father, Alexander III, a mountain of a man who had dominated Russia at once by his size and his ruthless aggression to all who dared oppose him, would have said. Yet Nicholas, however short, with his handsome features and neatly clipped beard, his splendid uniforms and his compelling eyes, looked capable of ruling as forcefully as his father had done. Only those who knew him as well as Alexei, or Sergei Witte, the Minister of the Interior who stood beside the Tsar's desk, were aware that he entirely lacked strength of character, would make a decision and then change it at the slightest hint of opposition – save where that decision had been made by the Tsaritsa, the real ruler of Russia. But, no doubt fortunately for the country as a whole, the Empress Alexandra confined her interests to domestic matters and the continuing worry over the health of the Tsarevich. Unfortunately, that involved the continuing prosperity of Rasputin. "It is the talk of Petersburg," Nicholas grumbled, flicking the various newspapers on the desk. "That a staretz should be attacked in his own chambers, horsewhipped . . . that

87

a prince of Russia should be thrown out into the gutter . . ." He looked up. "How is your head, by the way?"

Alexei touched the bandage. "I am told there is no permanent damage, sire. But I cannot accept that I am in any way in the wrong. My wife . . ."

"And how many other wives, do you suppose? Oh, do not remind me, this lout is an uncouth sex maniac . . ." Suddenly the Tsar smiled. "Did you really horsewhip him?"

"Unfortunately I was prevented from doing so properly, sire. But I did hit him." Alexei raised his right hand to show the cut knuckles.

"Capital. Capital, eh, Witte? But the Tsaritsa is furious. And the scandal." He frowned at Alexei. "You have dragged your wife's name into the gutter. Not to mention that of your sister and your sister-in-law. What's to be done about that, eh?"

"I do not think anything needs to be done about the Princess Dowager, sire," Alexei said. "She glories in her association with the staretz. My sister is already on her way back to Bolugayen, from whence she will be departing, with her husband and children, for England or America. She will not be returning."

"I should not have let her come back in the first place," Nicholas grumbled. "You asked me to do that, Prince Bolugayevski."

"I know that, sire."

"And your wife?"

Alexei gazed straight in front of him. "I have instituted proceedings for a divorce, sire."

"My God! Have you considered the scandal? A prince, divorcing his wife?"

"I have also considered the scandal of the Princess Bolugayevska allowing herself to be debauched by the staretz, sire."

"She has admitted this?"

"No, sire. She denies it. But then, does she not *have* to

88

deny it? And the facts are there. There are also . . . other matters to be considered."

"Hm," Nicholas said. "I have heard of these other matters." He pointed. "But I will have no duelling. It would be beneath your dignity, anyway, to challenge such a fellow. And, Alexei Colinovich, I am very afraid he might kill you. Captain Korsakov is one of the best shots in the army."

Colour flared into Alexei's cheeks, caused partly by surprise at how much the Tsar knew about his affairs. "The world will think me a coward, sire."

"Then the world will be wrong. And I will make it known that it was I who forbade a duel. Now we must look to the future. You have elected to divorce your wife, and we must be prepared to ride the scandal. I may disapprove of the necessity, but I cannot disapprove of the cause. May I say that I regretted your marriage in the first place, Alexei Colinovich. It is possible that this whole ghastly mess may turn out for the best in the long run. As I say, my wife is very angry. Therefore you will return to your estate and remain there. She is speaking of five years." Alexei's head came up. "However," the Tsar went on. "It may be possible to review the situation much sooner than that. When this scandal has died down, when your divorce is completed . . . and perhaps when you have married again." He gazed at Alexei, who swallowed. "Had you not considered this?"

"Frankly, no, sire."

"Well, I would if I were you, Alexei Colinovich. We live in troubled times, which are only going to grow more troubled. Consider this business in the Balkans. We could find ourselves at war with Austria at any moment." He cleared his throat and glanced at Witte; all three men were well aware that Russia, still not recovered from her shattering defeat at the hands of the Japanese, was in no condition to go to war with anyone, even decrepit Turkey, much less the Austro-Hungarian Empire, which also had deep interests in the Balkan Peninsular and was most definitely prepared to fight to protect those interests. "The point is, Alexei Colinovich, that Russia is going to need the total support of all good men over the coming years. I count you one of those men."

"I thank you, sire."

"But no man can give of his best while his domestic situation is in disorder. I will be frank with you. I think you are doing the right thing in getting rid of your Jewess. There is, however, the remaining point that your children, and most especially your present heir, are half-Jewish. I cannot help but feel that it would be best for everyone should this be different."

"You would have me disinherit Count Colin?" Alexei was aghast.

"I think it might be best if your *next* son were to be the future Prince Bolugayevski, Alexei Colinovich. I am sure you are in a position to make ample provision for Count Colin Alexeivich." Alexei bit his lip. "Well, I shall not detain you any longer," the Tsar said. "You will return to Bolugayen, and remain there until summoned by me. However, when I say remain there, I mean that you will not return to St Petersburg, until summoned by me. I will raise no objection to you leaving your estate, for, shall I say, matrimonial purposes. Good-day to you, Prince Bolugayevski."

Maitre Polonowski adjusted his spectacles and bent over his desk. Although she knew it could not be true, Sonia thought that he looked dusty. That was because the entire office was redolent of dust, to which could be added coal dust from the roaring open fire; the snow had at last arrived and St Petersburg was shivering under a white blanket. It was warm enough in the lawyer's office, but not warm enough to thaw her out; Sonia did not suppose she would ever be warm again.

Polonowski cleared his throat. "I would say this is all

in order. I would also say that Prince Bolugayevski has been most generous. Quite absurdly so, if you will pardon me, Your Highness." He peered at her over the tops of his glasses.

"And it does me no good to swear that I am entirely innocent of the charges brought against me," Sonia said.

Polonowski frowned. "You do not mean to contest the suit?"

"Should I not? He is taking away my children. I am not even to have access."

"Your Highness, I must advise most strongly against it. In the first place, it would mean washing a lot of dirty linen in a most public fashion, and would involve your total ostracism. In the second, it would cost you this most generous settlement offered you by the Prince. In the third, you would still lose. And in the fourth, well, Your Highness, you must realise that there are certain irregularities in your past, which have been entirely overlooked, because of your status as the Princess Bolugayevska. Your husband guarantees that they will never be raised again, even when you cease to be the Princess Bolugayevska. If you were to anger him . . . Take the money, Your Highness. Five million roubles. It is a fortune. You can live wherever you choose, ah . . . do whatever you choose. You could, ah, return to your own people, and, ah . . ." He flushed as Sonia gazed at him. "Will you not sign, Your Highness?" He pushed the paper across his desk.

At one stroke, she thought, I cease to be a mother. That was the hardest to bear. Beside that, her implicit condemnation of the fact that she appeared to be accepting of everything of which she was accused, was quite irrelevant. But then, that was the story of her life, as the lawyer had just reminded her. Seventeen years ago she had been forced to accept the charges made by the Okhrana, of which, then too, she had been entirely innocent. That had cost her four years in Siberia and a lifetime as a fugitive. She was at least being offered

91

an escape from that. She picked up the pen and signed at the indicated place.

"Thank you, Your Highness." Polonowski made sure everything was in order. And then flushed some more. "You understand that you must be out of the Bolugayevski Palace by tonight. I assume you will be going to an hotel?"

"I have not really thought about it."

"Yes. Well . . ." His expression indicated that it was time she did think about it. "His Highness has agreed that all your clothes and effects will be packed up and forwarded to you as soon as you inform me of your new address. I am speaking of your effects on Bolugayen, of course. I assume you will be taking your effects from the palace here in Petersburg with you."

"I am all packed," Sonia said absently.

"Well, then, that is most satisfactory. You will be pleased to know that I have been instructed to open an account for you, the moment you signed the paper, and that the money will be paid into this account immediately. So you really have no financial worries whatsoever. I hope you appreciate that, Your Highness." He was clearly anxious to see the back of her as well as debating whether he should continue to address her as Your Highness, in view of the fact that she had just signed away her right to be known as the Princess Bolugayevska.

What am I to be known as, then? she wondered, as she took her leave and went down the stairs. Plain Sonia Bolugayevska? Or do I not even have that right? Then do I call myself Sonia Cohen? After all these years? The chauffeur opened the door for her and she got in. "I should like to drive through the ghetto," she said.

"The ghetto, Your Highness?" He was alarmed. And he did not yet know that she was no longer Your Highness. She had perhaps another six hours of enjoying the omnipotence of being the Princess of Bolugayen, before disappearing into total anonymity.

"Just take me there," she commanded. He drove, slowly, through the streets she remembered so well. Until they arrived at the street she remembered more than any other. "Stop a moment," she said, and the car drew up outside the house in which she had been born. And where she had been arrested by the Okhrana, raped and beaten and humiliated. That was seventeen years ago, and she had never been back. She had never dared go back, as the Princess Bolugayevska, because, as the Princess, she had had to turn her back entirely on her past. Now she had been told, go back to that past. As if she dared do that, now. She leaned out of the window to look at the house, and the man standing outside it. "Good-morning," she said.

The man looked at the car, and her clothes, and touched his cap. "Good-morning, Your Nobility."

"Can you tell me who lives here now?"

"Rabbi Djerkin owns this house, Your Nobility."

"Ah! I was here a long time ago, once, and I seem to remember a family named Cohen . . ."

"Oh, yes, Your Nobility. There were people named Cohen living here once. Terrible people, Your Honour. Terrorists!" He lowered his voice. "Communists."

"How awful," Sonia said. "Whatever happened to them?"

"Oh, I wouldn't know, Your Nobility. There was talk some were executed, and some sent to Siberia . . . the daughter it was. Then there was a story about how she escaped and married a prince. Pure fairy-tale, Your Honour. There's none here now."

"I see," Sonia said, and pulled back into the car. "Home, please, Tomislav." Pure fairy-tale. How very true.

The house was quiet in the middle of the morning, although Sonia could hear the children playing in the garden. Dmitri greeted her as gravely as if nothing had

93

happened, although he, and indeed all the servants, had to know just what had happened. He could not resist asking, however, "Will Your Highness be going out again?"

"Yes," Sonia said. "I will be going out again."

"Of course, Your Highness. The Countess Patricia left this letter for you."

Sonia took the envelope, went up to her apartment, and sat down to open it.

My dearest Sonia, Patricia had written. *What a terrible bore!* Sonia raised her eyes to heaven. *I feel so responsible! Alexei is behaving like a silly schoolboy! Or a Russian prince! Well, that is all he is, on both counts. These men and their absurd notions of honour! And princes are worse than anyone else. I am sure he will regret what he is doing, and come running behind you. However, until then, should you have any difficulty, please be sure that you have·always a home with Duncan and me, whether it be in London or Boston. I can assure you that Duncan joins me in this invitation. I just know we are going to meet again, and laugh again, and even, perhaps, adventure again, together. Until then, yours ever and ever and ever, Trishka from the Steppes.'*

Sonia was amazed at her composure, the fact that her eyes were absolutely dry, while her mind was spinning half out of control. Dearest Trishka! As ebulliently confident as ever in the past. But then, why should she not be? Nothing that had ever happened to Patricia, and there had been a great deal, and nothing that *could* ever happen to her in the future, could alter the one simple fact that governed her life: she was the Countess Bolugayevska, born and bred. There was no stroke of the pen, her pen or anyone else's pen, that could possibly alter that. That she also happened to be married to a totally loving and *committed* man, who seemed prepared to forgive her anything, was just the icing on her cake. While she . . . but she was still the Princess Bolugayevska, at this moment. Although she had agreed to all the terms set out in Alexei's letter, agreed not to contest the divorce or any of the accusations contained in the petition, agreed to surrender her children, the matter still had to go through the courts, and even more important, the church. Alexei might have the power immediately to exile her from his houses, separate her from her children, but for some months yet she would remain his legal wife.

She walked to the window and looked down at her son and daughter. How could any man be so heartless as to separate a mother from her children? But Alexei would not see things that way. To him they were not her children so much as Bolugayevskis; that she happened to have given birth to them was an accident of history. But to walk away from her darlings . . . she did not think she could do that. Nor did she have to. If she were to summon them up here now, and tell them all three of them were leaving that afternoon, to catch a ship for England, there was no one in this building with the authority to stop her. But she could not do that. She could not take away their birthrights as boyars, nobles of the Russian state, with all the power and prestige that implied. Colin would one day be Prince of Bolugayen. Anna would be married to one of the highest men in the land. Theirs was a future which not only glowed, but was filled with responsibility.

Her eyes filled with tears. Then she thought: Aunt Anna! So much had happened so quickly that it had not occurred to her to appeal to that greatest member of the Bolugayevski family. Anna had had so many peccadilloes in her own life surely she would condone Sonia's curiosity? But Anna was a Bolugayevska to the toes on her feet. Whatever she had done had been undertaken with but a single aim – to control the future of Bolugayen. She had abandoned the comfortable life of a Boston matron to plunge back into the family politics when she felt they needed her, and she had stayed and suffered with them when at any time she could have opted out and returned to her American family. She was also fond of reminding everyone that however many lovers she had had, she had

95

never committed adultery: as Charles Cromb's wife she had been absolutely faithful. She would never condone the Princess Bolugayevska even contemplating committing such a sin. As for dragging the family name in the dirt by visiting Rasputin . . .!

Sonia sighed, and turned at the knock. Grishka entered. "Ah, Grishka. Have my bags sent down, will you. I shall be leaving in an hour or so."

"Of course, Your Highness. And the children?"

"No, Grishka. The children are remaining here for a while." The two women gazed at each other. "You know that I shall not be returning to Bolugayen," Sonia said.

Grishka bit her lip; undoubtedly she did know that. "May I ask where Your Highness *is* going?"

"I think I shall take a suite at the Hotel Astoria, for the time being. Perhaps you would have Dmitri send someone over to make a reservation."

"I will attend to it right away, Your Highness." She half turned to the door, and hesitated.

"I would be very grateful if you would accompany me, Grishka," Sonia said.

Grishka faced her again. Sonia could imagine the thoughts tumbling through her mind. It is not possible for a woman to keep any secret from her personal maid, any more than a man can from his valet. Grishka knew Sonia was innocent of having had an affair with Captain Korsakov. She also knew that on the one occasion her mistress had visited Rasputin, she had returned without a single garment, exterior or under, much less a single hair, out of place. But Grishka had been a Bolugayevski servant long before Sonia had first seen Bolugayen, and her family remained living on the estate. "I must do as His Highness wishes, Your Highness," she said.

"I know," Sonia said. "Then I must say goodbye."

A last look around the room. Sonia wished she could take a last look around Bolugayen. But what she was really doing was bracing herself to say goodbye to the children. She could not even explain to them what was happening. It was part of the agreement she had just signed that all explanations were to be left to the Prince. God alone knew what he would tell them. He would be free to describe her in the most wanton terms. But she could not believe Alexei would do that. He might be absurdly jealous, and behaving, as his sister had written, like both a prince and a schoolboy, but he was not a vicious man. But that did not help her, now. She was to say she was going away for a few days. A lie, to her children, on the occasion of their last meeting. But that was being absurdly pessimistic. If they were her children, then they would seek her out, one day. She had to believe that. Her door was swept inwards. "I am told you are going to the Hotel Astoria," Nathalie announced.

"It is the only one I know."

"I believe it is very nice there." Nathalie wandered about the room, fingering ornaments, as was her habit. "I suppose you think I am responsible for all this."

"No," Sonia said. "You are not responsible."

"Ha! That idiot Patricia thinks I am responsible. She has left me the most offensive note. But I do not wish to talk about the past. That is a waste of time. Only the future matters. Your marriage is over. Thus I would hope to see something of you in the future."

"I am forbidden the use of this house."

"Then I shall come to see you. And perhaps now you will come with me to Father Gregory." Nathalie had the grace to blush. "He is really very fond of you, you know. Probably this is because he has never had the chance to . . . well . . ."

"Get his hands on me," Sonia suggested.

"If you wish to be vulgar, yes. My dear Sonia, what do you have to lose, now?"

"Only my honour," Sonia said, and left the room.

*　　*　　*

97

"Really," Anna commented. "I don't know what to say." She sat in a rocking chair, which she moved carefully to and fro; although her bones had all but knitted she still needed to be careful. Nor would Dr Geller allow her to go out of doors until the spring, and the chair was placed in front of the window so that she could look out at the garden, although the window was of course closed, as the garden was submerged beneath a thick layer of snow.

Alexei waited, glancing nervously at Alexandra Robbins. This cousin he had never met before, but she was every inch the smart Boston matron in her kimono jacket and peg-topped skirt, her velvet-laced boots. She was, as he recalled, considerably older than Duncan, forty-one in fact, and her soft blonde beauty had just about reached an apogee. But her eyes were cold; she had wasted no time in conveying that she did not approve of the Tsar, or of the Russian aristocracy which supported him – which, he knew, represented fairly average American opinion. Yet Alexei was very glad she was here. He really was afraid of Aunt Anna's reaction to what had happened. As he also knew that when Aunt Anna said she did not know what to say, she was about to say a great deal. "I have never known Sonia to lie," Anna remarked.

"Now, Aunt," Alexei protested. "You yourself said that Korsakov came here to have an affair with her."

"Yes, I did," Anna agreed. "I also said that I was quite sure Sonia would not agree to it. If you are so sure of the matter, why have you not challenged the lout?"

Alexei bit his lip. "I was forbidden to do so by the Tsar."

"Because of the scandal. I quite agree with him. But you also believe she went to see this charlatan Rasputin. Despite her denial."

"She has not denied going to see him, Aunt Anna. She has denied that anything improper took place. Well, on the evidence I have been able to gather, if nothing did take place then her visit was unique."

98

"Duncan has forgiven Patricia."

"With respect, Aunt Anna, Duncan is not the Prince Bolugayevski. The Princess Bolugayevska must be like Caesar's wife: above suspicion." He looked at Alexandra for support.

But she was concerned with what she considered more important matters. "How have the children taken it?"

Alexei gave his aunt another anxious look. "I have not yet actually told them. Just that their mother had to go away on a visit."

"Do you realise that you are an arrant coward?" Anna enquired. "You, a soldier who has been commended for bravery in the field, cannot tell the truth to his own children?"

"The question is, what is to be done, Mother?" Alexandra pointed out.

"They will have to be told that their mother has behaved very badly, and that she therefore can no longer be their mother. Or the Princess Bolugayevska."

"But you cannot *do* that," Alexandra cried. "There is no proof. Even you admit there is no certain proof, Alexei."

"It does not matter whether there is proof or not," Anna said. "I may personally disagree with what Alexei has done, but he has done it. There can be no going back now. Therefore there can be no going back for the children either. They must be made to put their mother quite out of their minds. Colin will one day be Prince Bolugayevski . . ." She did not notice Alexei's sudden flush. "It will not do for his mother to one day reappear and claim any privileges from him. The same goes for little Anna. They simply have to accept that their mother never was, and that can only be done by making them reject her."

"Mother, you are a terrible old woman," Alexandra said.

"I am a Bolugayevska. Sometimes I think that I am the only Bolugayevska. Only the family matters. You

99

would do the same if there was a matching scandal in Boston."

"Are you telling me I should drop Duncan and Patricia should they ever return home? Anyway," she hurried on before her mother could make a pronouncement on that, "children need a mother." She glanced at Alexei.

His flush deepened. "It has been suggested to me, by the Tsar, that I should marry again, as soon as possible."

"And no doubt you have a princess in waiting," Alexandra suggested, coldly.

"I have not. It is a matter to be considered."

"And while it is considered, I will be a mother to the children," Anna declared.

"I think I will stay and help you, at least for a while," Alexandra said.

"And your own children? Do they not need a mother?"

"James is a grown man, Mother; he does not need me any more. As for Priscilla, I think I will send for her to join me here. She'll enjoy seeing how the other half of the family live."

Alexei looked at his aunt in consternation. He did not really want the upbringing of his family overtaken by Americans. Anna smiled reassuringly. "I shall still act as their mother, until you are again suited, Alexei," she promised.

Alexei was at the foot of the gangplank in Sevastopol to greet his stepniece. "Welcome to Russia, Priscilla."

"Gosh," Priscilla said. "Wow! I mean, I'm just happy to be here. Say, Mom says you're a prince."

"Unfortunately, that is true."

"Gee! Do you think I should curtsey or something?"

"I think it would be delightful for you to curtsey. But I don't want you to. I'm your uncle."

"Oh, yeah. I guess you are. You speak awfully good English."

100

"That's because I am English."

"Of course. That was stupid of me. Please forgive me."

"My dear girl, I will forgive you anything." Her eyebrows arched, delightfully, and he tried not to stare at her. Alexandra had told him that Priscilla was nearly eighteen, but he had not actually related that to the obvious fact that she would be a grown woman, certainly physically, and that she would also be the spitting image of the painting of Aunt Anna as a young girl, which hung in one of the downstairs reception rooms at Bolugayen. Or that she was just the age he was seeking in a second wife. How odd that the Tsar had given him permission to leave Bolugayen to seek a wife, and this was the first time he had availed himself of that permission. What an absurd and vaguely obscene thought. But was it? His sister had married her cousin with the blessing of the family, himself included. This girl was only his half-niece. That was a long way away in terms of consanguinity. But the very idea made him embarrassed. "Your maid?" he asked. Again she raised her eyebrows. "You haven't travelled all the way from America by yourself?" He was aghast.

"No, no, Uncle Alexei. I came on one of Uncle Charlie's ships, in care of Captain Lomas. Believe me, I was chaperoned by the entire crew. And then in London I stayed with Uncle Duncan and Aunt Patricia. And I came here on one of your ships, in care of Captain Iyinski. Again, I was protected, believe me."

"But still, a lady must have a maid."

For a third time she arched her eyebrows, even more delightfully. "Then I guess I'm not a lady."

He grinned at her, even more delighted with her spirit. "I am sure you are. Let's board the train."

"I have a couple of bags."

"My people will see to those."

Alexei leaned back in the first-class compartment while

101

they waited for the bags, smiling at Priscilla; in the background the train hissed impatiently, but gently. She smiled back, but was more interested in looking out of the window, at the platform and the harbour beyond. She knew he was old enough to be her father, of course. And at this moment saw no necessity to regard him as anything else than a very wealthy uncle. But she had to know more about him than that. "Was this the first time you had met your Aunt Patricia?" he asked. "In London?"

"Oh, no," she said. "I met her when she came to the States, a few years ago. She's very lovely, isn't she?"

"Not half as lovely as you," he said without thinking.

Her head turned, sharply, and she blushed. "That's very kind of you, Uncle Alexei."

"I meant it." He debated whether to tell her not to use Uncle, but decided against it; he was too good a horseman to rush his fences. "Did Duncan and Patricia tell you anything, well . . . about what has been happening here?"

Now she sat down. "I guess it's the current family skeleton. I'm so terribly sorry, Uncle Alexei."

"Please don't be. My wife . . . my ex-wife, and I, were never really suited. We were thrown together by circumstances, and, well . . . one thing led to another."

"It often does," Priscilla agreed. "But still . . . Who is this guy, Rasputin, anyway? One of the newspapers back home was running a story on him. Sounds a regular Bluebeard."

"Save that he neither marries nor murders his victims," Alexei said. "He doesn't have to."

"Yeah. I'm still so sorry about your wife, Uncle Alexei. Mom showed me a photo of her. She looked such a kind person. And Aunt Pat thinks she's the bee's knees." She bit her lip. "I guess I shouldn't have said that."

"Sonia and Patricia are very old friends. They went through a lot together. Do you know anything about *that*?"

"Some." But she was flushing again. He wondered just

102

how much she did know about it. She giggled. "I don't think Mom approves of Aunt Pat. Neither does Uncle Charlie."

"I don't think anyone approves of Aunt Pat," Alexei said.

"Save Uncle Duncan, I guess. Is it true she was once a Communist?"

"I sometimes wonder," Alexei said, "if she is not still a Communist, at least at heart."

"Holy Smoke!" Priscilla stood in the front hall of the Bolugayevski Palace in Poltava, and looked around herself with enormous eyes. "You mean you own this, Uncle Alexei?"

"I own several houses," Alexei said. "This is the one we use when we are in Poltava. Madame Tchernitska will show you to your apartment. Would you join me in the winter parlour, whenever you are ready?" The housekeeper curtsied, and led Priscilla up the grand staircase. Alexei watched the girl's hips swaying beneath the form-hugging skirt, and thought that the best thing that had happened in the last dozen years was when bustles went out of fashion.

He went into the winter parlour, followed by Mtislav the butler, with a tray of champagne and several glasses. "Did you have a pleasant journey, Your Highness?"

"I had a very pleasant journey," Alexei said, seating himself before the fire and drinking deeply.

"The weather has not really been conducive to travelling, Your Highness," Mtislav ventured; the snow was six inches deep on the street outside.

"I never noticed," Alexei said. He was telling the simple truth. For the twenty-four hours they had spent on the train, he had been entirely absorbed by Priscilla Robbins. It was not merely her very real beauty which made her so compelling; more important was the essential unworldliness of her mind, at least as regards Russia . . .

103

and her eagerness to learn. He had understood very early on that as regards matters on which most young Russian girls were totally ignorant, she was well informed. She was an American, she had been to a girl's school rather than being educated at home, she had an elder brother, and more important than any of these, she had a mother who called a spade a spade. Perhaps fortunately, she did not know her grandmother very well, having only met her on a couple of occasions, although she clearly had been brought up to worship the ground on which Anna walked. But she really knew nothing about living in a country where the rich were not only very rich – there were sufficient millionaires in America, her Uncle Charlie amongst them – but were allowed the license to impose their wealth upon others, without fearing the result of the next election: if the Tsar continued to call Dumas whenever he was persuaded it was what the country wanted, he always dismissed them again whenever they attempted to erode his prerogatives. Alexei had always been vaguely ashamed of that. Now he found himself thinking what a delight it would be to teach this young woman the pleasures of omnipotence.

Because now he sat beneath yet another portrait of his aunt, which Priscilla noticed as soon as she entered. "Gee," she remarked. "That's Grandma as a girl."

"Indeed it is." Alexei stood up, and himself held out the glass. "Welcome to Russia."

She sipped. "We've already drunk to that."

"This is the real Russia. The Bolugayevski Russia. *Our* Russia."

"Oh." Pink spots gathered in her cheeks, and she carefully studied the portrait. "Wasn't she lovely? I mean, she still is lovely. But then . . ."

"She turned many heads. As I have no doubt you will do."

"Me?"

"You are a reincarnation of her."

"Oh! Well . . ."

104

"So I say again, welcome to Russia." Alexei drained his glass and hurled it into the fireplace, where it exploded into a thousand slivers of crystal.

"Oh!" Priscilla said again. "Do I do that?"

"When you have finished your drink."

Priscilla drew a long breath, drank, and drew another long breath. "You don't reckon it's kind of extravagant?"

"It is not possible for a Bolugayevski to be extravagant."

"Oh," she said. "Gee!" She hurled her glass.

"I really do not know what to say," Alexandra commented, unconsciously apeing her mother. "As you know, Mother, I have had nothing to do with the Russian half of the family."

"Because you have never approved of us," Anna said, equably.

"I'll go along with that. The fact is, your family is a representative, and a relic, of a dying civilisation. Me, I believe in the future."

"I would say you are looking at it."

Through her binoculars Anna could just make out the four horses and their riders, topping the distant rise. In March, the snow was thicker than ever, but Alexei rode every day, with his children, and Priscilla. "She is absolutely terrified," Alexandra pointed out.

"Nonsense. Priscilla is not the sort of girl to be terrified by anything. Besides, she loves Bolugayen."

"She has had her head put in a spin, you mean. She has never come into contact with such wasteful opulence in her life. She was almost in a state of shock the other day when she realised her underwear had been burned simply because she had had her period. As for Alexei . . ."

"She seems very fond of Alexei."

"Do you know what she said to me, almost the day she arrived? Do all Russians come on that strong, Mom? I

105

must have been crazy to allow him to go to Sevastopol to meet her. You talked me into that, Mother."

"I did. And does her question mean that she doesn't like him?"

"It means that he is deliberately setting out to turn her head. I'm sorry, Mother, it's not on."

"What's not on?"

Alexandra glared at her. She was well aware that her seventy-four-year-old mother's brain was as sharp as a new pin, and that *she* would find herself on the defensive if she wasn't careful. "Any idea of marriage between Alexei and Priscilla. Don't tell me he hasn't got that in mind. Quite apart from the relationship angle, he's old enough virtually to be her grandfather, they come from different backgrounds and cultures, and he's a monster!"

"Oh, really, Alix."

"Listen to me, Mother. He's a Russian, right?"

"Wrong. Both his father and mother were English. Alexei has not a drop of Russian blood in his veins."

"You have to concede that he was brought up as a Russian. And a prince. Right?"

"I will accept that," Anna said.

"Well, we have lots of evidence of his ideas on things. Wife steps out of line, in his eyes, and she is condemned on flimsy evidence and out she goes."

"I think there was more to the divorce than you really understand. Or," Anna added, equally well aware that Alexandra numbered quite a few Jews amongst her friends in Boston, "than I am prepared to discuss."

Alexandra ignored the diversion. "Russian husbands beat their wives, right? If you think I am going to sacrifice Priscilla to some wife-beating monster . . ."

"I wish you wouldn't keep using that word, Alix. To my knowledge, Alexei has never raised his hand to any woman in his life. Least of all his wife. He is too much of a gentleman."

106

"You mean you would go along with the idea?" Alexandra was aghast.

"I think it might work out very well. Colin and Anna are really fond of Priscilla. She would be just what they need as a stepmother."

"For God's sake, she's only old enough to be their sister!"

"Quite. That means she'll be able to look at life with their eyes."

"I think you're crazy. And immoral. Well . . .." Alexandra flushed.

"Say it," Anna requested. "Everyone knows I am immoral, do they not? Or is not amoral the word?"

"He's her *uncle*, for God's sake!"

"Her stepuncle," Anna corrected. "Those things do not matter as much in Russia as they do in Boston. It is the blood that matters. Alexei married the wrong blood, first time around. Now he has the opportunity to correct that mistake."

"Well, Mother, I am sorry to disagree with you so strongly. I want you to understand that there is no way I will ever agree to a marriage between Priscilla and Alexei. So, in all the circumstances, I think we will leave as soon as the necessary shipping passages can be arranged."

"I do wish you would reconsider," Anna said, mildly.

"I do not intend to do that," Alexandra said.

Little flecks of snow flicked away from the horses' hooves as Alexei and Priscilla cantered up the slope above Bolugayen House. The snow was hard-packed still, although as March entered its second half, the temperature at noon was beginning to edge above freezing, and the grey skies were beginning to break and allow the sun to peep through, from time to time.

"Would you believe," Alexei asked, "that in another six weeks this will all be exposed earth, and a month after that, nothing but green for as far as the eye can see?"

"I wish I could be here then," Priscilla said.

Alexei guided them towards a little copse, set in a dip, and private to the world. As always when he rode his estate, he was accompanied by two grooms, but they kept a discreet distance, and now they remained on the far side of the rise, where they could neither see nor be seen from the copse – but from where they could still prevent their master from being interrupted. Today the children had been left behind. "But your mother will not let you," Alexei remarked.

"She says we go, so we go. She's all excited. She has tickets on this new liner, the greatest ship in the world."

"The *Titanic*. I have read of her. Won't your Uncle Charles be annoyed that you are sailing in a ship belonging to another line?"

"I guess. But that won't stop Mom."

Alexei drew rein, and dismounted, then held up his hands for her. "We are stopping for a purpose?" she asked.

"Just to stretch our legs."

She grinned, and allowed herself to be lifted from the side-saddle. Her boots crunched on the snow as the skirts of her habit settled about her ankles. "You know what I like about Russia, Uncle Alexei? It's the way you don't use foolish words to cover what you want to say. In Boston, no one ever refers to a lady's legs."

"I think you mean the Boston society to which you belong," Alexei suggested. "Not to the city as a whole. But surely it is sometimes necessary to do that? Speak of legs, I mean. How would they put it?"

"Well . . . limbs, I guess."

He tethered their horses and walked beneath the trees. "This is one of my favourite places on the estate."

"Romantic, huh?"

"Why, yes, it is romantic." He turned to face her. "I

108

would like you to tell me, with absolute honesty, what you think of Bolugayen."

"Why, it's just out of this world, Uncle Alexei." She hesitated.

"Go on. I asked for absolute honesty."

"It's out of this world," she said again. "If your name happens to be Bolugayevski, even if removed a couple of times."

"You don't think my people are happy?"

"Oh, sure, they give the impression of being happy. Maybe they are. But . . . as you just said, they're *your* people, not their own."

"Hm. Do all American girls of your tender years think as deeply as you do?"

"Not many American girls have ever seen a place like Bolugayen, Uncle Alexei. I guess most of them have no idea places like this exist. And when they do read of it, they automatically reject it. This kind of master/servant business isn't really our idea of what life should be about."

"Does it offend *you*?"

"In the abstract, maybe it does. In the concrete, like I said, I'm a Bolugayevska. Even if a couple of times removed."

He took her hat from her head, and her breathing quickened. "I should be the happiest man on earth if you were to remove those couple of times." The bodice of her habit was rising and falling even more quickly. "Does *that* idea offend you?" he asked.

"Gosh! That's kind of sudden, Uncle Alexei."

"Is it? You're a very intelligent girl, Priscilla. You know what's going on about you."

"Yes, but . . . well, I knew you found me attractive. But you never, well . . . ."

"It would not have been polite, to attempt to take advantage of you while you are a guest in my house. I would not have raised the matter now had you not been about to leave."

109

"You realise I can't stay. Not if Mom says we're going." Priscilla gave a quick frown. "You haven't spoken to her?"

"No. I understand that I am going about this quite the wrong way. But it is necessary. I mean, I must know whether you could consider the possibility, before I take it any further."

"What exactly are you asking me, Uncle Alexei?"

He smiled. "First of all, I would ask you to drop the 'uncle'. But what I am really asking you is to marry me. I know there are many objections to a marriage between us. Or there could be, if one sought them out. I am forty-seven years old, you are seventeen."

"That's not important," she said, perhaps without meaning to, for colour flared in her cheeks.

"That you should hold such an opinion pleases me greatly," he said. "I am also a representative of everything you say you and your friends instinctively reject, thus I am asking you to reject *them*, or at least their point of view, as you will have to if you become the Princess Bolugayevska."

"The Princess Bolugayevska," she muttered, then smiled. "You are a rogue, Uncle Alexei. Oops, Alexei. You are twisting my head right off my shoulders."

"Is there not a saying that all is fair in love and war?"

"I guess that's true." She hadn't said no. He could hardly believe it. She was standing there, gazing at him, waiting . . . "Do you think we could do something," she suggested. "My feet are freezing."

"Have you ever been kissed?"

"Well of course I have." She gave that unforgettable arch of her eyebrows. "Does that rule me out?" He took her in his arms and kissed her mouth, felt her body against him, wanted to hug her and hug her and hug her. Had ever a man known such happiness, he wondered. She moved her face back to catch her breath. "Mom will never allow it."

110

"Do you wish it, Priscilla?" His hands drifted gently up and down her back.

"Oh, gee," she said. "I don't know. I . . . do you love *me*, Alexei? Or just, well . . ."

"If I did not wish to possess your body, Priscilla, I could not love you in any other way. But I do love you. I think you are everything I have ever dreamed of." He kissed her again. "And I have been dreaming a very long time. I understand that you can hardly love me. But if it might be possible that you would grow to do so . . ."

She kissed him herself. "It's all academic. Mom will never agree."

Had she said yes or not? He could not be sure. But she had definitely not said no. On the other hand, she was absolutely right in her judgement. "I am afraid the idea simply cannot be entertained, Alexei," Alexandra said. Alexei looked at Anna; Priscilla was not present. "I have already explained this to my mother," Alexandra said.

"I will make your daughter a good husband. And she will make a brilliant Princess Bolugayevska," Alexei said, keeping his emotions carefully under control. "I realise that there is a considerable difference in our ages, but she does not seem to find this a difficulty."

"May I take your points in order?" Alexandra asked. "I am sure you will make Priscilla a good husband, according to your understanding of what makes a good husband. That is someone who requires absolute obedience, not to mention subservience, from his wife. That is slavery. I am sure Priscilla will make a brilliant princess, but I do not happen to believe in people being princes and princesses, at the expense of others. And however much you may have dazzled her, Priscilla also does not believe in that order of things, deep down. And lastly, as you say, you are old enough to be her father with a good deal to spare. I would say, looking at you, Alexei, that you are in very good health and only just past the prime of life. But

111

in twenty years time you will be an old man, and Priscilla will just have reached *her* prime. I cannot condemn my daughter to living the second half of her life tied to a corpse."

Alexei stared at her with his mouth open; he had never been spoken to like that in his life before. Then he looked at Anna again. "I should remind you," Alexandra went on, "that as Priscilla is only seventeen, she can undertake no marriage without my consent. I am sure you are gentleman enough not to attempt to force yourself upon her, but I think it would be best if we were to leave Bolugayen tomorrow morning. We can stay in an hotel in Sevastopol until our ship is ready to sail." Now at last she looked at her mother. "I am sorry, Mother. But I should prefer not to discuss this matter further."

Alexei sat in his study long after the servants had gone to bed, dismissing Gleb when the old butler would have stayed up with him. Never had he been subject to such mixed emotions.

From birth he had accepted that, as the half-brother to the heir to Bolugayen, his life would be lived in a minor key: the army, and hopefully a general command at the end of it. That limited ambition had been shattered by the family's disgrace following Patricia's arrest for treason, and he had resigned himself to being nothing more than an estate manager. Then had come Peter's death in Port Arthur, and his unforeseen elevation to Prince Bolugayevski, with all the privileges that went with the rank restored. Since then he had lived an extraordinary life. Yet always in the background there had lurked the knowledge that he was compromised, through his marriage to a Jew.

He had been desperately in love with Sonia. He suspected he still was. One of the reasons he had cast her out so completely was that he did not know how he would react were she ever to walk through his front door. But it had had to be done, whether she was truly guilty or not, because only the family mattered. He was at one with Aunt Anna on that. However unintentionally, Sonia had compromised the family even more deeply than through her racial background. She had had to be repudiated, and be seen to be repudiated. That done, he had been encouraged to believe that he was again climbing the highlands of royal approval. All he needed was the domestic bliss and social solidity to accompany it. And he had found it, miraculously. It had never occurred to him that a cousin of his would not jump for joy at the thought of her daughter becoming Princess Bolugayevska. There was not a mother in the world could resist such an offer, surely. Save for Alexandra Robbins.

And now . . . easy to say there were many other beautiful and desirable young women, Russian young women, just waiting to be invited to rule Bolugayen beside him. That it was merely a matter of putting Priscilla out of his mind. But he did not want to do that. She filled his mind more than any woman had done since he had first seen Sonia Cohen, freezing and frostbitten, huddling in his cellar, seeking sanctuary. And with Priscilla there would be no shadow lurking in the background. But it was not to be. Not to . . . he raised his head as the study door opened, because there she was.

She wore a robe over her nightdress, and was silhouetted against the electric light that still burned in the hall. She stood still for several seconds, then came into the room, softly closing the door behind her. "I wanted to say how sorry I am."

And how much I wish to be your wife, she thought. She dared not analyse her emotions, because images of the power he possessed, and would transmit to her, together with the enormous wealth that would be hers as Princess of Bolugayen, kept intruding on his attractiveness as a man, which far transcended his mere good looks and

113

perfect bearing. He was so gentle, so very nice, so very much everything she had ever dreamed of in a man.

But those were not things a Boston schoolgirl could say to a Russian prince.

He got up, went round the desk, and she was in his arms. She kissed him with a desperate urgency, and he responded, while his hands roamed over the shoulders and back, down to her buttocks, hardly protected by the thin material, round in front to caress her surprisingly large breasts, even less protected, nipples hard darts of flesh against his hands. She gave a little shiver, and he released her. "I'm sorry. I don't know what came over me."

"It came over me too," she said, and scooped the skirt of her nightgown and robe from around her ankles, lifted them to her thighs. "If you were to take me, now," she said, "Mom couldn't do anything about it."

He could not stop himself looking down. Had even Sonia ever had more perfectly shaped legs, so white they all but glowed in the light. And above . . . "You are too much of a gentleman to attempt to take advantage of my daughter," Alexandra had said.

"That would be to do you a great wrong," he told her.

She bit her lip, and let the skirts fall again. "Now you think I'm common."

"I think you are the most wonderful woman in the world." He held her shoulders. "Will you marry me?"

"I can't."

"Because you are seventeen, and your mother will not give you permission. When is your birthday?"

"6 June."

"Well, then, on 6 June 1915, your mother will not be able to stop you marrying whoever you chose. Am I not right?"

"Three years," she muttered.

"Three years and three months, actually. I know, a very long time when one is seventeen. I am not asking you to

114

wait for me, Priscilla. I am saying that I will wait for *you*, for those three years and three months. If you do not come to me then, I shall look elsewhere for my wife. Until then, I shall hope."

"Oh, I'll be here," she said. "Do please wait."

Chapter Five

The Bride

"There is a gentleman to see you, ma'am." Antonina hovered in the doorway of Sonia's drawing room. She was a tall, somewhat raw-boned young woman, who was still finding the position of lady's maid to a divorced princess both exciting and embarrassing. Sonia took the card, and felt a sudden quickening of her heartbeat. But obviously this had to happen. In the couple of months since she had left Alexei she had kept a very low profile. She had bought this small house in a quiet suburb of St Petersburg and considered herself fortunate that Nathalie had not sought her out.

"I will receive Captain Korsakov," she said, and stood up.

Korsakov stood in the doorway and bowed; it was snowing outside and although he had given his cap and cloak to Antonina and carefully wiped his boots, he looked, and smelt, damp. "Your Highness."

"I am no longer entitled to that form of address, Captain."

"And it is my fault." He came across the room, and took her hands to kiss each in turn. "I am devastated."

"There were other factors involved." Sonia gazed at him as he straightened. "Or do you know of them also?"

"I only know that I am innocent, save of adoring you.

116

As you are innocent, of me. And yet, I am the cause of all this catastrophe."

"I would not blame yourself," Sonia said. "Will you sit down? Champagne?" He sat down, but raised his eyebrows. "Old habits die hard," she explained with a wry smile. "My husband was good enough to make me a wealthy woman." She rang the bell.

"That is good news." He waited for Antonina to serve and raised his glass. "I am so pleased that things have worked out."

"I was not aware that things have actually worked out," Sonia remarked. "But I am an optimist."

"You do not mind my calling?"

"Of course not. It is good to see you again." She finished her champagne. "Was there something you wished to say to me?"

He licked his lips. "Well, you see, Sonia . . . you do not mind my calling you Sonia?"

"It is my name, Captain."

"Well . . ." Another circle of his lips. "You, I, are both innocent victims of circumstance. But the circumstance is there. Now you no longer have a husband, while I . . . I am still as much in love with you as ever. So . . . well . . . I would take it as a great honour if you would dine with me."

"Where?"

"I thought of the Restaurant de Paris. The food is very good there."

"It is a very public place."

"It is a popular restaurant, yes."

"You mean you wish to be seen with me, in public?"

Korsakov smiled. "I am hoping you will allow me to see you in private as well, Sonia."

"I do not think that would be a good idea." Sonia rang the bell.

"My dear woman," Korsakov said. "What have you got

117

to lose? Your marriage is over. And I adore you. I would make you very happy."

"I doubt that, Captain. Only one man has ever made me very happy: my husband. Antonina, Captain Korsakov is leaving."

Korsakov glanced from her to the maid, then stood up. "Do you find me that unattractive, Princess?"

"I do not find you unattractive at all, Captain. You are a very attractive man."

"But you cannot accept that you are no longer married."

"I am married, Captain, until my husband marries again. Thank you for calling."

"You are doing very well, Your Excellency," Dr Geller said, carefully folding the bedclothes back over Anna's shoulders.

"You mean I am going to live," Anna remarked. She and Geller had known each other for many years. Ewfim Geller's father had been doctor on Bolugayen before him, and it had been the obvious, and natural, step for his son to succeed him as soon as he had qualified.

"For many years yet, Your Excellency," he assured her.

"Well, when may I leave the house? I am beginning to feel as if I were in prison. I have been in prison, you know, Geller, and I did not enjoy it."

"I think you may now leave the house, Your Excellency. Why, I would say that you can attend Easter service. Father Valentin will be most pleased, I know."

"Well, that is good news." Anna dismised the doctor, had her maid dress her, and went in search of Alexei. She knew where she would find him: sitting in his office with the estate books open in front of him. But that was a subterfuge. He would not be reading the books.

"Why, Aunt Anna," he said. "You are looking very bright this morning."

"I have just received my usual pummeling from Geller,"

she said. "And the news is excellent. I am fit again. I can go out. I am going for a ride. Will you accompany me?"

Alexei frowned at her. "Geller said you could ride?"

"Well, he said I can go to church in the village. How else am I to get there? I certainly do not intend to walk."

"I will drive you there in my automobile."

"Ha! That is far more likely to do me a mischief than any horse."

"I do not think a woman of seventy-four should ride, even if she is as fit as a fiddle," Alexei said. And smiled. "After all, Aunt Anna, you are once again chatelaine of Bolugayen, and are likely to remain so for a considerable time. I cannot afford to lose you."

Anna went to the sideboard and poured them each a goblet of brandy. "This brooding is doing you no good. When last did you have a woman?"

"Is that any concern of yours?"

"Of course it is." She handed him the goblet. "A healthy man should have a woman not less than twice a week. And a healthy woman should have a man not less than that either." She chuckled as she sat down. "Although perhaps not at seventy-four. Brooding on that child is a waste of time, and *un*healthy."

"She said she would come to me when she is twenty-one."

"What, you expect her to keep that promise? Three years? A lovely girl like that? Be sensible. You turned her head, with your wealth and position, with the immensity of Bolugayen, with your aura. Once she gets home she will very soon forget all about you. You really were very naughty, and very stupid, to have attempted to get her in the first place."

"Thank you, Aunt Anna. Now, if you do not mind, I am very busy."

"Busy! Poppycock. Why . . ." Anna turned her head at the sound of the horn. "There's the post!" She finished her drink and stood up. "They should be home by now.

119

I asked Alix to wire me once they reached Boston, to let me know they got there safely." She went to the door, towards which Gleb was hurrying, carrying his silver tray laden with letters and newspapers.

"There is a telegram, Your Excellency."

"Just what I expected." She frowned at Gleb's expression. "Well? Give it to me." Gleb licked his lips as he held out the envelope; it was edged in black. Anna tore it open. TERRIBLE NEWS STOP ALIX DROWNED AT SEA STOP TOTAL DISASTER STOP LETTER FOLLOWS JAMES.

Alexei was standing behind her. She handed him the paper without a word. "It is in the *Gazette*, Your Excellency," Gleb said.

Anna took the paper, not quite sure that this was actually happening.

'DISASTER AT SEA,' the headline read. 'TITANIC HITS ICEBERG AND SINKS IN HOURS. OVER A THOUSAND LIVES LOST.'

"Good God," Alexei said. "They said she was unsinkable."

"They! Who are *they*? My daughter is dead. My daughter!" Anna's voice did not rise, but her knees gave way, and Alexei had to catch her and seat her in a chair.

"Brandy," he told Gleb.

"I must go," Anna said.

"You cannot go," Alexei told her. "Geller may say you are well enough to go to church in the village, but you are certainly not yet strong enough to travel six thousand miles and cross an ocean."

"She is my daughter."

"Who is dead. You cannot bring her back to life. I will go," Alexei said. Anna raised her head. "Your son-in-law does not mention Priscilla."

"You think . . ."

"While there is life there is hope."

120

Anna continued to gaze at him. "You mean to bring her back?"

"If she is alive, Aunt Anna, I will bring her back."

"Then let us send a wire, and find out," Anna said.

"Alexei?" Priscilla's eyes were enormous. "Oh, how splendid to see you."

It had taken Alexei three weeks to reach Boston, travelling by train from Poltava to Sevastopol, then by ship from Sevastopol to Southampton via Naples, and then again by ship from Southampton across the Atlantic. He had only stopped in England long enough to change ships, as Duncan and Patricia had already left for the States more than a week earlier. "To come so far," Priscilla said.

"Do you realise," Alexei said, "that I am forty-eight years old, and this is the first time I have ever been out of Russia?"

"I thought Mom said you had been in Port Arthur?"

He grinned. "When I was in Port Arthur, we thought of it as part of Russia." He held her hand. "Do you wish to speak of what happened?"

They sat on the verandah of the Robbins' house on Chestnut Hill, and could look down at the harbour. As with all the survivors of the disaster, Priscilla had been confined to bed after reaching America, suffering from both exposure and shock. But now she looked almost as well as ever he remembered her, save that her cheeks were unnaturally pale. "I don't remember much about it," she confessed. "It was so unexpected. The ship was just great, you see. It was like travelling in a good hotel. Everyone was so kind and attentive. And that night . . . Mom and I went to bed early. We always did. We were sharing a cabin." She looked at him anxiously; perhaps Bolugayevskis never shared cabins.

"Go on," he invited.

"Well, neither of us heard the impact, or even felt it. We didn't wake up until the steward knocked on the door and told us we had to go on deck, wearing our lifejackets. We thought it was some kind of drill, and Mom was quite

121

annoyed at the idea of having to go on deck, well, virtually at midnight. The steward had said we had to go right up, but Mom absolutely refused to go up in her nightclothes. So we dressed. That took some time, I guess, because by the time we left the cabin it was obvious something was wrong; the ship was down by the head and walking up the stairs was difficult. Then there was such a crush of people on the next deck. I think the passengers from the lower classes had been allowed up. Anyway, we were separated. I remember calling for her, and then shouting and screaming. Some sailors put me in a boat. One of the last boats, I think. But I couldn't see Mom. I never saw her again." She stared at him with enormous eyes.

"I'm sorry," he said. "Not only about your mother. I didn't mean you to have to relive such an ordeal."

"I'm glad. I've never really talked about it, before. I wanted to. It seemed like the end of the world," she muttered. "It *was* the end of the world. I'm not talking about Mom, about all the other people who drowned. I'm talking about all of us. We were so secure. We had so much. We had everything. We were so happy. Even the steerage passengers were happy, Alexei. We used to look down on them, on the after well deck, playing their games. Most of them were Irish, but one of the pursers told us there were some Russian emigrants as well. That ship was a big city, a huge chunk of society. A happy society, because everyone believed they were going to a better life. And then . . . it was gone. It makes you feel, well . . ." she bit her lip. "If such a thing could happen, well don't you see, it could happen to all of us, at any time. If the *Titanic* could sink in a couple of hours, well . . . is there anywhere on earth that is really secure?"

"Yes," he said.

She glanced at him. "I'm so glad you came, Alexei."

"Would you like to come back with me? To Bolugayen?" Her eyes seemed larger yet. "I know it'll mean crossing the ocean again," he said. "But I'll be at your side. And you'll

122

never have to go to sea again in your life after that, unless you wish."

"I'd love to come back with you, to Bolugayen. But Pa . . ."

"Did your mother tell him about us?"

"No. I'm sure she didn't. Mom would never tell Pa anything like that in a letter. I think she intended to when she got back, though."

"Then all it needs is a little lie. A white lie, Priscilla, my darling. For your happiness."

"To Pa?"

"Don't you think he'd like you to be happy?"

Her eyes were bigger than ever. "And Mom?"

"I think she would probably be happy too."

It was easier than she had dared hope. "Shucks, baby," James Robbins said. "You're aiming to fly right out of sight of us ordinary folk. Princess Bolugayevska! But say, don't get me wrong, this prince seems a nice fellow, and I know he's sort of being family, but . . . he's kind of old, isn't he?"

"I don't find him old at all," Priscilla said. She had convinced Alexei that this exploratory meeting, as it were, should be conducted tête-à-tête: Alexei had accepted that she would know best how to handle her father.

"And then there's this business of changing your religion. I'm not sure your Mom would have approved of that."

Priscilla drew a deep breath. "Mom thought it would be all right."

"You know," James Robbins said, "that's what's puzzling me. The way your Mom never mentioned it in any of her letters. I mean to say, it's a mighty big step."

"Mom was going to discuss it with you when we got back. She didn't feel it was the kind of thing one could put in a letter."

123

"It's a point. But hell . . . you'll have to change your style a little. Quite a lot."

"Grandmama will be there to help me."

"Yeah." Like so many men, James Robbins had always felt vaguely nervous in the presence of his mother-in-law. He peered at his daughter. "You're sure it's what you want?"

"More than anything else in the world," Priscilla assured him.

Sonia decided that the Restaurant de Paris was a place people went to in order to see and be seen; they could hardly go there for the food. When she remembered the mouth-watering meals that had been prepared on Bolugayen by Boris the chef, the pressed caviar and salted cucumbers, the smoked sturgeon and milk piglets, the ice cold champagne . . . not that there was any shortage of such delicacies, but nothing was quite the same – even the champagne was not really cold. But Bolugayen was not a place to be thought of, ever again.

Over the past year she had almost allowed herself to be lulled into a false sense of security. She had bought herself this little house, and she had waited. She had actually hoped that Alexei would come back for her and tell her that all was forgiven; they had shared so much, and so much love, it was impossible that it should just end, that she should never see her children again, that she should never see Bolugayen again either.

Polonowski's letter had come like a slap in the face. That nearly a year had drifted by without contact was not because Alexei was punishing her, and he would, in time, forgive her; it was simply because even for princes, obtaining a decree nisi had required time. That time had now elapsed.

That letter had been devastating, but the following week's *Gazette* had been worse. Alexei had wasted no time in marrying again. He had, it seemed, had his next wife already in residence, long before the decree became final. Sonia wondered if he had waited until then to possess her. But of course he would have. She had lived several months on Bolugayen before *their* marriage, and he had never laid a finger on her until their wedding night. Alexei was, above all else, a gentleman. Had he not been so complete a gentleman, he would never have divorced her for not, as he believed, being a lady. Certainly he would not have set her up as a millionairess, even if in a minor key. Thus this Priscilla Robbins would have gone to the altar a virgin. But now she was Princess of Bolugayen. An eighteen-year-old girl! But one who already had the Bolugayevski blood in her veins. Alexei would be quite sure that *she* would never step out of line, although with a sister like Patricia he was perhaps being optimistic.

The wedding of Alexei and Priscilla had been in a very low key, socially. Not only was she not a member of the Russian aristocracy, but the Prince was still officially in exile, and divorced men did not remarry in a church. Which did not mean he had not been married in great splendour, by his own priest, in his own drawing room, with all of his family around him. Sonia wondered if Sophie had attended. She imagined all of his servants bowing obsequiously, and all of his tenants gathered outside in the yard to praise their master and their new mistress. How that little girl's head must have spun.

But as she had once said, that column in the *Gazette* had meant the end of the line for her. Korsakov, of course, had merely been waiting, and watching, and reading the newspapers. He had called the day following the announcement. And this time, truly, she had had no reason to refuse him. Now he was like a dog with two tails. "See how they look at you, behind their fans," he said. "You are the most beautiful woman in the room."

"They are staring at me because I am the most notorious woman in the room," Sonia pointed out, and emptied her third glass of champagne. And why not there, either? She had been drunk often before, many years ago, when she had been escaping across Siberia, and the men she had been forced to lie with had given her vodka, and kept giving her vodka, in the winter so cold it had to be sucked through lumps of black bread held in the mouth. Now it seemed a good idea to get drunk again, because she was on her way to suffering the same fate. "And because they assume, as I have been divorced for it, that I am your mistress. Do you wish me as your mistress, Paul? Or as your wife? I assume I also am now free to marry again."

"Certainly. And I would very much like you to be my wife. But I am concerned about this trouble in the Balkans. There is a rumour that we may have to become involved and that my regiment will be amongst the first sent to Rumania if that should happen."

She studied him, wondering what the truth of the matter was. But then, did she want to marry this man, or any man? The only man she wanted to have as a husband was Alexei Bolugayevski, and as that was now impossible . . . she was not even absolutely certain she wanted to have sex with any man save Alexei. But that also was now impossible, and this man was so desperate . . . He was watching her, anxiously.

"I think," she said, reaching for her fourth glass of champagne, "that we should begin at the beginning. I shall be your mistress, until you return from the war, if there is one, at which time we may reconsider the situation."

Korsakov was obviously unused to having the decisions in his personal life made for him by a woman, but he was prepared to overlook the issue where Sonia was concerned. As they drove home from the restaurant in the hired carriage, he took her in his arms to kiss her. She was pleasantly surprised. His touch was both gentle and experienced. The door was opened for them by Antonina, who made a point of never going to bed until her mistress had retired; Sonia only employed four servants – there was no necessity for more, as her needs were few, and while she still enjoyed drinking champagne on every possible occasion, her instincts and background were all against unnecessary expense.

Now it was Antonina's turn to be surprised, as Korsakov gave her his cap and gloves and cape: it was already just on midnight. "You may go to bed, Antonina," Sonia said. "I will see Captain Korsakov out."

Antonina backed away, then turned and scuttled for the stairs to her attic quarters.

"You mean you are not inviting me to breakfast?" Korsakov asked.

"I may."

He took her in his arms and again kissed her, and now for the first time, he allowed his hands to wander, across her shoulders, under her arms to caress her breasts. What am I doing? she wondered.

He continued to fondle her as they went up the stairs, only released her, in the bedroom, to remove his clothes. They undressed together, gazing at each other. He was a fine figure of a man, not as powerfully built as Alexei, certainly, but perhaps even better endowed. While she . . . "You are exquisite," he said, coming against her. Once again his hands slid over her body, but now she was naked. She could not resist a shiver. "Are you afraid of me?" he asked, his mouth against her ear.

"No," she said. "I am afraid of myself." He swept her legs from the floor and laid her on the bed. "I am thirty-five years old," she said.

"You are a monument to womanhood." But, kneeling beside her, he could not prevent himself from looking at the two little white lumps that had once been her toes. "Do you find that repulsive?" she asked. In reply, he arched his back to kiss them, then continued to kiss her legs as he moved up to her thighs. "Will you love me forever?" To her surprise, that was suddenly important to her.

127

He had reached her thighs. "I will love you until the day I die," he told her.

Of course he knew all about her escape from Irkutsk, but he never asked about it, or even mentioned it. He was every bit as much a gentleman as Alexei. However, he did assume that she had nothing to learn about the sexual act. And he was correct in that; she even found it a pleasure to do whatever he wished, without the slightest feeling – such as she had always had with Alexei – that if she let herself go he might be silently critical of her. For the first time in a very long time she felt sated, as she lay with his head against her breasts, and watched the sky lighten. It was summer, and thus very early. "*Would* you like to stay to breakfast?" she asked.

He raised his head. "Would you like me to?"

"I think, as this is the first occasion, it would be best if you did not," Sonia said.

"But you will dine with me again?"

"I should like that."

He dressed himself, while she put on a dressing gown. "You have made me the happiest man in the world," he said.

"Then I am pleased." She led him down the stairs, unlocked the front door. "You have no transport."

"I will walk to the tram; it is not far." He kissed her fingers. "Adieu, my dearest Sonia. Adieu."

She half closed the door to watch him walk up the street. It was not yet five, and there was no one about. She wondered what he *would* be like as a husband. She made to close the door and was startled by a sound. It came from beside the steps leading down to the pavement, and Sonia hastily slammed the door shut and shot the bolt, leaning against it while she got her nerves under control. Could Alexei be spying on her?

"I must speak with you," a man said through the door.

"Who are you?"

"A friend of Patricia's."

Sonia was so surprised she opened the door again, gazed at a slightly built man with a black goatee beard. He wore wire spectacles and had pinched features; his clothes had clearly not been removed for some time, even for sleeping. "Who *are* you?"

"Please let me in. I will not harm you. I swear it. I am a Jew like you."

Sonia opened the door; he certainly looked desperately in need of a square meal. And if he was a friend of Trishka's . . . but how could such a fellow be a friend of Trishka's? *She* certainly wasn't Jewish. He came into the house, and himself closed and locked the door behind him. "Was that your lover?" he asked.

There did not seem any point in denying it, if he knew Korsakov had spent the night. "Yes, he is, if it is any business of yours."

"And now you are alone?"

"No, I am not alone," Sonia told him. "My maid is sleeping upstairs. She is a large, strong woman, and she will be with me in ten seconds if I cry out."

"Please do not cry out," the man begged. "May I have some food? I have not eaten in twenty-four hours. And I am . . ."

"A Jew," Sonia said. "I do not know why that should make me help you. I have been repudiated by my people."

"You mean, you repudiated your people, when you married the Prince of Bolugayen," the man corrected.

Sonia glared at him. But that was nothing more than the truth. She led the way into the kitchen, placed bread and cheese and a bottle of vodka on the table. "You need a bath," she remarked.

"I would like that very much," he agreed. "When I have eaten."

Sonia raised her eyebrows at his calm assumption that she would let him use her bathroom; but he was not

129

looking at her as he concentrated on the food. "How do you know Mrs Cromb?"

"We were in Moscow together, in 1905. She escaped. I was sent to Siberia." He raised his head. "You were in Siberia."

Sonia sat opposite him, across the table. "Patricia told you that?"

"Trishka. That's what we called her. Trishka. We had no secrets."

"What is your name?"

"Lev Bronstein. But you may call me Trotsky. Leon Trotsky. That is how I am known, now." She caught her breath. "Ah! You have heard of me."

"I have heard the name. Why do you not use your real name?"

"Trotsky is the name I have at the moment."

"Very well, Mr Trotsky. I believe you possibly did know Mrs Cromb at some time. Thus I have fed you. Now I must ask you to leave."

"But I must stay here," he protested.

"You *what*?"

"I too have escaped from Siberia," he said proudly. "They are looking for me. You must help me."

Sonia was aghast. Again to become involved . . . but when she, in this man's position, had begged for help, Alexei had given it to her. Because of course he had, even then, wanted her as a woman: he had confessed that to her, later. She certainly did not want this Trotsky as a man. But the principle remained. But . . . keep him here? That was impossible. "Who sent you to me?" she asked.

"I was given your name, as a possible refuge."

"By whom?" If Patricia was still involved with these anarchists . . .

"That is not important. I was given several names. I have tried the others, but they are not available. Only you are left." He leaned across the table, reached for her hands, but she withdrew them. "Listen to me," he

130

said. "You are one of us. You were born one of us, and you will die one of us. I know you tried to escape into the aristocracy. I do not hold that against you. But they betrayed you, as the aristocracy will always betray those not born into their class. You have nothing now, save us. That is why you must help me. And when the Revolution comes, you will be greatly honoured." His total confidence, both in her and in the future, was amazing. Trotsky stood up. "Now," he said. "I should like to have that bath."

"The woman Cohen has finally succumbed," Klinski said. Michaelin raised his eyebrows. "I have just heard from St Petersburg. Korsakov spent the night with her, in her house," Klinski explained.

Michaelin snorted. "That is going to get us nowhere. Korsakov is not involved in politics. He is a soldier, through and through. And a lover, to be sure. Your man is certain no one else has called there?"

"Well, there was another man. The woman is insatiable."

Michaelin frowned. "What other man?"

"Our man has never seen him before. But he estimates him to be a Jew."

Michaelin stroked his chin. "Trotsky is a Jew."

"You think this man could be Trotsky? But there is no link between the Princess and Trotsky."

"You are making a mistake, Feodor Petrovich. This woman is no longer a princess. She is an angry and humiliated Jewess. As for links, she was in Siberia. Trotsky was in Siberia. They both escaped from Siberia."

"Several years apart," Klinski argued. "Anyway, finding Trotsky is not our business."

"Finding Trotsky is the business of every policeman in Russia," Michaelin pointed out. "The man is desperate, and dangerous. And he is an anarchist. How long did he stay with the woman Bolugayevska?"

131

"As far as I know he is still there. Do you wish me to have the place raided and arrest them?"

Michaelin considered. "No. You would have to obtain authority for that from General Bor-Clemenski, and that would lead to questions as to why we are keeping the former princess under surveillance in the first place, and then the General would take all the credit. I think we will be patient, Klinski. It will all turn out to our advantage, sooner or later."

"May I ask, madam, how long this, ah, gentleman will be staying with us?" Antonina asked.

"It will not be very long," Sonia said, sitting in front of her mirror to allow her hair to be dressed for dinner.

"He is not actually a relative, is he, madam?"

"We were childhood friends," Sonia lied.

"I was just wondering what the Captain might say, next time he calls?"

"The Captain, Antonina, has absolutely no say in how I conduct my affairs," Sonia said.

Yet it was on her mind as well. She did not know how soon Korsakov's manoeuvres would be over, and she did know that he would give her no advance warning of his intention to call. She should have thrown Leon out long ago. A week was really too long. And yet . . . it was not merely the implicit power that he held over her: were he to be arrested, and tell the Okhrana why he had sought her out, her past would once again be raked up. Alexei might have promised that it never would be, but that had been upon the reasonable assumption that she would never again break the law. She had done so by admitting Leon into her home.

And it was not even that he was a Jew or that he claimed to be a friend of Patricia's, or that he had served time in Siberia. It was the man himself. She realised that deep down inside her, partly because of her birth and upbringing, partly because of her experiences,

132

there lurked a hatred of the tsarist regime far more deep than anything ever felt by Patricia. Patricia had dabbled in anarchy and terrorism because she felt guilt at having been born an aristocrat; the thought of actually throwing a bomb which might kill or maim someone had horrified her. Sonia, in her youth, certainly, had been prepared to do anything necessary to bring down the regime.

But then she had been shown both the futility of it, where the secret police had infiltrated every aspect of the movement, and the consequences of it, when she had been arrested. Equally had she been shown the sunlit uplands of belonging to the ruling elite. So, as Leon had pointed out on their first meeting, it had been she who had turned her back on her people and her very religion, and looked to what she had wanted to be her future. Most selfishly. Now that future had been ripped up and thrown in the gutter. She would not have been human had hate not returned in full vigour.

But still she had been obsessed by the futility of it all. The Tsar was there. He had been there for hundreds of years. This Tsar's family alone had been there for three hundred years, all but. He was supported by a huge army and an all-pervading secret police. The foreign press might make a great fuss about assassination attempts and civil disturbances, but the fact was that these were nearly all inspired by the Jews, her people, after some particularly violent piece of repression by the Tsarist agents.

The country as a whole, the vast mass of the peasants, the muzhiks as they were called, might have been shattered at the defeat by Japan, might be ground down by poverty and occasionally even actual starvation, might grumble that their 'Little Father' was not doing enough about it. But by no stretch of the imagination would *they* ever do anything about it. Sonia suspected that they mistrusted the dumas far more than did the Tsar himself. So, resistance, nonacceptance of one's fate, was an exercise in futility. Until one met someone like Leon Trotsky. His

133

fervour had an almost romantic quality. He believed! He believed that one day tsardom would be brought down, that one day the people would be the masters. He could not put a time span upon his dream, but that did not make him any the less certain. And his belief made her believe. But he was still endangering her life.

"You simply have to go," she told him at lunch.

He had bathed every day since his arrival, and she had managed to procure for him some changes of clothing by shopping in the ghetto. In that sense they were intimates. But in no other. He slept in the spare bedroom, and he had never attempted to touch her, after that first morning. But he had touched her with his mind! "I know," he said. "I am leaving tonight." Sonia's head jerked. He grinned. "I have surprised you. Now you will ask me to stay."

"No," she said. "I shall not ask you to stay, Leon. For both our sakes. But I will be sorry to have you go. Can you understand that?"

"Of course. But I will return, you know. In triumph."

"Before I am not too old to enjoy your triumph, I hope."

"It will be *our* triumph, Sonia. And you will be there, just as beautiful as you are now. Because you will never grow old."

She raised her head, flushing, and he held out his hand.

"Here they are," Anna said. She was sitting in her favourite summer position, on the upper verandah at Bolugayen, looking out over the garden and the wheatfields and the road curving round from Poltava. Down the road Alexei's Rolls-Royce was coming, driven by its chauffeur, its course marked by a huge plume of yellow dust rising from its rear wheels. Anna glanced at the Princess Bolugayevska, who had just joined her. "Does she frighten you?"

But she knew it was a rhetorical question; Priscilla was

not a woman who was frightened by anything, it seemed. Anna, remembering her granddaughter as a child, and then as a girl on her first visit to Bolugayen, suspected it had something to do with the sinking of the *Titanic*. One does not look death in the face, slowly and over a time span of several hours, and then survive, without becoming either a permanent nervous wreck, or totally unafraid of anything else life might do to one. Priscilla was definitely not a nervous wreck.

Thus she had ridden with total equanimity the ordeal of suddenly ascending from being a Boston schoolgirl to the Princess of Bolugayen. Anna had noted only one tremor throughout all the ceremonies that had accompanied that elevation; the morning they had knelt before Father Valentin for her to be inducted into the Orthodox Church, and her gloved hand had stolen into her grandmother's for support. Anna did not know, nor had she dared attempt to find out – although she was desperately curious – how Priscilla enjoyed sharing a bed with Alexei. But the Princess always looked happy enough, and Alexei had spent the past eighteen months walking around looking like the cat who had swallowed the canary – and now she was within three months of her first delivery.

All before she was twenty! But she would actually be twenty before the child was born, as her birthday fell during this very month of June. Hence Sophie and the dreadful Janine. They had been here for the wedding, of course, and had come last summer as well: they clearly found the new Princess more acceptable than her predecessor. They had fawned upon the lovely young girl who was so inexorably climbing on to the pedestal as female head of the family. Anna had suspected they even meant to seduce her, and had bristled to interfere. And had then realised that Priscilla did not need protecting, either from others or from her own desires. Now she asked, "Shall I go down?"

"No, no," Anna said. "They will come up."

135

"Because I am the Princess, or because I am pregnant, Grandmama?"

"Because you are the Princess. People must come to you, unless they are your superior in rank, and there are only a few of those, the Grand Duchesses, the Tsaritsa Dowager, and the Tsaritsa herself, in this entire land."

Priscilla seated herself beside her grandmother and watched the car disappear beneath them into the shadow of the porch overhang. Even if she knew Sophie and her lover were condemned by the rest of the family, she looked forward to their visits, which had become yearly events. She enjoyed them for their very difference; she could not possibly imagine a pair like that openly living together in Boston. But then, she enjoyed everything about Bolugayen, and even more, everything about being the Princess Bolugayevska, because it was so different to anything she had ever suspected to exist. She still occasionally had to pinch herself. When she remembered how enormous it had all seemed . . . but then, it *was* enormous. Pa had been a reasonably wealthy man, and Mom, as a shareholder in Cromb Shipping Lines, had been a reasonably wealthy woman, in her own right. Uncle Charlie was a millionaire. As, presumably, was Grandmama, as she was principal shareholder in the Line. But none of them had the slightest idea of what it was like to be Mistress of Bolugayen. Except of course Grandmama, who in many ways still was Mistress of Bolugayen. But Grandmama never interfered in any way in Priscilla's handling of her position, save to encourage her to be more assertive, where necessary.

It actually was not necessary to be assertive at all. Priscilla remembered how she had been terrified at the thought of having to order this huge household, but it was not necessary for her to have anything to do with that at all, either. Gleb and Madame Xenia were most efficient managers, Xenia of the household and Gleb of the food and drink. Priscilla had read often enough of young brides

136

being taken advantage of by old family retainers, and Gleb and Xenia were certainly those, both in their fifties and both having been born and bred into the service of the Bolugayevskis. They knew secrets, such as the mysterious appearance out of the snow of Aunt Patricia and the ex-Princess Sonia which had led to Alexei's first marriage, which she did not think even Grandmama had truly penetrated. She had never tried. If she felt guilt about anything it was the woman Sonia Cohen, who had had all this, and then lost it all – to her. But she had never even laid eyes on the woman, and she certainly did not wish to think about her or discover anything about her. So she merely dabbled in household management. When she had first come here to live she had felt obliged to pay a visit to the kitchens, and had been appalled at the amount of food consumed every day. But Alexei had accepted that as normal, and she had never commented again. Equally had she been appalled at the waste of glass, the family habit of never having more than one drink from the same goblet. But she had very soon become used to that as well.

Just as she had become used to the outlandish clothes she was required to wear, certainly on public appearances or visits to Poltava or even the village, heavy brocade gowns which weighed a ton, more underclothing than she would have supposed it was possible to fit on a single body, thick stockings and boots so vast she was sometimes not sure her feet were actually in there. Or to spending an hour every day having her hair dressed, loose for around the house, piled on the top of her head for evening, arranged in a smart snood for riding. Often as not, in the evenings, her hair would be surmounted by a diamond tiara, but this was only a small part of the quite fabulous jewellery which was now hers to wear, rings of every variety, sparkling with diamonds and rubies and sapphires, gold necklaces, amethyst pendants, and huge, heavy gold bangles. Fortunately, there was a ritual connected with the jewellery as well, a special piece to be

137

worn for every occasion, or she would never have been able to make up her mind.

Then what of her relations with the man two and a half times her own age who had given her all of this? The figure was suddenly more alarming than ever, in cold terms: if she was about to celebrate her twentieth birthday, Alexei would next year be fifty. Remarkably, that aspect of the situation, which, Grandmama had told her, had most concerned Mom, had never entered her calculations at all, until very recently. Alexei was a most attractive man, and a perfect gentleman. She had never been the least afraid of him, of what he might do, or might wish to do, even to her virginal body. She suspected that, as an American, she had been more prepared for that than the average Russian girl of noble birth. Her brother James Junior had had a succession of girlfriends, many of them friends of hers, and if they had apparently always rebuffed his most ardent advances – it was just as important for a Boston young lady to marry as a virgin as it was for a Russian – they had been equally eager to confide what it was he had wanted. Actually, all James had ever wanted was to get his hand inside a bodice or under a skirt, preferably in a darkened room; Alexei had never shown the slightest interest in that, in a clandestine sense. For the several months she had lived on Bolugayen as a bride-in-waiting he had never been more than a considerate uncle. Thus perhaps her senses had been dulled, her awareness of what would eventually happen to her left in a once-removed world.

That cocoon had been ripped away on her wedding night. In one way she had been shocked. That her prince would want to possess her was obvious – she had not stopped to think what the word 'possession' meant. He had wanted to kiss and suck her toes; she had not been sure whether or not to giggle at that. Then he had wanted to kiss her all over. Lips, nipples, these had seemed more appropriate than toes. Under her arms and between her legs had been an experience she had never imagined possible; it was quite *im*possible imagining Pa doing that to Mom. Perhaps he never had done. The actual entry, when he had had her on her knees, his groin thumping against her buttocks, had been no doubt the most shocking thing of all, looked at it Bostonian terms – she had felt it was somehow unChristian – but it had been something of a relief after what had gone before.

Then she had been left with a feeling of guilt that perhaps she had not responded with sufficient enthusiasm. But she had soon learned to do that. So, now she was in every way a Russian princess, all considerations of Anglo-Saxon puritanism banished from her mind. Did she love her husband? She was sure she did. She would not have been human – or a woman – had she not occasionally yearned for the moonlight and roses aspect of love, for something over and above the physical desire Alexei expressed on almost every occasion. But she was prepared to be patient. She had been an usurper – she was in another woman's bed, and every time Alexei held her naked in his arms he must have had some reflections on the last woman to lie there. She was very young; Alexei could not help but regard her rather as a daughter who had so delightfully strayed into his bed. Obviously he regarded her as too young to be involved in either the management of the estate or discussions on the political situation; she had to glean what she could from dinner table conversations between Alexei and Grandmama and Father Valentin and Tigran Boscowski, the estate man-ager, an enthusiastic young man who was utterly in awe of her. But these aspects of her situation would pass, she knew. Were already passing. She would soon be a mother; not even Alexei could then suppose she was still a girl.

They were passing, too, in her acceptance by the children. In many ways this had been the most difficult of her tasks. When she had come here permanently, in the summer of 1912, as a girl of eighteen, Colin had been fourteen. Little Anna, being only four, had been no problem, and had welcomed the appearance of an older sister, as it had seemed. Little Anna had perhaps not really taken in the fact that her mother was gone forever, and having lived her brief life entirely surrounded by nannies and servants with a ceremonial visit to Mummy and Daddy once a day for a hug and a kiss, was unaware that anything had really changed. Colin had been too old to accept at once a sister and a stepmother. Equally he had been too old entirely to accept the fact that his real mother had somehow turned out to be a 'bad' woman. He was too well disciplined, too much the Bolugayevski, ever to enquire after Sonia Cohen, but he had been disturbed by the situation, very evidently.

Fortunately, he had already been a cadet at the military academy in St Petersburg, and spent a good deal of time away from home. When he had come home, in those early days, he had been stiffly polite. But gradually he had warmed to her. She had been very careful at all times to preserve the dignity required of a princess and a mother towards him, however much, in his absence, she enjoyed romping with little Anna. She had felt she was building a relationship, in which he would be able to respect her as a stepmother while acknowledging that they were close enough in ages also to be friends. But then had come the pregnancy. She had clearly conceived during the last Christmas festivities, as she was due in September, but it had not become certain until Easter. Then Colin had been home on holiday, and Alexei had naturally wanted a great celebration. Colin had taken part in that, if in a rather subdued fashion, but had found an opportunity to be alone with her soon afterwards, and had asked, ingenuously, "Will your baby be a boy or a girl, Priscilla?"

"No one knows, until he actually emerges."

"You said he. You would like him to be a boy."

"Well, I suppose every mother wishes her first-born

140

to be a boy, because she knows that will please her husband."

Colin had stared at her. "If it is a boy, will he be the next Prince of Bolugayen?"

Priscilla had been so taken aback she had been unable to answer for several seconds. Then she had said, "Of course not. You are the next Prince of Bolugayen."

But she hadn't felt he was convinced, and had taken the matter up with Alexei. It was the first time she had ever seen her husband disconcerted. "It is something to be considered," he had said.

"But . . . Colin is your eldest son."

"He is also half-Jewish, my dearest girl."

Priscilla had stared at him with her mouth open. "Is it that important?"

"I'm afraid it is, here in Russia. Don't worry. Colin will never want for anything." She had wanted to say, that's not quite the same thing as being virtually disinherited, but hadn't. Because she did not want to argue with Alexei, on a subject of which she really knew very little? Or because, however guilty it made her feel, deep down inside the thought of her son being Prince Bolugayevski was too heady to be resisted? She had reflected that it would probably be a girl in any event. Colin had left soon after to return to school, and she had not seen him since. But he would be home in a few days. She must be especially kind to him.

Meanwhile, there were Sophie and Janine. They were at the top of the stairs, now, beaming at her. "Your Highness," Janine said, "you look positively obscene. Have you twins in there?"

"Ladies and gentlemen," Prince Alexei Bolugayevski said, standing and raising his glass. "I give you the Princess Bolugayevska. You too, Gleb. And Madame Xenia." The housekeeper looked thoroughly embarrassed, as she did not as a rule attend dinner. But she took her glass from

141

Gleb's tray and raised it, like everyone else beaming at Priscilla, who remained seated at the head of the table.

It was strictly a family party. The Countesses Anna and Sophie and Janine, Tigran Boscowski, Father Valentin, Count Colin, even Anna in a party frock, looking half asleep, Prince Alexei, and of course, Princess Priscilla. The toast was drunk and the glasses hurled at the fireplace, while Gleb hastily served fresh ones. "Speech!" Janine called.

Priscilla stood up, as they sat. "I thank you, and am deeply grateful, for your sentiments," she said. "I will offer you a toast in return." She raised her own glass. "I give you the name of Bolugayevski. May it never diminish!"

Priscilla awoke to find Alexei standing beside her bed. She blinked at him, uncertainly. Since she had begun to show, they had used separate apartments. She sat up. "Is there something the matter?"

"Not really. But I must leave, this morning. I am required in St Petersburg."

"But . . . why?"

"Nothing of great importance. But it is gratifying, is it not, that at a moment of crisis the Tsar should wish to see me?"

She grasped his hand. "What crisis?"

"Oh, some Austrian archduke has got himself shot and killed, together with his wife, and there is a possibility that the Balkan business may start up again, with Austria this time one of the players. Well, obviously we cannot permit that."

She was aghast. "You mean we will fight Austria?"

He leaned over and kissed her. "There is almost no chance of that. We will threaten to mobilise. We may even do so. And as Austria cannot match us for strength, she will climb down. I shall not be away long."

Part Two

The Swirling Clouds

'Where thou perhaps under the whelming tide visit'st the bottom of the monstrous world.'

Milton: *Lycidas*

Chapter Six

War

Priscilla stared at the telegram in consternation. This was about the best summer anyone could recall. The sun shone every day, the wheat was already high, people smiled as they went about their work, even the sheep seemed happy. Only the absence of the Prince in any way impinged upon the general feeling of contentment, and everyone expected the Prince to return, momentarily. Now . . .? Priscilla clutched her stomach.

"Not bad news, I hope?" Anna enquired.

"We are at war with Germany. And Austria."

Anna leaned forward and took the telegram from her granddaughter's fingers, scanned the words. "This is madness," she remarked.

"Madness! My God!"

"I meant it is madness on the part of that imbecile Kaiser. Both imbecile Kaisers. How can they hope to fight Russia? Especially if Alexei is right in assuming France will fight with us."

"Does that matter?" Priscilla asked. "If there is to be a war then Alexei could be killed!"

Anna had never seen her so upset; she had not supposed Priscilla could *be* so upset. "You are concerning yourself needlessly. Alexei is a general. Look what he says: he has been given a place on General Samsanov's staff.

Officers on the staff of the commanding general do not get killed."

Priscilla supposed she was right. But at the very least they were going to be separated for a very long time. Alexei would not be here for the birth of their child. And there were other aspects of the situation to be considered. Colin was running up the stairs, followed by his sister. "Is it true what the postman says, Priscilla? Grandmother?" He looked from face to face.

"That there is to be a war?" Anna asked. "Yes. It is true." Six-year-old Anna clapped her hands in excitement.

"Then I must leave immediately," Colin declared.

"You?" Priscilla demanded. "You cannot fight in a war."

"I am a soldier!"

"You are a cadet and you are fourteen years old. Besides, you have not been called up."

"Grandmother!" Colin appealed to Anna. The children always addressed her as their grandmother although she was actually their great-aunt.

"We shall have to see," Anna decided. "We will send into Poltava and ask the Governor." Colin pouted, but he was not going to argue with his great-aunt; nobody ever did.

When he and Anna had left the verandah, Priscilla sat beside the old lady. "Will it really be all right?" she asked.

"Of course. Nobody is really going to fight over Serbia. All we have to do is show the Austrians, and the Germans, that we are not going to be pushed about, and they will negotiate a settlement." Anna stroked the girl's head. "You've never seen a war, have you?"

"Well . . . I remember a lot of shouting and flag-waving and ballyhoo when we went to war with Spain. But I was only four years old."

"This will be my fifth war," Anna said. "I was a girl

146

during the Crimean War, which we lost. I went to America in the middle of the Civil War, which your grandfather's side won. I was in Port Arthur for the Sino-Japanese War, which China lost, and we were supposed to be on China's side, and I was again in Port Arthur for the Russo-Japanese war, which we lost. So you see, Priscilla, I have lost more wars than I have won. And do you know, I am still here, Bolugayen is still here, Russia is still here. I would not be too afraid of wars, if I were you, Your *Highness*." It was essential, at a time like this, that the child remembered who she was. Priscilla shuddered.

The city was filled with the ringing of bells. "One would suppose it was Christmas," Sonia remarked to Antonina.

The street outside, even in this normally quiet suburb, was constantly crowded, with parading soldiers, groups of young men hurrying to volunteer for the colours, and of course their female admirers. "May we go down to see the troops being blessed by the Tsar, madam?" Antonina asked.

"Yes, I think we should do that." Sonia wondered if Alexei would be there? And Korsakov? She hadn't seen her lover for some days, since the crisis had blown up. Her lover, she thought. Paul knew nothing of Leon. But at least Leon was safe in Vienna. Safe! According to the newspapers, that was precisely where the Russian armies intended to march, taking Berlin on the way, to be sure. But Leon, with his capacity for survival, would surely move on long before the Russians could get there.

They went out and joined the throng, flocking towards the Nevski Prospect. There they found a huge area cordoned off by police. Within the area, which was in front of the Winter Palace, were a large number of soldiers. They wore the new Russian military uniform, created for modern warfare. Gone were the reds and greens and whites and blues that had made warfare such a romantic business only a few years before. The

147

Russians had learned from the Japanese machine guns in Manchuria, much as the British had learned from the Boer sharpshooters in South Africa. Now everyone wore a drab khaki, copied from the British, a colour named after the Hindustani word for dust, meant to tone in with the background against which they would be exposed. Even the general officers, even the Tsar, wore khaki, although there were still a lot of red tabs and medals flashing in the midday sun.

Sonia had brought her opera glasses, and she used these as the soldiers knelt before their Tsar, who stood on a dais with the Patriarch and Tsarevich beside him, their attendants holding aloft the religious ikons and the battle flags; this was the first time Sonia had seen the Tsarevich. The boy – he was just ten years old – wore a uniform like his father and stood rigidly to attention. He looked perfectly well, if a little pale, and it was difficult to believe the rumours that swirled about him, that he was too chronically ill ever to rule.

Most of the watching crowd knelt, as did Sonia and Antonina, but Sonia kept looking through her glasses. She could indeed make out Alexei, in the midst of a group of staff officers, standing behind Generals Samsanov and Rennenkampf, commanders of the Second and First Russian armies, and General Jilinski, the commander-in-chief, charged with overseeing the Russian advance firstly into East Prussia and thence into Germany proper. With them was the Minister of War, General Sukhomlinov, also wearing uniform, as elegantly groomed and, no doubt, perfumed, as usual. They had taken off their caps and stood with heads bowed, not looking at each other, although they shared the command; all St Petersburg knew that the four men loathed each other. Sonia swept her glasses over the ranks of junior officers, but could not make out Korsakov; there were too many of them. But she was glad she could not make him out. She really only wanted to look at Alexei. Riding off to battle, looking as

148

noble as ever. Well, he had done that once before, against the Japanese, and returned alive and well. To marry her. This time he would be returning to the arms of another woman. But she still loved him.

"Isn't it exciting?"

Sonia turned to look at Nathalie, accompanied as always by Dagmar, who had grown into a quite beautiful if overly-voluptuous sixteen-year-old, her mother's somewhat coarse looks being tempered by the finely-chiselled features of the Bolugayevskis. Only her mouth and eyes, which regarded the world with a kind of slack laziness, indicated that she was not all she should be. Nathalie herself was looking amazingly well although she was larger than ever. And she certainly found it exciting; her cheeks were pink and her eyes gleamed – although, Sonia reflected, that might have been caused by either vodka or champagne. "I saw you looking at Alexei," Nathalie said. "Are you still carrying a torch? Or hoping he will get his head blown off?"

"I would not like anyone's head to be blown off," Sonia said.

"Ha! Well, quite a few of these are going to be, that is for certain. Why have you been avoiding me?"

They were all standing again now, the blessing having been completed, and the troops were forming up before marching off, while the bands struck up to obliterate all other sounds. Thus Sonia merely raised her eyebrows. Avoiding you? she wanted to ask. I loathe and abhor you, you obscene creature, for ruining my marriage and losing my children to me. But it seemed pointless to go on hating now; in any event, she was not a woman who could sustain hatred. The crowd was also starting to dissolve, people moving along the prospect. The four women were insensibly carried with them. "You have never called," Nathalie shouted.

"You have never called on me," Sonia countered. "I am sure you know where I live."

149

"I should like to see your home. I will take you there. My car is just round the corner."

Sonia considered briefly. But she did not feel like being alone, today.

"Quaint," Nathalie remarked, wandering from room to room. "It cannot require many servants."

"It does not require many servants."

"Do you have champagne?" Dagmar asked. "I should like a glass of champagne."

"Antonina, will you serve champagne, please," Sonia said, and showed her guests into the drawing room. "But I must warn you, we do not smash our glasses here."

Nathalie sat down with a sigh of relief to be off her feet. "Father Gregory keeps asking after you."

Sonia sat down as well. "How interesting."

"He would very much like you to visit him again."

Antonina served the drinks. "You had better leave the bottle," Sonia told her.

"You have a busy time," Nathalie remarked, as the doorbell rang.

"Today is a busy day." Sonia stood up. "Paul! I did not see you at the service."

Korsakov wore a khaki tunic over blue breeches and looked almost drab. But as handsome as ever. He kissed her hand. "I did not know you were there. Have you bought yourself an automobile?"

"That belongs to my sister-in-law. Ex-sister-in-law. Come inside, do." She went to the drawing room door. "Major Paul Korsakov. Her Highness the Princess Dowager Bolugayevska, and the Countess Dagmar Bolugayevska."

"Ladies!" Korsakov bowed over their hands, and then straightened to look more closely at Dagmar.

"Why, Major," Nathalie said. "Your name is familiar. Why . . ." She gave a peal of laughter. "You are the co-respondent!"

Sonia flushed with embarrassment, but Korsakov was not the least put out. "I have that honour, Your Highness."

"How exciting. You must come to call. I invite you to dinner, Major Korsakov. Oh, please bring your, ah . . ."

She looked at Sonia. "My fiancée, I think you mean," Korsakov said. "However, sadly, Your Highness, I am unable to accept your invitation, at least for the next few weeks. My train leaves for Warsaw in two hours." Antonina gave him a glass of champagne, and he raised it. "I give you, the Tsar, and damnation to the Germans."

"Absolutely," Nathalie said, drinking. "But not all the Germans, surely. Is not the Tsaritsa a German, which makes the Tsarevich and the Grand Duchesses at least half-German?"

Korsakov looked confounded, and Sonia stepped in. "How long can you stay?"

"Ten minutes."

"Then I am sure you ladies will excuse us." Sonia ushered him from the room. "I do apologise. She is quite impossible. And incidentally, so is Dagmar."

"She is very good-looking."

"You would get your fingers burned, at the very least, dear Paul. And I would not entertain you again." She showed him into the small parlour which she used as a study. "Are you going to have to fight?"

"Of course. I am going to kill a few Germans. Do you know, my dearest, that I am not sure I have ever killed a man? I got to Mukden in time for the big battle against the Japanese, but although I fired my revolver several times I do not know if I hit anyone."

"You should count that a blessing."

"I am thirty years old, and a soldier, and have never knowingly killed anyone? That is a confession of failure." He took her in his arms. "Oh, Sonia, Sonia, I must have you now. I cannot leave for a war and not have you."

"It would be difficult with them here," she protested.

151

"They are there and we are here."

"You mean . . ." she looked left and right. "There is no room."

"Room enough." He lifted her to sit on the desk, then scooped her skirts up to her waist and pulled down her drawers. She had to raise herself to allow the silk to be drawn from under her buttocks.

Not for the first time with this man she found herself wondering: what am I doing? But he was so enthusiastic and persistent, so sexual in a way she had never known before; every time his hands touched her naked flesh she experienced a sensation she had never known with any other man. And to think that he could do it standing up – but his breeches were round his ankles as were his drawers, and he was pulling her against him as he entered her.

It was at once exhilarating and vaguely frightening. He panted into her ear and she found herself panting into his, then moved her head to kiss him on the mouth as she felt the heat surge into her. "I am thirty-seven, a mother and a divorced woman, and you are yet teaching me things I never knew," she said.

"I will teach you a lot more, I promise you. When I come back." He kissed her again. "When I come back, we will be married."

Sonia returned to the drawing room after he had left.

"We need another bottle of champagne," Nathalie said.

"Are you staying to lunch?"

"But of course. I wish to hear all about your young man. I think he is very attractive. And so does Dagmar. Don't you, darling." Dagmar licked her lips.

"What are we going to do?" Duncan asked.

"Precisely who do you mean by we?" Patricia countered. "From what I gather America has no intention of getting mixed up in this war."

"I was thinking of Mom."

"Mom is in Bolugayen, Duncan, dear. That is five hundred miles from the Polish frontier, which is a good deal further than we are from Paris, which the Germans seem set on taking. And the Polish frontier is a good distance from the Austrian frontier quite apart from the German. Anyway, we are invading them, not them us."

"I still worry about it. It would be quite in keeping for her to get involved. Anyway, aren't you worried about Alexei and Sophie?"

"I am quite sure they can look after themselves," Patricia said. "I am far more worried about Sonia."

"What harm can possibly come to Sonia? She's in St Petersburg, isn't she?"

"She is also a Jew, Duncan. She may have had a permanent exemption from persecution up till now, but in a war all of these things get broken down. I told you about that mob I saw throwing stones at that shop off Piccadilly yesterday. All because it had a German name. Someone told me the shopkeeper had lived in England for thirty years, but the mob was still out to get him. And the police, the English police, the best police in the world, we are constantly being told, just stood by and watched."

"They did arrest someone for breaking the peace," Duncan said defensively.

"That was because he inadvertently threw a brick through the window of the shop next door," Patricia pointed out.

"Well, Britain does happen to be at war with Germany. Russia isn't at war with the Jews."

"But should anything go wrong, they will *blame* the Jews. They always do. And things always go wrong. Duncan, would you object very much if I invited Sonia to come and stay with us for the duration?"

Duncan frowned. "You did that, two years ago."

"Things are different now. I think she may accept."

"And how is she supposed to get here? The Germans are saying they control the Baltic."

"Well . . . she can go to Sevastopol, and take a ship from there. May I, Duncan?"

Duncan stroked his chin. "Charlie was wondering if I should go home. He reckons the shipping front is going to be pretty busy."

"Then we'll take her with us. I think America is probably the best place in the world for her to settle. They don't persecute Jews in America, either. May I, Duncan?"

"Well, of course you may, darling. If you want to."

"I'll do it right away." Patricia hurried to her desk.

"I'd like to join up." Joseph had been sitting on the far side of the room, listening.

"Don't be ridiculous," Patricia said. "You're only sixteen years old."

"Well, as soon as I can."

"You're not English, or French, or Russian, old son," Duncan pointed out. "You're American, and we're not involved. And, hopefully, we'll have the sense to stay that way."

"I'm really half English, and half Russian," Joseph argued.

Duncan looked at Patricia, as he was inclined to do in moments of stress, certainly when they involved Joseph.

"Yes, darling," Patricia said. "I think it is very good of you to be so patriotic. And of course you may join up, the very day you are eighteen." Duncan raised his eyebrows, and she winked. There was no possibility that the war would still be on in two years time.

"Ah, Michaelin." General Bor-Clemenski stood up to shake hands. "Welcome to Petrograd. Or should I say, welcome *back* to Petrograd."

"It is a pleasure to be here, Your Honour." For this meeting Michaelin had left his monocle at home.

Bor-Clemenski gestured him to a chair, and sat down himself, behind his desk. "How was life in Ekaterinburg? A trifle quiet, I imagine."

154

"A trifle, Your Honour."

"Well, I doubt you will find it quiet here. As I am sure you know, there are a great many people in Russia of German extraction, or indeed, who are still German citizens. These have got to be listed, and evaluated. Those who retain German nationality will be interned. Those who merely have German ancestry, will, as I have said, be evaluated. This is not your task, of course, Colonel. Your task will be to investigate any of those who, having been evaluated, may be deemed to require investigation. It is a line of work at which I am told you are expert."

"I do my best, Your Honour." But Michaelin's brain was tumbling. "May I ask how high these evaluations will go?"

"Not as high as I suspect you are thinking, Michaelin. Besides, the Tsaritsa is a Russian citizen. She has already been evaluated, and removed from our lists."

"I was thinking more of people like Rasputin."

Bor-Clemenski frowned. "Rasputin is a Russian muzhik."

"Of course, Your Honour. But I have heard that there are many German ladies among his clientele."

Bor-Clemenski stroked his chin. "I take your point. But you would be playing with fire. Rasputin is more than ever in the confidence of the Empress. No, you must leave him alone. But there is no harm in investigating his clientele."

"And the Jews?" Bor-Clemenski raised his eyebrows. "The Jews have very close links with Germany," Michaelin said. "Half the Reichstag are Jews."

"The Reichstag does not rule Germany, Colonel. The Kaiser does that."

"The Reichstag is behind the Kaiser in this war, Your Honour. They have declared that support, publicly. And you can be sure most Russian Jews support the Reichstag."

"Hm. However, we need their support here, now," Bor-Clemenski said. "It is also important that we present the proper image to our allies, the French and the English, who are also riddled with Jews. By all means investigate those you consider possible risks, but I want no wholesale arrests, and certainly no pogroms. In fact, I want no arrests at all without the sort of proof that will stand up in court. And Colonel . . ." He pointed, "that excludes confessions which everyone will know were obtained under torture. We want the entire country, the entire neutral world, behind us in this war. I hope you understand me."

"Entirely, Your Honour. I have brought my principal assistant with me. Feodor Klinski. He served with me when I was in St Petersburg before, and has been with me in Ekaterinburg. He is an utterly reliable man."

"By all means install your own assistant, Michaelin, providing you make sure that he plays the game by the new rules. My rules. Oh, and Colonel, do try to remember, this is no longer St Petersburg. It is now to be called Petrograd. More Russian than German, you understand. Carry on."

"Oh, how I wish Alexei were here," Priscilla grumbled. "What am I to do, Grandma?"

"I think, what this fellow Levenfisch wishes," Anna said. "It is most patriotic."

"And Colin?"

"Send Colin to be with me."

Priscilla went downstairs to where Colonel Levenfisch and his aides waited, boots shuffling uneasily on the parquet. "Very good, Colonel. You may address my people. Gleb, you will send into the village and inform Father Valentin and Monsieur Boscowski that Colonel Levenfisch will address the assembled male population in one hour; they will have to get them in from the fields. Haste, now." She looked at Levenfisch. "What are you going to say to them?"

"I am simply going to explain the situation to them, Your Highness, and tell them that their Little Father requires every able-bodied man to volunteer for the colours. I will tell them what a glorious task it is to fight for the Motherland, and what a hideous, cruel and brutal tyranny we are going to fight against."

"I see." Priscilla frowned. "Forgive me, but is Germany really a hideous, cruel and brutal tyranny? I was under the impression, just for instance, that Germany takes better care of its working people than any other country in the world."

Levenfisch looked dumbfounded. He had been dumbfounded anyway at the sight of the Princess Bolugayevska carrying the entire world before her, it appeared, even more than at learning that she was actually an American. And now, to hear her defending Germany! "They are Huns, Your Highness," he said. "All the world says so. In any event, it is necessary to make your people believe this, or they will not volunteer."

Priscilla sighed. "I suppose so. But, Colonel, none of our people have ever been to war. They will have to be trained for several months before you can expect them to fight. Is it not possible to have them trained here? We have the harvest coming up in a few weeks, and will need every man."

"I am sorry, Your Highness. I am required to despatch every man I can raise to Kiev just as quickly as possible."

"My people are to be trained in Kiev?"

"They will be inducted into the army in Kiev, Your Highness. As for training, well, they will be taught how to shoot their rifles, as soon as there are sufficient rifles, and they will be taught how to march in step, as soon as there are sufficient boots, eh? Ha ha."

"Ha ha," Priscilla agreed faintly. "But that is not training."

"There is no time for training, Your Highness. We have a war to fight."

The horses kicked muddy water to left and right, but the

mounted men were better off than the foot soldiers, who had to slog through the water itself, often up to their calves. To their right the railroad was in constant use, but the trains were carrying food and munitions; there was no room for men. And beyond the railroad, to the north, there was even more water. Up there were the Masurian Lakes, absolutely impenetrable to any large bodies of troops. Up there too was a huge forest, growing around and in places out of the water. In the mist caused by the low cloud from which seeped a steady drizzle, and the immense amount of steam given off by men and horses, there might have been no one for a thousand miles. Apart from this Russian army, tramping steadily to the west.

General Alexander Vasilievich Samsanov drew rein and slapped water from his gloves. "Is this not the most gloomy country in the world?" he asked of his staff. Samsanov was one of those forcefully handsome men, whose face appeared as all nose and moustache and flashing eyes. He had commanded a cavalry division against the Japanese ten years before with great élan, and he was popular with his men.

"It is better than Manchuria," Major-General Prince Bolugayevski suggested.

"Why, that is absolutely correct, Alexei Colinovich. And this time we know what we are doing, eh? We will cross the border tonight. We are ahead of schedule."

"And not an enemy in sight," Alexei murmured.

"Ha! They are all attacking Paris. I do not believe there is more than a division here in East Prussia. And what they have is facing Rennenkampf. Ha ha."

Alexei had to suppose his commander was correct in his estimation of the situation. The two Russian armies had advanced across northern Poland together, a huge mass of men, guns and horses, before deliberately allowing themselves to be separated by the lakes. Alexei could have wished there had been more guns, especially that there had been more rifles. There were some infantry

158

battalions where whole platoons were armed with wooden models. To be sure, they had bayonets, and equally to be sure very few of the hastily assembled troops were capable of accurate or even volley fire, but it was a disturbing reflection that they were about to face the most highly trained and disciplined, as well as best armed, soldiers in the world. On the other hand, as Samsanov had suggested, there was no evidence that there was any German strength before them. Every Russian officer knew of the famous Schlieffen Plan, the German device for conducting a two-front war against Russia and France at the same time. This plan predicated that the Germans would fight only a delaying action against the huge but – as they well knew would be the case – ill-armed Russian masses in the east while delivering a knock-out blow to France in the west. Then their full might would be hurled against Russia. And certainly all the immediately pre-war intelligence had indicated that this plan was being carried out, and more important from Alexei's and Samsanov's point of view, that here on the East Prussian border what German forces were available were massed north of the Masurian Lakes, facing Rennenkampf's First Army.

If that were the case, then the Germans had been completely outmanoeuvered, and Samsanov had the chance for glory, as if there were really nothing in front of him he could smash his way through to Berlin, leaving the German army cut off in East Prussia. This would entirely negate the strategical drawback of the forced separation of the two Russian armies, caused by the lakes, which left them quite unable to assist each other if necessary. But the plan was that whichever army was opposed in strength, the other would carry out the advance into Germany.

So why was he feeling so dispirited? Alexei wondered. It could be the weather. It could be the knowledge that at any moment now Priscilla would be commencing labour, with all of the dangers that were involved. Or it could be simply the fact that he was aware that commanding a regiment in the cavalry screen out in front of the army was Major Paul Korsakov. Of course in an army of a hundred thousand men there was no reason for them ever to meet; Korsakov was not senior enough to attend any staff conferences. But just the knowledge that he was *there* . . .

A halt was called for the midday meal. Camp fires were lit, giving off more smoke than flame in the steady drizzle. Men huddled around their company samovars. However, the general officers lunched in the command car attached to the train, out of the wet and discomfort. "I wish to know General Rennenkampf's position," Samsanov said. "Ask him to confirm what enemy forces are opposing him."

Perhaps even Samsanov was feeling uneasy about the lack of opposition south of the lakes. Alexei himself went to the wireless compartment, and waited while the enquiry was tapped out by the morse key; the Russian army did not use code, and regarded the German efforts to conceal what they were doing with contempt. The answer returned very rapidly, and Alexei took it back to the command car, where Samsanov studied it. "Map!" The staff officers spread the map in front of him while he lit a cigar and his aide poured him another brandy.

"Right Wing Sector 7b, left wing Sector 6C," Alexei said.

"General Rennenkampf's right wing rests on the village of Gumbinnen, his left on the village of Darkehman, Your Excellency." The staff officer placed a marker across the designated position.

"But that is absurd," Samsanov grumbled. "He has advanced not more than a mile in the past twenty-four hours."

"General Rennenkampf confirms that he is faced by both the German First and Seventeenth Corps, Your Excellency, and that they are retiring slowly before him."

"His last message only mentions a strong cavalry screen," Alexei commented.

160

"We must assume he has taken sufficient prisoners to identify the enemy forces," Samsanov said. "I do not understand why he does not attack. Everyone knows von Prittwitz is so timid he would never stand and fight. However, as Rennenkampf *is* advancing, even at a mile a day, it seems obvious that they *are* retiring before him, hoping their cavalry will delay him. Which is just what they are doing. But really . . . he is fifty kilometres behind us."

"Does that matter, Your Honour?" asked another officer. "If he is continuing to contain the main German army, our task remains an easy one."

"Yes," Samsanov agreed. "Yes."

As if he is trying to convince himself, Alexei thought. Because his instincts as a soldier are telling him there is something wrong. As are mine. The Germans are the finest soldiers in the world. Their General Staff is the envy of all other armies. And they have left their entire frontier unguarded, when they must know there is a Russian army south of the lakes? "Permission to take out a reconnaissance in force, General?" he said.

"Hm," Samsanov grunted. "Hm. Yes, you may do that, General Bolugayevski. Take a regiment of cavalry." He turned to his adjutant. "Recommend."

"The Actirski Hussars, Your honour. They are the best mounted."

Alexei swallowed, but Samsanov was already issuing the order. "You will reconnoitre due west, that is, away from the railway, until you encounter any enemy forces, General Bolugayevski. Then you will report back to me."

Alexei knew he had to put Korsakov out of his mind; there was no room for personal feelings in a war. "Here, General?"

"Wherever I am, General Bolugayevski. This army will continue its advance."

Alexei swallowed again, this time for no personal reason. Presuming there was an enemy in force out

161

there, somewhere, it was military nonsense for the army to blunder forward into the mist until the exact nature and disposition of that enemy was discovered. But it was not his business to argue with his superior officer. He called for his horse. "Am I to accompany you, Your Highness?" Rotislav asked, awkward in his uniform.

"Yes. Bring my shaving gear and a change of clothing." Alexei mounted and rode to where the regiment of Hussars, six hundred sabres strong, awaited him. They were a smart-looking body of men, who had retained their blue breeches under their new khaki tunics, but had changed their busbies for peaked caps. They were armed both with swords and rifles and, unlike too much of the rest of the army, looked thoroughly professional. Major Korsakov saluted him, face rigidly impassive. "Our orders are to find the enemy, Major," Alexei said.

"Yes, Your Highness." Korsakov raised his gloved hand, and the regiment moved forward in column of fours, Alexei, Korsakov, his adjutant, trumpeter and two staff officers out in front, Rotislav immediately behind them, while a sergeant and four troopers cantered out in front of them and indeed disappeared into the rain mist to act as an advance guard.

"No bugle calls, Major," Alexei reminded Korsakov.

"Of course not, Your Highness."

Not that it would make much difference to the knowledge any enemy would have that they were approaching, Alexei reflected, as the morning became filled with the splashing of hooves and the jingle of harnesses. He could not stop himself glancing at Korsakov, who rode beside him, staring fixedly ahead. Alexei did not know if Sonia was innocent of adultery or not, but he had no doubts, judging by the reports he had received from St Petersburg naming this fellow as a regular caller at her house, that since the divorce they had slept together. This youth, he thought, for Korsakov was really hardly more than that, has held my wife naked in his arms.

162

The thought made him feel quite sick. And quite angry, as well.

They rode for some two hours, seeing nothing save already harvested fields, although it was mid-August, and occasional copses emerging from the mist, and then one of the advance guard returned to say that they were approaching a village. "Is it defended?" Korsakov asked.

"I do not believe it is, Your Honour."

Korsakov looked at Alexei.

"Assume it is defended, Major."

Korsakov summoned his troop captains. "Troop A will circle to the right, and assault from the north. Troop B will circle to the south and attack to the north. Troop C will follow me into the village. There will be no further orders and no bugle calls. I will advance in thirty minutes."

"No firing," Alexei said. "Use steel."

The captains saluted and rode off to join their commands. Korsakov took out his fob watch and checked the time, then restored it to his pocket. "It is odd, do you not think, Your Highness," he remarked, "that we have come some twenty miles and not encountered a German? We are certainly well across the border."

"Yes," Alexei agreed, but did not comment further.

The half-hour passed, and they led their men forward. They advanced with drawn swords but no shouting, and were overtaken by the noise to either side as the other troops charged in, drawing their reins to come steaming to a halt as they discovered only their own comrades. And a few terrified villagers, to be sure. But far less than there should have been, while nearly all the livestock had been driven off. There were not even any barking dogs. But there was a railway station, for the line had curved back in front of them. Alexei and Korsakov had their men dismount, and did so themselves, summoning their prisoners. "Where is the mayor?" Alexei demanded, speaking Polish.

163

The men gazed at them with wide eyes, so he changed to halting German, a language he had learned at military college, but had not often used since. "The mayor has left, Your Honour," said one of the men.

"When did he do this?"

"Four days ago, Your Honour."

"With all of your women and children and your animals," Korsakov remarked. "Four days ago? Four days ago you could not have known we were coming. Why did the mayor leave?"

The man rolled his eyes. "He was told to do so, Your Honour."

"By the German soldiers? So, the Germans soldiers were here four days ago. Where are they now?"

"I do not know, Your Honour."

"Well, tell us how many there were," Alexei said. "Mounted, or on foot?"

"They were in an automobile, Your Honour."

Alexei frowned at him.

"How many automobiles?" Korsakov snapped.

"One, Your Honour." It was Korsakov's turn to frown.

"You are saying that one automobile containing German soldiers came to this village, and told the mayor and your women and children to leave?" Alexei asked.

"They were officers, Your Honour. Four officers."

"Very good. Four officers came to your village and told you to evacuate. Was this evacuation carried out by the train?"

"Yes, Your Honour."

"Were there soldiers on the train?"

"A few guards, Your Honour."

"So, your village was evacuated. But some of you stayed. Why?"

The man shuffled his feet. "We did not wish to leave our homes, Your Honour."

"They have clearly been left behind to act as spies," Korsakov remarked in Russian. "We should hang the lot."

164

Alexei ignored him while he tried to work out what was happening. This village had been evacuated four days ago. If the Germans had been retreating then, they could be fifty miles away by now. But fifty miles would mean they had retreated almost into Germany proper, and certainly far beyond the lakes. All without tearing up the railway line. If they had done that, they were allowing Samsanov's army to swing up to the north behind the troops opposing Rennenkampf, and gain an enormous, possibly a decisive, victory. So they *could* not have done that. Therefore . . . they had not torn up the railway line. There was the key. "We will camp here for the night, Major Korsakov," he said. "I want you to send a squadron of your men north, for twenty miles."

"With respect, Your Highness, that will take them into the bog."

"Well, twenty miles or the bog, whichever is closer. They must report to us tomorrow morning what they find. And send another squadron south for twenty miles."

Korsakov made a movement with his hand, almost as if he wished to scratch his head. "You think the Germans are to the north of us, and to the south of us, but not in front of us, Your Highness? Would they not use the railway to advance their people?"

"I am sure they intend to. The Germans are somewhere, Major. I am certain of that. I am also certain that they wish us to continue our advance. Thus it is up to us to find them, and find out what they are at. You will also send a galloper back to General Samsanov. I will give him a written message."

"May I ask what you will tell the general, Your Highness?"

"Certainly. I am going to recommend that he halt his advance immediately, until we can give him some positive information."

The Russians made themselves as comfortable as they

165

could in the abandoned village; those Germans who had remained behind were placed under guard so they could not sneak off. Alexei and Korsakov chose the mayor's house as their quarters, although even this was hardly more than a cottage. "At least it will keep the rain off," Alexei said, sitting before the hastily laid fire while Rotislav and Korsakov's batman prepared supper.

Korsakov offered him a cigar, and after a moment's hesitation he took it. Korsakov struck the match, and then leaned back in his chair, inhaling deeply. "Do you expect my men to discover the Germans, Your Highness?" he asked.

"I know they are there, Major. They have to be there."

Korsakov considered. "In that case, Your Highness, we may well be fighting a battle tomorrow."

"I would estimate the day after, at the earliest. Once we have established the German position and numbers, we will fall back on the army."

"If they allow us to. What I am trying to say, Your Highness, before we go into battle, is that I would like to apologise for any misfortune that I may have brought upon your house. And to avow before you, and in the sight of God, firstly that I am innocent of any wrongdoing with the Princess Sonia, before your divorce, and secondly, that I love her and intend to marry her the moment this war is over."

"Major Korsakov," Alexei said. "The Princess Sonia no longer exists. I do not wish to hear this matter mentioned again."

Alexei slept heavily. But then, the ability to sleep soundly and well, no matter what the conditions or the events that might be whirling around his head, had always been one of his greatest assets. And tonight, apart from the discomfort of lying down in his wet clothes on an uncomfortable bed far too small for him and entirely lacking, despite

166

Rotislav's turning of the house upside down, in sheets or pillows, he was angry. The effrontery of the fellow, daring to raise Sonia's name between them as if they were of equal rank. And now confessing that he was seeking to marry her! She might have fallen from the heights, but she could never be used as a stepping stone to higher things by a man like Korsakov.

He was awakened to uproar, before dawn, scrambled into his boots and ran into the front room, where Korsakov was confronting a mudstained and excited trooper. "From the northern troop, Your Highness," Korsakov said. "Repeat what you have just said to General Bolugayevski," he commanded.

"Germans, Your Highness. A huge number of Germans."

"Be specific," Alexei said.

"I cannot say for certain, how many, Your Highness. We heard them before we saw them, and then, when we saw them, we were ourselves seen, by a troop of uhlans. They charged us, Your Highness, and Captain Averbach commanded me to return here as quickly as possible to inform Your Highness."

Alexei looked at Korsakov; the fellow could just have run away. "This is a good man, Your Highness," Korsakov said. "I am sure he is telling the truth."

"Very good," Alexei said. "You saw a large number of Germans. What were they doing? Besides attacking your comrades."

"They were marching east, Your Highness."

Alexei pulled on his gloves, and heard hooves. He went outside, followed by Korsakov, and saw several horsemen galloping into the village, from the south. The lieutenant commanding them dismounted and saluted. "Verbal message from Captain Vronski, Your Highness. We have encountered a large body of Germans."

"Marching east?"

"That is correct, Your Highness."

167

"Was it possible to identify any units?"

"Yes, Your Highness. We identified the flag of the Eighteenth Saxon Light Infantry."

"Rotislav!"

"Here, Your Highness." Rotislav was delving into the knapsack to find the list provided by Russian intelligence. "The Eighteenth Saxon Light Infantry is part of General von Prittwitz's Seventeenth Corps."

"But that is north of the lakes, facing our First Army," Korsakov protested.

"It was, Major. Mount your men." He smiled at Korsakov's stricken expression. "It need not be a disaster. General Samsanov will have halted by now. But we must accept a defensive battle. And we must hurry."

The hussars cantered out of the village and proceeded back along the road. If down to this morning they had not known the Germans were there, at least, Alexei reflected, the Germans could only just have realised they had been discovered. They would surely halt their advance to reconsider their dispositions, given that they were still some twenty miles from the Russian army. But how had they got south of the lakes without anyone knowing? Simply because Samsanov had accepted Rennenkampf's repeated assurances that he was facing the main German army. While all the time, leaving only a cavalry screen to continue hoodwinking Rennenkampf, they had been shifting their main force to the south. If that were so, then they were being commanded by a general of high skill. He found that hard to reconcile with the tales of Prittwitz ordering panic-stricken retreats.

"Permission to halt the column, Your Highness," Korsakov said. Alexei looked at him in surprise. He had been entirely wound up in his thoughts. "I think I can hear something," Korsakov explained.

"Halt the column."

Korsakov raised his hand, and the horses came to a

stop. Then the major looked at the major-general. There was definitely noise out there in front of them, a huge amount of noise, varying from the hissing of a steam engine through the clopping of hooves to the tramp of boots. "Germans, Your Highness?" Korsakov enquired.

"The Germans do not have a train to the east of us," Alexei snapped, and kicked his horse forward. A few minutes later he was in the midst of Samsanov and his staff, while the army moved forward to either side of them. "I sent you a galloper," Alexei said.

"You are too cautious, Alexei Colinovich," Samsanov said. "Your man reported you had found no enemy. To stop where there is no opposition would be criminal."

Alexei had a tremendous urge to tear his hair out by the roots. "I have found the enemy, General," he said. "They are to either side of us. And as you have continued your advance, they are probably behind us now, as well."

"For God's sake keep your voice down, Prince Bolugayevski, if you intend to be alarmist," Samsanov snapped. "You have found our enemy," he sneered. "Where?" Almost as if he had asked his question of the gods, there came a whine, and the first shell exploded amongst his people. It was the first of many.

Samsanov was neither a coward nor a total incompetent; he was merely overconfident. Now he reacted with energy, commanded his men to deploy, sent his Cossacks ahead for another, equally belated, reconnaissance. But he would not retreat immediately, as Alexei begged him to. "You wish me to withdraw before an enemy I have not even seen, Prince?" he demanded. "I would be cashiered. The best form of defence is attack, is it not. We shall advance."

The Russian army was already disorganised, both by the shelling and the sudden discovery that they were in the midst of a battle. Staff officers, Alexei amongst them, were despatched to all units, commanding them to stand firm if attacked, but to continue the advance where possible. But all the time shells were bursting in their midst, destroying men and horses and material in a welter of blood and screaming horror. And now there came the chatter of machine guns as the opposing infantry made contact. Alexei could see the morale of the troops draining away like water from a holed bucket. They had advanced so confidently, relying on what their officers had been telling them. Now they had been struck on all sides out of the mist, by an enemy their officers had not known to be there, an enemy of whose strength they had no idea, but which naturally, unable to see in the mist and rain, they multiplied out of all proportion to the actual firepower to which they were exposed.

He galloped back to the command train, where Samsanov was sending urgent radio messages, back to Jilinski, inform-ing him of the situation, and north to Rennenkampf, imploring him for help. But there was no way Rennenkampf could possibly reach them in time, even supposing he was likely to disobey his orders, which were to keep on advancing west, to go to the aid of a man he in any event loathed. "General," Alexei said. "We *must* retreat while there is still time."

"Their shells have broken the line behind us," one of the staff officers said. "We would have to abandon the train."

"We would save the army," Alexei shouted.

Samsanov pulled his beard. He knew as well as anyone this catastrophe was of his doing, because he had not sent out a reconnaissance until it was too late, because he had not accepted the finding of the reconnaissance when it had been sent out, because he had made the cardinal sin in warfare of believing things were as he wanted them to be instead of finding out what they actually were. "The army will retreat," he said. "We will fall back on Bialystok. General Prince Bolugayevski, you will organise the advance guard of the retreat. Leave

170

now. Haste is imperative. Report to me when you are ready to move out."

Alexei saluted and ran back to his horse. Around him shells continued to burst, and now he saw soldiers milling about, lacking officers to command them, throwing down their weapons. He urged his horse into their midst. "Follow me," he shouted. "Pick up those rifles. We must fight our way out."

"We are lost," someone bawled. "We are surrounded. We must surrender."

Without hesitation Alexei drew his revolver and shot the man dead. "You and you," he shouted at junior officers who were emerging out of the mist. "Rally these men or I will have you shot." He galloped into the mist, wondering where Rotislav was. Or Korsakov, for that matter. In front of him he found a group of mounted officers. "Where are your men?"

"We have taken cover over there." The colonel pointed to the south-west."

"And you are here," Alexei remarked. "Well, follow me."

"You'll be killed," the colonel said.

"Correction," Alexei replied. "*We'll* be killed. Perhaps. But is that not why we are soldiers? To die for Tsar and Motherland?"

He walked his horse forward, and the officers followed. He came upon a regiment of infantry, lying or kneeling, firing into the mist. In the mist there were flashes of light, and every so often a man would collapse to the ground, mostly without a sound. But they were holding. "If only we knew where they were," the colonel complained, reining his horse behind Alexei's. The animals were neighing and occasionally rearing as bullets whistled by or sent up spurts of mud or earth from close at hand.

"They are there, Colonel. And you can be sure they are dying as often as any of our people. Where is your brigade commander?"

"I do not know, Your Highness."

"Well, hold your men here. I will return in a little while with orders." He rode alongside the track, which was now filled with several trains, all stopped and helpless, unable to go forward or back as there were great gaps torn in the line. Everywhere there were men milling about, wounded – men and horses – screaming, officers bawling orders which were not being obeyed. The Second Army had become a disorganised mob. Then he saw Korsakov. The major had lost his hat, and there was blood on his face. But he looked as efficient as ever, even if he now had no men at his back. "Where is your regiment?" Alexei demanded.

"They are there, Your Highness. What is left of them. I must tell you, there is no way through; the Germans are behind us in force. We are surrounded."

One of the officers who had followed Alexei gave a great shout. "We are surrounded! The army is lost!"

Alexei turned in the saddle, drawing his sword as he did so, and swung the weapon. The officer gave another shout, and attempted to drag his horse round, so vigorously that the beast went down on its haunches and he was unseated. He freed his feet from the stirrups and ran into the mist, but the damage had been done. His cry was taken up, wailing its way through the ranks.

"What do you wish me to do, Your Highness?" Korsakov asked.

"Join your men, and lead them out, if you can."

Korsakov wheeled his horse, and then checked. "Will you not come with us, Your Highness?"

"I will come if I can," Alexei told him. "But do not wait for me."

He rode back towards the command train, through masses of panic-stricken men. No one attempted to stop him, except inadvertently by being in his way; no one took any notice of him, either. There was still a good deal of firing going on, but the bombardment had ceased. The Germans knew the battle was won. He galloped up to the command train, flung himself from the saddle, burst into the compartment. "General, this army is disintegrating into a mob. You must take personal control. You must . . ." He looked left and right, at the frightened staff officers. "Where is General Samsanov?"

"The General has left the train, Your Highness," one of the officers said. "He told us he was going for a walk in the woods, to think."

"To . . . my God!" Alexei leapt from the open door and ran into the trees. "Alexander Vasilievich!" he shouted. "Where are you?" For reply, he heard the flat sound of a revolver shot. He stumbled towards it, and came upon Samsanov, lying on his back. The general had placed his revolver muzzle in his mouth and pulled the trigger. The whole top of his head had been blown off and only a bloody mass remained.

Alexei stared at him, while a million thoughts tumbled through his brain. Samsanov had killed himself because he knew his army was lost, and he could not face that fact. But as he had killed himself, the command now devolved on his deputy: Prince Alexei Bolugayevski. Then, as the army was lost, swallowed up as if it had never existed, should not he also blow out his brains? But to do that would be never to see Priscilla again, or his children, including the one not yet born, or Bolugayen. It would also be a gross betrayal of all the men who now had to depend upon him for salvation.

Alexei straightened and squared his shoulders, and listened to footsteps, all about him. He saw grey-green uniforms coming through the trees and heard barked words of command.

"Your Highness!"

He turned, and saw Rotislav, peering at him from some bushes. Hastily he joined the valet. "I thought you were dead."

173

"It is my business to be where you are, Your Highness. But what are we to do? If we do not surrender, we will be killed."

"We must surrender," Alexei agreed. "But there is something I must do first."

Chapter Seven

The Arrest

Gleb Bondarevski stood on one leg as the Countess Anna read the newspaper. The entire house, the entire estate, was hushed, as the news had spread through the servants' quarters and down to the village. But then, perhaps the whole of Russia was hushed.

"A hundred and twenty-five thousand men," Anna muttered. "Swallowed up in a single day. Do you know, Gleb, our total casualties in the war with Japan were less than double that? And Samsanov, disappeared! Then where is the Prince? Why is there no word of the Prince?"

Gleb looked more distressed yet. "Here is the later paper, Your Excellency. There is a rumour that General Samsanov, when he realised that his army was surrounded and would have to surrender, went into the woods and committed suicide."

Anna raised her head. "The man is a coward. Was a coward." She snorted. "I am not interested in General Samsanov, Gleb. I wish news of the Prince."

Gleb licked his lips. "It is said that Prince Bolugayevski followed General Samsanov into the wood, Your Excellency. And has not been seen since."

Anna stood up. "Are you saying that the Prince committed suicide, Gleb?"

"I am reporting what the newspapers are saying, Your Excellency. But they are only rumours."

They gazed at each other. Of all the servants on Bolugayen, only Gleb would dare put such a possibility to the Countess. And looking at her expression, the old butler began to wonder if he had exceeded the bounds of even their twenty-year-old friendship. But she merely said, "The Prince Bolugayevski does not commit suicide. Where is Count Colin?"

"He is out riding, Your Excellency."

"I wish him sent to me the moment he comes in. To me, Gleb, and no one else. Where is the Countess Anna?"

"At her lessons with Mademoiselle Friquet, Your Excellency."

"See that she stays there until Count Colin comes in."

"Yes, Your Excellency." Gleb shuffled his feet. "Will you tell Her Highness?"

"Of course I must tell Her Highness, you old goat." Anna hesitated for a moment, her mouth twisted. Then she said, "Send into the village and tell Dr Geller I wish to see him. Now." Gleb hurried off, and Anna climbed the stairs, as slowly and painfully as she did most things nowadays, one hand on the bannisters, the other clutching the newspapers. Oh, she thought, to be young again. To be the girl who had defied the world, laughed at it, conquered it as much with her fearless energy as with her beauty. Now . . . Alexei dead? She could not believe it. But if it was true . . . young Colin was the Prince. Half-Jewish and sixteen years old, in the middle of a war which was again turning out to be a disaster for Russia. There was a problem.

On the first floor gallery a clutch of maids ceased whispering to curtsey as she reached them. They would have heard the rumour, of course. She could only hope it had not reached Priscilla's sewing room, before she did.

Anna opened the door and stepped inside. Madame

176

Xenia was seated beside the Princess with notebooks before them both; obviously they had been going over household matters. Xenia rose and gave a brief curtsey as the Countess entered. Priscilla looked up with a bright smile. "Was that the post, Grandma? Were there any letters?"

Her tone was wistful. In the past month she had received but a single letter from Alexei, written before the campaign had properly started. Anna had explained that he could not write once the march on Germany had begun, for fear of giving away the army's position and progress, but it was nonetheless upsetting for the girl not to know what her husband was doing, and how he was faring. Well, she would have to know now. "Leave us, if you will, Xenia," Anna said. "I think you should have a word with Gleb."

Xenia raised her eyebrows and gave her actual mistress a glance, as if to say, am I being dismissed? But Priscilla responded with her usual bright smile. "I will send for you in a few minutes, Xenia," she said. Xenia curtseyed, and closed the door behind her. "You have that poor woman terrified out of her wits, Grandma," Priscilla said with mock severity. "Now, what has happened? I know that something has."

Anna sat beside her and placed the newspapers on the table. Priscilla picked up the first broadsheet, a frown slowly gathering as she read. She raised her head. "How can our army have been defeated, just like that?"

"Incompetence, I would say. It has always been incompetence."

"But . . . there is no word of Alexei. And Samsanov has disappeared . . ."

"Samsanov appears to be dead. They are saying he committed suicide."

"My God! That is a reversion to barbarism."

Anna shrugged. "In many ways the Russians are still a barbaric people, and proud of it. Priscilla . . ." She rested

177

her hand on the girl's. "There is a rumour that Alexei may also have done this."

Priscila had been reading some more. Now she raised her head again. "Alexei? I do not believe that. I will never believe that. He . . . he has too much to come home to."

"I do not believe it either. But, as he also has disappeared, we must face the fact that he may have been killed."

Priscilla stared at her for several seconds, then she grimaced at the same moment as she grasped her swollen stomach. Anna squeezed her hand. "Geller will be here in a little while." She rang the bell for the maids.

"Is it true that we have lost the war, Grandma?" Anna asked. Behind her, Mademoiselle Friquet was wringing her hands. Elene Friquet was a young woman, and not at all unattractive; she had a well-nourished figure which expanded lavishly at hip and bust, and thick black hair which promised much but which she invariably wore in a tight bun to match her tight features. She was unmarried, and as far as Anna was aware, a virgin: certainly she had never shown the slightest interest in any of the men of Bolugayen since coming here the previous year.

Alexei had considered her the perfect governess for his daughter. Anna was not so sure, if he wanted his daughter to be a Bolugayevska. There was also the undoubted fact that Mademoiselle Friquet, being French, regarded such things as tsars and aristocracies with deep suspicion, and was critical of the lavish lifestyle of the family with which she now lived. But her heart was undoubtedly in the right place when it came to hating Germans, and she was as horrified as anyone by the news of this catastrophic defeat suffered by France's allies.

It was time to put things in perspective. "Of course we have not lost the war," Anna snapped. "We have lost a battle, and, it appears, one of our armies. A hundred

178

and twenty-five thousand men. Do you know how many men Russia has under arms at this moment, Anna? Eight million! That is to say, we have lost one sixty-fourth of our total strength. What nonsense. Where is Count Colin?" she asked the governess.

"I have not seen him, Your Excellency. May I ask if there is any news of the Prince?"

"There is no news of anyone, at the moment," Anna said. "It is all rumour."

"I saw Dr Geller arriving . . ."

"Her Highness is in labour, Friquet." Anna forced a beam in the direction of her namesake. "You are about to have a baby brother." Pray heaven, she thought, it is a baby brother.

She went downstairs again. Gleb was waiting in the front hall, with his black tie and tails suggestive of a messenger from hell awaiting a summons from his master, she thought. "Am I to understand that Count Colin has not returned from his ride?" Anna demanded.

"I have not seen him, Your Excellency."

"Then he has heard the news and taken himself off."

"Off, Your Excellency?"

"He wants to fight. He will have gone into Poltava to get the train. Silly boy. He could be the Prince of Bolugayen." She bit her lip, and glanced at the butler. "You will forget I said that, Gleb. But you will summon Monsieur Boscowski and have him send men into Poltava to bring the silly boy back. Discreetly. But it must be done." Gleb bowed.

Anna returned upstairs to the Princess's bedroom, from whence a stream of anxious maids came and went, carrying cloths and hot water, whispering amongst themselves. She went through the sitting room, where there were more anxious women, and opened the bedroom door, just in time to hear the slap and the thin wail. She stood by the bedside and kissed Priscilla's sweat-wet forehead. "It's a

179

boy, Grandma," Priscilla said. "A boy. Oh, I wish Alexei were here."

"He will be," Anna assured her, and turned to Geller. Madame Xenia actually held the babe, like all newborn babes, a wizened scrap of humanity.

"I have a wet nurse waiting," Geller said. "Until Her Highness's milk comes in. That is, if . . ." He hesitated.

"Yes, I intend to feed him," Priscilla said.

"You must rest," Anna told her. "I will come back later, and we will talk about a name." She nodded her head to the door, and Geller followed her into the sitting room. "Well?"

"The babe is a month premature, Your Excellency. Obviously brought on by the terrible news."

"Obviously. That is why I sent for you even before Her Highness began labour. Will it survive?"

"I think, with care . . ."

"Then give it care. Move in if you have to. But be there, all the time."

"I will do that, Your Excellency. May I ask . . ."

"No," Anna said. "Ask nothing. Just make sure that boy lives."

The future Prince of Bolugayen, she thought, as she returned downstairs and called for a bottle of champagne; Alexei had confided part of his problem to her. But now Alexei was gone. She was still sitting, by herself, sipping her drink – she was on her second bottle – when Boscowski was admitted. The bailiff was twisting his hat in his hands. "I am sorry to say, Your Excellency, that we have been unable to find Count Colin. Or should I be saying Prince Colin?"

"I think that would be premature, Boscowski. Count Colin will do for now. You say you cannot find him. You checked the train?"

"He did not take the train, Your Excellency."

180

"Because he knew that is where we would look. Very good, Boscowski. You have done all you could."

"I shall, of course, continue the search," Boscowski said. "I will send to both Kharkov and Kiev. We will find him, Your Excellency."

"No," Anna said. "I do not wish you to do that, Boscowski."

"But, Your Excellency, if he were to join the forces, he could be killed."

"To bring him back, virtually in chains, would be more humiliation than he could stand. Besides, is it not the duty of every Russian, whether he be prince or peasant, to fight for the Motherland? And if necessary, to die for the Motherland? I think we should let Count Colin follow his own instincts." Boscowski so far forgot himself as to scratch his head. This woman had sent him out in great haste only a few hours previously, just to prevent the boy following his instincts. And to let the man who could possibly already be the Prince Bolugayevski just disappear into the sunset . . .

"Thank you, Boscowski," Anna said. "I am very pleased with you. Now drink with me a toast to the new . . . to Princess Priscilla's child."

A single bell tolled, but the sound seemed to travel all over St Petersburg. Every day's report was worse than the last. Every day's rumour was more horrifying than the last. Following the disaster at Tannenburg, the Government had attempted to put the best possible face on things, pointing out that the offensive against Austria in Galicia had been a great success, that the huge fortress of Premszyl was besieged and surely about to fall. Premszyl had indeed fallen, but everyone had expected to be able to beat the Austrians, an antiquated army in which officers and men spoke differently languages, literally. It was the Germans who mattered, and Tannenburg had been followed by yet more disasters, fought out in the winter snows.

181

It had in any event been a grim winter, quite apart from the news from the front. There had been shortages of food and fuel. Again the Government had pointed out that Russia was the wealthiest country in the world, in terms of food and fuel. The difficulty was getting those essentials of life into the cities, where so much of the available transport, from trains to carts and wagons, was being used for conveying men and matériel towards the front. But such explanations did not prevent people from feeling any the less cold or hungry, or discontented with the way things were going. The Russian people, Sonia knew, had always been discontented. But they had responded to the call to arms against Germany with tremendous enthusiasm. Now that enthusiasm was gone, and the discontent was back, more strongly than ever.

Now there were mutterings that the so-called defeat by Japan had been a colonial war which had not been taken seriously enough. These continuing defeats, these unending shortages, could only be caused by treason. Petrograd, it was remembered, was filled with Germans; it had even had a German name, which was why it had been changed to Petrograd. And top of the list of Germans resident in the capital was the Tsaritsa herself. Useless to point out that she had an English mother, and that her grandmother was the most famous Englishwoman of all time.

Equally did people mutter about her continuing relations with Rasputin. Once upon a time the muzhiks had been proud of the staretz, as a man of the people who had risen to be courted in the salons of the great. Now, too many of them had seen with their own eyes some of his drunken excesses, which overflowed into the restaurants and streets, and as the tales of his sexual excesses grew, there were even those who whispered that he too must be in the pay of the Germans. But the coming of spring had brought a lift in everyone's spirits; it always did. At least the question of heating one's house was no longer a perpetual worry. It had almost been possible to smile. Until that cursed bell had started tolling again.

Sonia was downstairs to greet Antonina on her return from the shops. "Well?" she demanded.

"A loaf of bread, madame. And some coffee. Look!" Her tone indicated, haven't I done well?

"But no meat."

"There is no meat, madame. I have a paper."

Sonia took it. "What is the news? Why is the bell ringing?"

"The Germans are advancing again. They have recaptured Premszyl."

"Oh, my God!" Sonia sat down with the newspaper, but she hardly read the words. She knew there would be nothing about what she wanted to know. There had been no word of either Alexei or Paul since the Battle of Tannenburg. She had read the speculation that Alexei was probably dead. No one had done any speculating about the possible fate of a major in the Actirski Hussars; there were too many other majors who had simply disappeared, with their entire commands. She wondered what Trotsky thought about it all? Or Lenin? How they must be chuckling at the misfortunes of the countrymen who had thrown them out. Never had she felt so utterly alone.

But, if Alexei were dead, then Colin was Prince Bolugayevski. That was a quite tremendous thought. It had grown on her slowly during the winter, but as it had not been possible to travel anywhere because of the winter, she had put the thought away at the back of her mind. Now the sun was shining and the snow had gone. And not all the trains were filled with soldiers.

To be on Bolugayen, where she knew there would be food, wine and warmth, and above all else, security! Did she dare? Obviously Alexei and this new wife of his would have denigrated her as much as possible to the children. But yet, they were her children. They could not, surely, turn their own mother away? She did not seek any kind of role. She asked only an apartment and the privilege of seeing them from time to time. Surely . . . But supposing they did reject her, why not take up Trishka's invitation? She had, in fact, received the letter before Christmas, but that too she had put away for the winter. For all her misfortunes, Sonia yet loved Russia, considered it her home, considered herself a Russian. To run away in the middle of a war, even when no one seemed to want to know her, was somehow cowardly.

But now, what did she have to lose? If Alexei was dead she had nothing left to dream about, and if Paul was also dead, she had no companionship to look forward to. Only another winter, now again only a few months away, in which there would be even more shortages and more grumbling. And more hatred of the Germans, and those associated with the Germans – the Jews. To be free of anxiety was certainly a dream. Patricia did not suffer from anxiety. She never had. But a good deal had happened since her oldest friend had extended her invitation. For one thing, leaving via Sevastopol was out, since Turkey had joined the German side: the Dardanelles were closed. She would have to go via the trans-Siberian railway to Vladivostock and then across the Pacific to America, an immense journey. It certainly made more sense to try Bolugayen first.

She wrote Patricia a letter, apologising for not having replied before, telling her how sorry she was about Alexei, giving her some idea how miserable conditions were in Russia, and asking if she was serious about the invitation, and if so promising to come as soon as she could.

'To be with you is like a dream,' she wrote. *'We have so much to talk about, and perhaps, even to do, together.'*

She knew Patricia had been on her side over the divorce. With Alexei dead, she thought, Patricia might even be willing to help her get back to Bolugayen – if her initial attempt failed.

The letter mailed, she went to her bank and drew out some money. She asked if it might be possible to convert some of it, and was told no. Nor could she withdraw as much as she wanted, however substantial her balance remained. There were restrictions. But she obtained enough to get her down to the south. She would have to take things as they came; she still had several valuable pieces of jewellery, which she was prepared to use, if necessary. Even as she thought, what a topsy-turvy world it is that I, a wealthy woman by any standards, should have to contemplate selling my jewellery to escape from Russia. But then, she supposed, looked at objectively, her life had always been topsy-turvy. "I am leaving Petrograd," she told Antonina that evening. Antonina's eyebrows went up and down like yo-yos. "In the first instance, I am travelling to the south, to Poltava," Sonia said. "I may be staying there. If not, I shall be leaving Russia and travelling to England."

"England, madame?" It might have been the moon.

"I have a friend there, who has asked me to visit with her," Sonia explained. She did not wish to get involved in explaining relationships to her maid at that moment. "Now, I should very much like you to accompany me, Antonina. But I shall not hold it against you if you decide you cannot do this."

"Madame is selling this house?"

"No, no. I propose merely to shut the house up for a' while. I shall be coming back to it. I shall be leaving most of my clothes and all of my books, in any event."

"Will madame not require someone to look after the house for her?"

"You would prefer to do that?"

Antonina shuffled her feet. "Petrograd is my home, madame."

"I understand that. Very good. You may remain here as caretaker. I will arrange with my bank for you to be able to draw money every month, both for your salary and for any expenses regarding the house. But I cannot travel without a maid."

"I will find one for you, madame."

"I would appreciate that. But, Antonina, she must not know anything of my plans. When we interview, we will merely say that I intend to leave Petrograd, and that therefore whoever gets the post must be prepared to travel."

It was a great relief actually to be doing something. Running away! The last time she had run away, it had been from Bolugayen, seeking to escape meeting Paul. That had been a disaster, and Paul had still wound up in her bed. This time . . . in any event, the decision was taken, and she could only wait for a reply from Patricia. She knew this would take several weeks, if not months, but as long as she was out of Petrograd by the end of September she felt she would be all right. And there was a great deal to be done. She consulted train timetables and shipping schedules. She sorted through her wardrobe, determining what she could take – she wanted to travel as lightly as possible. She interviewed the various women Antonina produced without finding anyone she really wanted to travel with. And she began to worry as the weeks went by and she did not hear from Patricia. She kept reminding herself that in time of war, letters were obviously going to take a long time, but she either had to leave in September or sit out another winter.

It was a much better summer than anyone had dared hope. The Grand Duke Nicholas, the Tsar's uncle, who was Commander-in-Chief of the Army, finally brought the German offensive to a halt, even if in doing so he had had to yield virtually all Poland. This brought praise and condemnation in equal proportion, but everyone was taken aback when it was announced that the Grand Duke was being removed from his command and sent to the Caucasus to confront the Turks; his place as

Commander-in-Chief in the field was to be taken by none other than *the* Commander-in-Chief, the Tsar himself. Opinion was divided about this as well. The Tsar had absolutely no military experience, and would therefore be entirely at the mercy of the advice of his staff. What worried people even more was that he announced his intention of leaving the Tsaritsa in command at home as his regent. The question was immediately asked, is this to be government by Rasputin?

Sonia was more than ever convinced she was doing the right thing. There had still been no letter from Patricia, but she had found herself a lady's maid, a young woman named Irina, who came from a good lower middle-class family. Irina was small and dark and intense. She was also inquisitive, according to Antonina, always asking questions about madame's affairs, about her past, and certainly curious about where she was intending to travel. However, she was clean and efficient. Sonia went to the bank to make the necessary arrangements to enable Antonina to be able to draw sufficient money to manage the housekeeping, and was shown into the manager's office. "May I ask where you are going, Madame Bolugayevska?" he enquired.

"You may. But that is surely my business. Are my affairs not in order?"

"Certainly. Oh, certainly. It's just, ah . . ." He looked at the door, which was half open, got up, and closed it. Sonia raised her eyebrows. "What I have to say must remain entirely confidential, Madame Bolugayevska."

"I shall respect your confidence, Monsieur Ragosin. You have something to tell me?"

"Well . . ." He drummed on the desk with his fingers. "When last month, you withdrew a fairly large amount of money, and at the same time enquired as to the possibility of converting that money into English pounds, well . . . I was required to inform the authorities."

187

Sonia frowned. "Is that not against all banking practice?"

"In normal circumstances, yes. But these are not normal circumstances. We are at war. Besides, when I say the authorities . . ."

"You really mean the Okhrana."

"It is their business to maintain the internal stability of the Motherland."

"And by withdrawing my own money, I am endangering the Motherland?"

"I am required to advise the Okhrana of any unusual banking business I may observe. In the circumstances, you understand, madame."

"Oh, I understand," Sonia said. "So now you are required to inform them that I am planning to leave Petrograd, is that it?"

"I am afraid so. You realise that I am not supposed to tell you this, that I am taking a great risk. If it were ever to come out . . ."

"I have said that I will respect your confidence, monsieur. I am grateful for learning this."

"May I ask you to be careful, madame?"

"You may, and I shall. However, if it will put your mind at rest, and the minds of your masters in the Okhrana, you may inform them that I am travelling to Bolugayen, to see my son. You understand, monsieur, that if, as seems likely, my husband . . . my ex-husband, is dead, then my son is the Prince Bolugayevski. He wishes to see me," she lied. "And thus I am going there, and I do not know how soon I will be able to return."

"Ah!" Ragosin smiled. "Well, then, that is a perfectly reasonable explanation. Of course. I thank you, madame, for being so co-operative."

Sonia went to the central station herself and bought the tickets for Kharkov. "There is no first-class available, madame," said the clerk.

"You are saying there is no first-class carriage on the train to Kharkov?"

"I did not say that, madame. There is a first-class carriage, of course. But it is entirely reserved for military personnel. Senior military personnel."

"Going to Kharkov," Sonia remarked, beginning to get annoyed. "Are the Germans invading the Don Basin?"

"I do not know why these gentlemen are going, madame. I only know that all first-class carriages are fully booked. I can give you seats in a second-class carriage."

"That will have to do. Yes, I will have a second-class compartment."

"I am sorry, madame. I cannot give you a compartment to yourself. I can give you a seat."

Sonia could not believe her ears. "It is two days from St Petersburg to Kharkov, is it not?"

"No, madame, it is nearer three nowadays. There are many delays, you understand."

"And you expect me to share a compartment with strangers, for three days? And nights?" she added.

"Perhaps madame has an alternative means of transport."

I am the mother of the Prince of Bolugayen! Sonia wanted to shout. But she kept her temper. She was back where she had been so often before, where only survival mattered. "Very well," she said. "But I will need two seats." The man raised his eyebrows. "I am travelling with my maid," Sonia snapped.

She stepped outside, and had to stand very still for several seconds to allow her blood pressure to decline from its near explosion level, and realised she was holding the two tickets in her hand. She opened her bag, put them in, and looked up, at two men, one to either side of her. They were very well dressed, in silk hats and frock coats and spats, while each sported a gold watch chain.

189

Yet her stomach was suddenly filled with lead. "Madame Bolugayevska?" asked one of the men.

Sonia looked from one to the other. Again she wanted to shout that she was the mother of the Prince Bolugayevski. But as they knew her name, they would know that. Indeed, they would know everything about her. "That is my name," she said, relieved that her voice was so steady.

"Will you come with us, please?"

Again she looked from face to face. "Are you arresting me?"

"We are inviting you to come with us, madame."

"And suppose I do not wish to come with you? Do you have a warrant?"

"We do have a warrant, madame. But I am sure you do not wish to make a scene."

Did it matter? she wondered. Everyone on the platform was looking at them. Even a train which had just pulled into the station seemed to be delaying its departure again, while people looked out of the windows. There was no one in Russia unable to recognise Okhrana agents. And if I do not make a scene, am I just to be led away like a lamb to the slaughter? She could remember her last arrest, twenty-one years ago, as if it had been yesterday. The utter savagery of it. These men did not look like savages, but she was not yet alone with them. And yet, she was already moving with them, between them, to the gate. Princesses, even ex-princesses, did not make scenes on railway platforms.

There was an automobile waiting. A door was held open for her, and Sonia bowed her head so as not to dislodge her hat as she got in, expecting every moment to feel their hands on her hips and legs, to be thrown forward as they sought to beat her, rape her, terrify her, to make her their slave. But neither of them touched her. One sat beside her, the other faced her in a jump seat. They both actually looked vaguely embarrassed. And, now that she looked past the carefully waxed moustaches, terribly young. Perhaps they did not know how to begin raping a thirty-eight-year-old ex-princess? "Where are you taking me?" she asked. As if she did not know.

The man facing her smiled at her, nervously. "There is someone wishing to speak with you, madame. An old friend."

Sonia was surprised at how little the building had changed. She had of course passed it often enough, but always had looked away. Most people did, when they passed the Okhrana headquarters, even while noting that the facade remained always the same. But she would have expected more differences inside the building, if only a change in decor. But the only differences were in faces, and manners.

When she had been dragged in here, beside a panting Patricia, incoherent with outrage, as a seventeen-year-old girl, everyone had been older than they were. Now everyone seemed younger. Save for the Tsar, staring down at them from huge framed photographs, clearly taken just before the start of the war. The other difference was that she was not being dragged, but rather, invited, to move forward. She knew that should be reassuring, but it wasn't. There was always the threat of what was coming next: she knew only one member of the Okhrana who might be described as an old acquaintance.

And there he was, standing at the top of the stairs up which she was being taken, smiling at her. She remembered above all else the monocle. But she remembered too being forced to stand naked before his desk, and his slow rising and coming round the desk. Suddenly she could go no further, and checked, so suddenly that the man behind her bumped into her, and muttered an apology. "Will you not come in, Madame Bolugayevska?" Michaelin invited. "Or should I call you, Sonia, after all these years?"

191

Sonia had to swallow, and lick her lips, before she could speak. "Why have you brought me here?"

"Because I wish to speak with you." He stepped back and indicated an open door. Sonia reflected that as she had decided against making a scene on a crowded public platform, it really made no sense to consider one now, in hostile privacy. Despite the trembling in her legs, she mounted the last of the stairs and went into the office. She did not look at Michaelin, but she heard him follow her in, and close the door. Yet they were not alone. When she looked to her right she saw another man standing against the wall. Perhaps the Colonel was afraid she might scratch his eyes out. The other man's face was also vaguely familiar.

She did not think she had ever been in this room before, but it too had a familiar look. There was a desk and a comfortable chair, and no other furniture; it was not part of the Okhrana's method to make their victims feel comfortable. But at least there was no inlet for a hose, she saw, remembering the dreadful, piercing stream of water with which she had been tortured twenty-one years ago. Michaelin might have been able to read her mind. "Twenty-one years," he mused as he sat down. "Do you know, Princess, that you are just as beautiful now as you were then? Perhaps more so. Then you were a trifle scrawny. Now . . . I like my women to have tits and hams. Give me your handbag."

Carefully Sonia controlled her breathing as she placed the bag on the desk. Control in all things was vital, until she got out of here. "What do you wish of me?" she asked. "I have committed no crime. Your men said you had a warrant for my arrest. I should like to see it."

"It is sufficient that I have it," Michaelin said, and emptied the bag on his desk, flicking through her intimate belongings. "As for crimes, one could say that you committed a crime by being born, Princess."

192

"You are out of date," Sonia told him. "I am no longer a princess."

"To me, you will always be a princess," Michaelin said.

"However," Sonia went on, "I believe I may well be the mother of a prince. I think you should bear this in mind, Colonel."

"Even the mothers of princes can be charged with offences against the state, Princess, especially in time of war. That is, with treason." He gestured at some papers on his desk. "I have been keeping an eye on you, Princess. The saying goes that a leopard never changes his spots, and a leopardess even less so." He picked up the train tickets. "Tell me why you are leaving Petrograd."

"I am going to visit my son on Bolugayen," Sonia said. Her legs were starting to grow weary of standing still, but she did not wish to move and suggest fear.

"I do not believe that is the truth," Michaelin said. "I believe it was your intention to leave Russia."

"Supposing I were, is that treason?"

"It might be, depending on where you were going to, and who you were going to. Do you realise that every letter posted in Russia today is subject to examination by censors? As is every letter coming in to Russia." Sonia caught her breath, and frowned as she tried to see what was in the papers. Michelin smiled, and picked one up. "This is a copy of your letter to the woman Cromb. What is it you wrote? We have so much to do together. Oh, the original was sent." He picked up another sheet of paper. "This is her reply, and this *is* the original. I thought I had better keep this until you were able to collect it yourself, Princess. Would you care to read it? Oh, and Princess, please do not attempt to destroy it. That would make me very angry. Feodor!"

Sonia stopped herself from looking over her shoulder; she heard the man come to stand immediately behind her. She took the letter from Michaelin's outstretched hand. It was undoubtedly from Trishka. And what the idiot had written . . . Michaelin had obviously taken a copy of this one as well.

"What is it she says?" he asked, picking it up. "Ah, here we are . . .

"'*I am so looking forward to having you in England, my dearest Sonia. There is so much going on. So much for us to do. You will never believe who called the other day. Vladimir. Or Nicolai as he likes to be known nowadays. Olga was with him; she insists upon calling him by his second name, Ilich. I did not even know they were in England, but I suppose if you are going to lay plots England is safer than anywhere else, although it is all apparently very hush-hush; the authorities do not know they are here, and they are afraid of being arrested should they be found out. Nicolai is in despair. He says he had such hopes of this war, of the proletariat refusing to fight, because those in the opposing ranks would also be proletarians, but both sides would unite to overthrow kings and governments and above all, tsars. Instead they have all gone marching off to war, singing songs! Of course he is right. (When I think of Alexei, lying dead in some ditch – I wonder how that little girl he set up in your place is coping? Aunt Anna writes that she has had a son, whom she has named Alexei, after his father.) But Nicolai still hopes, and dreams. I know he will love to meet you again.*'"

Michaelin raised his head. "So, Princess, you will understand that there is no point in attempting any further subterfuge."

"I have no idea what you are talking about. My sister-in-law invited me to go and stay with her, and I accepted."

"To meet this fellow Lenin, your old associate in treason."

"That is not true," Sonia snapped. "I had no idea Lenin was in England. Mrs Cromb's letter confirms that. She didn't know he was in England, either, until he called."

Michaelin leaned back in his chair. "I am afraid I do not believe you." He grinned. "To be honest, I do not wish to believe you. I have here sufficient evidence to place you under arrest, and thus, you are under arrest. I was very foolish twenty-one years ago. I saw you then only as evidence against the Bolugayevskis. Now you are again evidence against the Bolugayevskis, but now I know how to appreciate you. Enjoy you. And I am going to do that."

"I demand to see my advocate," Sonia said. But now her voice was trembling. "It is my right."

Michaelin wagged his finger to and fro. "Traitors to the state have no rights."

"I am not a traitor."

"You will have to prove that."

Sonia suddenly felt deathly tired. If she did not sit down she was going to fall down. "Is it possible to have a chair?"

Michaelin looked left and right. "There is no chair. Have my questions exhausted you?"

"I am tired, yes. If you are going to continue questioning me, I would like to sit down."

"And I have said you may not. But I am a generous man. You may *lie* down, Princess, if you wish."

"Are you mad?"

"Lie down!" Michaelin snapped. "Feodor, assist the Princess Bolugayevska."

Sonia turned. "Don't touch me," she snapped. Slowly she dropped to her knees, hesitated there.

"On your back," Michaelin told her.

Sonia bit her lip to stop herself from screaming. She took off her hat and placed it on the floor, then sat down, and then lay down, her head on the bare boards, staring up at the ceiling. How can this be happening to me? she asked herself. Again. And this time, alone. When she had been arrested, twenty-one years ago, it had been with Patricia. What had happened to them had been terrifying, horrible, but they had been together, even if then they had hardly

195

known each other. Equally, because they had been so savagely ill-treated, it had been a matter of survival; they had not had the time actually to consider their positions, save that she had felt that as she was with the Countess Bolugayevska there had to be an end in sight. She had been wrong, of course. But yet she had had that hope to cling to. Since then she had scaled the very heights, with a hundred servants waiting to do her every bidding. And now she was back to where she had begun. Only without Patricia. But still Michaelin. Who was now kneeling beside her, smiling at her. "Do you know, Your Highness, that I am under instructions not to ill-treat my prisoners? Isn't that a pleasant thought?" Sonia thought she was going to choke.

Michaelin delicately pushed her skirts up to mid-calf, and began to unlace her boots. "We are to use gentle persuasion to have the guilty confess their crimes. But do you know . . ." He pulled the boot off, caressed her stockinged instep. "It is actually more enjoyable, to persuade someone through kindness. They always do confess." He took off her other boot, again caressed her foot. "Ah, yes," he said. "The effects of a Siberian winter. You were very lucky to survive, Princess. But I am so glad you did. I think I should inspect this foot more closely. The leg as well. Who knows what other injury you may have suffered?"

He moved with sudden speed, gathering her skirt and petticoat and pushing them up to her thighs. Sonia sat up, and was thrust flat again by Feodor, standing behind her. Her head hit the floor and for a moment she was dazed. She felt Michaelin's hands on her thigh, pulling garter and stocking down past her knee. "What I am doing," he explained. "Is searching you. I have not been forbidden to do that, and it is very necessary. Who knows what weapons you have concealed about your person. Or even a bomb?"

Sonia exploded in fear and outrage and attempted to

196

kick him. But he caught her ankle, and forced her legs back down. "If you attempt to do that again," he said, "I shall call some more of my people in here to hold you down. Do you really wish me to do that?" Sonia panted. "Because you see, I am going to strip you naked, Princess. To search you, you understand. I am going to search you very carefully. Every nook and cranny." He drew her stocking right off, turned his attention to her other leg, sliding his hands up to the garter and then beyond, to seep beneath the hem of her drawers. "Every nook and cranny," he said again.

Chapter Eight

The Mistress

The Princess Dowager Nathalie Bolugayevska knew the glow of anticipated pleasures as she got out of her car in the forecourt of Rasputin's apartment house, and smiled at her daughter. Afternoons with Father Gregory were all they really lived for. And when they had been summoned on a non-regular day, it was even more exciting. Winter had come down with a blast from the north; snow was thick on the ground and even with chains it had taken them nearly an hour to drive from the Bolugayevski Palace to this house, only a few blocks away. The car had slithered to and fro, and such passersby as were out had scurried to and fro as well to avoid being mown down.

Nathalie thought winter was the best time of the year, in Petersburg – she refused ever to call it by its new name – providing, of course, that one was a princess. Or the daughter of one. Nathalie endeavoured never to see a newspaper, much less buy one or read it. But even she could not be unaware that things were not right with Russia. It was not so much the war. The front had been stabilised along a line stretching roughly from Riga to the eastern end of the Carpathians; this left an enormous amount of Russian territory in German hands, but it was a lot better than what had at one time seemed likely, and with the Tsar himself in command great things were hoped of next year. Of course, people were saying that Russia had suffered more than two million casualties in the first year of the war – some people put the figure as four million – but most of these were prisoners and they would one day be coming home. If they survived the German prison camps. But there could be no escaping the great hunger that was sweeping across the capital, accentuated by the chill. Nathalie made a habit of driving through the streets with the curtains closed in the back of the car, so that she would not have to look at the emaciated faces, staring at her and her furs and her plump, well-fed body. Rasputin liked her plump, well-fed body. As he liked Dagmar's plump, well-fed body. At eighteen, Dagmar was an only slightly smaller edition of her mother.

Nathalie had not the slightest reservations about prostituting her daughter to the staretz. Physically, there was no reason to *have* reservations; she knew that Dagmar was still a virgin, however she had become used to a man fondling her body. Morally, there could be no crime involved, as long as one believed in Rasputin's message. But Nathalie knew she would not have had reservations in any event. Born the daughter of a wealthy Georgian merchant, and of a Circassian mother, she had been brought up in the hot heady atmosphere of Tiblis. *Her* virginity had been equally well protected, but simply to ensure a good marriage, not for any moral reasons.

And the marriage, when it had come, had been beyond her wildest dreams. True, Prince Peter Bolugayevski had been in disgrace; everyone had known the disgrace had been temporary. True, he had left her in no doubt that he was marrying her because he had been commanded to do so by the Tsar, that he did not love her, and never would; Prince Peter had been desperately in love with the one woman he could never marry, his Aunt Anna. This had not bothered Nathalie. No wife of a Russian boyar expected to be well treated by her husband, and at least he never beat her. Peter could do what he liked,

199

incestuously or not: she was the Princess Bolugayevska, and as she had been less than half her husband's age, she would one day surely be the Princess Dowager.

She had not reckoned on having to accompany her husband to Port Arthur, much less that he would die there, in that stupid war with the Japanese. But that would have been entirely acceptable, had she then been able to rule Bolugayen. She had forgotten that Prince Peter had a half-brother, Alexei, who had been a favourite of the Tsar. She suspected that Anna, another favourite of the Tsar, had had a good deal to do with what had followed, the upshot of which had been that while she was undoubtedly the Princess Dowager, entitled to the rank and a commensurate income for life, her daughter had been set aside as the Bolugayevski heir and Alexei elevated to the princedom in her place.

Nathalie could well remember the vicious anger she had felt when that had been made clear to her. She was still angry whenever she thought about it. But she had thought about it less often as the years had rolled by, even if it had been a pleasure to destroy Alexei's marriage, and to light a candle to mourn his disappearance and almost certain death at Tannenburg. She had then actually given a thought to attempting to regain what she still regarded as Dagmar's inheritance, but had very rapidly abandoned the idea. She was most certainly *not* the Tsar's favourite, and was liked even less by the Tsaritsa. Besides, it would be a tiresome business, and she had actually had everything she wanted, right here in St Petersburg.

She had always been given to self-indulgence. But the pleasures of overeating and getting drunk were entirely passive. She had wanted a lover. In the years immediately following Peter Bolugayevski's death she had been afraid to take one, engaged as she had been for most of those years in fighting to obtain her daughter's inheritance. The final rejection of her claim, which might have driven her over the top, had coincided with the appearance of the staretz in St Petersburg. Like most of the Russian nobility, Nathalie was at heart an atheist, only taking part in the country's endless religious festivals – apart from Sundays, there were ninety religious holidays in every year – because everyone else did. But Rasputin's coming had almost turned her into a Christian. Rasputin's version of Christianity, in any event. And thus for seven years she had been utterly happy. He totally satisfied her sexuality, from the sublime, when he caressed her, to the lowest level of obscenity, when he let her watch him mauling other women, including her own daughter. Going to visit the staretz made what was happening in the rest of Russia, much less the rest of the world, quite irrelevant.

As usual, she swept through the antechamber with hardly a glance to left or right at the clamouring women. Anton waited obsequiously to open the door for Dagmar and herself, and they marched into the inner room, where, to her surprise, she found the staretz alone, sitting on his settee, drinking Madeira and obviously drunk. He blinked at her, and then pointed. "I have been waiting for you, Nathalie Alexandrovna."

"I came as soon as I got your message, Father." But Nathalie was frowning. "Is something the matter?"

"The matter?" Rasputin gave a huge shout of laughter. "I have a task for you to perform."

"Of course." Nathalie started to unbutton her blouse, and nodded to Dagmar to do the same.

"Not that, you silly bitch," Rasputin said. "Do you not know that your precious sister-in-law, the Jew who spurned me, has been arrested by the Okhrana?"

"Sonia?" Nathalie smiled. "How interesting. I hope they cram so much broken glass up her ass she never shits again."

Rasputin finished his wine and tossed his glass to Dagmar, who hurried to the table to refill it. "I want her out of there. Go and fetch her."

201

"Me?"

"You will go to see General Bor-Clemenski and tell him that I wish her released, into your custody. I don't care what she has done or is alleged to have done. You will tell the General that I will take full responsibility for her."

"Do you suppose he will do as you ask? Or certainly, as I ask?"

"Yes, he will. Firstly because you will tell him that you are acting for me, but that I prefer this informal approach. And secondly because you will tell him that if he does not give you the Princess, I *will* make formal application for her release through the Tsaritsa, and he will probably find himself sent to the front."

Nathalie licked her lips. "And, suppose I secure her release, what am I to do with her? Take her home?"

"You will bring her here." Rasputin took the glass from Dagmar's hand.

"Even if she has already been reduced to a gibbering wreck?"

"If she has been harmed in any way I will have the head of the man responsible. Make that very clear. But whether she has been harmed or not, you will bring her here. Once I have rescued her from the Okhrana, she will not be able to refuse me. You should explain that to her, before she gets here."

Nathalie snorted. She had never supposed the staretz could be so much at the mercy of his desires that he would go to this length to obtain a woman like Sonia, when he had the pick of virtually every other woman in Russia. "You do realise that this woman is very nearly forty years old? What are you going to do with a forty-year-old Jewess?"

Rasputin grinned. "How old are you, my dear Nathalie?"

"Well . . ." Nathalie pouted. "I am thirty-seven."

"And Sonia is thirty-eight. I can still find the odd thing to do with you. Go and fetch her."

Nathalie snorted again. "Come along, Dagmar," she said. "Uncle Gregory wants us to work for him."

"No, no," Rasputin said. "Leave Dagmar here. I wish to be amused until you bring me the Princess."

Sonia listened to the sound of boots hitting the floor of the corridor outside her cell, and hugged the blanket more tightly around herself. The blanket was a concession to the onset of winter; Michaelin did not wish her to die, or even become seriously ill. He enjoyed having her in his power too much. He was clearly a pervert. He had made her strip, that first day in his office, and he had kept her stripped; he had even, from time to time, touched her, stroked her breasts or bottom, put his hand between her legs. But he had never attempted to rape her, he had not beaten her, and he had not inflicted upon her any of the horrendous methods used by the Okhrana, methods she remembered well enough from twenty-one years before. She had survived them then. Surviving humiliation, more than surviving pain, is a good deal easier to achieve at seventeen than at thirty-eight; she had not supposed she would survive them now. But nothing had happened to her, save the humiliation of constant exposure, whenever he felt like it.

And the hose. But even that had been beneficent. When she remembered the way he had used the hose twenty-one years ago – had she not already lost her virginity to his savages she would certainly have lost it to the hose, sometimes a spout of water broad enough to knock all the breath from her body, at others a blade thin enough almost to perform surgery. The hose remained a toy for him to use, but thus far it seemed only for his amusement and her cleanliness. In the beginning she had assumed that he was playing with her as a cat might play with a mouse, choosing his moment to torture her; every day had begun with terrifying apprehension. But over the weeks she had been in here she had slowly begun to realise that he really

203

did not intend to harm her body, no matter what he might be doing to her mind. She was actually being very well treated, given the use of a brush every day to keep her curling dark hair under control, given two square meals, which included two jugs of vodka, a day, given an hour's exercise in the prison courtyard every morning. For that she was allowed to dress, but she was never allowed to encounter any of the other prisoners, and on being returned to her cell she was forced to strip again. It was as if he wanted her as some living pin-up picture, which he could look at whenever he felt the urge, but which must always be preserved in its original, immaculate form.

But the apprehension remained. What he was doing had to have an end in sight. And the fact was that she had simply vanished off the face of the earth, as far as anyone who did not know the truth was concerned. Even more frightening was the realisation that there was no one in the world who would make the slightest effort to find her. No one on Bolugayen knew anything of what had happened to her, or, presumably, cared; Patricia was in England, and would put the fact of her not having turned up to a change in plan; and Antonina would be living quite happily in her house, drawing money from her account as she needed. Even if Antonina had become aware of her mistress's disappearance, Sonia doubted she would do anything about it; certainly if she had spoken to Ragosin, he would have warned her off – it did not pay to be inquisitive about the Okhrana. So here she was, and here she would stay, until Michaelin made up his mind what to do with her. Thus she could not hear boots in the corridor without having to control a violent urge to shiver.

The door opened. She remained sitting on her pile of straw, back against the wall, blanket wrapped around her shoulders. But it was not Michaelin today; it was his sidekick, Feodor Klinski. And Feodor was carrying her clothes in his arms. "Kindly dress, Princess." It pleased both Michaelin and Klinski always to address her by her

204

former title; no doubt it tickled their fancies to be in such total possession of a member of the aristocracy.

Sonia discarded the blanket to pull on her clothes; dressing and undressing in front of this man was no longer the least embarrassing. But she was curious. "It is not time for my exercise," she remarked.

Feodor gave one of his cold smiles. "You are not to exercise today, Princess. At least, not in this prison." He even had her hat. Sonia put it on, as best she could; they were not so careless as to leave the long pins she normally used. But how good it felt to be fully, warmly dressed. "Upstairs," Feodor commanded.

Sonia obeyed, brain tumbling. She had not been upstairs since the day she had been arrested. But it remained familiar. Here there were people, clerks and agents, stopping whatever they were doing to stare at her as they had stared at her the day she had been brought in. She ignored them as she had learned to ignore all humanity in here, and climbed another flight of stairs to Michaelin's office, her apprehension growing with every step. Then she stood in the doorway and stared at Nathalie. "My dear," Nathalie said. "You look perfectly all right, to me." She sounded surprised.

"I am perfectly all right," Sonia said, and looked at the desk.

"The Colonel has taken himself off," Nathalie said. "But he signed the paper before leaving." She picked it up. "Your release." She smiled. "Into my custody."

"I do not understand," Sonia said.

"I would not worry about it right this minute," Nathalie said. "I think we should leave this place. It makes me shiver."

She went through the doorway, and Sonia hesitated only a moment before following. Again the clerks stared at her as she went down the stairs, but no one moved. Feodor was not to be seen. It was cold in the courtyard and she had only a light coat; she caught her breath and shuddered. "You will soon be warm," Nathalie promised.

The chauffeur was holding the door of the Mercedes for her. Sonia wondered where, if there was as serious a fuel shortage in Petrograd as people said, Nathalie managed to obtain her petrol from – and the penny dropped. She hesitated, and Nathalie urged her forward. How good it was to sit on the soft leather cushions, to have the door closed, to shut out the world behind the drawn curtains. But . . . she looked at Nathalie, sitting beside her. "It is Rasputin who has had me released."

"As I tried to tell you so long ago, my dear Sonia, Father Gregory is the best friend a woman can have."

"And what will he require in return?"

Nathalie's smile was cold. "You." She shrugged. "There is no accounting for tastes."

Sonia's nostrils flared. "If you think I am going to prostitute myself to that horror . . ."

"Oh, really, Sonia," Nathalie snapped. "Your sanctimonious purity makes me sick. Why do you not get a grasp of reality? Consider one or two things." She held up her gloved hand and began to tick off the fingers. "One: you are a Jew and therefore by definition an enemy of the state. Two: you are a convicted anarchist and therefore a condemned felon. Three: you are a prostitute. You prostituted yourself to live. Well, do not all prostitutes do that? And once you have sold yourself once you are a whore forever more; you may as well wear the yellow card of a licensed streetwalker and be done with it. Four: Michaelin has found the wherewithal to arrest you again. Five: Father Gregory is the only person in all Russia who wishes to help you, or who *can* help you. And six: if you do not reward him for his generosity, he is going to return you to Michaelin. I do not know what the Colonel has already done to you, but I can tell you that he was both angry and humiliated at having to let you go. Whatever Father Gregory wishes of you, it will have to be better than what Michaelin is going to do to you if he ever gets his hands on you again." She parted the curtain as the car came to a halt. "We are here. So, now, tell me, Sonia, are you going to get out and go upstairs and be a good girl, or are you going to have me tell the chauffeur to drive you back to the Okhrana?"

Sonia stared at her for several seconds. But she had to survive, if only, now, for vengeance on all those who snapped at her like a pack of savage dogs. Including this woman.

She opened the door and got out.

Patricia Cromb pushed open the dingy doorway leading into the equally dingy shop; this was not a part of London she knew at all. But it was the address she had been given, and for all the stares she had attracted as she had alighted from the taxi in her blue serge costume with its black velvet trimming, her blue felt hat with its ostrich feather, her fur muff and the gaiters over her black patent leather shoes, she was not the least embarrassed by or apprehensive of her surroundings. Wherever Patricia was, or whatever she was doing, she always felt entirely at home. The storekeeper peered at her from behind his counter and a pair of horn-rimmed spectacles. "Can I help you, ma'am?"

"I wish to see Mr Lenin."

The storekeeper's forehead wrinkled. "I know no such person."

"Yes you do, little man. Go and tell Mr Lenin that Patricia Cromb is here." She gave a brief smile. "I will mind the shop for you."

The storekeeper gave a gulp, then turned and hurried through the bead curtain over the inner doorway. Patricia took a turn around the shop, moving restlessly as she always did when the adrenalin was flowing. The storekeeper returned. "If you will come through, Mrs Cromb."

Patricia followed him through the bead curtain and up

a flight of steps. Olga Krupskaya waited at the top. Once she had been an attractive girl, Patricia remembered, with full features and a full body too. Now both features and body looked scrawny, and were not helped by the wire spectacles, behind which her eyes in recent years had started to bulge in a most unattractive fashion – she claimed it was the result of a thyroid condition. She had also, over the years of exile, lost much of her humour. "You were told not to come here except in an emergency," she remarked by way of greeting.

"I always ignore what people *tell* me to do, Olga," Patricia pointed out. "And even less what they tell me not to do. Besides, this *is* an emergency."

Olga looked frustrated, as she invariably did when trying to converse with this aristocrat who had always, even in the direst extremity, managed to convey the impression that she was slumming in even talking to people so far beneath her. "What is this emergency?" Lenin asked from the doorway.

Patricia smiled at him. She really was very fond of him, although the years had perhaps been even less kind to him than to his wife. He was now quite bald except for a fringe of red hair, although he had attempted to make up for the absence of hair on his head by growing a straggly beard. He had also lost weight, and wore a perpetual air of strain. "I will tell you about it," she promised, and swept past them both into the small, badly furnished living room, taking the bottle from her handbag and placing it on the table. "Vodka."

Olga made a face. "I am trying to get him to drink less."

But Lenin was already unscrewing the cap, nodding to his wife to close the door. "I did not suppose people like you ever had problems." He held out a glass.

Patricia sat down, sipped, and shuddered. She never drank vodka at home, as Duncan did not like it. "Everyone has problems," she pointed out. "I have a son who

208

is determined to join up the moment he is eighteen, and that will be in a week's time."

"What do you expect, of a bourgeois?" Olga asked, contemptuously.

"That sort of problem does not concern us," Lenin said.

"I am sure it does not," Patricia agreed. "However, I am equally sure that Sonia does concern you."

"Sonia? She is not even a bourgeois. She is an aristocrat. She is our enemy."

"Sonia is no longer an aristocrat, and she was never your enemy. She shared our exile with us. She is one of us. That she married my brother was an act of necessity, to save her life. And he treated her shamefully. Now she is in deep trouble."

"What sort of trouble?"

"That is what I want you to find out."

"Me?" Lenin sat down, pouring himself a second glass of vodka and topping hers up. Olga, apparently working on the theory that if you can't beat them join them, poured one for herself.

"Listen," Patricia said. "When this stupid war started, I wrote Sonia and invited her to come to England where she would be safe, until it was over. It took her some time to make up her mind, but in the summer she wrote and asked if the invitation was still open, because she would like to come. I wrote back and said of course she must come. That was in August. And I have never heard another word. That is eight months ago."

"So? She has probably changed her mind."

"I do not believe that. When I did not hear from her, I wrote again. And this time I got a reply. Last week."

"From Sonia?"

"No. From some woman called Antonina Rospowa. She says that she is Madame Bolugayevska's housekeeper. She says that in September, Sonia just disappeared. She said

209

she was coming to me, had made all the arrangements, and then just disappeared."

"When was this letter dated?"

"Just before Christmas. It took three months to get to me."

"The Okhrana," Olga said.

"That's what I think, too," Patricia said. "I mean, if she had been taken ill or something, this woman Rospowa would have heard. I did think she might have gone down to Bolugayen, because, since Alexei died, Sonia's son Colin is now Prince. So I wrote my mother-in-law, Anna Bolugayevska. And got a very odd reply. Aunt Anna said they knew nothing of Sonia, nor did they wish to. Nor did she say anything about Prince Colin. Or his sister or his stepmother. The letter said nothing at all, except to enquire after Duncan and our children."

"She does not wish to know Sonia, since the divorce," Olga said.

"Well, that is obvious. But if she is again in the hands of the Okhrana . . . Michaelin . . . my God, can you imagine what they will do to her?"

Lenin poured himself a third glass of vodka. "I can imagine very well," he said.

"I must know where she is, Vladimir."

"What do you suppose you can do about it? You? An exile."

"We are all exiles," Patricia pointed out, with great patience. "Will you help me?"

"You mean, will I help Sonia. I do not see what I am supposed to do."

"Last time we spoke you were boasting of the agents you had in Russia. In Petrograd. Even in the Okhrana."

"Well," Lenin said. "Maybe I was exaggerating."

"But you do have agents in Petrograd," Patricia insisted. "Surely they can find out something."

Lenin got up, picked up the bottle of vodka, by now half empty, and then corked it and put it down again, to be

210

enjoyed later on. "You are asking me to risk my people," he said over his shoulder. "To help someone who turned against us, no matter what you say. If I do this, what do I get in return?"

Patricia raised her eyebrows and glanced at Olga. In all the twenty-one years she had known this man, which included sharing prison and exile and then escape with him, he had never once shown the slightest sexual interest in her. While she . . . he had a magnetic personality. She loved magnetic personalities, which was a characteristic Duncan entirely lacked. I am probably an even more wicked woman than Aunt Anna, she thought. But then, have I not always intended to be that? "What do you wish?" she asked, heart pounding.

Olga snorted. "Your money, of course."

"I will tell you what I wish, when the time comes," Lenin said. "All I wish now is your promise that you will give it to me."

Patricia smiled. "Yes, I promise. But my promise only takes effect when you bring me news of Sonia."

Gleb Bondarevski stood on the lower porch of Bolugayen House and squinted up the hill. It was again summer. The second summer of the war. And at last things were going well: Russia had found a general who could win battles! His name was Brusilov, and his offensive, begun without any of the usual preliminary bombardment or mass movement of men, had taken the Austrians entirely by surprise; they were fleeing in every direction, so it was said.

Gleb supposed one had to credit the Tsar with the victory; it was he who had selected Brusilov. So then, long live the Tsar. And even the Tsaritsa, no matter what they said of her in Petrograd. Gleb was a monarchist, simply because he was entirely against change. His father had been butler on Bolugayen, and before that, his grandfather. Gleb, born towards the end of his

211

father's life, could not remember his grandfather. But his father had told him of the upheavals of sixty years before, when Tsar Alexander, coming to the throne at the end of the disastrous Crimean War, had endeavoured to free the serfs, and when the Countess Anna and the Princess Dagmar had fought each other for control of the estate, with the Englishman Colin MacLain in the middle, until Maclain had taken them both over, so to speak. Old Igor Bondarevski had endeavoured to avoid choosing sides, had always obeyed whoever had been in power, however briefly. It had not merely been a matter of survival. It had been a matter of the family – the Bolugayevskis – and the preservation of Bolugayen. That was all that was important in life. And Gleb had determined that that was all would ever be important in his life, too.

In this regard he was at odds with a good many people in the village, people he had known all his life and who in many respects were his friends. But it distressed him to observe, and to hear, how so many of them had virtually no loyalty to the family. They were concerned only with their own small prosperity, and remained on Bolyugayen and obeyed the Princess and Monsieur Boscowski simply because their parents and grandparents had always obeyed the Bolyugayevskis, and they could think of nothing better to do. They did not seem able to realise that the smallest prosperity of the average *muzhik* on Bolugayen depended entirely upon the prosperity of the family, and that this went for all the big estates throughout Russia. They did not seem able to appreciate that were power to be taken away from the Tsar and the boyars, in the name of that scurrilous word democracy – which might have worked for a few thousand Greeks in an unsophisticated age but which had to be a catastrophe for over a hundred million Russians scattered over twenty million square kilometres in an age of newspapers, radios and rapid transport – the whole fabric of the state would collapse, and with it their livelihoods.

212

Gleb knew there were princes and counts, barons and mere gentry, who were difficult men, and harsh to their tenants and underlings. By the word of his own father he knew that there had been Bolugayevskis like that, and not all in the distant past: from what old Igor had had to say, the Princess Dagmar had been a devil incarnate, as had her father. But they were dead. There was the saving grace of humanity, they always died. Even monsters like Ivan the Terrible and Peter the Great had eventually died. As no doubt would this present day monster, Rasputin. One simply had to wait for the enemies of mankind to die, and make sure one did not die first. One had this problem even within one's own family. Gleb would never forget his brother Rurik, not because Rurik had been his brother, but because the poor fool had had the temerity to lust after the Countess Anna, and then the Countess Patricia, and when brought up short had been dismissed.

Gleb was no different to any other heterosexual male: he also lusted after the beauty with which he was surrounded. He thought the Countess Anna the second most beautiful woman who had ever walked the face of the earth, and the second most desirable, too, even in her seventies – once he had placed her at the top of the list. Now she was surpassed by her granddaughter. But he had more sense than even to dream of being anything more than a valuable servant to such goddesses. Rurik's excesses had led him into the ranks of the Okhrana and an assassin's bullet in the Moscow rising of 1905. Gleb was still alive.

It followed therefore that he regarded the war with disfavour. He had no great personal feelings about the death of Prince Alexei, or about the disappearance into the Army – and thus also the probable death – of Count Colin. Or should it be Prince Colin, despite what the Countess Anna had decreed? In that respect life on Bolugayen had not changed, nor did he expect it to. But, remembering as he did the upheaval that had followed defeat by the Japanese in 1905, the war itself

213

threatened the life he so cherished. That bothered him. More, it frightened him. He was childless and his wife was dead. He had only himself to think about. But he had every intention of ending his days in his own pantry with his own bottle of vodka and the fairly regular leavings from the Prince's table of bottles of champagne and brandy and port. Anything that threatened that desirable termination of his years was unacceptable.

He watched the man coming down the road and through the gates with a frown of annoyance. He had first of all made out that the man was on foot, which meant that he must be poor. That he was limping, which meant that he was an invalid. And that he wore the tattered remnants of a uniform, which meant that he had been a soldier. Or perhaps, still was a soldier. And now he recognised the man himself, and felt a very curious sensation. He was not a superstitious man, at least, any more than the average Russian, but as nothing had been heard of him for two years, the fellow he saw walking wearily towards him was surely dead.

Gleb cast a hasty glance left and right, but the verandah and front garden were deserted. So many men had been recruited from Bolugayen that even the fields were being worked by women, nowadays, and there were no men in the house at all save for Oleg the bootboy. In the middle of the afternoon the women would all be drinking tea, even the Princess and the two Countesses. It might be possible . . . all manner of ideas went through Gleb's mind – he even thought of loosing the dogs, who were in any event barking. This man had no right to be returning without the Prince . . . but he knew he was not going to do anything more than welcome the stranger he knew so well. He went down the steps, and hurried up to the gates, which as always stood open. The man was quite close now. "Rotislav?" Gleb asked. "My God, man. What has happened to you?"

"I have come home," the valet said. "Have you anything to drink?"

Rotislav wanted vodka more than even food or a bath, although he certainly needed a bath. Gleb took him into the pantry, watched him gulp at the alcohol and then tear at the food he put in front of him, like a wild animal. "Where have you been?" he asked.

"I have been to hell," Rotislav said.

"But . . . where is Prince Alexei?"

"I must speak with the Countess Anna," Rotislav said.

"Should you not speak with the Princess?"

"Her too," Rotislav said.

"When you have had a bath and a change of clothing," Gleb decided.

So much for keeping the valet's return secret. Gleb told Madame Xenia, supervised Rotislav's bath, found him some clean clothes and then hurried upstairs. The Princess and the two Countesses were in the summer parlour, as he had supposed, drinking tea, while Count Alexei Junior played on the floor at their feet.

Anna was now entirely recovered from her accident of five years ago, and her eyes were as bright as ever; even the tiny wrinkles which crisscrossed her seventy-eight-year-old cheeks could not detract from the essential beauty of her features, supported as they were by her immaculate bone structure. The Countess Anna Junior was an extremely pretty child of eight, with the golden hair and strong features of her family. But Gleb had eyes only for the Princess, and not only because of what he had to say. He had regarded this young woman with grave suspicion when she had come here permanently, as an eighteen-year-old. She had not been Russian. In fact, she had been American, a nation Gleb held in the deepest distrust, if only because they did not have a tsar. But more important than that, she had been taking the place of a woman he had respected and loved. Gleb had no idea if the Princess Sonia was guilty of everything or indeed anything of which she had been accused; he had never known, and he had never expected to know, anyone quite as charming and as beautiful.

On the other hand, he had reminded himself, he had also disliked the Princess Sonia, in the beginning, because she was Jewish. Thus he had been prepared to wait, and been rewarded. He had watched the Princess Priscilla grow from a somewhat uncertain girl into a quite entrancing woman. She was indeed a reincarnation of her grandmother, judging by the painting hanging in the downstairs parlour – but with a vital difference: where the Countess Anna had always had the morals of an alleycat – or a Russian countess – the Princess Priscilla had always had the morals of a Boston matron. She never swore, and she drank little, while since the disappearance of her husband she had never looked at any man in more than passing. Even the fact that she clearly supposed Prince Alexei dead, and thus routinely wore black, had not, to his knowledge, caused her ever to consider sharing her bed; she had remained concerned only with managing of Bolugayen, and with bringing up her son and stepdaughter. And even the widow's weeds, in such stark contrast to her pale complexion and yellow hair, did nothing more than enhance her beauty. But now he might be the one to bring a smile to those habitually sombre features.

"Is there news, Gleb?" Anna asked. "I did not hear the post horn."

"There is news, Your Excellency, Your Highness. Your Highness . . ." Gleb licked his lips. "Rotislav is here."

Priscilla stared at him with a faint frown, as if she could not quite place who he meant.

Anna reacted more quickly. "Rotislav? Rotislav is dead!"

"He is here, Your Excellency. He came an hour ago."

216

"An hour? And you have only just told us?"

"I have had him bathed and fed. He needed food, Your Excellency, and he stank."

"Rotislav. My God!" Priscilla stood up; all the blood had drained from her cheeks. "I must speak with him."

"He is outside, Your Highness." Gleb opened the doors, and the valet came in, moving hesitantly, as if he had forgotten the luxury in which he had once worked.

"Rotislav!" Priscilla impulsively reached for his hands, and just as impulsively he kissed her knuckles, and then dropped to his knees before Anna. Little Anna gathered her half-brother into her arms and retreated across the room.

"Two years," Anna said. "Where have you been?"

Rotisav kissed her knuckles in turn. "I was taken by the Germans, Your Excellency. I was sent to a prison camp. But when they discovered I was Polish, they made me enlist in a Polish regiment they were raising from amongst our prisoners. They made me fight with them, against our own people. They made me kill Russians."

Anna gazed at him. "They also allowed you to survive."

"I was lucky, Your Excellency. The time came when I was able to desert. I ran away and got through the Russian lines. Then I did not wish to fight any more, so I came here."

"You walked through the Ukraine and the Donbass, wearing a German uniform?"

"I took a uniform from a dead Russian. And his papers. I only wished to live, Your Excellency. Say that you forgive me."

Anna looked at Priscilla. "Have you news of the Prince?" Priscilla's voice was low. But Rotislav got the message; forgiveness would depend on what he next had to say.

"His Highness is a prisoner, Your Highness."

Priscilla stared at him, and the blood, beginning to

217

flow back into her cheeks, faded again. She sat down, heavily.

"You are lying," Anna snapped. "If Prince Bolugayevski had been taken prisoner, the whole world would know of it."

Rotislav nodded. "That is what he feared, Your Excellency. He feared the Germans would gain a huge propaganda coup if they could claim to have captured a prince. Thus, when he realised we were going to be captured, he took off all his badges and discarded anything which could identify him, and surrendered as an ordinary soldier. I was with him when he did this, Your Excellency," Rotislav said. "We were in prison together, but he told me to treat him as an equal, not as his servant. Then the Germans made me enlist."

"How long ago were you enlisted?" Anna asked.

"Over a year, Your Excellency."

"Then you have not seen the Prince for over a year. And he has spent all that time in a prison camp, where we are told men are dying like flies?"

"He was well when I had to leave him, Your Excellency," Rotislav insisted.

Priscilla stood up again. "He is alive," she said, and flushed as her grandmother looked at her. "If he survived Tannenburg, then he is alive." She hurried from the room into her own apartment. Her heart was pounding so hard she was quite sure the others could hear it.

Alexei was alive! But had she not always believed that, refused to accept the fact of his death? For two years she had lived in a limbo of uncertainty, but always with that one dream to occupy her mind, at the expense of all else. She had refused the pleadings of her father and brother that she return to the safety of Boston until the war was over. She knew her attitude had frustrated Grandmama. Not the decision to remain: Anna had expected that of the Princess Bolugayevska. But Anna was a woman to whom action was the elixir of life. She gloried in it herself, and

218

expected those around her to do so as well. She had been
unable to understand why Priscilla had not exerted herself
as Princess of Bolugayen, why she had not consciously
instilled in her son the understanding that he was prince in
fact, rather than in waiting. For Priscilla it had *been* simply
a matter of waiting. As she had survived the catastrophe
of the *Titanic*, so Alexei would survive the catastrophe of
the war. The pair of them had been chosen by Fate to be
indestructible.

And now it was certain. She fell to her knees, clutching
the cross given to her by Father Valentin when she had
become an Orthodox Christian. She had not believed
then, had secretly dismissed the whole thing as a lot of
mumbo jumbo, especially if this religion could throw up
someone like the monk Rasputin, who everyone seemed
agreed was ruining the country. But she believed now,
because this was the cross to which she had prayed, every
night for two years, to bring Alexei back to her.

She heard the door of her sitting room open, but did not
turn her head; there was only one person on Bolugayen
would dare enter the private apartment of the Princess Bolugayevska without knocking. "Are you praying
because you are pleased, or sorry?" Anna asked.

"How can you ask that, Grandmama?"

"Answer me, and we will both know."

"I am the happiest woman in the world," Priscilla said.

Anna snorted. "He has not yet come home," she
pointed out.

Sonia supposed she was the most depraved woman on the
face of the earth. She was far more depraved than any
of those who shared her lot, because they had never
attempted to resist. Naked, she knelt beside a tin bath
tub and bathed a man. No, not a man. Never a man. A
beast from the steppes. At the moment she soaped his
back. But it would soon be time to soap his front, and
then go lower. When she did that, he would drive his thick

219

fingers into her hair, and pull it, hard enough to cause discomfort. He enjoyed causing discomfort. When he was bored with her hair, he would fondle her breasts, pulling the nipples, again hard enough to cause discomfort, and then roam between her legs, squeezing and pulling. There was nothing gentle about anything he did.

But everything *she* did had to be gentle. She sometimes wondered just what he would do if she squeezed his testicles while washing them, or scratched his penis with her nails. He would certainly beat her. But it was what else he might do to her that held her back. So then, she was, on top of everything else, a coward. She wanted to live. And even, perhaps, one day, prosper all over again. It was too easy to tell herself that survival was the key, survival to avenge herself on all those who had wronged her. Then she would need to live forever. But in her heart she knew she would do anything to save herself from being returned to the clutches of the Okhrana, of Michaelin, to the constant fear and the constant humiliation.

As if she did not suffer constant fear and even more, constant humiliation, here! But here was different, because here she shared, and was yet humiliated, in private. Besides those with whom she shared did not seem to be aware of being humiliated, and therefore did not consider her to be humiliated either. So, when she began to soap Rasputin's right shoulder, she could look across that great mass of hair at Nathalie, busily soaping his left shoulder, or she could turn her head and look down the length of that enormous body at Dagmar, busily soaping the staretz's feet. Two princesses and a girl who should have been a princess, abasing themselves before the almighty – at least in Petrograd. It was a mystery to Sonia why Dagmar did it. She herself had no choice, if she wanted to live. Nathalie had no doubt abandoned the concept of any other man, lost as she was in her mountains of fat. But Dagmar, if undoubtedly overweight, was still young enough to be called voluptuous. She was, in fact, an

220

extremely attractive young woman. She could have the choice of virtually any young man in Petrograd, and there were a surprisingly large number of these, when one would have thought they should be at the front. But she preferred to be here, pandering to the obscene lusts of her master, racing her mother and her aunt by marriage to be the first to reach the elongated goal.

The door behind them opened. None of the women even raised their heads; they were as used to being naked in front of Anton as they were to being naked in front of Rasputin himself. But Rasputin lazily opened his eyes. "A message, holy Father," Anton said. "From Tsarskoye Selo. Her Majesty requests your presence, urgently."

Rasputin snorted. "The little brat is bleeding again. Very well, Anton. I will leave immediately. Have the automobile brought to the back." He stood up, scattering water in every direction. "Now I am aroused and unsatisfied," he remarked. "To please a woman." His tone was contemptuous. "You will accompany me."

Sonia realised he was pointing at her. "Me, Father Gregory?" She could not believe her ears.

"Yes, you, you silly bitch. Go and dress yourself. Put on some decent clothes." If he had not allowed her to return to her own house, he had sent for her belongings, no doubt bewildering Antonina even more.

"Her Majesty hates me," Sonia said.

"You are wrong. She has asked after you. She told me to bring you to her, next time I was summoned."

"Why can't I go with you?" Nathalie asked.

"Because Her Majesty has never told me to bring you, that is why. Now dry me and help me dress." He glared at Sonia. "Hurry, woman."

Sonia had never been to the Summer Palace. It was situated some distance outside of Petrograd, a place of utter quiet, shrouded from the world by huge stands of trees as well as extensive fields, under both flowers and

221

vegetables; the Tsar was an enthusiastic gardener, who enjoyed the pastoral life – there were those who said that was what he had been born to do, rather than attempt to rule a country as turbulent as Russia. Not that there was much evidence of pastoral life as they neared the complex of buildings themselves, and had to stop time and again to be inspected by soldiers and flunkies. No one smiled at the holy man, or gave him more than the most cursory of greetings. Sonia they ignored altogether. "They do not like us," she muttered.

It had been a strange experience, for in all the months she had lived at Rasputin's apartment that summer, he had never taken her driving before. But then he had never had a reason to take her driving before. Whatever could the Tsaritsa want with her? She supposed she should be apprehensive – if the Empress knew she was living with Rasputin she would surely know what she was called upon to do – but she was not apprehensive at all. She did not think there could be anything done to her or said to her, or even thought about her, which would hurt her or embarrass her, ever again. But she could not help but wonder how intimate *was* the staretz with the Tsaritsa, and just how much *did* she know about his lifestyle, about what went on behind the closed doors of that infamous apartment?

She herself had had no idea what to expect. She remembered the day she had arrived at the apartment, how he had slowly looked her up and down, and then undressed her, again slowly, and carefully, with obvious pleasure, uncovering her as a child might have unwrapped a Christmas present promised him by his parents, knowing what lay beneath the paper and yet savouring every second of approaching it. He had dismissed Nathalie, to her obvious chagrin, and they had been alone. Sonia had thought she would faint, but she had not dared faint, lest he perform some unacceptably obscene act on her body. Thus she had stood there while he had fingered her. There had been

222

nothing else. He had not even attempted to kiss her. He was truly interested only in what lay between the neck and the navel, save for the hair. He found hair exciting, whether on the head or at the groin. But for the rest, it was look, and touch. And hurt, to be sure.

It was difficult to understand his motivations. Clearly he found his greatest pleasure in women. But he would never take one to his bed. Some, those who had never been admitted to his inner sanctum, whispered it was because he suffered a physical disability. Sonia knew better than that: she had never known a man with so much sexual power, either in size or performance. Nathalie claimed it was because he would not break his vows of chastity, but as he continually broke every other vow he might ever have taken that didn't make sense either. Sonia had her own theories. One was that he genuinely enjoyed being masturbated by a beautiful woman; that was in fact not such an unusual masculine desire. The second was more important. She was sure he felt that actually to enter one of his acolytes, to gasp and pant his way to orgasm while holding her naked in his arms, would somehow be to surrender his power over her. When he lay, or sat, or even stood to be fondled, while playing with her hair or body, he remained in command, even at the moment of climax. To *share* that moment, to risk losing his own pleasure in hers, as Korsakov had so enjoyed, and even more, Leon, would be weakening. She wondered if she would ever see Korsakov or Leon again?

The automobile threaded its way through the buildings and stopped before a private doorway. Sonia found herself in a hall of enormous splendour, with bowing servants to either side. Rasputin ignored them, so she did likewise, but it was difficult to ignore the huge Nubian, dressed in a red and white uniform and wearing a turban, who opened an inner doorway, which was quickly closed behind them again. A secretary waited inside the private apartment. "Her majesty is in the study, holy Father."

223

Rasputin raised his eyebrows. "The Tsarevich is not ill?"

"Not today, holy Father. This is an affair of state. Goremykin has got to go. He simply cannot do his job. Thus Her Majesty must find a new prime minister. She wishes your recommendation."

"You had best remain here for the moment," Rasputin told Sonia, and followed the secretary along a corridor, feet soundless on the thick carpet.

Sonia selected a chair and sat down, allowed herself to be absorbed by the utter quiet of the palace. To her left there was a staircase leading up. To her right, a liveried flunky stood by the door, but he might have been a statue, as he never moved and indeed hardly seemed to breathe. The walls were hung with ikons and the light was muted. There was sound, but it too was muted, and very far away. She wondered what it must be like to live one's entire life in such security, such a sense of belonging, of being above such mundane concepts as wealth or poverty, social acceptability or social disgrace, having nothing more to worry about tomorrow than which hat to wear. And having to seek advice from a man like Rasputin? Then at least some of the rumours were true: the Mad Monk, as they called him, did indeed rule Russia! And of course, not even the most omnipotent of humans could avoid illness. How bitter must the little prince be, she thought, to have so much, and know it was for such a brief time.

"Hello!"

Sonia looked up, and then leapt to her feet. She had not heard the young woman approach from behind the staircase, but she knew who she was: the Grand Duchess Olga, eldest of the Tsar's daughters. Olga would be about twenty, she supposed, a quite beautiful girl, who wore a simple white house gown, and was smiling at her in a totally unaffected manner. Sonia curtseyed. "You're Sonia Bolugayevska," Olga remarked. "We met at Kiev, on that dreadful night Monsieur Stolypin was killed."

224

Sonia gulped. "Yes, Your Highness."

"Mother said you'd be coming today, with Father Gregory. She says you're his housekeeper. Do sit down." Olga sat herself, in the chair beside Sonia's, and Sonia obeyed. "I'd love to be the housekeeper of a man like Father Gregory," Olga confided. Was it possible this girl was so innocent she did not know what being 'housekeeper' to Rasputin entailed? "Is he difficult?" the Grand Duchess asked.

Sonia swallowed. "Sometimes, Your Highness."

"But I suppose you're used to that. Having been married. Tell me, what it's like?"

"Your Highness?" Sonia's voice had risen an octave.

"Being married. And then divorced. You see," Olga went on, "I have to be married, some time soon. I should have been already, but for this dreadful war. There's talk of one of the King of England's sons, perhaps the Prince of Wales. Of course, I don't suppose I could ever be divorced." She paused, as if expecting Sonia to say something. Sonia couldn't imagine what. She had never encountered such innocence. She had been three years younger than this girl when she had been on a train to Irkutsk, her life already in tatters, her experience already ageless. "I really would like to know," Olga said. "About marriage?"

Sonia licked her lips. "Your mother . . ."

"Mother doesn't talk about such things. And the women, well, they drop all manner of hints. But they won't tell us anything. If you told me, I could tell my sisters," she added, ingenuously.

"I . . ." Sonia had never in her life been so relieved to hear a door open. She sprang to her feet, and Olga also rose.

The Tsaritsa was speaking as she and Rasputin entered the hall. "The people will complain, of course. They think Sturmer is pro-German. But if you are sure he is the right man . . ."

225

"The people will always complain about something, Little Mother," Rasputin said. "It is always best to direct their complaints. This is Madame Bolugayevska." Sonia curtseyed.

The Tsaritsa's undoubtedly handsome face was cold. "I see you have been speaking with my daughter. What have you been telling her?"

Sonia looked at Olga, who came to her rescue. "We have been discussing the war, Mama."

"What do you know about the war?" Alexandra asked, contemptuously. "Or you, madame. Or does Father Gregory discuss it with you?"

"From time to time, Your Majesty," Sonia said.

"Well, keep your thoughts to yourself. I knew Prince Bolugayevski. He was a misguided young man. How are you faring, madame?"

This time Sonia had to prevent herself from glancing at Rasputin. "As well as can be expected, Your Majesty." Did this woman, who now ruled Russia in the name of her husband, not know that she had been arrested by the Okhrana, not once, but twice? And had thus been blackmailed into becoming the mistress, in effect, of the most reviled man in the Empire?

"That goes for all of us, in these dreadful conditions," Alexandra agreed, as if she were living in a hovel. "I do not know, I do not wish to know, the truth of your relations with your ex-husband, madame," she went on. "But I do not believe in divorce. You have my sympathy." Her tone softened. "I understand your son is also in the army."

"Your Majesty?" Sonia was taken entirely by surprise. "My son is only just sixteen years old."

"He is a patriot, and a Bolugayevski. You should be proud of him. Good-day to you, madame." Sonia gave another curtsey and nearly overbalanced and tumbled to the floor. "And you, Olga, rejoin your sisters. I should be grateful if you would look at the Tsarevich before you

226

leave, holy Father," Alexandra said. "He does so like to see you."

"Of course, Little Mother." Rasputin followed the Empress up the stairs.

"I must go," Olga whispered. "I have so enjoyed meeting you, madame. Please, if you can ever find the time to visit us again, I should be so grateful."

She hurried off, leaving Sonia uncertain whether she was dreaming or not. The Empress, actually apologising far the part she had played in ending her marriage? The Grand Duchess Olga actually extending the hand of friendship? And above all, Colin, in the army? If he also were to be killed, while she was trapped in this obscene pit . . . but was she trapped? If Olga would be her friend, might it not be possible to escape?

"They like you," Rasputin remarked, as the car drove them back to Petrograd. "Does that not please you?"

"It pleases me very much."

"Poor woman, she has not the mentality to rule," Rasputin said. "Oh, she has the will, and the personality, and the desire. But not the talent. As for Nicholas . . . I very much fear this dynasty is doomed. Certainly in its present form."

Sonia turned her head, sharply. "But . . ."

Rasputin gave a shout of laughter. "Oh, *we* are not doomed, my little Princess. Not you and I. When Nicholas and Alexandra fall, we shall simply take up with whoever succeeds them. That is why a relationship between you and the Grand Duchess might be useful. She may well have to play her part in replacing her mother and father. I wonder . . ." He brooded out of the window.

"You *want* Nicholas and Alexandra to fall," Sonia said, hardly believing what she was hearing. "That is why you are recommending Sturmer as the new prime minister. He is not only pro-German, he is dishonest and incompetent."

227

Rasputin shot her a glance. "Women should not have opinions about great matters," he remarked. "Now be quiet and let me think."

And let me think as well, Sonia thought. Life had suddenly taken on a new meaning. She had always dreamed of escaping to Bolugayen, to the protection of Colin. But if Colin was in the army . . . Anna was too small to protect her. She would be at the mercy of the Countess Anna and the Princess Dowager. The other Princess Dowager, who would undoubtedly be a more deadly enemy than Nathalie had ever been. But escape, to Tsarskoye Selo – there was a heady thought. Yet it had to be considered very carefully, if only because she had no idea whether or not the Grand Duchess really wanted to be friends with her, as Sonia Bolugayevska, or with Rasputin's housekeeper. In which case, she would be no protection at all.

Meanwhile, winter once again descended upon the capital, while the news of Brusilov's defeat as he encountered a German counterattack came trickling in to increase the despair caused by hunger and cold, while the bread lines lengthened and the police and the Cossacks had to use more and more force to disperse the angry mobs, swollen by the endless succession of strikes. "I really think the Tsar should come home and take control," Nathalie grumbled. "This man Sturmer is a fool."

"Sssh," Sonia recommended. "He was Father Gregory's choice."

"Oh! Well, then, I suppose he is not as bad as all that." She looked up as Anton entered. They were in the inner room, but Rasputin was in his bedroom, with one of his more attractive young women callers, with whom he wished, for once, to be private.

"Prince Yusupov is here, Your Highness," Anton said.

Nathalie raised her eyebrows. Felix Yusupov was married to one of the Tsar's nieces, the Princess Irina, and was not a usual visitor to the staretz, although Sonia knew the two men occasionally dined together. Felix Yusupov was, in fact, a somewhat disreputable figure, whatever his wealth – his family owned more land than even the Bolugayevskis – or his royal connections: he was rumoured to have been a transvestite in his youth, which was only a few years ago, and although married to one of the most beautiful women in Russia was seldom seen in her company. "What does he want?"

"To see Father Gregory. He says it is important."

"Oh! Well . . ." Nathalie looked at Sonia.

"I will see if Father Gregory can receive him." Sonia got up and went to the inner door, checked as Yusupov himself entered the room, thrusting eager women away behind him.

"I am not accustomed to being kept waiting," he remarked. He was a remarkably handsome man, clean-shaven and with crisp features.

"Your Highness." Sonia bobbed in a brief curtsey, while Nathalie merely snorted. "I was going to see if . . ."

To her relief, the door behind her opened and Rasputin emerged, pulling up his pants. "Felix!" he said. "You are slumming."

"One never slums in the company of beautiful women," Yusupov pointed out. "I have come to invite you to a party."

"*You* have come?" Rasputin sat down beside Nathalie, and whatever the condition of the young woman he had just left, immediately began fondling her.

"I did not wish to confide this invitation to a servant," Yusupov said. "It is a small dinner, at my house, the day after tomorrow, 16 December."

"I am already dining out the day after tomorrow," Rasputin said. "With Sonia. At the Restaurant de Paris."

It was Sonia's turn to raise her eyebrows. This was the first she had heard of it, and Rasputin had never taken her out to dinner before. That visit to Tsarskoye Selo must have been more important than she had supposed.

229

"Surely, as you can take Sonia out to dinner on any night of the week," Yusupov argued, "you can change that date and come to me instead."

"Why do you not change *your* date instead? Or will you extend your invitation to Sonia as well?"

"Certainly, if you wish. The reason I cannot change my date is that my wife has agreed to attend." There was a moment's silence. Everyone in the room knew that Rasputin had wanted to get his hands on the Princess Irina from the moment he had first seen her at a court function. "Shall we say, seven?" Yusupov asked, knowing he had won the day. "And *will* you be bringing Madame Bolugayevska?"

Rasputin glanced at Sonia, and gave one of his great shouts of laughter. "I think I shall come alone," he decided.

"Of all the cheek," Nathalie remarked. "He treats you like dirt, Sonia."

"Because I am dirt," Sonia agreed. "I am not complaining. I am going to have a night all to myself. There is a blessing."

"I think you should be very rude to him," Nathalie recommended.

She did not seem to realise that it was not possible to be very rude to Rasputin. Or even ordinarily rude. Besides, Sonia had meant what she said; the idea of having an evening entirely to herself was a delight. She ate a light meal, declined to drink a single glass of wine – when she dined with Rasputin she was invariably forced to drink herself insensible – and retired early to her own two-roomed apartment within the building awaking with a start to realise that although it was winter it was light outside. She tumbled out of bed, pulled on her robe, and ran into the outer room. "Anton!"

"I am here, madame."

"What time is it?"

230

"Ten of the morning, madame."

"But . . . where is Father Gregory?"

"He has not returned as yet, madame." Anton gave a discreet smile. "The Princess Irina must be even more attractive than one hears."

Sonia sat down to drink her coffee. But why should she worry about what he might be doing, even if he was debauching a royal Princess? Yet when Rasputin did not return by that evening, she felt obliged to telephone Prince Yusupov's house. She got the butler, who told her that the Prince had left the city, with his guests. "And the Princess?" Sonia asked.

"The Princess Irina is at her country estate, madame. She has not been in town for over a month," the butler pointed out, clearly wondering who this foolish woman was.

Sonia hung up, and stared at the wall for several seconds. Rasputin had been invited to meet the Princess at her town house. But she had not been there. Had never been there. Yet Rasputin had stayed the night. And now the Prince had gone off into the country with his friends. Including, presumably, Rasputin. Well, she thought, it merely prolonged her opportunity to rest and relax.

And wait for him to return. She dared not even leave the apartment, without Rasputin, because the Okhrana had released her into his custody, and she was quite certain that Michaelin was only waiting for the staretz to tire of her and put her out, to rearrest her. Even to be arrested by mistake, and taken to that prison for only half an hour before he came to get her, was not something she could contemplate. While if he were to leave her there for twenty-four hours or more . . .

There was no word from Rasputin the next day, either. The day after, Sonia was still in bed when there was the sound of doors banging. She sat up, scooping hair from her face. Oh Lord, she thought. He's back. But her door was thrown open, not by Rasputin, but by Nathalie. A Nathalie, Sonia had never seen before, wide-eyed and panting. "Sonia!" she screamed. "Sonia! Get up. Haven't you heard? Father Gregory is dead!"

Part Three

The Red Tide

'But such a tide as moving seems asleep,
Too full for sound and foam,
When that which drew from out the boundless deep,
Turns home again.'
                    Tennyson: *Come Not When I Am Dead*

Chapter Nine

Fall of a Dynasty

Sonia could only stare at Nathalie in total consternation.

"Dead!" Nathalie shouted. "Can't you understand? Rasputin is dead. They pulled his body out of the Neva, this morning. Through a hole in the ice. My God!" She sat down, shivering violently although the room was warm as toast.

Sonia looked past her at an equally thunderstruck Anton, standing in the doorway. "Brandy," she suggested.

Anton hurried off, and Sonia sat beside Nathalie. "You say he was in the river? But that's not possible. He was in the country, with Prince Yusupov."

"He was in the river," Nathalie insisted. "He was murdered."

"Murdered? But if he was in the river . . .?"

"Oh, he drowned. But before that he had been shot and stabbed, more than once. They put his body in the river because they thought he was dead. Then he drowned."

Anton was back, with a tray and glasses, and again he and Sonia stared at each other. Rasputin had been to dinner with Felix Yusupov. Then the Prince had gone off into the country. Taking Rasputin with him? Or having shot him and stabbed him, thrust him, still alive, beneath the ice of the Neva? Suppose she had gone after all? Yusupov had raised no objection. Would she now also

235

be drowned in the Neva? But where did his death leave Rasputin's acolytes, hitherto protected by his powerful presence and through him, the favour of the Tsaritsa? Those who came and went could just stay away out of sight, and hope never to be identified. Those who had lived in the same house . . . .

"You had better go home," Sonia told Nathalie.

"I shall kill myself," Nathalie moaned.

"Do it at home," Sonia recommended. "But go there, now. Don't you realise you are in danger here?" Nathalie's head came up. She might be contemplating killing herself, but she did not want to be lynched by a mob. "Hurry!" Sonia said. Nathalie stumbled from the room.

Anton did not bother to close the door behind her. "What are we to do, madame?" He was white with fear.

"Get out of here," Sonia told him. "As quickly as possible."

"But where can we go?"

Sonia hesitated, biting her lip. Her instincts were to run and run and run. At least as far as Bolugayen, no matter what kind of welcome might await her there. Besides, once she reached Bolugayen she would be able to leave the country, and get to Trishka. But she knew she would never reach Bolugayen. Certainly not if she tried to take Anton with her, and however much she despised him for serving such a master, he had never done any harm to her. But they would both be recognised, very quickly. She had no more desire to be lynched by a mob than had Nathalie. So then, her house? But the mob would find her there too. That left . . . she snapped her fingers. "Can you drive an automobile, Anton?"

"Oh, yes, madame."

"Then drive me, us, out to Tsarskoye Selo."

"The palace, madame?"

"We will find shelter there," Sonia said. She could only pray she was right.

*　　*　　*

236

"Mother is distraught," the Grand Duchess Olga explained. Her sisters, and her brother, stared at Sonia, as did the flunkies who had shown her into the royal presence.

"Is it possible for me to stay here?" Sonia asked. "At least for awhile."

"You're a Jew!" the Tsarevich Alexei pointed out.

Sonia sucked in her breath as she continued to look at Olga. "People on the streets recognised the automobile," she said. "And threw stones at it. If I were to go back out . . ."

"Of course you must stay here," Olga said. "You were Father Gregory's friend. So you will be our friend."

"Thank you, Your Highness. I am asking on behalf of the valet, too."

"Oh, him as well," Olga agreed. "I will speak to Mama."

"Are you really a Jew?" asked the Grand Duchess Anastasia, youngest of the four sisters.

"I was," Sonia said. "But I became a Christian when I married Prince Bolugayevski."

"I thought Jews never changed their religion," remarked the Grand Duchess Marie.

"They don't," Sonia acknowledged. "Usually."

"Stop asking Madame Bolugayevska silly questions," Olga admonished, and signalled one of the waiting maids. "Show Madame Bolugayevska to an apartment. And see to quarters for the valet."

"I shall be eternally grateful, Your Highness," Sonia said.

Olga gave a curious smile. "No one has ever said that to me before," she said.

The Tsaritsa was more than distraught. She had had Rasputin's body brought out to Tsarskoye Selo and spent the next forty-eight hours kneeling beside it, strewing flowers on the corpse. On the Thursday the staretz was buried, in the palace gardens, with as much honour as

237

if he had been a grand duke. Then Alexandra sought vengeance. "I wish Prince Felix arrested, charged, convicted, and hanged," she declared. "Now!"

Prime Minister Sturmer, a heavy-set man who exhaled frightened incompetence, twisted his fingers together. "Only the Tsar can order the arrest of a member of his own family, Your Majesty."

"My husband left me full powers to act in his name," Alexandra asserted.

"I know that is true, Your Majesty. But not everyone believes it. In any event, in this instance, may I beg Your Majesty for restraint. The fact is that Prince Felix is at this moment a hero to the people; they are kneeling outside his house to give thanks to God for their deliverance from that . . . from Father Gregory."

Alexandra pointed. "Do you realise that you are standing there, holding the powers you do, simply *because* of Father Gregory? He recommended you to me. And you would not have me avenge his death?"

"I am merely suggesting prudence, Your Majesty. Prince Felix has fled to his estates. Why not simply command him to remain there, until further notice?" Alexandra snorted, but Sturmer could tell he was winning. "We do have the name of one other person who was present, Your Majesty. A doctor, named Purushkevich."

"Then he, certainly, will pay."

Sturmer coughed. "The doctor cannot be charged with the murder of Father Gregory unless the Prince is charged also. The people would not stand for it."

"The *people*," Alexandra said contemptuously.

"But there is a war on, Your Majesty, and medical men are urgently needed at the front. No one could object to that."

"Yes," Alexandra said. "Send the swine to the Polish front, and perhaps he will get his head shot off." She gave a great sigh. "But what is to happen, Sturmer? Without Father Gregory to guide me . . ."

"We must do the best we can. With God's aid . . ."

"God's aid," Alexandra said, more contemptuously yet. "And when the Tsarevich has another attack? What do we do then, Sturmer? Tell me that."

"I am sure Dr Botkin has absorbed sufficient of Father Gregory's methods . . ."

"Methods? You are a fool, Sturmer. Our friend did not have methods. He was a holy man, and he prayed. Oh, Botkin is a good doctor, and an able man, so far as he goes. But he is not a holy man. I am lost. Alexei is lost. The Dynasty is lost."

"I do assure Your Majesty that my colleagues and I will serve you to the last."

"The last," Alexandra sneered. "Then go away and serve me, to the last. Go away! Get out!" she shouted.

The children had been listening in the next room, with Sonia. She was old enough to be their mother herself; she was only a few years younger than the Tsaritsa. But they had adopted her as a kind of large toy, female equivalent of the French sailor, Derevenko, who was Alexei's nurse. "*Are* we lost?" Anastasia whispered, tears in her eyes.

Olga rubbed her sister's head. "Of course we are not lost. Mama just talks like that."

"It is almost impossible to believe," Anna remarked as she studied the newspaper.

"This makes it sound as if he was a great man," Priscilla commented, reading the other newspaper. "Did you know him, Grandma?"

"Thank God, no. Great man! Ha! He was a lecherous rogue, by all accounts. You do know it was he caused the divorce?"

Priscilla bit her lip. "I thought there was another man."

"You do not call Rasputin a man? Yes, there was another. Your predecessor was not very selective in her love affairs. I wonder what has become of her?"

Priscilla got up and left the breakfast table; she did not

239

have any desire to consider what might have happened to her predecessor. Little Anna joined her on the gallery. "Does the death of Monsieur Rasputin mean that the war will end, Priscilla?"

"If only it would. But I don't think so."

"Oh!" The little girl pouted. "I was so hoping Colin would come home."

"I know, darling." Priscilla hugged her. "He will be coming home, I promise. Soon." She went to the huge French window looking out over the porch and the drive, and a waiting footman hastily drew the drapes so that she could see out. She smiled at him, as she always smiled at all the servants, and gazed at the snow covering the estate. Bolugayen was at its most beautiful in the winter, but it was also at its most isolated.

They'll soon be coming home, she thought. Both of them. She had to tell herself this, every morning. In a curious way Rotislav's news, while raising her spirits, had also made her the more anxious. She believed Alexei was still alive. But she did not *know*. She believed he would come back to her. But she did not *know*. So many emotions tumbled through her mind, continually, but were most insistent in the early hours of every morning, when she lay alone in the huge bed she had once shared so enthusiastically. She wanted, with both mind and body, and had to exist on memories. She even, daringly, considered alleviations. She reminded herself that had Grandma been in her position at her age she would have had a constant stream of all the handsome young men in the village knocking on her door. But she was not Grandma, and could never be.

However, she did try to rationalise her situation, to tell herself that it was absurd for her to remain hopelessly in love with a man twice her age when her life was there to be lived. But there it was, life had ceased to be lived, as a wife or a woman, when Alexei had gone away. Since then she had lived only as a mother . . . and a princess, to be sure. But, oh, how she longed for her life to be

240

complete again. So she stood at the window and looked out at the snow-covered road down from the hills, all the while knowing that there could never be anyone coming down that road in December, and feeling her heartbeat quicken, because there *was* a vehicle on the road . . . a horse drawn wagon, moving slowly through the snow.

For a moment she could not believe her eyes, then she turned to the patiently waiting footman. "He's coming!" she shouted. "The Prince is coming. Ring the bell. Summon the servants. The Prince is coming!"

He hurried away, but she was herself running along the gallery, almost bowling over little Anna, summoned by the shouts. Grandmama was in the breakfast room doorway. "Whatever is the matter?"

"Alexei! He's here," Priscilla panted. "Grishka! Grishka! Bring baby down to meet his father."

The house bustled as it had not done for a long time. Priscilla went downstairs, baby Alexei in her arms. Gleb was marshalling the servants, lining them up to greet their returning master. Anna also descended to the ground floor, assisted by her namesake. "Are you sure it's Alexei?" she asked.

"Of course I'm sure, Grandma," Priscilla said. "Who else would be coming to Bolugayen in December? Home for Christmas. Home for . . ." She stared as the double doors were thrown open, and several people got down from the wagon at the foot of the steps. Two of them, wrapped up in furs, hurried towards her. "Sophie?" she asked. "Janine? But . . ."

"Oh, it's been terrible." Sophie embraced her, while snow fell from her coat and hat to gather on the parquet. "Oh, it's so good to be here."

Priscilla looked past her at Janine Grabowska. "Burned out," Janine said. "We've been burned out." Priscilla was speechless.

"You mean the Germans are in the Ukraine?" Anna demanded.

241

"No, no," Sophie said. "These were Russians."

"They were rioting because there was no bread in Kiev," Janine explained. "My husband was in Petrograd. It was terrible. We felt we had to get out while we could."

"They were after our blood," Sophie explained.

"Well . . ." Janine gave one of her pretty little giggles. "They were after something."

"So you came here," Anna said, with some grimness.

"This is my home," Sophie said, with dignity.

"If we could stay, for a while, until things sort themselves out," Janine begged.

"Of course you may stay," Priscilla said.

"Riots," Anna commented. "It really is absurd. You say they burned your house, Countess?"

"We saw it go up, after we had left," Janine said.

"Ha! You should have stayed and defended it. Well, I can tell you, that will never happen here."

"We know that. Which is why we came."

"Gleb, you will see to apartments for the countesses," Priscilla instructed. Gleb bowed and hurried off, beckoning the bewildered servants to follow him.

Priscilla found herself staring at Rotislav. She often found herself staring at him, as, while he was a member of the house staff, in the absence of the Prince and with baby Alexei still too small to require a male servant, he had no specific duties. But he was always there, staring at her. He gave her the creeps. She did not know what had happened between him and Alexei during their imprisonment. But something had. Something that had dissipated Rotislav's innate subservience. Now he looked at the family almost as if he was their equal. At her, as if he were her equal! And today his stare seemed to have redoubled in intensity.

She wanted to weep with fustration and anger; but they would also have been tears of fear. If only Alexei would come home.

* * *

242

Christmas was not celebrated at Tsarskoye Selo. There was a Rumanian chamber orchestra in residence at the palace, and the Tsaritsa spent her time listening to them playing mournful music, or writing long letters to the Tsar. She wanted him to come home, but she didn't want him to give up the command of the army. She didn't know what she wanted. As she confessed to Sonia, with whom she had become amazingly friendly, because she supposed Sonia, having lived with Rasputin, had been as fond of the staretz as she herself – and Sonia was not about to disabuse her of that idea – she really just wanted to weep and weep and weep.

The girls did what they could, handing out little presents to each other and their favourite servants, who included Sonia, and when by themselves singing carols, but without decorations the palace remained a vast, exquisitely furnished, empty cavern. Yet strangely, as it seemed, Rasputin's death had no immediate impact outside of the royal family. The supposition, shared by Sonia and the Empress, that with his demise the mob would immediately take to the streets, was proved wrong. The mob certainly did take to the streets, but this was simply in the search for bread, as had happened the previous winter. They were beaten and shot and driven back to their lairs by the police and the Cossacks. But everything else remained static, while the winter had stopped operations on the front and equally shut down the rest of the country.

Sonia wondered what Patricia thought of it, but she did not dare write any letters. Equally, she wondered what Lenin, and more important, Trotsky, thought of it. But, in, as it appeared, their permanent exile, they could do nothing about it. As for her own future, she did not dare contemplate it at the moment. As Rasputin's housekeeper she was apparently welcome in the royal palace, especially as Alexandra discovered in her someone to talk to. Being with the royal family also meant that she was beyond Michaelin's reach. But equally, as Rasputin's mistress, she would not be welcome anywhere else, and she had no doubt the Okhrana were waiting, with their invariable deadly patience, for her to fall out of favour. She could not risk that happening, because if Colin was not on Bolugayen then she had nowhere to hide, save right where she was. And it was where she wanted to be. Whatever might be happening in the outside world, Tsarskoye Selo was the most peaceful place she had known for a long while. It reminded her of Bolugayen when she had first gone there, and been taken in by Alexei. She had been so tormented, physically and mentally, by her existence in Irkutsk and then when escaping that perhaps she had overvalued the security offered her. She would not make that mistake here, because she knew how temporary this was likely to be. But she still needed it, desperately, after the trauma of the previous year.

And Tsarskoye Selo offered attractions even Bolugayen had never possessed. Here she was not required to act either the princess or the chatelaine – or even the wife or mistress: she was simply a companion. And the grand duchesses were such delightful girls. If they took their positions and their perrogatives for granted – there was never any shortage of bread or indeed any other commodity at Tsarskoye Selo – they remained amazingly unaffected by the omnipotence they possessed through their parents, laughed and joked with their servants and their tutor, an anxious young Frenchman named Gaillard, and talked frankly and openly with Sonia about every subject that came into their heads.

Sex and men topped the list, not only because the older girls were approaching the age of marriage.

Another attractive aspect of their personalities was the way they sought to protect their young brother. Not only in a physical sense, although the risk of a fall which might bring back the dreadful internal bleeding was present in all of their minds all the time, but in loving and giving. What was sad was Alexei's inability to respond. Obviously, as

244

he knew he trembled on the edge of life, he could hardly be expected to possess his sisters' gaiety, but he was in any event a much more serious character. He was now twelve, and very well aware of the responsibilities of his position. He often sat with his mother when she was receiving Baron Sturmer or one of the other ministers, and was quite willing to air his own opinions.

Sturmer invariably painted a grim picture of life outside the palace walls. Sonia knew of this because Alexandra often discussed the situation with her. The new year was one of the coldest on record, even in Petrograd: the ice lay thickly on the streets, and people were starving and freezing to death daily "I feel we are sitting on a powder keg of resentment, Your Majesty," the Prime Minister said.

"You are an alarmist old woman," Alexandra riposted. "Answer me a few questions. Is it not true that just about every winter this century there have been food and fuel shortages in Petrograd?"

"Well, Your Majesty . . ."

"And nothing has changed. Is it not true that every winter this century there have been strikes and riots in Petrograd?"

"Well, Your Majesty . . ."

"Which have always been ended by the police and the Cossacks. Is it not true that there is normally a garrison of perhaps eighty thousand troops in Petrograd?"

"That is so, Your Majesty, but . . ."

"And what is the present strength of the garrison?"

"One hundred and seventy thousand, Your Majesty."

"So that is more than double the usual figure. Now tell me this: what is the present population of Petrograd?"

"Well, Your Majesty, excluding the garrison, there are about a million people resident in the city."

"Then, unless I have forgotten my simple arithmetic, you are telling me that there is one soldier, armed with

245

rifle, bayonet, lance and revolver, to every six inhabitants, including women and children. Are you seriously supposing that one soldier cannot keep six people, of whom probably two are children, two are women, and two are elderly, under control?"

Sturmer licked his lips. "That is supposing the troops are all loyal, Your Majesty. I have officers' reports which indicate that a large part of the garrison is composed of totally inexperienced recruits, many of whom are of bad character." Alexandra snorted, but she had not made an immediate riposte, so he hurried on. "I also have police reports which indicate that some of the officers are fraternising with the people."

"And why should they not do that? They are not an occupying army."

Sturmer persevered. "Then there is this fellow Kerensky, making all manner of inflammatory speeches . . ."

"Kerensky? I have heard the name."

"He is a lawyer, Your Majesty. He made a reputation denouncing the government over the deaths of those miners in the Lena goldfields before the war. He has always been on the side of the Jews. Now, unfortunately, he is a member of the Duma, and is denouncing the conduct of the war."

"Is that not treason?"

"As a member of the Duma he is not subject to charges of treason, Your Majesty."

"I remove his immunity. Arrest him, for treason or something. Hang him. Oh, go away and govern. That is what I am paying you to do." She flounced into the inner chamber, where Olga and Tatiana were waiting, with Sonia for support. "That man drives me up the wall. What possessed our friend to recommend him defeats me." She glared at her daughters. "And if you propose to raise the matter of the Radziwill party, the answer is still no."

"Oh, Mama!" Olga protested. "Princess Radziwill gives such lovely parties."

"We are in mourning," Alexandra announced. "I think it is in extremely bad taste for that young woman to be having a party at this time in any event. Now I do not wish to discuss the matter further. I need to write to your father." She swept from the room.

"Oh . . . boo!" Tatiana stuck out her tongue at the door being closed by the waiting flunkey.

"There is no point in getting upset about it, Your Highness," Sonia suggested.

"I *am* upset. I am very cross. I am angry!" Tatiana shouted. "Oh . . . I feel all, odd."

She half turned and gave such a shudder that Sonia caught her before she fell down. "Oh, dear," she said. "You're very hot. You have a temperature."

"Tattie? Ill?" Olga hurried up to her.

Sonia waved at the waiting maids. "Help the Grand Duchess to her room. And summon Dr Botkin."

"Shall we tell Mama?" Olga whispered.

"Let's hear what Botkin has to say, first," Sonia decided.

"Measles," Botkin pronounced.

"Oh, good Lord!" Olga complained. "Where on earth could she have got measles from?"

"I feel dreadful," Tatiana grumbled. She had been undressed by her maids and tucked into bed; they were now tucking her up again as the doctor had finished his examination.

"Are you sure?" Sonia asked.

"Absolutely. Look." Tatiana's nightgown had not been tied at the neck, and now he pulled it down far enough so that Sonia could see the tiny spots. "There is no doubt about it. Her Majesty will have to be informed," he now decided.

"I'll do it," Olga volunteered.

"Ah, no, Your Highness," Botkin said. "I think you should remain in these apartments. You see, if the Grand

247

Duchess Tatiana has contracted measles, it is extremely likely that you also have got the disease."

Olga stared at him with her mouth open, as if he had just been rude to her. The two younger sisters had come hurrying in at the news that Tatiana was ill. Now Anastasia gave a shout of laughter. "You wouldn't have been able to go to the Radziwill party anyway! You'll be all spotty like Tattie." Olga glared at her.

"Ahem!" Botkin remarked. Everyone looked at him. "I'm afraid you must remain in these apartments also, Your Highness. And the Grand Duchess Marie."

It was their turn to stare, just as it was Olga's turn to laugh. "You beast!" Marie shouted.

"I will inform Her Majesty," Sonia said. "Don't worry, doctor: I had measles as a child."

Predictably, Alexandra was not amused. "Oh, really," she remarked. "Measles! How common. For how long will they have to be confined?"

"Botkin says for at least two weeks, possibly longer, Your Majesty."

"Oh, good Lord!"

"Were you planning to go anywhere, Your Majesty?"

Alexandra glared at Sonia, and then smiled. "No. Of course not. You will stay and nurse them, won't you, Bolugayevska?"

"Of course, Your Majesty." She had no plans to go anywhere either.

By Saturday the other three girls were infected. But they were remarkably good patients, probably because they were feeling so ill. Alexei was not allowed near them, and Sonia marshalled half a dozen of the maids who, like her, had already had the disease. She was kept quite busy, and was only vaguely aware that there was some agitation in the palace. "There's been shooting in the city," Botkin muttered at her.

"The police firing on the mobs, I suppose."

"Yes. Trouble is, it seems this time the mobs are firing back."

"Does Her Majesty know?"

"Of course. But she takes the view that it is just high spirits. Also, it is a fact that all the restaurants and theatres were full last night, as well as the ballet, and that the Princess Radziwill has not cancelled her ball, so it really cannot be very serious."

Sonia presumed he was right; it had all happened before. Sunday was a quiet day out at Tsarskoye Selo, but she awoke with a start on Monday morning to a great clamour. She had been given a bed actually in the Grand Duchesses' apartments, and they were also awake, although none of them was up to leaving their beds. "Do ask them to be quiet, Bolugayevska," Olga begged.

Sonia went downstairs, to find the Tsaritsa, wearing a dressing gown and with her hair in pigtails, standing in the main hall surrounded by anxious officers. "It is true, Your Majesty," one of these was saying. "There was shooting yesterday, so this morning Captain Lashkevich called out his battalion of the Volynski Regiment to put an end to this trouble, and, Your Majesty . . ." The captain seemed unable to go on.

A lieutenant took up the tale. "When cartridges were issued to the guardsmen, Your Majesty, they loaded their rifles, and then turned and shot the captain. Then they marched off to join the mob."

Alexandra stared at him, then looked at Sonia, as if she was the only sane person present. "The Preobraschenski, Your Majesty," Sonia suggested. She knew Alexei had in his youth been an officer in Russia's premier regiment, and had always spoken highly of it.

"Of course," Alexandra agreed. "There is a detachment of the Preobraschenski in the city. Turn them out, and the Cossacks, and have these mutineers dealt with." The

249

officers saluted and hurried off. "We'll soon have this mess at an end," the Empress declared. "Mitlin!" One of the secretaries came forward. "You'll send a telegram to His Majesty, informing him of what is happening. But tell him I have it under control."

Mitlin bowed.

Alexandra returned to her apartment to get dressed, and Sonia went back up to the girls, who were by now extremely agitated. She persuaded them to remain in bed, then dressed herself, had breakfast, and went out on to the terrace to look in the direction of the city. As she watched, a smoke-pall began to build above the distant houses; someone must have authorised a special release of fuel, she thought.

She spent some time with the girls, then heard the growl of automobile engines and went downstairs again. The officers were back, some of them, looking more agitated than ever. "The Preobraschenski have bayoneted their colonel," one of them said. Sonia's stomach seemed to do a complete roll. The Preobraschenski! "The mob have fired the Duma building." The smoke! she thought. Oh, my God!

Alexandra entered the room; her face was pale but she looked at her most regal. "I have just received a telegram from the Tsar," she announced. "His Majesty's train is on its way back to Petrograd, now. He will be here tomorrow, and will settle this matter himself. You may return to your duties, gentlemen."

The officers exchanged glances. "We feel we should remain here, Your Majesty, with our men. It is our duty to defend Your Majesty and your family."

Alexandra glared at him. "Do you seriously suppose we are in danger?"

The captain bit his lip. "The mob is in control of Petrograd, Your Majesty."

Alexandra continued to stare at him for some seconds,

250

then she repeated, "His Majesty will be here, tomorrow," and left the room.

Anton knocked on Sonia's door. Like her, he had been keeping a very low profile in the two months they had been at Tsarskoye Selo. "What are we do to, madame?"

"The Tsar will be here tomorrow," Sonia told him.

"Do you really suppose the Tsar can end this revolution, merely by appearing, madame?"

"Anton, if you do not believe that, then you had better leave here, immediately, and join the mob."

Anton licked his lips. "And you, madame?"

"I have promised to stay, with the Grand Duchesses. Besides, I believe in the Tsar." What a lie, she thought, as the major-domo shuffled off. I hate this tsar, for what his policemen have done to me. But then, does that not mean I must hate his family? She could not bring herself to do that.

"What will Papa do, when he gets back?" Marie asked.

"I'm afraid he will probably have to shoot a lot of people, and hang a lot more," Sonia said.

"How awful," Anastasia said. "I wish he didn't have to do that."

"Those people are in rebellion," Olga said severely. "They need to be hanged and shot. Some of them."

"Time to take temperatures," Sonia said, producing the thermometers.

Olga had not even been born when she had been sentenced to death by the Tsar's court. That her sentence had been commuted to exile had been the merest chance, simply because Patricia had been condemned with her, and the Tsar had not wanted to hang the daughter of one of his most noble families. But presumably, had Olga been alive and able to understand, she would have declared, that woman Cohen is in rebellion against us, she should be hanged. Or shot. Yet she was such a charming girl!

* * *

251

The palace remained in a state of suspended animation throughout the rest of the day. From the terraces they could see that Petrograd was burning in several places. From the various officers who from time to time arrived, clearly terrified, they heard the most horrendous tales of murder and mayhem in the city. Yet at Tsarskoye Selo all remained peaceful. It was the next morning, as Sonia was helping serve the Grand Duchesses their breakfasts, that they heard the sound, as if a huge sea was gathering force to break on an empty beach.

They gazed at each other in wonder, while Sonia's stomach did another of those somersaults. But she was becoming used to coping with them. "I think, Your Highnesses," she said. "That it might be an idea for you to get up and get dressed."

"But we're ill," Tatiana protested.

"Yesterday you said we weren't to get up," Marie pointed out.

Sonia looked at Olga. Now they could hear a succession of sharp cracks, rising above the approaching tumult. Olga swallowed. "I think Bolugayevska is quite right," she said. "It is time we got up and got dressed." She got out of bed herself, and beckoned her personal maid to help her remove her nightgown.

One of the maids had gone to the window. "People!" she gasped. "Thousands and thousands of people! Marching on us."

The Grand Duchesses insensibly moved closer together. "They wouldn't dare come in here!" Tatiana said, putting her arms round her two younger sisters.

"Get dressed!" Olga shouted. It was the first time Sonia had ever heard her shout. Now, as her maids held her drawers for her to step into, she beckoned Sonia closer. "What is going to happen to us?" she whispered.

"Pray God, nothing, Your Highness."

"But suppose . . ." Olga bit her lip.

"If they cannot be stopped, if they come in here . . ."

252

Sonia took a deep breath. "You must remember you are Romanovs. Whatever they do to you, you are royal princesses. You must never scream or shout or beg." Olga looked past her at her sisters. "They will do what you do, Your Highness," Sonia told her.

The petticoat was raised to Olga's shoulders, the straps settled in place. "Will you stay with us?" she asked.

Sonia hesitated. But she had nowhere to run. And she had suffered what she feared was going to happen before, when she had been younger than this girl, or Tatiana. *She* had screamed and shouted and begged. But she would not do so again, and perhaps she could set them an example. "I will stay," she promised.

"Thank God!"

"What must we do, Your Highness?" asked the maid.

Olga looked at Sonia. "They cannot help us, Your Highness." What she really meant was, do we want them here, watching us being raped?

"You may go," Olga said. "All of you."

"But I'm not dressed," Anastasia complained.

"Bolugayevska will finish dressing you. Off you go now, all of you." She clapped her hands. The maids fled from the room, and Sonia closed the door. "Lock it," Olga commanded.

"No," Sonia said. "That lock will not keep anyone out. And if they break in, they will be the more inflamed." She finished dressing Anastasia. "Now, brush your hair," she told them all. They obeyed. "Now," she said. "I think we should all sit together, on the settee."

"Can't we look out of the window?" Marie asked.

"No. If we can see them, they can see us."

They sat together, Olga in the middle, her sisters to either side. Sonia stood behind them. "If they come in, will they . . .?" Tatiana hesitated, then touched her breast.

"You must be very brave, and treat them with contempt," Olga said. "No matter what they do to you."

Marie burst into tears. Sonia supposed they must all

253

be on the edge of a complete breakdown. Up to yesterday they had been omnipotent, inviolable, almost, one could say, untouched by human hand, unless it had been washed, perfumed, encased in a new glove, and utterly gentle as well as servile. Now they faced a mob of human hands which would would be filthy and grasping, brutal and degrading. The mighty, thrown to the floor to be trampled into dust. And their fate would be compounded by their beauty, their sheer desirability.

The noise was growing all the time. Now the firing was almost continuous, but then it died. The palace had had insufficient guards, and perhaps not all of them had been had been sufficiently loyal. Now they listened to shouts and screams, close at hand; perhaps the maids had not got away, after all. They listened too to the sound of tearing drapes and smashing wood. And bawdy laughter. Olga suddenly sat straight. "Mama! Alexei!"

"Don't think about them, now," Sonia snapped. "Don't think." Exist, she thought. These may be your last minutes on earth. Exist, and if you are alive in an hour's time, you may live forever.

The doors were thrown open, and they gazed at the mob. The sisters insensibly rose to their feet. Perhaps they had never seen the lower classes of their father's subjects before, close to.

The noise slowly died, as the five women stared at the mob, and the mob, both men and women, stared back. Sonia knew it would require only a single movement, perhaps a single word, to set the whole unthinkable scenario moving; she was almost afraid to breathe. "Aside! Stand aside!"

Sonia's breath was released in a rush, as the people moved away from the door, before a group of men in uniform. Sonia could not tell if they were officers, for they wore no insignia, but they certainly moved with authority, and the man at their head, a tall, somewhat cadaverous looking fellow, exuded arrogance. "Close the doors," he commanded, and the men behind him obeyed. "I am Alexander Kerensky," he announced.

The Grand Duchesses had heard their mother denounce that name; they huddled closer together. Not for the first time Sonia felt utterly isolated. "I have assumed responsibility for your safety," Kerensky said. "But you must co-operate with me. You will remain here, and there will be a guard on that door. Food will be sent to you."

Olga drew a deep breath. "Is our mother safe? And our brother?"

"Yes."

"When will Papa get here?" Tatiana asked. "The Tsar," she explained.

"Monsieur Romanov will be here today, I should think. You must understand, young ladies, that your father is no longer the Tsar. He abdicated two days ago. There is no longer a tsar in Russia. Therefore there are no longer any Grand Duchesses. You are plain Mademoiselles Romanov, now. You must understand this, and accept it." Sonia could not believe her ears; three hundred years of history had come to an end, just like that. And while she believed that Kerensky did intend to protect them, she could also tell that he had enjoyed stripping them of their power. The Grand Duchesses stared at him, almost uncomprehendingly. Kerensky turned to Sonia. "Who are you?"

"That is Bolugayevska," Olga said before Sonia could frame a reply. "She is our lady."

"Bolugayevska," Kerensky said, putting a frightening amount of meaning into the word. "You'll leave the room, madame."

Sonia bit her lip as she looked at the girls. "You cannot send her out to the mob," Tatiana shouted. "She is our friend."

"She will not be harmed," Kerensky assured her. "If she does as she is told. Open the door," he commanded.

255

One of his aides opened the door. Kerensky nodded to Sonia.

She looked at the Grand Duchesses. "You will have to do without me for a while," she said, keeping her voice steady with an immense effort.

"Oh, Bolugayevska!" Olga ran forward to embrace her, and her sisters followed.

"We shall miss you so," Anastasia wept.

"Do come back to us as quickly as you can," Marie admonished.

"Of course she will," Tatiana said, and kissed her.

Kerensky waited patiently by the door. Olga and Sonia looked into each other's eyes. They both had the same feeling, that they were not going to see each other again. Then Olga embraced her a last time. "We shall pray for you, Sonia," she whispered.

"And I for you," Sonia promised. Then she walked through the door.

To her surprise, the hallway was empty, save for armed men, lounging in a not very military fashion, but straightening as they saw Kerensky. Sonia wondered if they would trouble to pick her up if she fainted; she certainly felt as if she might, from sheer relief at the realisation that she was not immediately going to be torn to pieces. "What is in there?" Kerensky pointed at one of the doors leading off.

"The Grand Duchess Marie's apartment," Sonia said.

"You mean Marie Romanov's apartment, madame. In there."

My God! Sonia thought: can he mean to rape me himself? But she opened the door and went into the room. Kerensky followed, and closed the door behind him. They both inhaled Marie's scent. "Sonia Bolugayevska," he said. "Ex-Princess of Bolugayen. Rasputin's mistress."

"As you are Alexander Kerensky," she retorted. "But I know nothing more than that. Are you now President of Russia?"

"I am Minister of Defence in the new government. I control the Army. As long as I do that, there is some hope for all of us. What have you to say for yourself?"

"You mean you have not yet decided whether or not to have me shot, or thrown to the mob. I was never Rasputin's mistress. I was his slave. I had no choice, as he rescued me from the Okhrana. Will you send me back to them?"

"The Okhrana no longer exist, Madame Bolugayevska." He gave a grim smile. "The mob has done that. Is still doing it. But I know you were arrested by the secret police, not once, but twice. That makes you one of us. What were you doing here?"

Sonia shrugged. "They offered me sanctuary. Because I worked for Rasputin."

He nodded. "But they can no longer offer you sanctuary. Do you have anywhere to go? Bearing in mind that you are no longer subject to arrest by the Okhrana."

"You mean I can leave here? By myself?"

"I would recommend very strongly that you leave here. Leave Petrograd, in fact. And do not ever come back."

Sonia licked her lips. "My things . . ."

"Things can always be replaced. A life cannot. Run for your life, Sonia Bolugayevska."

Sonia went to the door, hesitated. "And the Romanovs?"

"Those girls are splendid creatures, aren't they?"

"You cannot mean to give them to your men?"

"No," he said. "My aim is to restore civilisation in Petrograd. Not destroy it entirely. I will do whatever I can do for them. They have relatives. The King of England is their cousin." This time his smile was wry. "So is the Kaiser. But as it is my intention that we should continue the war with Germany, that would not be a good idea. I will do what I can. But you, Madame Bolugayevska, you must hurry away from this place."

Chapter Ten

Going Home

One of Kerensky's soldiers used his bayonet to help Sonia tear a drape into pieces and secure her a length of the material to use as a headscarf. This she could legitimately wrap around her face, as it remained very cold. The rest of the material she wrapped round her shoulders, thus concealing the fact that her clothes were of good cut and allowing her immediately to look as ragtail as the rest of the women milling about the palace complex. But even so, reaching Petrograd was immensely difficult, and painful. Memories of her escape from Irkutsk kept rising up and threatening to overwhelm her with despair. She could only take comfort from the fact that now she was surrounded by people, angry but yet good-humoured, swearing they would hang every Romanov or Tsarist they could lay hands on yet solicitiously helping Sonia back to her feet when she slipped and fell. Soon after that she found a place on a cart filled with loot from the palace, and travelled in comparative comfort.

Going where? Regaining Petrograd was instinctive. But what would she find there? She had a house which she had not visited for over a year. She had a bank account with enough money in it to take her round the world in luxury, but she did not suppose any bank would be doing business today. And at the moment she had no money. But getting back to her house, and some warm clothing, remained her first priority.

The cart rumbled into the city, and she looked around herelf with a growing sensation of horror. People lay dead on the streets, attracting no attention at all, save from the children who were kicking them or pulling at them with an almost maniacal glee. Then she saw a man hanging from a lamppost. From his tunic she could tell that he had been a policeman, but he was naked from the waist down, and he had been castrated before death. And the children were poking at his body, too. I have sought refuge in hell, she thought. Over all there was a pall of smoke from the burning public buildings. Yet the private dwellings seemed, remarkably, untouched.

She recognised the street they were on, and when the cart was slowed by a group of men armed with rifles, shouting and asking questions, she slipped from the tailgate. Someone called after her, but she ignored him and hurried round the corner. She was only a few blocks from her own house. And here there were less people, and no corpses, either lying or hanging. Here the revolution might never have been. She wondered if Michaelin had been dragged from his office and stretched on the snow to have his breeches torn off and his genitals cut away? She wondered why she did not go and find out, and do it herself if he still lived? But she was too exhausted, emotionally and physically. She wanted rest, and safety.

She stumbled up the steps to her front door, and banged on it. She had to do this several times before she elicited a reply. "Who is there?" asked a voice.

"Korsakov!" she shouted, too bewildered to do more than pronounce the name. "For God's sake let me in."

There was a moment's hesitation, then the bolts were released. Sonia had been leaning against the panels and fell on to her hands and knees as they swung inwards. With very little ceremony she was dragged into the hall and the door shut and bolted behind her. Only then did

Korsakov kneel beside her. Standing behind him was a terrified Antonina. "Sonia? Is it really you?"

Sonia rose to her knees. "What are you doing here?"

"I came looking for you. But Antonina did not know where you were. She said you had been arrested by the Okhrana . . ."

Sonia stood up. "I need something hot to drink. Tea. And vodka. And I need a bath. Do those things, Antonina." The maid looked at Korsakov, and received a quick nod. She hurried off. "So, you are the master here," Sonia remarked. "How long have you been here?"

"Since last summer."

"Last . . . are you wounded?"

He was not wearing uniform, but rather a collection of odd garments. "A few scratches."

"You mean you deserted? You?"

Korsakov sat down, hands dangling between his knees. "You were not there. You cannot criticise, unless you were there. You know nothing of the filth and the lice. You have never heard the sound of the guns, constant, always coming closer. You do not know what it feels like to know there is an enemy, not a hundred yards away, and when you go to load your revolver, you find you have no bullets left, and there are none to be had. You have not lived with the smell of death, the screams of the dying. You cannot *know*."

Sonia stood above him. While she understood what he was trying to convey, she felt no pity for him, simply because there were millions of men who had *not* run away. "You were with Samsanov," she said. "Tell me what happened."

He raised his head. "That was more than two years ago."

"Tell me what happened."

He shrugged. "We walked into a trap. We were surrounded and butchered. Those who survived, surrendered."

260

"But you were neither butchered nor surrendered."

"I cut my way out. With what was left of my regiment. I commanded men, then. Under Brusilov I was expected to command boys. Frightened boys."

So you became frightened yourself, Sonia thought. "Did you see Alexei at Tannenburg?"

"We rode together for a while. We talked about you."

"What about me?"

"I told him we were to be married."

"And what did he say?"

"He did not wish to discuss it."

"Did he get out, with you?"

"No, he did not. He told me to get out if I could, then he returned to be with Samsanov. I am afraid he was killed. Or killed himself. Oh, very gallant."

"Alexei would never kill himself," Sonia snapped. Although she could not be sure about that. Alexei was so bound up in notions of honour that the defeat of an army in which he held a command might well have been too great a humiliation for him to bear.

Antonina produced the tea. "I will draw your bath, madame," she said. But she was again exchanging glances with Korsakov.

"Thank you, Antonina," Sonia said. She waited until the maid had left the room, then said, "So, having deserted, you came here, and took up with my maid."

"Well . . . I came looking for you, Sonia, my dearest Sonia."

"You had better not let Antonina hear you calling me that," Sonia suggested.

"But you were not here. And I needed some place to hide. If they had caught me . . ."

"They would have shot you. Which is what you would have deserved. What you still deserve."

"You were not here," he said again. "Antonina gave me shelter. And, well, we were two lonely people together."

"And one thing led to another. I know. I do not

261

imagine you made too great an effort to find out where I was."

"You were in the hands of the Okhrana. If they had caught me . . ."

"They would have shot you. Well, I am here, now. What are your plans?"

"What are *your* plans?"

"I am going down to Bolugayen. How much money do you have?"

"I have nothing. We have nothing. Antonina went to the bank yesterday to draw money, but the bank was shut."

"And is likely to stay shut." Sonia chewed her lip. She actually didn't even know if there were any trains running. But she had to get out of Petrograd, with or without Korsakov. She did not care whether he came or not. However could she ever have contemplated marrying such an ignoble creature? "I am going to have my bath."

There was not enough fuel to spare for more than a luke-warm bath – the entire house was like an ice-box – so it was a quick in and out for Sonia, while Antonina hovered, and chattered, aimlessly. Antonina was in a highly agitated state, but Sonia could tell that she was also waiting for a lead from her lover, and with that understanding she also realised that she might be in some personal danger. As Sonia lacked a friend in the world, now, she needed to tred with caution. "I intend to leave Petrograd," she said, as she stepped out of the tub and was wrapped in a towel-robe. "And go down to Bolugayen. I think it will be much safer there. Would you like to accompany me, Antonina?" Antonina did not reply for a few seconds, and as she was standing behind Sonia, massaging her through the towel, Sonia could not see her face. "Major Korsakov would be welcome to accompany us, of course," she added.

"How would we travel?" Antonina asked.

"Well, if I can raise some money, we would go by train."

"I meant, would I continue to be your servant?"

"Well, of course, Antonina." Sonia stepped out of the towel. "I am not going to sack you."

"The people on the streets are saying that there will be no more mistress and servant, in the new Russia," Antonina remarked.

Sonia had opened her wardrobe, looking for the clothes she had left here, a year ago. She wanted a warm nightdress, and then a warm bed. She wanted to sleep for a week. But now she turned, frowning. "If you do not wish to work for me Antonina, then you may leave."

"Leave! Ha! Madame, it is time we understood certain things. Paul is my lover, not yours. This is my house, not yours."

I must not lose my temper, Sonia thought. But she could not carry on such an argument standing naked and goose pimpled before this woman. She selected a nightdress, dropped it over her head, settled it around her hips while she did some rapid thinking. But anger still predominated. "You may find that difficult to prove in a court of law," she remarked.

"Court of law," Antonina sneered. "Those courts of law no longer exist. They have been burned down. You are an aristocrat. In the streets they are saying, death to all aristocrats."

Sonia lost her temper. "Then why do you not get out there and shout it with them?" she snapped. "Go on. Get out. You are dismissed."

"You cannot dismiss me," Antonina asserted.

"I have just done so," Sonia told her.

"I am here by right of occupation," Antonina said. "You are a wanted felon." Sonia picked up her largest hairbrush, backed with heavy silver. "Paul!" Antonina bawled. "Come up here!" She certainly had taken on a lot of airs, Sonia thought. Korsakov hurried up the stairs. "She thinks she can throw us out," Antonina said.

263

"Now, Sonia," Korsakov said placatingly. "I am sure you do not wish to do that."

"I do wish it. Out!"

"We'll just tell the people out there who is in here," Antonina threatened. "Then we'll see."

"Do that, Paul, and you're a dead duck," Sonia warned. "Russia is still at war with Germany, and you are a deserter."

Korsakov chewed his lip. "Listen," Antonina said earnestly to Paul. "Why don't we do her, now. Nobody knows she's here. And nobody cares. Now's our chance, Paul. People are being killed all over the place. One more corpse in the streets isn't going to concern anyone. And then she won't bother us again."

Sonia looked from one to the other in horror; she could not believe they would actually murder her. Korsakov continued to look uncertain, and there came a knock on the street door – a loud authoritative knock. "Oh, my God!" Korsakov said. "The police!"

The knock was repeated. "We will have to open it," Sonia said, "or they will break it down. Antonina!"

She had no idea who it could be, but even the police would be a help. Save that the police were also fugitives, now. Antonina went down and unbolted the door. "Woman, you have not changed at all," said the man on the step.

"Leon!" Sonia screamed, and almost threw herself down the stairs, ignoring the fact that she was wearing only a nightdress. She endeavoured to check herself at the foot, if only to take him in. He did not seem to have changed all that much either, physically, but he had lost the furtive air she remembered. He was not in uniform, although he wore the invariable Russian belted tunic and peaked cap, but he looked well-fed as well as confident.

"I told you I would come back for you, dear girl," he said, and took her in his arms.

She kissed him, several times. "But . . . have your people taken power?"

"Not yet. But the power is there for the taking." He was looking over her shoulder, at Korsakov, slowly descending the stairs. "I remember you."

Behind him, Antonina closed the door. "Who is this man?" Korsakov demanded.

Sonia looked at Trotsky. "Lev Bronstein, at your service," Trotsky said. "But you may call me Trotsky."

"What do you want?"

"I have come to see my mistress," Trotsky announced.

Sonia caught her breath. But Trotsky's appearance had undoubtedly saved her life, whatever might happen after. "Get them out of here, Leon," she said. "They were threatening to kill me."

"He knows you!" Antonina shouted. "You must kill them both Paul!" Korsakov turned to run back up the stairs; no doubt he had his revolver concealed in the bedroom. But he was not quick enough. Trotsky pushed Sonia to one side, and from beneath his tunic drew his own revolver. A single shot brought Korsakov tumbling back down the stairs. "Aaaagh!" Antonina screamed, and reached for the door. Trotsky turned, and shot her also. The range was so close Antonina's back seemed to dissolve in blood and bone, and she hit the floor without another sound.

Sonia could only stare, as Trotsky turned again. Korsakov had fallen right down the stairs, and now lay in a heap at the bottom, moaning. "My God, I'm hit. Sonia . . ."

"I am out of practice," Trotsky complained, and fired again. This bullet hit Korsakov in the head. Again Sonia watched something living explode in a cloud of blood and grey matter. Her stomach rolled, and she sat down heavily on one of the straight chairs in the hallway. "Bourgeois scum," Trotsky remarked, and emptied the three used cartridge cases on to the floor, carefully reloading his weapon with bullets taken from his pocket. He glanced at Sonia. "You are shaking. Have you never seen a man killed before? Or a woman?"

"A long time ago. In Siberia."

"One thing about life never changes, and that is death. That is good, eh? I must use it in a speech." He went into the sitting room and poured a glass of brandy, brought it back to her. "Drink." She obeyed, gulping the burning liquid down her throat. "Now come upstairs," Trotsky said. "I wish to fuck you. I have looked forward to this moment for so long. My God! It is four years."

He held her hand, and she pulled it free. "No. I cannot! Not now. Please, Leon. Not with . . ."

"When you're upstairs, you won't be able to see them." He returned to the sitting room for the brandy decanter, and just for good measure brought a bottle of vodka as well. "We will get drunk together."

What am I doing? she asked herself. What have I done? I have plunged headlong into hell. But how long ago did I do that?

She could not resist him. Her only aim was survival. "You are already exhausted," he commented, when he was temporarily sated, and lay across her, his head on her shoulder. "What did the Okhrana do to you?"

"They exhausted me," she said.

"How long were you in their cells?"

Sonia did a hasty calculation. She did not think it would be a good idea to tell Trotsky either about being Rasputin's housekeeper or her stay at Tsarskoye Selo; of course he would find out about Rasputin soon enough, but she did not intend to be here when he did. "Over a year."

"God, the thought makes my blood boil. Well, most of the scum have been destroyed."

"Michaelin?"

"I do not know for certain. But we will find him out, you may be sure of that."

266

"We? Is Lenin with you?"

"No. He wishes to be with me. But I do not know how he is going to get here. When he heard of Rasputin's death, he wired me to enter the country and see what I could do. I was in Helsinki. But as he is in Switzerland, there is all of Germany between him and us."

"And now you will lead another revolt? Against men like Prince Lvov and Kerensky?"

He grinned, and began kissing her breasts. "Not immediately. They suppose that by removing the Tsar they have cured all the evils of this country. They propose to continue the war with Germany and Austria, and hope to gain Russia a seat at the peace conference. Well, let them try. The Army is already in a state of near mutiny. When they have lost a few more thousand men they *will* mutiny, and that will be the end of Prince Lvov and his demagogues. Then it will be our opportunity." He chuckled. "We'll shoot the lot."

"What about the Royal Family?"

He raised his head. "There is no such thing any more, my dear Sonia. You should forget that you were ever an aristocrat. In fact, you must, if you are to survive. But you will always survive, my dearest Sonia, because I have said that you will. I love you. I adore you. I will love you, always, and forever. Listen: I swear this."

"Yes," she said. "Thank you. What will you do with the Royal Family?"

Trotsky put on his glasses. "We will shoot them too. Every last one of them."

It was mid-afternoon before he was ready to leave. By then she had fed him, and he had dragged the two bodies together by the front door. "I will send people to take these out on to the streets, when it gets dark," he said. "They will clean up this blood, too. You do not have to do it. You do not mind a few more hours?"

"No," Sonia said. "I do not mind." As there were no

fires, inside the house it was very nearly as cold as outside, and the bodies were not offensive, so long as one did not look at them. Or thought about them. She had lain naked in Korsakov's arms as she had just lain naked in Trotsky's. Now one was a bloody apparition. And Trotsky . . .

"You must stay here until I can come for you," he told her. "It is not safe on the streets. I will come later this evening, and take you to a place where you will be safe and we can be together."

"I have no money."

He kissed her. "You do not need money. I will look after the money. I will look after everything. Just go upstairs and stay in your bedroom until my people come. They will be absolutely trustworthy." He kissed her again, and left.

Sonia went upstairs immediately, dressed herself as warmly as she could. She knew she could not take anything apart from what she could wear. Then she stood at the window and looked out. The evening was already drawing in and in an hour it would be dark. Then Trotsky's people would come. She dared not risk waiting for them. Where Korsakov had been a cad, Trotsky was a monster, who thought nothing of shooting people out of hand, and who planned to shoot a lot more. Including those lovely girls, if he could ever get his hands on them.

She opened the front door and stepped outside, closing and locking the door behind her. She wondered if they would break it down. More likely they would report back to Trotsky for orders. Well, then, what would he do? The important thing was that he should not know where to look for her. She hurried along the streets. Some were crowded, some were empty; few people paid any attention to the lone woman who, wrapped up in a coat and with her head encased in a scarf, could have been any age and any class. The burning buildings still glowed, and the air was heavy with smoke. Every so often there was a gunshot or a scream, but in the gloom there was little evidence of

268

revolution or atrocity to be seen, save for the burning buildings.

She refused to allow herself to consider what would happen if the Bolugayevski Palace had been burned, or if Nathalie was not there, or if . . . there were so many ifs. But Nathalie was now her only hope. Nathalie! The palace stood, foursquare and undamaged, so far as she could see, although the gates were open. She looked left and right, then hurried through them and up the drive. The palace was also in darkness. Her heart began to sink, but to her amazement, and relief, the front door was also open. Whoever had left had left in a hurry. They must have left *something* of value behind.

She entered the open doorway, her boots clicking on the parquet. She stood still, and listened. She knew this house very well, and had no need to use a light, not that she supposed, as there had been no electricity at her house, there would be any here. There was not a sound. She closed the front doors, discovered that the lock was undamaged, and carefully locked them. She walked across the parquet and up the grand staircase. Above her head the great crystal chandelier still hung, undamaged. Nothing was damaged.

She reached the first floor gallery, and again stood still to listen. And heard a sound. The merest suspicion of a noise. There was someone, or something, in the house with her. For a moment the hair on the nape of her neck prickled, then she drew a deep breath. "Nathalie!" she said. "Is that you?"

"Sonia!" Nathalie squealed, from behind her.

Sonia turned, sharply. Her eyes were accustomed to the darkness, and she could just make out the two figures standing in one of the reception room doorways. She also saw that Nathalie was holding a revolver. "For heaven's sake stop pointing that thing at me," she requested.

"Oh, Sonia!" Nathalie lowered the gun and hurried forward to embrace her.

269

Then it was Dagmar's turn. "We have been so afraid!" the girl sobbed.

"It's a common complaint right about now," Sonia agreed. "What happened here?"

"The servants left," Nathalie said. "Even Dimitri and Rykova. They just left."

"I think you should say, good riddance," Sonia suggested. "They would only have got in the way. Have you any money?"

"Of course I have money," Nathalie said. "But there is nothing to spend it on."

"Get all your money together," Sonia told her, "and all your jewellery. You too, Dagmar. We have got to get out of Petrograd, and the only way we are going to do that is bribe and buy our way. But it must be done now, before things get any worse."

"What do you think?" Joseph Cromb asked his mother, taking a turn up and down the drawing room carpet before her.

"I think you look tremendous," Patricia said.

Joseph had been commissioned into an infantry regiment, and certainly looked very smart in his new khaki uniform, even if Patricia's romanticism would have preferred to see him wearing proper boots rather than puttees. Jennie ran up to her big brother to throw both arms round him and give him a hug. "I wish I could come with you."

"Well, you can, as a nurse. Whenever you are old enough."

"Oh, can I, Mom?" At thirteen Jennie was a most attractive child, who had inherited the auburn hair and pale complexion of both her mother and her grandmother.

"Whenever you are old enough," Patricia agreed. This war had to end some time. "Here's Daddy. He's home early!"

270

Duncan Cromb burst into the room, waving various papers, and checked at the sight of his adopted son. "Hello, Joe. I didn't expect you to be here."

"Embarkation leave," Joe explained.

"Heck. When do you go?"

"Tomorrow."

Duncan looked at his wife, and Patricia shrugged. "Had to happen, darling."

"Yes." Duncan absently put his arm round Jennie's shoulders to give her a hug. "If you could've waited a couple of months, you would have found yourself in another uniform. Seems even Woodrow Wilson is prepared to go to war, now."

"Duncan!" Patricia cried. "That would be terrific."

"Yeah," Duncan said thoughtfully. "We'll be with you in a moment, kids, but your mother and I need to have a word."

Patricia raised her eyebrows as her husband held her arm and almost pushed her into the study. "Are you bothered about the news? I think your people coming in is the best thing I've heard in a long time."

"I agree with you. But it's obviously going to be some time before they can have any effect. We don't really have an army, you know. We have to create one."

Patricia frowned. "You won't be involved, will you? For heaven's sake, Duncan. you're forty-one years old!"

"I don't think I'll be drafted, if that's what you mean. But I'm going to be pretty damned busy. The Navy Department wants every ship they can lay hands on for convoying troops, and Charlie's been on the wire; we've volunteered our entire fleet."

"I hope you're being paid for them," Patricia remarked. "So what's eating you?"

Duncan dumped the various papers on the desk. "Things aren't good in Russia."

"You mean the Tsar abdicating? I can't believe that's a

bad thing. This fellow Lvov declares he intends to continue the war on our side."

"I believe he means to try. But there's horrendous news coming out of the country. Petrograd is a charnel house, by all accounts."

"Oh, gosh, I hope Sonia's all right."

"I thought your friend Lenin was going to find out about her?"

"I haven't heard a thing from that bastard. I went to the bookshop a couple of weeks ago, and was told he and Olga had gone back to Switzerland."

"Yes. Well, if Sonia was really arrested by the Okrana, then she's all right now: according to these, the Okhrana no longer exists."

"Gee, I wish I could be there!" Patricia's eyes gleamed.

"And I am damned glad you're not. But I'm not bothered about Petrograd, or even Sonia. It's down south. Seems there are mutinies and riots and God knows what going on. The peasants are burning manor houses, looting and murdering . . ."

"Is there word from Bolugayen?"

"Nope."

"Well, I should think they're all right. Our people have always been utterly loyal."

"Maybe. But Mom's too old to get involved in a revolution."

Patricia kissed him. "Then we must get her out of there, just as quickly as possible."

"I couldn't agree with you more. The problem is, how?"

"She can take a ship from Sevastopol."

"Of course she can't. Russia is at war with Turkey, and the Dardanelles are closed."

"Well, then, she can take the Trans-Siberian train and go to Vladivostock. That would be best, anyway, because there are no submarines in the Pacific, and she can go back to Boston and total safety."

"God, that would be a relief. The real problem is, how are we going to persuade Mom to leave Bolugayen, darling? She certainly isn't going to do that if we just ask her to by wire."

"I see what you mean." Patricia appeared to consider. "Well, I suppose we'll just have to go and get her. There's no Tsar or Okhrana to keep me out of Russia now. We'll just go in, and come out, with Mom, even if we have to carry her."

"But . . . that'd mean crossing the Atlantic and then the Pacific."

"Sounds enormous fun. I'll make arrangements right away."

"What about the shipping line?" Duncan's voice was almost a wail. "Charlie says I must run the operation from here."

"I know," Patricia said sympathetically. "The war must come first. But not to worry, my dearest. I'll get Aunt Anna out."

"You?"

"For heaven's sake, I know my way in an out of Russia, and Poltava."

Duncan looked as if someone had hit him on the head. He sat down behind the desk. "You can't go into a country filled with anarchists and revolutionaries, all by yourself."

"Oh, come now, don't you think I know how to deal with anarchists and revolutionaries?" Patricia bit her lip, and then hurried on, realising that she might have said too much. "If you're worried, let Morgan come with me. I'll take Giselle as well," she added, just to square propriety. Remarkably, although both valet and maid knew all about her adventure with Rasputin, since then they had been more loyal to her than ever.

Duncan gazed at her. "You want to go back, don't you?"

"Well . . . I always want to go back to Russia."

"And the children?"

"Oh, really, Duncan, darling, Joe's going off to war. And you'll be here to look after Jennie."

He pointed. "You're dreaming of finding Sonia and joining in whatever absurd activity she's up to. Tell the truth, now."

"I am going to Bolugayen to get your mother out of Russia," Patricia said with dignity. "To get Priscilla and the children out as well, if they'll come. I have no intention of going near Petrograd. Or any revolutionary."

"Will you give me your word on that?"

"Absolutely," Patricia said, eyes gleaming with excitement.

"What are we going to do, Grandma?" Priscilla asked.

"Oh, they should be hanged, all of them," Sophie declaimed, somewhat shrilly. Janine Grabowska leaned across the breakfast table and squeezed her lover's hand, while little Anna looked from one to the other of the four women with enormous eyes. She did not really understand what was happening, although she did realise that it was an earth-shaking event.

Anna also looked from one to the other; she included a glance at Gleb, standing as immobile as ever by the doorway to the breakfast room. "What do you propose we should do, Your Highness?" She directed her question to Priscilla. "We shall do what we have always done, sit it out."

"But if the Tsar . . ."

"Do you not suppose tsars have been forced to abdicate before? Abdication is at least a civilised way of giving up the throne. This Tsar's grandfather was murdered. So was his uncle. So was his great-great-grandfather."

"Yes, but they were always replaced by other tsars," Priscilla argued. "Not by Socialist governments."

"There will be another tsar," Anna said firmly. "Things are in a state of turmoil at the moment, because of the

274

war. But there is no possibility of a country like Russia being ruled by a committee. It has to have a tsar. And it will have a tsar."

"Oh . . . you always talk as if you were giving an historical lecture," Sophie said. "It's the here and now that matters. What's going to happen to us. Poor Janine's house has already been burned. She doesn't know what's happened to her husband . . ." She burst into tears, while Janine looked at the other two in embarrassment.

"I hope you will forgive me, Countess," Anna said – despite the close social circle into which the four women had been thrown over the past few months she remained stiffly formal – "but I feel I must point out that your house was burned entirely because you abandoned it."

"If we had stayed we would have been murdered," Janine protested.

"Again, I feel I should point out that if you feared being raped and murdered by your own servants and tenants, then you cannot have been a very good mistress."

Janine got up and left the breakfast room. "Oh, Grandma," Priscilla protested. "Now you've offended her."

"Someone should have offended that woman years ago," Anna declared.

"Oh, you . . . you wicked old woman," Sophie shouted, and ran behind her friend. Anna snorted.

"Darling, I think Mademoiselle Friquet is waiting for you," Priscilla told little Anna, who promptly rose, bowed to the Princess and the Countess, and left the room, Gleb gravely bowing in turn as he held the door for her. "Thank you, Gleb," Priscilla said. Gleb bowed again, and left the breakfast room. "What *are* we going to do, Grandma?" Priscilla asked again.

"I meant what I said, Priscilla. We are the Bolugayevskis. This is our house, and our land. We are surrounded by our people. We have been here for three hundred years. We will be here another three hundred years."

Priscilla shivered. "The Romanovs were on the throne three hundred years."

"Do you not suppose they, one of them, will be back on the throne in short order? That they are not there now is because Nicholas is a weakling. He would not lead. We have always led our people."

"If Alexei were here, or even Colin . . ."

"*You* will lead, because you are the Princess Boluga-yevska," Anna told her. "You will never reveal the slightest sign of weakness, or uncertainty. Promise me this."

Priscilla looked at her for several seconds. "I promise, Grandma."

"Then go into the village. It is time for your morning ride. Get dressed, and go into the village."

Priscilla was dressed by her maids – since being told by Rotislav that Alexei was alive she had abandoned black and today wore a pale blue habit – and then stopped by the nursery to say good-morning to Alexei. His nurse was a young woman from Poltava, named Constantina, cheerfully ugly, squat and heavy, but she clearly adored the little boy, and he adored her. Priscilla went downstairs. listened to the sound of the piano coming from the music room, where Anna was doing her scales. There was no sign of Sophie or Janine; they were probably solacing each other. But there was a row of footman bowing as she walked past them, smiling at them, to where Gleb waited on the porch.

Everything was so perfectly, reassuringly normal. If only those newspapers hadn't arrived yesterday, there would be nothing to worry about, because nothing would have changed. But today, everything had changed. There was no tsar, any longer, and everyone on Bolugayen knew that. And, for all of Grandma's bold words, that left the ultimate question to be answered: did the boyars hold up the tsardom, in which case there *was* nothing to worry about, or did the mystique of tsardom hold up the boyars, whom the tsars had created in the first place? If the latter were true, then she and Grandma, all the Bolugayevskis and indeed all the two thousand odd princes in the Russian Empire, no longer had any reason to exist. She wondered if her people were considering that at this very moment?

But she had her duty to perform, her aura of omnipotence to maintain. Gleb gave her a knee up, as he had done whenever she went riding from her first day here. Her two grooms mounted behind her, walked their horses out of the drive in time to hers. It was still only mid-March, and very cold. Women were working to clear the snow from the road into the village. It was one of the things about Russia which always surprised her, that the women seemed required to do all the heavy work . . . and that they did not seem to mind. This morning, as always, they stopped work to bow and then cheer their mistress, for all that their bare hands and arms glowed red with the cold. Priscilla smiled at them, and rode into the cluster of houses. As ever, she went first of all to the church, to kneel before the altar and be blessed by Father Valentin.

In his tall black hat and with his flowing black beard, he truly was a relic of the past, but he was the most reassuring of figures, not really in himself, but because of what he stood for. The Russians were the most religious people on earth. That had to be their salvation. And yet . . . "What is going to happen, Your Highness?" Valentin asked as she kissed his hand.

"The war will continue until the Germans are beaten," Priscilla said. "And we will plant the wheat crop as soon as the ground thaws."

"I meant, about the Little Father, Your Highness."

"There will be another Little Father, soon, Father Valentin."

She went on to the schoolhouse, and chairs scraped as the children rose to their feet. Komski the master bowed. "What terrible news, Your Highness. What will become of us?"

277

"We shall continue fighting the war, and we will continue farming our crops here on Bolugayen, Komski."

He bowed again. "Do I ask the children to hail the Tsar, Your Highness?" he whispered.

"Of course. Long live the Tsar," she called, and the children responded. Whoever he may be, Priscilla thought.

She went to the hospital, and was escorted through the ward by Geller, stopping from time to time to speak with a patient. "Will a Socialist government affect us on Bolugayen, Your Highness?" the doctor asked.

"I imagine we will have to pay more taxes," Priscilla said.

"Ah!" Geller commented. But he could tell she didn't want to talk about it.

Priscilla went outside, where the grooms waited with her horse. They had been stamping their feet and slapping their hands together because of the cold, but they hastily stood to attention as she emerged. Now she looked past them, and saw Rotislav, standing further down the main village street, on which the hospital was situated, and talking with a man. That they were talking about her she did not doubt for a moment, nor was she disturbed by this; she knew that the people of Bolugayen talked about her constantly, and the more constantly when she was in their midst. What interested her, and did disturb her, in a vague manner, was the fact that she had never seen the other man before, and if she could not always put a name to all of her husband's tenants, she certainly knew all of their faces. Even more disturbing, when she turned towards them, the stranger hurried off. "Rotislav!" she called.

The valet came forward, bowing as he reached her. "Your Highness."

"Who was that man, Rotislav?"

Rotislav looked bewildered. "Man, Your Highness?"

"The fellow you were speaking with, Rotislav. He was a man, was he not? And a stranger."

278

"Oh, you mean Viktor Nordenski, Your Highness."

"If that is his name, yes, it is he I am speaking of. He is not a Bolugayen man."

"No, no, Your Highness. He is a soldier. Was a soldier. We served in the same regiment."

"You mean he is Polish, like you?"

"No, no, Your Highness. He is a Ukrainian. But yes, we were in the same regiment."

"Fighting for the Germans."

"Well, yes, Your Highness. We had no choice. But we escaped together."

"You never spoke of him, before."

"He is of no account, Your Highness."

"A fellow deserter? What is he doing here, in Bolugayen?"

"He is looking for work, Your Highness. I told him there was none here."

Priscilla regarded him for some seconds. Obviously he was lying. The question was, what about. "I think you should go after your old comrade, Rotislav, and bring him up to the house so that I may meet him. If we cannot find him employment, I should still like to offer him a square meal."

Rotislav bowed. "Your Highness is too kind." He stood by her stirrup. The grooms stepped back. Because they remembered that once he had been their senior in the village heirarchy? Or because, for some reason, they still regarded him as their senior, Priscilla wondered. In any event, he clearly intended to give her a leg up. He had done this before, and she found it unsettling. As it was on this occasion. His hand, wrapped round the ankle of her boot, remained there a moment longer than was necessary, and his fingers moved, as if he were massaging her flesh through the leather. Oh, to know what secrets he and Alexei had shared during their imprisonment together!

She looked down at him. "Thank you, Rotislav. I shall look forward to meeting your old comrade." She turned

279

her horse and walked it out of the village, the grooms at its heels.

Priscilla drew rein and looked up the slope of the road to the hilltop above the valley. Standing there were three people, huddled together against the cold wind. More fugitives, she thought. Perhaps more comrades of Rotislav. Her heart went out to such dregs of humanity. But at the same time she understood that even Bolugayen's resources were limited; she could not offer refuge to every fugitive in Russia, whether they were fleeing the Socialists or the Okhrana or the Army: she had been told often enough how, during the great famine of 1907, Alexei had used armed guards to keep people off his property. She hated the idea of having to do that, but if it was a case of exposing her own people to want . . . She turned her horse and walked it up the slope. It did not occur to her to feel afraid of three hungry people: she was the Princess Bolugayevska.

They watched her approaching, and continued to stand there, waiting for her. Priscilla listened to the reassuring sound of her grooms' hooves behind her, and walked right up to them, frowning as she realised they were women, and that although their clothes were in rags, they had once been fine clothes. "Who are you?" she demanded. "What do you want here?"

One of the women pulled away the ragged strips of material wrapped around her face. "Who are *you*?" she demanded.

Priscilla's head jerked. "I am the Princess Bolugayevska."

Nathalie gave a hoarse laugh. "Why, so am I," she said. "So are we all, Princess Priscilla. Are you not going to invite us in?"

Chapter Eleven

The Wives

Priscilla slipped from her saddle before either of the grooms could react. She was aware of a most peculiar sensation. Over the past five years she had been steeped in stories of the various eccentric members of the family, the more so since Sophie had returned to Bolugayen to live. Thus she realised that this huge woman who had addressed her had to be the Princess Dowager, just as the hardly less well-built young woman beside her had to be the Countess Dagmar. But the third woman, tall, dark, slender, who had been walking with a slight limp . . . her head and hair and face were almost completely hidden by the protective headscarf, but Priscilla's stomach did a complete roll. "We have been walking for a long time," Nathalie said. "Would you be kind enough to offer us a ride?"

Priscilla looked at the grooms, almost in desperation. "You are welcome to use our horses, Your Highness," one of these said. "But I am afraid we do not have side saddles."

"Fuck that," Nathalie told him crudely. "Give me a leg up." She swung into the saddle, and a moment later Dagmar was also seated.

Priscilla looked at Sonia. "I am Sonia Bolugayevska," Sonia said.

Priscilla drew a deep breath. "I am Priscilla Boluga-yevska," she said. "Would you like to ride behind me?"

"What on earth are you doing here?" Anna demanded. She was asking the question of Nathalie, but she was looking at Sonia. Priscilla remained standing at the back of the room; not for the first time since coming to Bolugayen she felt completely out of her depths.

"We have decided to visit with you, Anna," Nathalie said. "For a season. Things are not good in Petrograd."

"But how did you get here?"

"Mostly by train."

"We understood there were no trains."

"When there were no trains, we walked, as we walked from Poltava." Nathalie sat down heavily, with a deep sigh. "I would like something to drink."

"Champagne, Gleb," Priscilla said. There were some things which nowadays came naturally to her. But her brain was spinning even faster. The thought of these three women, used to nothing but total luxury, walking through the snow all the way from Poltava . . . things must indeed be bad in Petrograd.

"Not champagne," Nathalie said. "Vodka. Lots of vodka."

Gleb looked at his current mistress. Priscilla nodded, and he hurried from the room. "What you need is a bath," Anna remarked.

"Oh, yes. A hot tub. Have three drawn, if you please." Anna snorted. Priscilla pulled the bell rope. "And then a warm bed. I want to stay in bed for at least a week," Nathalie announced.

Madame Xenia arrived, and Priscilla gave her the necessary orders. She hurried off again. Anna looked at Sonia. "You were not supposed to return here."

Priscilla bit her lip. Although Sonia had ridden behind her back to the house, she had not spoken, except to say,

"You are very kind, Your Highness." But she did not wish her to feel unwanted.

"There was nowhere else to go," Sonia replied. "May I see my daughter, please?"

"Of course you may," Priscilla said, before Anna could speak. Anna glared at her, but Priscilla ignored her grandmother. "Would you like to see her now, or . . . after you have bathed and changed your clothes."

Sonia looked down at herself. "That would be better, I suppose. Thank you, Your Highness. But I have no clothes into which to change."

"Madame Xenia," Priscilla said, as the housekeeper returned into the room. "Hunt through my wardrobes and find clothes for these ladies." Xenia looked at Nathalie in consternation. "Oh, get the seamstresses upstairs to make whatever alterations are necessary," Priscilla said. "Madame Xenia will look after you, Your Highness." Sonia and Xenia looked at each other. "But of course, you know each other," Priscilla said.

"Yes," Sonia said. "Thank you, Your Highness. May I ask, is Anna well?"

"Oh, indeed," Priscilla said.

"And is there any news of Colin?"

"I'm afraid not."

"Vodka," Nathalie said with great satisfaction, as Gleb returned.

"Of all the effrontery," Sophie declared. "Coming here. That fat pig is bad enough, but Sonia . . ." She glared at her aunt. "You're not going to let them stay?"

"You will have to ask the Princess," Anna said huffily.

Sophie turned to Priscilla. "Of course they are going to stay," Priscilla said.

"For how long?"

"For as long as it is necessary."

"Ha! What are you going to say to her?"

"I don't really know," Priscilla confessed.

283

Yet, oddly, she had always had the feeling that one day she and her predecessor would meet. Now it was necessary to be positive; they could not share the same house at arm's length, as it were. She retired to the study, sat behind Alexei's desk, and summoned Grishka. "Are you pleased to see your old mistress again, Grishka?"

"Oh, yes, Your Highness." Then Grishka bit her lip, wondering if she had said the right thing.

"I wish you to resume being her maid, while she is staying with us. I would also like to speak with the Princess, as soon as she feels able."

"The Princess, Your Highness?"

"I do not think one should cease to be a princess by a stroke of a pen, Grishka."

"No, Your Highness. I was just thinking . . . when His Highness comes back . . ."

"But we don't know when that is going to be, do we?" Priscilla asked. "You will of course invite the Princess to join us for supper, although I will quite understand if she would prefer to take it in her apartment. But I really would like to speak with her. I will go to her, or she may come to me. It is up to her."

"Yes, Your Highness." Grishka curtsied, and retreated to the door, and there curtsied again. "Your Highness is very kind."

Kind, Priscilla thought. Guilty, more like. She only knew that suddenly, and after all her earlier rejection of the very idea, she desperately wanted to get to know this woman, and if possible to help her. And when Alexei came back? He would probably be as angry as Grandma appeared to be. But she was in charge of Bolugayen at this moment, and she would do what she thought right. She returned to the study after she had been bathed and dressed for dinner; Grishka had told her that Madame Bolugayevska would indeed like to call on her, at her convenience. She had named six o'clock. That was before the rest of the family normally came down for the evening.

She had dressed with great care, as if she were throwing a party, and had chosen a dark blue gown with a deep *décolletage*, and her favourite necklace, a thin gold band from which was suspended an enormous pearl which seemed to nestle in her cleavage. Now she sat behind the desk. Here, she was clearly the one in authority. But she did not suppose Sonia would challenge that authority. "Please come in," she called when she heard the knock.

Gleb himself opened the door for Sonia, and closed it behind her. Patricia found that she had stood up. She had not intended to do that. But she was drawn to her feet by the sight of her visitor. When they had first encountered each other, and even when the fugitives had been brought to the house, it had been difficult to discern much about any of them, because they had been so wrapped up and generally filthy and miserable in appearance. Now she gazed at a tall, slender, and quite exquisitely beautiful woman, her black hair loose and curling on her shoulders. Her gown was one of Priscilla's own, with a *décolletage* which left bare her superb neck and throat as well as the curve of her full breasts. Priscilla knew that Sonia was about forty years old, just as she knew the Jewess had lived an intensely hard life, but there was no trace of either – apart from that limp. "Please sit down," she invited.

Sonia sank into a chair before the desk with a rustle of taffeta. "I must thank you for the loan of your clothes."

"It is the least I can do. Yours . . ."

"I have not changed them for four weeks. Grishka has taken them away to be burned."

"I will have the seamstresses up again tomorrow morning," Priscilla promised. "And we will make you a wardrobe of your own."

"You are very kind," Sonia said again. "I am sorry to have inflicted myself upon you, but . . ."

285

"This is your home. How do you feel? I mean, after your . . . journey?"

"As if I have been travelling all my life. But Nathalie and Dagmar have suffered more: I have made that sort of journey before. Did you not know that, Your Highness?"

"I was told of it." Priscilla was embarrassed. "Have you seen little Anna?" Sonia's lips twisted. Priscilla sighed. "What did she say?"

"When Grishka said, this is your mother, Your Excellency, my daughter replied, Priscilla is my mother."

"I am sorry. The family, well . . ."

"You mean Aunt Anna."

"I suppose so. She felt that was necessary. I am most awfully sorry about it. And now you are here, why, we shall set about reversing the situation."

"I do not think Prince Alexei would like that."

"Prince Alexei is not here." Priscilla saw Sonia's eyes flicker, as if for the first time she was realising that this apparent child she was facing was actually as much the Princess Bolugayevska as she had ever been. "And I do not know when he will ever return."

"Did you love him?"

"Would you like an aperitif? Champagne?"

"Thank you."

Priscilla rang the bell. "I do love him, very much."

"So do I," Sonia said. The two women gazed at each other. "I never betrayed him," Sonia said. "He acted upon rumour. He felt that was necessary."

"And you can forgive him that?"

"Is not love a business of forgiving?"

Priscilla looked up in some relief as Gleb entered with the tray and glasses. "Have you *any* news of Colin?" Sonia asked.

"I am afraid not. So you see, we live in a kind of limbo here. Waiting. And we do not even know for what we are waiting." She raised her glass. "I am so glad to have met you, at last, Sonia. I am so glad that you are here."

* * *

286

The first dinner was an icy affair. Nathalie did not come down, but Dagmar did, also wearing hastily adjusted borrowed clothing, and looking around her with an air of, this is all really mine, you know. Father Valentin and Tigran Boscowski also came up to greet the new guests, but were clearly very nervous at meeting Sonia again, the more so when they saw that Priscilla had seated the ex-Princess on her right. Anna, as usual, sat at the bottom of the table, with Sophie and Janine. The old guard forming up against the new, Priscilla thought. But Sonia had once been one of the old guard herself. After the meal she had a word with Valentin. "There was a stranger in the village this morning, Father. An old comrade of Rotislav's."

Valentin nodded. "I spoke with him."

"Rotislav said he was looking for work."

"We could do with extra help, Your Highness."

"I did not like the look of him," Priscilla said. "I told Rotislav to bring him up to the house. But he has not done so. Now I wish you to tell him to send him away."

"If that is what you wish, Your Highness."

Priscilla arched her eyebrows. "You do not approve?"

"It is not my business to approve or disapprove of your decisions, Your Highness."

"Except in matters of religion. But I would like you to speak your mind."

Valentin hesitated. "This man has been speaking against you. Not you, personally, Your Highness. Against all landowners. Against the very principle of princes, and counts, and barons."

"Then surely the sooner we get him off my property the better. He must be one of these Socialists."

"The government is now Socialist, Your Highness."

"Does that mean we have to accept them on my property? I want him off Bolugayen, Father. Tomorrow."

Valentin looked doubtful, but he bowed in acquiesence.

*   *   *

287

To Priscilla's great relief, none of the three fugitives appeared to have suffered any serious physical consequences from their horrendous flight. And it had, apparently, been horrendous. They had had to use all their money, and then sell their jewellery, to obtain seats in overcrowded third-class carriages, crammed cheek-by-jowl with people they would never have looked at on the street; once they had even had to travel by cattle car. It was Nathalie who volunteered all this information. "Of course," she said, "Sonia knows all about travelling by cattle car. That is how she went to Siberia, when she was exiled."

"I had no idea you and the Princess Dowager were so close," Priscilla remarked to Sonia, when they were alone.

Sonia gave one of those twisted smiles. "There have been times when I would cheerfully have strangled the woman, Your Highness. We are only close by force of circumstances."

Priscilla found the love-hate relationship shared by the three women interesting, but then, she found everything about Sonia interesting. There was so much she wanted to ask her, and not only about the journey from Petrograd or what Alexei had been like as a young man. It was the woman herself, her experiences, some of them so terrible, that fascinated her. But she knew it would have to be a slow and careful business; much of Sonia's life was locked away in a mental safe to which Priscilla wondered if even Sonia herself still held the key. But as winter turned into spring she felt a definite closeness was growing between them. Because Sonia knew so much, and so many people, and about recent events she was quite happy to speak, although even here Priscilla felt that her recollections were being carefully censored. Not only had she known Rasputin, quite well, apparently, but she had been intimate with the Royal Family, and had met Kerensky, who almost everyone agreed was the true head

288

of the new government. Sonia indeed was most anxious about the fate of the Royals, and eagerly devoured every bit of news that came out of Poltava. "He promised that they would be sent to England," she told Priscilla. "Oh, I so hope those lovely girls manage to get out."

But all they could learn was that the Romanov family had been removed from Petrograd 'to a place of safety.' For the rest, a certain stability seemed to have descended on the country. The front was being held in the west, and of course the news that the United States was now involved, on the Allied side, was enormously encouraging, while nothing else had really changed on the home front. As always with the coming of spring, food became more readily available in the cities, and living conditions generally improved. There had never been any food shortages on Bolugayen, but Priscilla was relieved to find her people smiling again, although not quite as readily as in the days before the war. She discussed the situation with Boscowski, and found him disturbingly pessimistic.

"The fact is, Your Highness, that everyone is unsettled. You know, with the deepest respect, when the Tsar was on the throne, while times might sometimes have been hard, there was a sense of stability. Now that has gone. The people are waiting to see what else will go, what Prince Lvov will be able to do to improve their lives."

"Surely they can understand that he can do very little until the war ends?" Priscilla asked.

"Ah, well, Your Highness, there is another point. Many people feel the war is the Tsar's war. Or was the Tsar's war. They cannot understand why Prince Lvov does not make peace. They do not understand about treaties with the English and the French. All they want is for their loved ones to come home – or at least to know whether they are alive or dead. As do you, Your Highness."

"Yes, Tigran Ivanovich," Priscilla said. "As do I."

Priscilla found herself sharing more and more of the

running of the estate with her predecessor, who knew so much about it. Anna of course did not approve. But then, Anna did not approve of Sonia's being on Bolugayen at all, and Priscilla was sure that it was the old lady who was keeping little Anna's mind closed to the reappearance of her mother. Sonia was desperate to regain some intimacy with her daughter, to discover some spark of love or even affection. But Little Anna steadfastly refused to treat her mother as other than a not altogether welcome guest. In that regard Priscilla placed her faith in time and nature, but she was saddened that she and the grandmother who had been her friend and mentor throughout her adult life should have drifted apart. Anna spent more time with Sophie and Janine nowadays, often joined by Nathalie and Dagmar, but they did nothing except drink tea or champagne, or in Nathalie's case, vodka. But Sonia was interested in everything that was going on. Everything that she had had to abandon; in the changes in the estate in the more than five years she had been away. She accompanied Priscilla into the village, and was warmly greeted by Geller. "He delivered both my children," she told Priscilla.

"As he delivered mine," Priscilla replied.

When she came face to face with Rotislav Sonia looked taken aback. "Were you not with Prince Alexei?" she asked the valet, who was now Boscowski's assistant as there remained nothing for him to do about the house.

"I was, Your Highness. But I escaped."

"It is a long story," Priscilla said, anxious to be away. "It was Rotislav who brought me the news that Alexei is still alive." They walked their horses back to the house, their grooms at a discreet distance. "Did he always look at you like that?" Priscilla asked.

"No," Sonia said. "Has he always looked at you like that?"

"Only since he came back from the war. It is as if . . . I don't really know."

"He looks at you like that because he wants to have you," Sonia said.

"To . . ." Priscilla was too taken aback to speak.

"And I would say he would like to have me, too. And you have only his word for it that Alexei is alive. Or, was alive, at any rate."

"What could he possibly hope to gain by saying that if it wasn't true? If, as you say, he wants to, well . . ."

"As you say, I don't know. I only know that he has changed. Why do you keep him? There is surely no valeting to be done?"

Priscilla considered. "I suppose I just never thought of not keeping him. Anyway, he is not around the house, now. He assists Boscowski. But this is his home. I could not possibly throw him off Bolugayen. I mean . . ." She flushed. "I do not suppose he is the only man on Bolugayen who has ever dreamed of well . . ."

"Holding you naked in his arms? I imagine not. And presumably it is a compliment, to be desired by every man who looks at you. But Rotislav . . . I sometimes wonder if men like him ever *have* homes," Sonia said thoughtfully.

Priscilla preferred not to think about Rotislav. She was only relieved that as the spring went into the summer, Bolugayen remained unchanged. For a great deal was happening in the rest of Russia. They heard first of all of how the Bolsheviks had attempted a coup, which had been smashed; all their leaders had been forced to go into hiding, including men with well-known names like Lenin and Trotsky. "Were you not exiled with Lenin?" she asked Sonia.

"Yes," Sonia said. "I did not even know he was back in Russia."

"And this man Trotsky? Did you ever meet him?"

Sonia hesitated before replying. Then she said, "Yes, I met him. He is a fool. He will get himself hanged, or shot." She spoke with a quite unusual vehemence. But apparently Kerensky was not having it all his own way either, and later on that summer they heard how, having taken over the government from Prince Lvov, he had been forced to flee Petrograd for Moscow, partly because the German advance through the Baltic States was threatening the capital, but also partly because of the unrest there. "Those poor girls," Sonia said. "He promised to help them get out of Russia."

"You mean you can feel sorry for them?" Priscilla asked. "Did not their father send you into exile? And was it not he who encouraged Alexei to divorce you?"

"I suppose that's true. But those girls were so sweet. And so lovely." She sighed. "And now so helpless."

"Maybe they've already left the country," Priscilla said encouragingly. "Or found a haven like Bolugayen, which seems like an island of peace and plenty in a sea of human misery."

The current harvest was one of their best ever. Priscilla was sitting at her desk checking Boscowski's returns on a day in September when she was summoned by a huge explosion of noise in the hall. She ran out on to the gallery, and looked down at Patricia. "Aunt Pat!" she cried. "What on earth are you doing here?"

"Recovering from my journey," Patricia said. "Before anything else. Do you realise that it has taken me four months to get here?"

Looking past her at the boxes being unloaded from the van she appeared to have hired in Poltava, and the smaller bags being manhandled by Morgan and Giselle, Priscilla could well understand that, although her aunt looked as flawlessly chic as ever. She went down the stairs. "You do realise there is a war on?"

Patricia gave her niece-in-law – who was also her second cousin – a withering glance. "I was nearly sunk by a submarine, but the beastly thing missed, thank God. Aunt Anna!" Anna had also appeared on the gallery. "It is is good to see you looking so well." And, as Anna was clearly not coming down, she gathered her skirts and went up the stairs.

Priscilla looked at Morgan. "I think I should leave explanations to madam, Your Highness."

"Well, you are welcome, of course. Madame Xenia . . ."

"I shall see to it immediately, Your Highness." Xenia bustled off to marshal her housemaids and prepare guest apartments.

While there was a fresh explosion of sound from above. "Sonia? Sonia! Oh, my darling Sonia!" Sonia was in Patricia's arms.

"Well, really!" Sophie commented from further along the gallery.

"But how on earth did you get here?" Sonia asked, when they were all seated in the summer parlour drinking tea.

"I took one of Duncan's ships across the Atlantic. That was when we had that fuss with the submarine. Then I had to visit the family in Boston. That took time. Then I had to cross America. That was fun. Then I had to find a ship from San Francisco to Tokyo. That took a month in itself. Then I had to get to Vladivostock. That wasn't too difficult. But the people! They were so rude. I felt quite ashamed to be Russian. Then I had to find seats on the train for the three of us. That took a week. Then the journey itself took a fortnight; the beastly thing kept breaking down. But it was all rather fun."

The other women exchanged glances. None of them had been so fancy free for a long time. "But why have you done all this?" Anna enquired. "It may have been fun, but it sounds dreadfully inconvenient."

"I have come," Patricia announced, including them all in her gaze, "to take you out of here."

"Out of where?" Anna enquired.

"Now, Aunt Anna, you know what I mean. You cannot possibly stay on Bolugayen."

"Why not?"

293

"Well . . . there is a war on. Revolution is in the air. The Germans might invade the Donbass at any moment. Besides, Duncan insists that you come out."

"If he is that worried, why did he not come himself?"

"Because he is fighting this war," Patricia said, beginning to show signs of irritation. "Ships are the lifeblood of the Allies. And he has ships. So he has to control them. I have come all this way, and been nearly drowned in the process. You *must* come out."

"I can see no possible reason for leaving Bolugayen," Anna declared.

Patricia looked at her sister. "England is a ghastly place," Sophie declared.

"How do you know?" Patricia demanded. "You have never been there."

"We need to be here," Janine explained. "So that as soon as things return to normal, we may go home. I expect to hear from my husband at any moment."

"What makes you suppose things are ever going to return to normal?"

"Oh, don't be ridiculous," Sophie remarked. "Of course they will. They always do."

Patricia turned to Sonia. "Surely you will come with me?"

Sonia looked across the room to where little Anna was following the argument with enormous eyes. "I have to stay, Trishka," she murmured.

"For heaven's sake, Priscilla," Patricia said. "You are the Princess. Tell them they must come away. *You* must come away. Think of the children!"

"I am thinking of the children, and thus I cannot leave Bolugayen, Aunt Pat," Priscilla said. "I am in charge here, until Alexei comes back. Or Colin." She glanced at Sonia.

"But don't you see," Patricia almost begged. "If you stay, they'll stay. At least tell them to go."

"I cannot *tell* them to do anything," Priscilla said. "Least

294

of all to leave their home. But . . ." she looked around the faces. "I think Aunt Pat is probably right, and it would be best for you all to go, while you can."

"Stuff and nonsense," Anna said. "None of us is going anywhere. Our place is here, with the Princess. You should know that better than anyone, Patricia."

"It is madness," Patricia said guiding her horse up the slope of the hill to the west of Bolugayen. "Surely you can see that? The Socialists are in power. They are going to make life very difficult for everyone with any money. I'm not talking about just putting up taxes. They're going to take away our land, give it to the muzhiks . . . they may even take away our titles. In England, people like Lloyd George keep talking about doing away with the House of Lords. And he doesn't even call himself a Socialist!"

"Is that a reason for running away?" Sonia rode beside her friend. They were alone: as neither was actually a ruling member of the family the grooms had not instinctively followed them. Besides, they wanted to be alone. Although Patricia had now been on Bolugayen for over a week, they had had very little time to themselves.

"Okay," Patricia said. "Maybe Priscilla has a reason for staying. She has a stake here; it's her business to salvage what she can from the wreck. Maybe Aunt Anna has a reason; she always was mule-headed, although Duncan is going to be hopping mad if I go back without her. As for Sophie and Janine, well, to hell with them." She giggled. "But you, Sonia . . . there is nothing here for you. Come with me. Please."

"I can't, Trishka. You know that. Priscilla has made me welcome here. I never really expected that. And Anna . . . I was forced to abandon her once. I am never going to abandon her again."

"Wouldn't Priscilla let you take her out?"

"No. Anna is also Alexei's daughter. And Priscilla

295

expects Alexei to come home, one day. And when he does . . ."

"Yes. When he does. Where do you think you will be then?"

"I shall be wherever Priscilla chooses."

Patricia drew rein. "You're really fond of her, aren't you. I find that incredible. When you think what she did to you, I don't see how you cannot hate her."

"She did nothing to me," Sonia said. "It was all done before Alexei even met her. And now . . . yes, I like her. But I also feel sorry for her. She's going through hell."

"What does she know about hell? When you think what you and I have experienced together, while she has only ever lived on the fat of the land . . ."

"There was the *Titanic*," Sonia protested.

"Oh, boo. Can you really relate a shipwreck to being a prisoner of the Okhrana? To trying to exist in Siberia?"

"All things are relative," Sonia argued. "I think she has a lot more guts than is immediately apparent. I also think things are going to get worse before they get better, and that she is going to need all the help she can get. Anyway, there's Colin. I don't believe he's dead. I know he's going to come home, one day. I mean to be here when he does. Or some place he can find me, anyway."

"If he wants to. Don't you realise that his mind has also been poisoned against you?"

"I am prepared to risk that."

"Well, of course what you do is up to you. But I am going to have to leave and go back, before winter sets in. I don't want to, but Duncan will be raising the roof if I don't. So . . . what's that noise?"

"People," Sonia said, and urged her horse to the top of the slope to look down into the valley behind. This was on the northern side of the estate, and the road into Poltava was some miles behind them. They looked at some fifty men, coming towards them across the black earth of the bare fields. Sonia frowned. The

296

men wore uniforms, and were armed with rifles and bayonets.

Patricia joined her. "Good lord!" she commented. "Those aren't Germans, are they?"

"They're Russians," Sonia said. "I think we should go home."

"But we must find out what they are doing on our property," Patricia insisted. "They could be retreating before the Germans."

"If the Germans have conquered the Ukraine and are invading the Donbass, we would surely have heard," Sonia said. "We would have heard the sound of gunfire, for a start. Those men are deserters. Come on, Trishka, let's get out of here."

"Oh, boo. Men don't desert in groups of fifty. I am going to find out where they're from, and where they are going." She kicked her horse and cantered down the slope. Sonia bit her lip. Patricia's innate aristocracy was surfacing. And however much she had suffered as a girl, she had never seen a mob at work. Or the results of its work. Sonia's instincts warned her that the men were dangerous. And they were armed. The soldiers were only a few hundred yards away now, and she could even make out their faces. As they could clearly discern that they were looking at two extremely attractive and well-dressed women. Patricia, indeed, with her auburn hair flowing out from beneath her silk hat and her blue scarf seeming to melt with the red, made a compelling picture. While she, in her white habit and her black hair loose beneath her hat . . . she should go down with her. Reluctantly she walked her horse down the slope. The men had now completely surrounded Patricia. Some were shouting and gesticulating, others were just staring at the Countess. And some were staring at her as well, Sonia realised. "No, no," Patricia was shouting to make herself heard. "This is very wrong of you. What are you, cowards, or Russian *men*?" She looked at Sonia. "You're right, they are deserters. They were supposed to entrain for the front in Poltava, and they ran away instead."

"Why should we be killed, fighting for England and France?" one of the men demanded. "It was the Tsar fighting Germany. Now the Tsar has gone. We have no quarrel with the Germans."

"I think you are disgusting," Patricia told them, while Sonia held her reins very tightly. Trishka, as always, was living entirely in a dream world. "Now, I command you, return to Poltava at once."

"We were told we'd find shelter here," someone said.

"Well, I can't imagine whu told you that," Patricia said. "Now, off with you. Don't do that, you wretched creature!" A man had put his hand on her boot.

"Trishka!" Sonia called. "Let's go home!" Patricia had freed her leg from the man's grasp, and now she kicked him away and wheeled her horse. But as she did so another man reached up and grasped her scarf. Patricia did not utter a sound; the sudden closing of the material on her neck prevented that. But she was plucked out of the saddle, seemed to hover in the air for a second while her hat flew away, and then crashed into the midst of the men. "Trishka!" Sonia screamed, instinctively kicking her horse forward, and then drawing rein again as Patricia was suddenly presented to her, having for a moment struggled upright. But her clothes were already half ripped from her back, and men were clawing at her again.

"Sonia!" she shrieked. "Get away. Tell the . . ." her voice faded into a choking gasp as she was pulled down again into their midst. Sonia saw some of the men looking at her. She had two choices. She could ride into that mob and be torn to pieces beside her friend, or she could warn the others. And die with *them*, when the time came. Certainly she could not help Trishka now. She wheeled her horse and whipped it up the slope.

Priscilla loved the peace of Bolugayen immediately before

luncheon. It was even more peaceful after the meal, when the entire estate seemed to sink into somnolence, but by then one's senses were dulled by vodka and champagne. Just before lunch one was fully aware of the pleasures that lay immediately ahead. One could smell the aromas arising from the kitchens, and knew that it was time to gather in one of the reception rooms to have an aperitif. She had just left the nursery, where Alexei, who was now two and a half years old, was being dressed by Constantina for lunch. Priscilla had insisted that Alexei attend the midday meal from his second birthday, seated in his high chair and interrupting the flow of conversation by banging his spoon. This was not usual in the homes of the Russian aristocracy, where children were required to be seen, but not more than twice a day, and *never* heard, and she knew that Grandma thoroughly disapproved. But it was how children were brought up in Boston, and Grandma had given up trying to cross the Princess Bolugayevska in anything. Now she opened the door of the schoolroom, where Anna was washing her hands and face preparatory to coming down, watched by Mademoiselle Friquet. Mademoiselle curtsied at the entrance of her employer. "What did you learn today?" Priscilla asked her stepdaughter.

"About how the French chopped off the head of their king," little Anna replied. "Is Monsieur Kerensky going to chop of the head of the Tsar?"

"Certainly not," Priscilla said, and looked at Mademoiselle Friquet.

"I am sorry, Your 'ighness, but it is 'istory," Mademoiselle Friquet said.

"I suppose it is. But only the French and the English cut off the heads of their kings," she told Anna. "It is not a Russian habit." She frowned. "What is that noise?"

"It is a gunshot, Your 'ighness. Several gunshots."

"Oh, really." Priscilla found herself becoming annoyed. She had always forbidden shooting close to the house, and certainly just before lunch. "I will speak with Boscowski."

She went to the door, and Mademoiselle Friquet said, "Those were rifle shots, Your 'ighness. Not shotguns."

Priscilla looked over her shoulder, frowning, then went on to the gallery, just as Anna herself appeared from another room.

"Someone is shooting," the old lady announced.

"Yes," Priscilla said. "I must . . ."

"Your Highness!" Gleb was standing in the hall beneath them. "Your Highness!"

Priscilla had never heard him use such a tone before. She gathered her skirts and ran down the stairs, as Gleb opened the front door. Now she could hear the sound of hooves, but as she went to the door, they stopped, abruptly. She stood beside Gleb and looked out at the drive, where a horse had just collapsed, pouring blood. Sonia, who had been riding it, had stepped out of the saddle as the animal had fallen, and was now running towards them. She had lost her hat, but her clothes did not look disturbed; it was the expression on her face and the way she was shouting incoherently that was alarming. Priscilla went to meet her. "Sonia! What's the matter? Where's Aunt Pat?"

Sonia stumbled, tripped, and landed on her hands and knees at Priscilla's feet. "Dead!" she gasped. "Dead. Oh, my God, she's dead!"

Priscilla couldn't believe her ears, looked at the dying horse and up the hill. But the road was empty, although guns were still being fired on the far side, and she thought she could hear men shouting. "Those shots . . .?"

"They were firing at me. But they hit the horse. But Patricia . . . oh, my God!"

"Lock the doors . . . Fetch brandy," Priscilla told Gleb, and helped Sonia towards the steps. On which Sophie and Janine had appeared, together with Madame Xenia.

"What on earth is going on?" Sophie demanded.

"Something's happened to Aunt Pat," Priscilla said. "You," she shouted at one of the grooms who had come

300

round the side of the house from the stables. "Go down to the village and tell Monsieur Boscowski I wish to see him, now."

"You don't understand." They had reached the porch and Sonia sank into one of the wicker armchairs. "Patricia is dead. She's been killed by a mob. They tore her to pieces."

The women stared at her for several seconds, then Sophie threw back her head an uttered a long, wailing screech, the like of which Priscilla had never heard before. They might not have cared very much for each other, but Patricia had been Sophie's baby sister. The groom had stopped at the noise. "Fetch Boscowski," Priscilla shouted again. "Sonia: inside!"

Sonia gave her a startled look, and then pushed herself up and stumbled into the house. By now every servant had appeared in the hall, summoned by Sophie's scream. And on the gallery there were Mademoiselle Friquet and Grishka, Madame Xenia and little Anna . . . and Anna herself, all staring down at them. Now Anna slowly descended the stairs. "What do you say happened?" she demanded.

"Grandma . . ." Priscilla began, giving the servants an anxious glance.

"Tell me!" Anna's voice was like a sliver of ice.

Gleb had brought a goblet of brandy. Sonia drank deeply, and drew a long breath. "Men," she said. "Soldiers. Deserters. In the next valley."

"How many men?"

"A lot. Fifty, at least. Patricia . . . she rode down to ask them what they were doing, and they pulled her from her saddle, and . . ." She stared at her erstwhile aunt-in-law.

"You saw this happen?" Sonia's head moved up and down. Anna walked past her on to the porch. "Where are these men?" she demanded. "Did they not follow you?"

"I think they are following me. They are on foot."

Anna looked up at where the road topped the hill,

and watched it fill with men. "They have guns," she remarked.

"They are soldiers," Sonia said again. Her knees gave way and she sat down.

"I have sent for Boscowski," Priscilla said.

Anna's face hardened, and she turned to the servants. "Which of you is the best horseman?"

"Oleg the bootboy, Your Excellency," Gleb said.

"Where is he?"

"I am here, Your Excellency." Oleg stepped forward. He was still in his teens, and eager to please his mistresses.

"Choose a horse from the stable," Anna commanded. "And ride into Poltava. Go to the Governor and tell him what is happening. Tell him we need help, immediately." Oleg hesitated, looking first of all at Priscilla, and then at Gleb. From both he received a quick nod. He ran from the room. "Gleb," Anna said. "Close and lock those doors. She summoned the four footmen. "Close and bar all the downstairs windows. Make sure the cellar doors are bolted." She went towards the gun room. "Come with me, Priscilla."

"You cannot mean to fight them," Janine protested.

"I do not mean to allow them into this house," Anna told her.

"But, fifty men, armed with rifles . . ." Janine looked from left to right. "We are seven women."

"There are the servants," Anna pointed out. "And your father, Sophie, once defended this house against two hundred Cossacks, with four men."

"Anyway," Priscilla said, as reassuringly as she could, "Boscowski will be here in a little while, with the men from the village. Until then . . ." She went into the study, took the keys from the drawer, and unlocked the gun cabinet. There were four rifles, two shotguns, and four revolvers, and several boxes of ammunition.

"They are going to the village, Your Highness," Gleb said from the porch.

"Upstairs," Anna said, taking one of the rifles and using it as a crutch to get up the stairs the more quickly.

"Oh, Your 'ighness," Mademoiselle Friquet said. "What am I to do?"

Priscilla had armed herself with both a rifle and a revolver, and was following her grandmother. "Take Anna up to her bedroom, and stay there with her. Grishka, you are responsible for Count Alexei." Grishka ran for the nursery. Priscilla found Sonia at her elbow, also carrying a rifle and a revolver. "Have you ever shot at a man?"

"No," Sonia said.

"Neither have I."

"But I am going to do so now," Sonia said, "because of what they did to Patricia."

Priscilla swallowed. "Did they . . .?"

"I imagine so," Sonia said.

They stood at the French window on to the upper porch, behind Anna. They could see out through the glass but it was difficult for anyone on the drive to see in. And the soldiers were not on the drive, anyway. They were trooping down the road to the village, waving their weapons and occasionally firing them into the air. "Boscowski will deal with them," Priscilla asserted. "And Father Valentin."

"We must hope so." Anna squinted into the noonday sunlight. "What is that they are carrying?"

Sonia stared at the men. "That is Patricia," she muttered.

303

Chapter 12

Red and White

Priscilla swallowed; she felt physically sick. "Is she alive?" she whispered.

"I hope not," Anna said, and turned from the window to survey the two women. "You are both Princesses of Bolugayen, You'll show no fear."

Priscilla licked her lips; she was trembling from head to foot. "No, Grandma."

"Should I have stayed with her?" Sonia asked.

Anna's lips twisted. "So you could have died holding hands? They would not have allowed you that privilege. Priscilla, you must take command. I will tell you what to do, but the orders must be yours." Priscilla nodded. "Then, as soon as the house is secure," Anna said, "have a footman placed up here to warn us the moment anyone approaches. I am going to sit down." She turned, and they gazed at Morgan and Giselle.

"Morgan!" Priscilla shouted in sheer relief; she had forgotten about the Englishman. "Where have you been?"

Morgan looked embarrassed, as did the maid. "We were in the orchard, Your Highness. Is it true . . ."

"Yes," Priscilla said.

Morgan swallowed. He had served Patricia and Duncan for seventeen years, ever since she had so mysteriously turned up in London, a fugitive from the Okhrana. He had even adventured in Russia with her, after her imperial pardon. They had been friends rather than mistress and servant. "Those bastards," he said. "With respect, Your Highness. If I could have them at the end of a gun . . ."

"You will have that privilege, Morgan. Now we have to defend ourselves. Aunt Pat told me you were in the British Army."

"A long time ago, Your Highness."

"But you defended Rorke's Drift against the Zulus. Thousands of Zulus."

"There were over a hundred of us, Your Highness. Welsh fusiliers."

"Well, there are only fifty of them," Priscilla told him. "I put you in command."

Morgan instinctively stood to attention. "My orders, Your Highness?" Priscilla looked at her grandmother.

"If we are attacked," Anna said, "your orders are to defend this house to the death, Morgan. To the very last man, Morgan." She gave a grim smile. "Or in this case, most likely, the very last woman. There can be no negotiating with those men. They raped and murdered your mistress. Do you understand me?"

"To the very last bullet, Your Excellency," Morgan said.

Morgan's appearance galvanised the defence. He surveyed the staff – he had come to know them all fairly well over the preceding week – and decided who should have which weapons. The four rifles were issued to the footmen; Gleb, whose eyesight and muscle control were going, received a shotgun, and Morgan kept a shotgun for himself. Anna insisted upon one of the revolvers and he issued them also to Priscilla and Sonia. Sophie and Janine had locked themselves in their apartment, as had Nathalie in hers, but Dagmar was excitedly keen on taking part in the defence. However, Morgan gave the last revolver to Grishka, who knew how to use it. She

305

was put in the nursery, with Mademoiselle Friquet and Giselle, and told to stay with the two children, although little Anna complained loudly about not being allowed to see the 'fun'. Constantina had disappeared, and it had to be assumed that she had run off.

The remaining maidservants were told to stay in the cellars, save for Madame Xenia and two of her least excitable women, who would back up the men and act as nurses if any of them was hit. Boris the cook was told to continue preparing lunch, as it was now well into the afternoon. He had a large accumulation of knives of all sizes as well as an axe, so he should be able to defend himself, if necessary, at least at close quarters. Morgan then explained his plan to the two Princesses and the Countess. "Two footmen and Gleb at the front, two at the back. I will be in reserve. If you, Your Highnesses, would attend to the upper windows. I do not wish you to expose yourself to any shots, but just to take care of anyone who might attempt to climb up."

Sonia and Priscilla nodded.

"I'll help you," Dagmar volunteered.

Morgan looked at Anna. "I will be the upstairs reserve," Anna said.

Morgan licked his lips. "You understand, Your Highnesses, Your Excellency, that should they break in, and cannot be immediately expelled again . . ."

"We know what to do," Anna said. "They will not have the children."

Priscilla forced a smile. "It is all probably a storm in a teacup. Mr Boscowski and Father Valentin will have sorted them out by now. I think we should have lunch."

But no one was the least hungry, although Boris had as always produced a delicious meal. They kept wandering to the windows to look out at the drive and beyond. They could not see the village, apart from the church spire. Priscilla and Morgan opened the front door to listen.

There was certainly a lot of noise from down there, but it was difficult to make out anything positive. What was disturbing was that the footman Priscilla had sent down earlier had not returned. "Do you think we should send another?" Priscilla asked Morgan.

"No, Your Highness. We cannot dissipate our strength. We must wait here."

"I know you're right. I suppose the troops from Poltava are already on their way."

Morgan did not reply to that, and Priscilla went up to her apartment, where she was joined a few minutes later by Sonia. "Do you blame me for not staying with Patricia?" Sonia asked.

"Of course I do not. And you must not blame yourself."

"She was so confident," Sonia muttered, sitting down. "She was always so confident. She had every reason to be confident. Until now. I feel as if the end of the world has come."

Priscilla squeezed her hand. "I know. I felt the same way about the *Titanic*. But . . . the world does go on."

Sonia glanced at her. "Aren't you afraid?"

Priscilla gave a crooked smile. "I'm terrified. But, as Grandma said, I'm the Princess Bolugayevska. Sorry, so are you. Or are you regretting having come back here?"

When I could be snug in Trotsky's arms, Sonia thought, listening to him tell me how many people he had murdered that day. The world might not be coming to an end, but it was certainly doing its best to stand on its head. "Do you really mean to kill your son before you will let him be taken by those men?" she asked.

"My God!" Priscilla said. "What else can I do?"

"And then no doubt you will kill yourself."

"How can you ask those questions? When you think what happened to Aunt Pat . . ."

"Patricia was murdered because she resisted them. She

307

had been raped before, many years ago, and survived. As was I. I am still alive."

"By not resisting? Have you no sense of honour?"

Sonia sat down. "Oh, yes, I had a sense of honour. Once. But is your honour of any value when you are dead? What does your honour stand for? Your position as the Princess Bolugayevska? That is over, Priscilla. This revolution has just begun. There are going to be no more princes and princesses when it ends."

"Oh, you . . . you are hateful," Priscilla shouted. "Go away. Leave me. If you do not wish to fight those men, give your gun to someone who will."

Sonia got up and went to the door. "I will fight them," she said. "But I will not kill my daughter. And neither will you, Your Highness, because if you try and I am alive, I will kill you first."

Priscilla's mouth was open. "You would rather have her raped, is that it?"

"Yes," Sonia said. "If it comes to that. I would rather have her raped, and beaten and even tortured, so long as there is a chance that she may survive, and live."

She closed the door behind herself, and Priscilla threw herself across the bed. She expected to weep, but she had never wept in her life. Not even when she had realised that Mom was dead. But to contemplate the possible future . . . it could not be going to happen. Alexei had described Bolugayen as the most secure place on earth, and she had believed him. Nor had she had the least reason to disbelieve him, until now. Oh, Alexei, she thought; if only you could be here. But with every second that passed, the troops from Poltava were coming closer. Surely.

She prowled the house, restlessly, spoke with each of the servants. They looked terrified, but for the moment, at least, steadfast. "We shall not fail Your Highness," Gleb promised.

Priscilla felt tears spring to her eyes. "I know you will not, Gleb," she said.

She went to the nursery, where Alexei was playing with his building blocks, apparently unaware of the crisis, while Mademoiselle Friquet and Giselle and Grishka kept going to the windows to look out; but the nursery was at the back of the house, and they merely looked down on the orchard and beyond, the stables. "Are we going to kill all of those men who assaulted Aunt Patricia?" Anna asked.

"Someone is," Priscilla promised her, and looked over the girl's head at Giselle's stricken expression. Giselle had probably known Patricia better than anyone.

She went out to the upstairs porch. Morgan was on the balcony, slapping his hands together. The footman opened the door for Priscilla, and she joined the valet. "What on earth are they doing?"

"Listen, Your Highness."

Priscilla listened, to the sound of music and laughter and voices, drifting up the slight slope from the village. "They sound . . . as if they were celebrating something. Do you think the war is over?"

"For them, certainly. But that is not what they are celebrating."

Priscilla glanced at him. "You cannot mean they are welcoming those scoundrels?"

"They are not resisting them, Your Highness."

"But . . . Boscowski . . ."

"Has either joined them or is . . . under restraint, Your Highness."

"And Dr Geller? And Father Valentin? Rotislav . . .?"

"I do not trust Rotislav, Your Highness."

"Then we must leave," Priscilla said. "All of us. We must ride for Poltava. We'll probably meet the troops on the way."

"If they are coming, Your Highness."

"What do you mean? Of course they are coming."

Morgan ignored her claim. "In any event, I imagine the house is being watched, even if we cannot see the watchers. If they were to catch us in the open we would not stand a chance. Nor could we possibly take the old Countess in such a flight. I think we must stay here, and defend the house. And pray that those troops *are* coming."

Priscilla drew a deep, slow breath. "Do we have a chance, of defending the house, Morgan?"

Morgan sighed. "It is the best chance we have, Your Highness."

Priscilla went back inside. We are going to die, she thought. I am going to die. And so is Alexei and Anna. None of them had really lived yet. And before they died – but that at least could surely be avoided, no matter what might be done to their bodies. Then why *not* make a run for it. After dark! Some of them would get through, surely. But not Grandmama, as Morgan had said. God, what a decision to have to make! "Your Highness." Morgan had opened the door. "Someone is coming."

Priscilla nearly tripped as she ran on to the balcony. Beneath her, on the drive, was Rotislav. Behind him, beyond the gates, was a mass of people. Her people. But she no longer believed that. "Good-afternoon, Your Highness," Rotislav said.

"What do you want?" Priscilla demanded. "Where is Monsieur Boscowski? I sent for him."

"Boscowski is no longer estate manager, Your Highness. He has been relieved of his duties, by the soviet."

"The what?"

"The soviet, Your Highness. The village council. We have formed one, to control our affairs. I have been elected its president."

"I see. But this is still my land, and those people are still my tenants, and . . ."

"No, no, Your Highness," Rotislav said. "That is what I have come to tell you. The soviet has voted that there shall be no more Prince or Princess of Bolugayen. All this land is now theirs, to be divided according to the needs of

310

each family. Do not fear. You will be alloted two acres for your own use, but you must work it yourself. If you do not, it will revert to the soviet."

"The man must be mad," Anna remarked. Priscilla had not heard her grandmother approach; Anna had a rubber ferule on the end of her stick. "Are you a good shot, Morgan?"

"With a rifle, Your Excellency."

"Then take this fellow's rifle . . ." Anna nodded at the footman, "and shoot that rascal down."

Morgan looked at Priscilla. "Wait," she said, and stood at the balustrade. "You know that is an absurdity, Rotislav," she said. "I am very disappointed that my people, and you in particular, should have listened to such claptrap."

"Claptrap, is it, Your Highness? Am I to understand that you do not wish the land? Very well," he hurried on before Priscilla could speak. "You have one hour to pack your belongings and evacuate the house. You and all your family."

"And what happens if we come out?"

"Why, you may go where you choose, Your Highness. You will have to walk, but . . . it is not so far to Poltava."

"If we leave the house we are all dead," Anna declared.

"I think the Countess is right, Your Highness," Morgan said.

"I still say, shoot him now," Anna said.

Priscilla looked past her at Sonia, standing silently in the hall. But Sonia had already given her advice. She turned back to the balustrade. "You are being very foolish, Rotislav. Do you not realise I have sent to the Governor in Poltava, telling him that there are deserters on my property? His men are already on their way here."

Rotislav waved his arm. Instantly some men advanced through the gates. Two of them held poles. On one of them was stuck Oleg's head. From the other were suspended his genitals. Priscilla gasped, and stepped backwards. Morgan had to catch her arm before she fell. "There will be no help from Poltava, Your Highness," Rotislav said. "And if you resist us . . ." he waved his arm again, and some more men came forward. These carried a large wooden cross, on which was suspended Patricia's naked body, by nails through each wrist, each ankle, her throat, her chest and her groin.

"Oh, my God!" Priscilla screamed, and fell to her knees.

"There is no blood. She was dead when they did that to her," Anna said. "Shoot him down!" Her voice was like a whiplash. Morgan snatched the rifle from the footman's hands, but Rotislav had seen the movement and hurled himself into the bushes behind the drive. Morgan fired twice, and immediately the men by the gate returned fire. The bullets smashed into the stonework and a window shattered. Morgan seized Priscilla's arm again and dragged her back into the house; the door was slammed shut and the shutter closed. "Did you hit him?" Anna demanded.

"I don't know, Your Excellency."

"Well, get downstairs. You too," she told the footman. Morgan led the footman down the stairs. The entire house was reverberating to the sound of the shooting, as those already in position returned fire. "Tell them only to shoot at what they can see!" Anna bawled. "Get up, girl! You are the Princess Bolugayevska."

Sonia helped Priscilla up. "Did you see?" Priscilla whispered. "Oh, God, I'm going to be sick."

"Then be sick," Sonia said. "And then come back here, and fight." Priscilla stumbled along the corridor.

"She will be all right," Anna said. "She is the Princess Bolugayevska. But you . . . you have always been the Princess Bolugayevska."

"Do you hate me?" Sonia asked.

"I have never hated you. Do you hate *me*?"

312

Sonia shrugged. "You are a hateful woman. But now . . . we have all to die like Bolugayevskas."

Priscilla found she could not vomit, after all. But she did not suppose she would ever forget the sight of Patricia nailed to that cross . . . and she was not going to be allowed to. When she peered from her apartment window, she saw that the soldiers had planted the cross in the earth of the drive, so that every defender had to stare at Patricia every time they looked out. The thought that in another hour her naked body might be nailed to a cross . . . would *she* be dead when they did that to her?

She slammed the shutters, even as she was spotted and bullets thudded into the wood. From downstairs there came the sound of shots as the defenders replied, and now shots came from the rear as well; they were surrounded. She went to the nursery, where the shutters had been closed. Little Alexei was very upset, and Mademoiselle Friquet was holding him in her arms, rocking to and fro, while Giselle had Anna on her knees. Grishka waited by the window, peering through the half-closed shutters, the revolver in her hand. "Have we a chance, Your Highness?" she asked.

"There is always a chance," Priscilla said. Now that she knew they were all going to die, she had regained her courage. She went back on to the gallery. Sonia remained by the porch window, waiting, while the house reverberated to sound and the smell of cordite drifted upwards.

"Maybe they'll shoot themselves out of ammunition," she said.

Priscilla went into Anna's sitting room, where as everywhere, the shutters were closed. Anna sat in her rocking chair, moving to and fro, a bottle of champagne in an ice bucket on the table beside her, a glass in her hand. "Tell them only to shoot at what they can see," she said again. "We must not waste bullets."

313

"Aren't you afraid?" Priscilla asked.

Anna snorted, and drank some champagne. "What have I got to be afraid of, child? I am afraid for *you*."

"Sonia says we should not kill the children. Or ourselves."

Anna turned her head to look at her. "Only you can make that decision, but . . . if you do not, you may have to experience a great deal."

Priscilla attempted a smile. "A fate worse than death."

"There is no fate worse than death," Anna told her. "But death can sometimes take too long to come. It would be a great boon if you could put a stop to that terrible racket."

Priscilla had been so preoccupied with the shooting that she had hardly been aware of the additional noise. Now she realised that there was a continual high-pitched screaming coming from close at hand. She went to the guest apartment occupied by Sophie and Janine, and found her sister-in-law lying on her back on her bed, screaming again and again. "I can do nothing with her," Janine said.

"Well, then, gag her," Priscilla said. "She is upsetting Grandma. Where is Dagmar?"

"I have no idea."

Priscilla went further along the gallery to the other guest apartment, knocked, and went in, paused in amazament. Nathalie sat in front of her dressing table, wearing only an undressing robe, and carefully painting her face with make-up. She saw Priscilla in the mirror and smiled. "One must look one's best when one is about to be torn to pieces, my dear," she explained. "That's what they did to your great-aunt, you know. The grandparents of those same people out there. They tore her to pieces. Isn't that something to look forward to?"

Priscilla slammed the door behind her and leaned against the panels, panting. She was surrounded by madwomen. Yet Nathalie had been speaking the truth; she

314

had forgotten the fate of Great-Aunt Dagmar. But Great-Aunt Dagmar had been hated by everyone. She was loved by everyone. Including Rotislav. My God, she thought: Rotislav. Dreaming of me! And now . . . She heard a shout, and the drumming of hooves. She ran back into her apartment to look out at the stables, and saw Dagmar galloping through the orchard, thick yellow hair streaming in the wind. "Shall I go after her, Your Highness?" called the footman on the back door.

"No," Priscilla said. A rat, deserting the sinking ship, and her own mother. But maybe Dagmar could reach Poltava, where Oleg had failed.

"Priscilla!" Sonia called. Priscilla hurried along the gallery. The firing had died down, and Sonia had opened the shutters far enough to peep through. "I think they are going to attack."

Priscilla peeped through as well. There were two bodies sprawled on the drive, a testimony to the good shooting of the defenders. Patricia's body still hung from its cross. And there was definitely movement in the shrubbery. Priscilla went down the stairs. "Is anyone hit?"

"Not yet, Your Highness," Morgan said.

"They seem to be advancing." He nodded, his face set in grim lines. "Can you hold them?"

"We can try, Your Highness."

Priscilla went back up the stairs to be with Sonia. "If we stop them now," she said, "do you think they will go away?"

"No," Sonia said. "Here they come."

With shrieks of "Oorrah!" a mass of men rose from the hedges and ran at the house. Priscilla's stomach lurched as she realised there had to be more than fifty of them, and that not only were there more shouts coming from the back of the house, but that a fair proportion of the attackers were women. Her people had entirely turned against her. Would they have turned against Alexei, had he been here?

315

Sonia had pulled the doors wide open, and was on the porch, firing her revolver into the people beneath her, heedless of the occasional shot being sent in her direction; she was shouting herself, with a kind of maniacal glee. Priscilla reckoned that for years her predecessor must have felt like firing a revolver into a mob. But she could do no less herself, and emptied her own weapon. Then the two women ran back into the hall where a box of bullets waited on one of the tables. Sonia reloaded quickly and expertly. Priscilla had never loaded a revolver before, and her hands were shaking; for every bullet she crammed into a chamber she dropped two on to the floor.

She heard Anna shouting something, but ignored her as she closed the chamber. "They are in," Sonia said.

Priscilla ran to the head of the stairs, looked down into the hall, where the doors had been opened and the doorway was filled with shrieking men and women; she saw Morgan fall to his knees and then on to his face. One of the footmen lay on his back, in a pool of blood. As she watched the other threw down his rifle and raised his hands. Of Gleb there was no sign. But who had opened the doors?

Priscilla gasped for breath as she saw the surrendered footman engulfed by angry bodies, heard him scream as he was thrown to the floor and trampled on. She watched Madame Xenia run for the stairs, to be seized by her hair and dragged back into the grasp of the eager men. She heard screams from the kitchens as the maidservants were discovered. She looked at Sonia, who had retreated along the hall to the nursery. Then the mob saw her, and uttered another roar and charged at the steps. Priscilla recognised Viktor Nordenski at their head, turned and ran, following Sonia to the nursery, encountered Mademoiselle Friquet and Giselle, shaking with fear and confusion. "Where are the children?" Priscilla shouted.

"In there, Your Highness," Giselle said. "She made us leave!"

316

Priscilla ran at the door, found it locked. She glared at it in frustration. It should be possible to shoot out the lock. But she did not know how to begin to do that. The mob reached the gallery. Giselle screamed. Priscilla looked back at the two women, and saw them being engulfed as the footmen had been. She gasped in terror, and ran further along the gallery to Anna's apartment. Anna had turned her rocking chair to face the door, and she brought up her revolver as it swung in; she still held a glass of champagne in her left hand. "Grandma!" Priscilla gasped, tripping and falling to her knees.

"Use it!" Anna snapped, and Priscilla realised she was still holding her revolver. She turned, on her knees, as the doors were thrown wide and men surged inside. Anna brought up her gun and fired into them and again. Blood flew and then she too was engulfed, the rocking chair flying into splinters beneath the weight of bodies trying to reach her. Priscilla rose to her feet and backed against the wall. Use it, Grandma had said. On herself? But little Alexei still lived. With Sonia. And Sonia had said, survive. No matter what, survive.

She dropped the revolver on the floor, and was surrounded by people, enveloped in breaths which were laden mainly with vodka. Her arms were seized and she was pulled forward into their midst to face Nordenski while fingers dug into her hair and her clothes. She shut her eyes and heard the material ripping even as she thought she was going to choke from lack of breath as other fingers clawed into her hair, pulling her head backwards. She felt pain in her thighs and her belly, her back and her breasts, where hands were clutching. She was lifted from the floor and then thrown down again, and was again breathless. She opened her eyes again and gazed at Nordenski, kneeling between her legs, unbuckling his pants, and realised that she was naked save for her stockings and boots and the wisps of material still hanging from her shoulders. She threw back her head and screamed, and heard a voice

317

shouting. Slowly the noise subsided, and Priscilla opened her eyes. Was she miraculously to be saved? But she knew she wasn't going to be that fortunate. "This is my prize," Rotislav said. "My reward, for leading you. Did I not say this?"

The men, and woman, growled at him, but they released Priscilla. Even Nordenski, still holding her thighs apart, hesitated. Rotislav grasped her wrist and pulled her to her feet. "Please," she whispered, hating herself for begging.

"Where are the children?" he asked.

"I don't know."

He hit her in the stomach, and she fell to her knees, retching and gasping for breath, while the men and women laughed. Rotislav pulled her up again. "Shall I hit you again?"

Priscilla panted. "They are in the nursery. With Sonia. Please don't harm them. Please."

"Little runts," Rotislav said. "Leave them there for the time being. Find the other women."

"For sport," shouted the men, and ran through the door.

"Please," Priscilla said. Rotislav pulled her across the room towards the bedroom. She tripped and looked down at her grandmother. But Anna was dead, her clothes ripped and slashed, a knife thrust into her chest. That long, turbulent, often shocking but also often glorious, life, had ended, in the most terrible circumstances. Now it was indeed up to her. Rotislav threw her across the bed. She landed on her face, lay there, and felt his hands on her buttocks. She twisted away from him and rolled on her back, drawing up her knees. Everyone had always said she was the spitting image of Grandma as a girl. Now she had to to think like Grandma, and act like her too, as well as resemble her. Or die like her.

Rotislav seized her ankles and pulled her down the bed; with his other hand he was releasing his belt. All the while he stared at her; never had she seen such

318

desire in anyone's eyes. "Listen," she said. "I know you want me."

"I am going to have you."

"I know. But would you not prefer it if I was yours?" His pants had dropped about his ankles, and he kicked them off. Priscilla kept her eyes on his face. The only naked adult male she had ever seen before was her husband. "I will be good to you," she said. "I swear it. I will be your woman in all things. I will do anything you command, without question. Only spare my children." Rotislav half turned his head; the house was a huge thunder of demonic sound, varying from screams of terror and outrage to bellows of obscene laughter. "I swear it," Priscilla said again.

He grinned at her. "Then be my woman," he said.

He had promised nothing. But she dared not press her point. She spread her legs and closed her eyes. "I like my women to caress me," he said. "Hold me. Kiss me." He knelt above her as she forced herself to obey, having to open her eyes to do so. Nothing in her relations with Alexei had prepared her for this; Alexei had only ever wanted to kiss *her*. "God, but you are beautiful," Rotislav muttered, driving her hands into her hair, letting it spill through his fingers as if it were indeed gold. Will it still be gold when this is finished? Priscilla wondered. Or will it have turned white. "Over," he said, holding her thighs.

She obeyed, grateful not to have to look at him, feeling his fingers groping at her body as he made room for himself. She chewed the sheet, which so terribly still carried Grandma's scent, to prevent herself from crying out, and felt him inside her, surging back and forth. She was being savaged by a wild animal. But he was the only one of the wild animals to whom she could appeal, who offered any hope of survival. He lay on her and panted, and now that he was finished she could listen to the noises too. There was so much that was beautiful in

319

this house, just waiting to be savaged. "The children," she whispered.

"Let's see what has happened to them." He pushed himself off her. "Up."

Priscilla pushed herself up in turn, sat on her heels. Alexei had always insisted on a bath after sex. But she did not suppose that idea had ever occurred to Rotislav. "I must get some clothes," she said.

He grinned. "I like you the way you are. Then those bastards can see what they're missing. Come."

Priscilla got out of the bed, pushed hair from her face. At the bedroom door she checked, stomach rolling. "Grandma . . ."

"She's past caring. They'll see to her." Priscilla stepped over the body, followed him on to the gallery. Her magnificent house was being torn apart. Men and women, and children, were pulling down the drapes, throwing the priceless paintings and ikons on to the floor and down from the gallery; she listened to the sound of shattering glass and knew her crystal was being systematically destroyed. And in the midst of the destruction there was death. She looked down at the footmen and Morgan, and Madame Xenia; all had been stripped naked, and all had been muti-lated. In front of her in the gallery, a naked Giselle lay on her face in a pool of blood. As she passed a reception room she heard Mademoiselle Friquet begging for mercy. And beyond them lay Nathalie, grotesque in death; like Giselle her body had been stripped and her breasts cut off – but her face was flawlessly made up. The Dowager Princess of Bolugayen, Priscilla thought, swallowing bile. But there were two more princesses, waiting to be savaged. "It is the vodka," Rotislav explained. "We gave them much vodka, to make them fight."

Priscilla listened to a tremendous screaming from the guest apartment. That was Sophie, suffering what to her would certainly be a fate worse than death. The nursery door remained locked. Priscilla stood in the midst of a

320

crowd of people, who fondled her body and pulled her hair, slid their hands between her thighs. She hardly knew they were there. Rotislav drew his revolver and fired into the lock, three times. There was a shower of splinters, and one of the bullets ricochetted along the gallery. No one seemed to mind. The door was open. "Go in," Rotislav invited.

Priscilla was not sure she wanted to; she had no idea what she would find. She drew a long breath and opened the door, gazed at the two children, and Sonia and Grishka. Grishka still held her revolver, and this she brought up, and then slowly lowered it again as she gazed at Priscilla. Rotislav made a mock bow, careful to remain standing behind Priscilla. "Your Highness," he said to Sonia.

"Priscilla!" Anna said. "You've nothing on."

Little Alexei started to cry. Priscilla ran forward and lifted him into her arms.

"Here's a present for you, Viktor," Rotislav called, looking at Sonia, who had remained standing absolutely still, her face expressionless. "She's no chicken, but there's meat on those bones."

Nordenski came into the room, and Grishka brought up the revolver again, face rigid with tension. "You promised you'd not harm them," Priscilla shouted.

"The children."

"I meant everyone in the nursery."

Rotislav glanced at her, and grinned. "Well, it'll be an experience, lying with two princesses at the same time. And you'll need a maid. Go find someone else, Viktor."

"I hate you," Anna said.

Rotislav ruffled her hair. "When you've grown a bit, I'll lie with you as well."

The crowd had followed Nordenski back on to the gallery. Only one man had remained, standing in the doorway. "Gleb?" Priscilla whispered.

321

Gleb would not look at her. "I am to be rewarded," he reminded Rotislav. "You promised me."

"Gleb?" Priscilla could not believe it. "You opened those doors? You? You betrayed us?"

Gleb licked his lips. "We could fight no more, Your Highness. Now . . ."

Rotislav gave a shout of laughter. "Now for your reward. Well, take your pick." Gleb looked at Grishka; he had known her all his life. Grishka's lip curled in contempt. Gleb looked at Sonia; he had known her for nearly twenty years. Sonia's face was stony. But both Sonia and Grishka remained fully dressed. Gleb licked his lips again and looked at the naked body of his mistress.

Bolugayen House burned. As it was a very large house, the smoke had to be visible for miles, Priscilla thought. And the flames, for now it was dark. But it had to burn, to take all its terrible secrets with it. Grandma and Sophie, Mademoiselle Friquet and Giselle, Madame Xenia and gallant Morgan. Even the crucified Patricia had been thrown into the flames. They would disappear without trace, all the horror that had been committed on their bodies vanished from human sight. But not from human memory. While the horror that had been committed on *her* body still seethed in her mind and between her legs.

She drew the blanket tighter about herself and Alexei. She had been allowed to dress, but only a single garment, and the night was chill. She sat on the grass on the hill above the house, looking down at the inferno. Sonia sat beside her, Anna on her lap. Sonia had said hardly a word since surrendering to Rotislav. When, as he had promised, he had lain with them both, it had been Sonia he had chosen to enter, and she had looked past his shoulder at Priscilla, lying on his other side, with enormous eyes. But the pain and sorrow those eyes had expressed were felt for her, Priscilla had realised. For what she had been forced to suffer, before them all, her children, and Sonia and

322

Grishka. At least, she thought and prayed, little Alexei did not know what had been happening.

Grishka sat on her other side, knees drawn up and clasped in her arms. Grishka had not even been raped, yet. Most of the men were incapable, now. And beside Sonia sat Janine Grabowska, her grey hair straggling down her back. She had certainly been raped, and beaten; like Priscilla she wore only a single garment. But unlike Sophie and Nathalie, and as Sonia would have recommended, she had not fought her tormentors, and thus she had lived. As she was a married woman, no doubt she was less traumatised by what had happened to her than had been her lover.

"What is to become of us, Your Highness?" she asked, not specifying to which princess she was speaking. "Do you think we could escape?"

"No," Sonia said.

"If we could steal horses, Your Highness . . ." Grishka suggested.

"We would still have nowhere to go," Sonia pointed out. "Rotislav says that Poltava is in the hands of the Revolution."

"Do you think Dagmar got away?" Janine asked.

"As far as Poltava, maybe."

Priscilla hugged Alexei. Whatever she had done, whatever she had accepted, had been for him. She could only pray his father would understand.

Priscilla had had a secret hope, that the soldiers, having helped themselves to everything they could from Bolugayen, would move on, and that most of the villagers would go with them; they had to know there would soon be retribution for their terrible crime. But she was disappointed. It was coming into winter, and to men who had never known anything like it, Bolugayen was a paradise. They were in no hurry to leave this bountiful estate. Well, then, she thought, surely men will come, from Poltava or Kharkov, but no one did. "I thought you said your friend Kerensky was going to civilise the country?" she asked Sonia.

"I don't think he was my friend," Sonia said. "And he certainly seems to be a failure."

"Get on with it," growled the guard.

They were required to work, with the other women, collecting firewood, cooking, caring for the animals. This was decreed by Rotislav, who had taken command; the soldiers just wanted to lie in bed, debauch the women whenever they felt like it, and drink all the vodka and fine wines they had managed to extract from the cellars when the building had cooled. Priscilla had to feel that she and Sonia were actually the lucky ones, because, having been appropriated by the colonel, as Rotislav called himself, they were not required to service any of the others. But he still made them work, and chopping wood was backbreaking to women who had never done any physical labour before; here again Sonia, with her wealth of experience, her years in Irkutsk as a political exile, was their leader, although she was considerably younger than Janine Grabowska. But Janine, revealing unexpected depths of strength and resolution, worked without complaining.

Wrapped up against the cold, they were indistinguishable from the other women. Priscilla had supposed that the muzhik women would make their life hell, but in fact they were surprisingly friendly. Perhaps it had, as Rotislav had said, been only the vodka had turned them in maenads that day. Or perhaps, deep inside their hearts, the sight of their princesses being exposed and raped had touched a chord of feminine sympathy. Now they laughed and joked, and took turns at holding Alexei and bouncing him on their knees. He enjoyed them thoroughly. Anna was not so forgiving. "Are we going to hang all these people when Papa gets home?" she asked.

"Sssh, sweetheart," Sonia said. "We'll talk about that,

when your father gets home." Then she gazed at Priscilla. Who felt an enormous urge to hold her in her arms and hug her and hug her and hug her. They had become utter intimates, and not only in being forced to share the same man. Where once Priscilla had rejected the very thought of Sonia, now she wanted to know everything about her. Because Sonia had endured so much – and she was still alive, so remarkably courageous and self-contained.

Sonia was in fact quite happy to reminisce, although Priscilla felt that her memories were a trifle selective. She would speak of what she had suffered at the hands of the Okhrana, beside which what they had jointly suffered, or were suffering, at the hands of Rotislav, appeared almost gentle. She would speak of her years as Princess of Bolugayen, of the various social and domestic problems which had cropped up. But she would never hear a word against Alexei. Could she really still be in love with him? Priscilla wondered. Sonia would also speak of her life in Petrograd, of the people she had met. She even, now that it was all so firmly in the past, spoke of Rasputin. But she would never speak of Korsakov, and Priscilla also felt that there was someone else from those years of whom she would never speak. But she had no means of finding out.

But Sonia was a constant pillar of support, in a way that Janine, for all her steadfast determination, and Grishka, for all her steadfast loyalty, could never be. Priscilla felt that without her support she might have gone mad. For the future was unthinkable.

The onset of winter was grim, even if they were given shelter in the house Rotislav had appropriated as his own. It had belonged to Father Valentin and was almost a palace compared with most of the houses in the village. Had her people always lived like this? Priscilla wondered, and realised that she had never entered any one of their homes before. She had become quite familiar with them now, with the single huge room built around the central

325

chimney rising out of its iron stove, on which the samovar constantly bubbled, and around which the muzhiks ate and slept, with their animals, in an atmosphere thick enough to be cut with a knife.

But they were alive, and in a singularly Russian fashion, seemed from time to time to be happy. That was more than could be said for Valentin, who had been hanged before his own altar. Once Priscilla had supposed that their deep-seated religious views would be the salvation of these people, and therefore of her. Now she had come to understand that while they might still be as superstitiously religious as ever in the past, they had regarded Valentin as a representative of the social system they had been encouraged to hate. As had been Boscowski. He had been shot on that very first day, when he had attempted to do his duty and restore his people to theirs. With him had died his wife and two small children. Madame Boscowski had been placed naked in a barrel studded on the inside with nails, and rolled up and down the hill. Priscilla could still hear her screams. Geller still lived; they needed him.

Then why was she, the greatest symbol of that dead past, still living? With her son and stepdaughter? Simply because Rotislav had decreed it. Thus, she owed Rotislav her life, and could not yet afford to dream of his death, if she would continue to live. But what did the future hold? The news filtered through soon after Christmas. Kerensky had fled and the Bolsheviks had taken power. Lenin now ruled Russia, with his henchmen, Trotsky and Stalin. Russia was in the hands of the terrorists. Priscilla thought it was a grim irony that Patricia's friendship with Lenin might have ensured their salvation. She mentioned this to Rotislav, as it was his friends who had murdered Patricia. "No one will ever know that," he had said.

Sonia took the news with some consideration. "Lenin was your friend," Priscilla reminded her.

"The Lenins and I were exiled to Irkutsk together. With Patricia. After that . . . one does not become the

Princess Bolugayevska and remain the friend of a man like Lenin."

"Oh. You mean he would not help us?"

"I doubt he even knows we are alive," Sonia said. "Or cares."

"Did you know any of the others?"

"Yes. I knew one of the others," Sonia said. "But he would not help us either, now."

So there is no hope for us, Priscilla thought. We are doomed to remain the sexual slaves of a monster. She, more than any of the others, because she was very much the youngest. But there was far more than herself to worry about. Anna was growing up; she might only be nine years old, but she was a most lovely child. Priscilla knew that Sonia worried about the little girl as well, and not only sexually. As the winter fastened its grip on the community they began to run out of food and fuel. Sonia's only solace was that their situation had brought her daughter back to her. But Priscilla's fears for Alexei were even greater. He was three years old and a sturdy little boy, and Rotislav was never cruel to him, although he did insist on giving him vodka to drink. But he too was not getting the right diet, or enough of what he did eat, and although he was still a small child Priscilla could not help but wonder how much he was taking in of their surroundings, so different to anything he had known before – or how much he was capable of understanding her relationship with Rotislav. In any event, he would soon *have* to become aware of it.

Sometimes Priscilla considered suicide. But it was not in her nature. She could not believe that God had allowed her to survive the tragedy of the *Titanic* in order to have her kill herself because she was being raped on a daily basis. Besides, life had been so good before, she had to believe it would one day be that good again. In any event, she could not possibly abandon little Alexei, or take him with her into the dark corridors of eternity before he had

327

had a chance to live. Even these sane reflections did not stop her from feeling she was going mad, despite Sonia's company. "Aren't you interested in this new government in Petrograd?" she asked Rotislav.

"I am as interested in them as they are in me," he replied.

"But . . . you cannot mean just to squat here forever?"

"Why not?" He squeezed her bottom. "I have everything I need."

"There is no medicine."

"You've been talking with Geller, have you? So we'll manage without medicine."

"But there isn't enough food."

"There is never enough food, in the winter. It'll soon be spring. Then we'll get some food in Poltava to tide us over to the harvest."

"What are you going to use for money?"

He grinned, and gave her another squeeze. "We'll use you and Sonia, on the streets of Poltava if necessary."

Geller shared her fears and her misery. He was doing the best he could, but without any medical supplies he had a hopeless task. "I suspect Rotislav *wishes* all the old people to die off," he told Priscilla. "Well, they are doing that."

"If only we had some news of what is happening, somewhere, anywhere," Priscilla said. "Even in Poltava. They must know we are here."

"They know Rotislav is here," Geller said. "I imagine they assume *we* are all dead. You at the least, Your Highness. As for Rotislav, as they know he is supported by fifty armed men, they are probably happy to leave things alone."

"But what about things like laws, and taxes. All governments need those things. Won't they come here eventually?"

"I am sure you're right, whenever next there is a

government. There's not much suggestion of anything more than anarchy, at the moment."

With the first promise of spring, Priscilla walked across to look at the snow-covered mound which had been the house. She had not done this before; the memory of that terrible day was too fresh. But now the snow was melting, and the gaunt timbers were pushing their way up. The gates still stood, but the gardens and the orchard were a mass of weeds. Worse yet, the cemetery behind the house, where the Bolugayevskis had been buried for three hundred years, had been desecrated, the coffins dug up and torn open, the skeletons thrown about as heaps of bones. Thank God Grandmama had never been interred there, Priscilla thought, and wondered what had happened to Dagmar, or if she was dead in a gutter in Poltava?

She heard a footstep, and turned her head. Sonia stood behind her. "They'll rebuild it," Sonia said. "When this is over. *You'll* rebuild it, Your Highness."

"You will help me, Your Highness," Priscilla replied.

They smiled at each other, and even moved towards each other, and heard the sound of hooves. They turned together to stare at the lone horseman, coming down the road from Poltava. Insensibly they now did move together, holding hands. He drew rein, looked at the gate posts and the trampled earth, the wreck of the house. "Where is Colonel Rotislav?"

"In the village."

"Take me to him," the horseman commanded. "Haste, women. This is urgent." Priscilla and Sonia exchanged glances, but they had become used to taking orders. Besides, this man wore uniform, was armed with both sword and revolver, and had an air of authority; there was a little red star in the front centre of his schlem. They led the horseman into the village, at times having to run to keep up with his trotting horse. But at the first houses he drew rein.

"There are no sentries or lookouts."

"No," Priscilla agreed.

He kicked his horse forward. One or two people came to their doorways to look at him. "I was told there were fifty soldiers here," the man said.

"There are," Sonia said.

"Where are they?"

Sonia waved her arm. "Around."

"Fools. Where is this so-called colonel?"

"This is the house," Priscilla told him, and opened the door.

The horseman dismounted and stamped inside. Priscilla and Sonia followed him. Rotislav was reclining on the bed they all shared. He had not yet dressed himself for the day. Anna and Alexei played in the corner, but looked up with interest at the appearance of a stranger. So did Grishka, who was making tea. Janine was in bed with Rotislav; she sat up in alarm, the sheet held to her throat. Rotislav also sat up. "What the devil . . ."

"You may well say that, Comrade," said the stranger. "You are he calling himself Colonel Rotislav?"

"I am Colonel Rotislav," Rotislav said, with an attempt at dignity.

"Then act like a colonel. Get up and get dressed. Summon your people and put this village in a state of defence. There is a regiment of White cavalry not fifty miles away."

"A regiment . . ." Rotislav scratched his head, clearly not understanding. "Who are you?"

"I am Commissar Denovich. I am from General Trotsky's army."

Priscilla heard a sharp intake of breath from Sonia.

"General Trotsky?" Rotislav asked. "Who the hell is General Trotsky?"

Commissar Denovich advanced to stand beside the bed. "Are you for the Revolution?"

"I am for the Revolution."

330

"Because if you are not, I will have you shot. I may have you shot in any event. I may shoot you myself." He rested his gloved hand on his revolver holster. Rotislav attempted to back across the bed, and bumped into Janine, who had lain down again, the blanket still held to her throat. "As you appear to be totally ignorant of the world in which you live, Comrade," Denovich said. "I will give you a last chance to prove that you *deserve* to live. Listen very carefully. The Tsarists and dissidents calling themselves the White Army are advancing from the Crimea, and as I have told you, there is at least one of their cavalry regiments not fifty miles south of here. They will arrive here tomorrow at the latest." Sonia's hand stole into Priscilla's. "Coming down from the north," Denovich went on, "is General Trotsky's Red Army, under the personal command of the general. His train will be in Poltava the day after tomorrow. It is his intention to smash this White advance, and he will do so, because they have no idea that he is anywhere close. It is therefore vital that they do not find out until it is too late for them to retreat. If they reach Poltava before the General, they will surely learn of his advance. Therefore it is the General's orders that you and your men hold this village against them, and prevent their further advance."

Rotislav gulped. "But . . . you spoke of a regiment."

"Six hundred sabres."

"I have only fifty men. We must be reinforced if we are to hold."

"There can be no reinforcement until the day after tomorrow."

"Then we will all be killed."

"If you are killed, you will have died for the Revolution. There is no finer end. Remember, you must hold out for at least twenty-four hours. Then you may retreat. Do you understand me?"

Rotislav swallowed. "Yes, Comrade Commissar."

"Very good. I will report to General Trotsky that the village will be held."

"But . . . suppose this regiment bypasses the village, Comrade Commissar?"

"It will not. It will come here before advancing on Poltava."

"How can you know that, Comrade Commissar?" Rotislav's voice was almost a whine.

"Because the commander of the White regiment comes from this village, and will certainly wish to return here. He calls himself Prince Alexei Bolugayevski."

The Commissar left immediately, unaware of the psychological bomb he had just tossed into the bedroom. Sonia followed him, and they spoke for some moments before he mounted his horse and trotted out of the village, watched by an increasing number of people. Then Sonia returned into the house. Rotislav appeared to be quite speechless, which Priscilla supposed had to be a blessing: if he had told the Commissar who they were they might have been shot on the spot. But then, she was speechless herself. Alexei was after all, alive, and coming towards her. And what would he find? A woman who had been raped and beaten. But he would also find . . . she glanced at Sonia. Sonia's face was stony. She had not expected ever to have to face her ex-husband again.

They both looked at Rotislav, who was slowly getting out of bed. Now he looked at them in turn. He was trembling as he pulled on his pants. "You think your knight in white armour is going to come galloping up to your rescue," he said. "We'll see about that." He buttoned his shirt, walked to the door, pushing them to one side. "Up, up," he bellowed. "Everybody up. We have a battle to fight." Now people poured from doorways; the last thing any of the soldiers had anticipated was having to fight a battle, on Bolugayen. They gathered around Rotislav, everyone talking at once.

"What are we going to do?" Priscilla asked. "Alexei . . ."

"The Prince!" Grishka said, eyes shining.

"Daddy!" Anna jumped up and down. "Daddy's coming!"

Little Alexei gazed at his sister with enormous eyes.

"They will murder us," Janine said. "Before they let us be rescued. You heard what he said."

Priscilla looked at Sonia. "We will have to see," Sonia said. "We must first of all discover what Rotislav plans."

Her calmness was quite startling, and almost frightening. Priscilla could not help but wonder if she was planning some kind of mass suicide. How the wheel does turn, she thought; now she was the one who would resist that.

Alexei was not fifty miles away, and coming towards her!

Rotislav was giving orders, and the men were reluctantly gathering their weapons, rusting now it was so long since they had been used or oiled. Sonia went outside. "Why did you let that man order you around?" she asked. "He was one man. You had fifty at your call. Yet you obeyed him like a slave."

He gave her an impatient glance. "He was a commissar. You do not understand these things. Commissars are the rulers of Russia under Lenin and Trotsky. They have powers of life and death. No one can oppose a commissar. Except perhaps Lenin and Trotsky."

"Is Trotsky that powerful?"

"You heard the Commissar. Trotsky commands the Red Army. He is the most powerful man in Russia. Only the fact that he is a Jew prevents him from being more powerful than Lenin."

"I see," Sonia said thoughtfully. "So you will fight and die, at his command. You will die, you know, Rotislav. You cannot hope to defend this place against a regiment of cavalry."

Rotislav grinned. "Maybe not. But I have resources the

333

Commissar knew nothing of. I know things that no one else knows. Your husband is coming."

"Not my husband," Sonia said. "Not any more."

"Do you think that matters? When we were in prison together, he told me, how much he loved you, how much he hated what he had had to do. How much he regretted it." He looked past her, and Sonia turned, to see Priscilla standing in the doorway, her face pale. Now he laughed out loud. "But he loves you too, Princess. He adores you. He dreams of your body every night. There is a confused fellow, eh? But his confusion is my power. I hold the two women he loves, and I hold his daughter. And I hold his son and heir. Oh, yes, he told me about that, too. Your babe is his heir, Priscilla, because he has no Jewish blood. So he will never take Bolugayen, if it would cost your lives. Rather will he turn back when I tell him to, and I will be congratulated by Trotsky, and perhaps made a general myself, eh?"

Priscilla but her lip, and looked at Sonia. But Sonia's expression had not changed. "Back in the house," Rotislav told them. "In there, and stay there. You and you," he bawled. "Mount guard on this house. Let no one in or out save on my orders. The rest of you, come with me." Sonia was pushed inside and the door shut.

"Isn't Daddy coming?" Anna asked.

"Yes, sweetheart, he is coming," Sonia assured her.

"We are going to be killed," Janine moaned. "I know it. I feel it in my bones."

"We should have been killed six months ago," Sonia reminded her. "And we are still alive." Grishka fell to her knees and began to pray. Priscilla sat on the bed, and Sonia sat beside her. "I would not let what Rotislav said upset you," she recommended. "You are Alexei's wife."

"I doubt that, in the eyes of God."

Sonia sighed. "I'm afraid it is difficult to believe in God any more, after what we have seen and experienced."

"Do you want to see him again?"

Sonia considered. "Yes," she said at last. "I would like to see him again. But I wish to see Colin more."

"I know. To have him so close, and yet . . . are we going to die, Sonia?"

Sonia's smile was grim. "Not if we are sufficiently determined to live."

Rotislav had apparently determined that only the village was capable of being defended, and instead of attempting to create a position to the south, he placed his men in the houses commanding the road. The women watched from the window of their prison. "He is laying a trap," Priscilla said. "They will all be killed."

"I do not think Rotislav is laying a trap," Sonia said. "He knows this rabble of his cannot stand up to a regiment of professionals, even if he manages to kill a few in an ambush. He wants to be close to his trumps." She smiled at them all. "Us."

Priscilla could not doubt that Sonia had determined upon a course of action, she was so composed and relaxed. The thought terrified her, because it could only be violent, and perhaps fatal. But as Sonia would not confide in her, she could only do the same as everyone else, and wait. Food was brought to them, but they were at least spared a visit from Rotislav. Priscilla spent the afternoon playing with Alexei, who was as usual totally oblivious that there was a crisis – the poor little boy had lived just about all his life in an atmosphere of crisis.

Sonia spent her time with Anna. They were both, Priscilla felt, saying goodbye to their children even if they would not admit it, even to themselves.

It was late afternoon when Grishka, who was at the window, said, "They are here, Your Highnesses."

All the women joined her. From the window they looked straight down the village street, and beyond, to the road which wound its way into the distant trees.

335

And along the road there came a body of five horsemen, walking their mounts, carbines drawn from their scabbards and hafts resting on their knees. Each man was also armed with a sword. "If only we could warn them," Priscilla muttered.

"They do not need warning," Sonia assured her. "Rotislav knows his only hope is to negotiate."

"Look there," Janine said.

The advance guard was almost up to the houses. Now the rest of the regiment debouched from the wood, a splendid body of men, similarly ready for a fight. At their head rode several officers. "Alexei," Priscilla breathed, and hugged her son to her breast. Alexei looked, as always, handsome, dignified and totally confident. Sonia said nothing, but she rested her hand on Anna's shoulder to prevent the girl from crying out.

The door of one of the houses opened, and Rotislav stepped on to the street. At the sight of him, the sergeant commanding the advance guard held up his hand, and the horsemen drew rein. "Who are you?" the sergeant demanded. The women could hear his voice quite clearly in the still afternoon air.

"I am Colonel Stanislav Rotislav."

"Serving with which army?"

"I serve the Red Army of General Trotsky."

"Then you are under arrest. Throw down your weapons."

Rotislav grinned at him. "I have fifty men armed with rifles in these houses." The sergeant looked left and right, and several rifle barrels protruded from the various windows. Priscilla found she was holding her breath, and Alexei so tightly that he was beginning to squirm. "Do not be afraid," Rotislav said. "I would speak with your commanding officer."

Alexei had been walking his horse forward while the parley was going on. He was followed by a youthful cornet. "Colin," Sonia breathed. Priscilla had to bite her lip to stop *herself* from precipitating a crisis by shouting.

"Rotislav?" Alexei asked. "By God, man, but it is good to see you. What nonsense is this?"

"No nonsense, Prince Alexei. I am for the Reds."

"Then you are a fool, and a traitor, and I will have to hang you."

"I would ask you to reconsider, Prince Alexei."

"Because of your fifty men?" Alexei asked, contemptuously.

"Because of my prisoners," Rotislav said.

Alexei frowned. "Prisoners?"

"Your family, Prince Alexei."

"My family are dead. Murdered by the Reds. Murdered . . ." he checked as the penny dropped.

Rotislav half turned, and gestured at the prison house. "In there, Prince Alexei, I hold both your wives, your son and your daughter."

Alexei stared at him. "*Both* my wives. And my son?"

"Oh, indeed, my lord prince. I have a full hand."

Alexei almost glanced at Colin, whose face was rigid. Then he looked straight again. "Do you expect me to believe you?"

"I expect that you will wish to see for yourself," Rotislav said. "I offer you free entry into my village for that purpose. But you will tell your men to cease their advance."

"You will return to the command, Cornet Bolugayevski," Alexei said. "And hold your men until further orders."

"But, sir . . ." Colin protested.

"That is an order," Alexei said, and walked his horse forward, accompanied now only by his standard bearer.

"Will you not dismount?" Rotislav invited. Alexei dismounted, handing his reins to the trooper. "This way," Rotislav said, with the utmost politeness. They walked up the street together. "Ladies," Rotislav called.

337

"Will you please come out. All of you. Including the children."

Sonia glanced at Priscilla; both women were terribly aware that in their torn and stained gowns, bare and dirty feet and wearing their bandannas, they looked less like princesses than the peasants they had been forced to become. Equally she could tell from Priscilla's pink cheeks and quickened breathing that the younger woman was every bit as nervous as herself. But this was the moment for which they had both forced themselves to survive. She held Anna's hand, in her left hand, and walked through the door. The guard stood to attention. Priscilla took little Alexei in her arms, and followed. Grishka and Janine brought up the rear.

"Your family, Prince Alexei," Rotislav said. "All that is left of them, at any rate." Alexei gazed at Sonia, his cheeks flushed, then he looked at Priscilla, and the baby boy.

"You will, of course, wish to regain possession of your women and children," Rotislav said. Alexei looked at him.

"I am perfectly willing to return them to you," Rotislav said. "If you agree to my terms."

"Which are?" Alexei's words were like drops of ice.

"That you withdraw your force for a distance of fifty miles. Some of my men will accompany you. Once your withdrawal has been made, one of my people will return to inform me, and I will send my prisoners to you."

"You expect me to trust you?" Alexei said.

Rotislav made a mock bow. "You have no choice, unless you wish to see your wives hanged before your eyes. I am being very generous, Your Highness."

Alexei hesitated. "As you say, I have no choice. I will withdraw my men."

He turned, and Sonia stepped forward. "Have we no say in this?" she demanded.

Rotislav grinned at her. "None at all, Princess. This is men's business."

"You are mistaken, wretched man," Sonia said, and drew her hand from beneath her shawl. It held a revolver, and before anyone could move she had levelled it and shot Rotislav in the groin; he gave a shriek and fell to the ground, clutching his shattered genitals. In almost the same movement Sonia continued to turn and shot the guard through the chest, while completing a full circle and shouting at the top of her voice, "Charge, Colin! Charge!" That done, she grabbed Priscilla by the shoulder and hurled her at the door, following her with the other women; Grishka paused long enough to pick up the guard's rifle and bandolier. Alexei took in the situation as the men in the houses began to stir into action, and ran behind the women. Sonia admitted him, and then closed and bolted the door.

"Sonia!" he gasped, and she was in his arms. Then he looked past her at Priscilla, and slowly released her. "Priscilla!"

Priscilla did not move. "Where did you get that gun?" she asked.

Sonia smiled. "I asked the Commissar for it. I told him we wanted to kill Whites as much as anyone, and he gave it to me." She went to the window, gazed at the writhing, moaning Rotislav, then levelled the gun and shot him through the head.

Bullets thudded into the walls of the house, but now they were overtaken by the bugle call as the cavalry charged.

Alexei continued to stare at Priscilla for a few seconds, then he drew his revolver and joined Sonia and Grishka at the window to return fire. But the Reds were already distracted by the charging cavalry, firing their carbines to smother the houses in bullets and then drawing their sabres to complete their victory. The Reds came out of their houses with their hands up, demoralised at once by the death of their leader and the sudden overturn in their fortunes. Nordenski was the first to emerge.

Colin brought his horse steaming to a halt in front of

339

the prison house, and leapt from the saddle, as his father and the women came out. "That was a very brave thing you did, Mother," he said, and was in Sonia's arms. It had been seven years since he had seen her, and then he had been only eleven – but it might have been yesterday.

Prince Alexei Bolugayevski stood in what had once been his front drive and looked at the burned-out shell of his house. "We fought virtually to the last bullet." Sonia was at his side. "But we were betrayed."

"Aunt Anna?"

"Died quickly, and in the midst of battle." ·

"Thank God for that."

"She was more fortunate than either of your sisters," Sonia said.

Alexei turned and looked back at the gate posts, gaunt in the gloom of the evening. "Yet I am more fortunate than most," he said, half to himself.

"You must go to her," Sonia said. "And make her realise that she is still your wife." He made no reply, continued gazing into the darkness. "She is every inch the Princess Bolugayevska," Sonia said. "She managed the estate for you all the while you were away. She bore you a son. She fought as hard as anyone. And when she surrendered, it was to save the children. Your children."

"How much did she surrender?" he asked.

"Everything. As did I. As did we all, to survive."

"Then those people in the village are all guilty."

"Every last one, save Dr Geller. But she is not guilty, Alexei. She is your wife, and you could not have a better one."

He sighed. "And you?"

"You must give me the time to think. I need a home. I was going to Trishka, but now . . ."

"This is your home, Sonia. I committed a great crime when I drove you away from it."

She rested her hand on his arm. "Alexei, Bolugayen is

340

nobody's home now. You and Priscilla and the children also have to find a new home."

"Sevastopol," he said. "They will live in Sevastopol, until we have won this war, then we will come back here and rebuild Bolugayen."

"I wish you joy of it."

"But you will not be here? Do you think I can ever let you walk away into the unknown, now?"

"Dear Alexei," Sonia said. "You cannot stop me walking away from you. I am no longer your wife."

The regiment bivouacked in and around the village. Camp fires were lit, and the men settled down to a comfortable night, after their arduous march. The prisoners, men and women and children, were herded together in adjacent houses under guard. Alexei embraced Geller, listened to the tale of the murders of Father Valentin and the Boscowskis with a grim face, but he smiled when he saw Gleb. "You old reprobate," he said. "You are a survivor."

"He raped the Princess," Grishka spat.

Alexei looked at the butler, then at Priscilla, who stood with shoulders bowed. Gleb fell to his knees. "Mercy, Your Highness," he said. "I have been a good and faithful servant, except for that moment of madness."

"He was also the one who opened the doors and let the Reds in," Sonia said.

Alexei's face hardened. "Put him with the others."

"Mercy!" Gleb howled as he was dragged away. "Mercy."

"Are you going to execute him?" Priscilla asked. They lay in bed together, but both had remained fully dressed. Neither knew how to resume their marriage. They had not even kissed.

"Are you going to ask for his life?" Alexei countered.

"No," Priscilla said. "Not for raping me. But for

betraying us all, including his own people, the servants."
She rose on her elbow. "Is that wrong of me?"

"That is right of you." Alexei continued to lie on his
back, staring up at the darkness.

She bit her lip. "About . . . what happened."

"Sonia has told me you had no choice. I understand
that."

"She is so brave, and so strong. She never wept. I wept.
I did not beg, Alexei. I never begged for myself. But I
told Rotislav I would not fight him if he would spare the
children. I thought that is what Aunt Anna would have
done."

"That is what Aunt Anna would have done, yes. I am
proud of you."

"If only we had known what had happened to you . . ."

"By the time the Germans released me, the Army had
already been taken over by the Reds. But I knew Denikin
was raising a counter-revolutionary force in the Crimea,
so I made my way there. I had been told you were all
dead, you see. I was seeking only revenge. But now, to
find you all alive . . ."

He had used the word, all. "Do you wish me to go back
to Boston? Then you and Sonia . . ."

At last his head turned, his face a blur in the darkness.
"You are my wife, and the Princess Bolugayevska. You
are also the mother of my son and heir."

"But Colin . . ."

"Colin understands the situation, and accepts it." She
heard him smile in the darkness. "I think he is rather
relieved."

"And for those reasons you wish me to stay." She lay
down again.

Now it was his turn to rise on his elbow. "I forgot to add,
that I love you, have always loved you, and will always love
you." He lowered his face to hers.

They were awakened by a rifle shot. Alexei leapt out

of bed, dragging on his clothes as he ran to the door. Colin was already dressed and on the street. They gazed at the sole horseman who had been checked by the shot from the sentry, and now sat his mount some fifty yards up the road leading from Poltava. "That is Commissar Denovich," Sonia said.

"You are our prisoner," Alexei called. "Dismount and raise your arms." Denovich obeyed. He looked totally confounded. But not afraid. "Now advance," Alexei commanded.

Denovich came towards them, hands held high. "That traitor Rotislav," he remarked.

"Rotislav is dead," Alexei said. "And his people are my prisoners. As are you."

"You are dreaming, Colonel," Denovich said. "You are *my* prisoners. I came here to tell Rotislav that he need no longer defend this village, because General Trotsky advanced more quickly than he had hoped. You are virtually surrounded."

It was Alexei's turn to look confounded. "Where is General Trotsky?" Sonia asked.

"He has made his headquarters in Poltava. He but awaits my information as to your whereabouts before resuming his advance."

"But as you will not be returning with any information," Alexei said, "he will not move."

Denovich grinned. "If I am not back by noon he will resume his advance in any event. You may be able to get out of here in time, Colonel, but General Denikin's army is lost. He does not know we are here. But we know where he is." Alexei bit his lip, knowing that the Commissar was stating nothing but the truth, in the circumstances. "Of course, you could sacrifice yourself and your men by attempting to hold this village," Denovich suggested, slyly. "Then, as General Trotsky is well supplied with artillery, you will all die. But . . ." he shrugged. "You are all going to die in any event."

343

"Take him away," Alexei snapped. Two of his men marched Denovich away. "You and the children at least must get out, immediately," Alexei said.

"No," Priscilla said. "After so long, to send us away? And what are we, without you?"

Alexei gazed at Sonia. "Walk with me," she invited. He hesitated, glanced at Priscilla, and then followed his first wife to the side of the road. "You are keeping Denovich a prisoner?" Sonia asked.

"I shall probably hang him. But as I expect he's telling the truth, I don't think it'll do us much good."

"Listen to me. Mount up your men, and Priscilla and the children, and leave Bolugayen. Get back to your General Denikin and tell him what is happening."

Alexei's expression was almost pitying. "Sonia, I am four days away from Denikin. Even supposing I can get to him at all. If Trotsky's men are already south of Poltava, then they are already south of Bolugayen. I cannot fight my way through with Priscilla and the children. I can ride round them, I think, but then I could only reach Denikin at virtually the same time as Trotsky's people. There would be no time either to retreat or set up an adequate defence."

"How much time would you need?"

"Oh . . . twenty-four hours start, certainly."

"I give you that time."

"You?"

"Leon Trotsky and I are old friends. We are lovers, Alexei. Don't look at me like that. When you turned me out to sink or swim on my own, I determined to swim, and to do that I had to accept some very strange bedfellows. But Trotsky is different. I am special to him. I ran away from him, over a year ago. Now I will go back to him. And I will guarantee that when I do that, you will have your twenty-four hours, at least."

His frown was the deepest she had ever seen. "But . . .

344

you say you ran away from him? How can you be sure he will not have you shot?"

I will love you forever, Leon had said. Had he meant it? "I cannot be sure. But I am sure he will not even do that, until he has . . . renewed our acquaintance. For at least twenty-four hours."

He gazed at her as if she were a stranger. Well, she thought, no doubt I am, now.

"You would take that risk, for me?"

"No, Alexei. Oh, I still love you, I think. But that is feminine weakness; you are not really worthy of my love. I will do it for the sake of Colin and Anna. I have nothing to offer them, now, and perhaps you still do. And I know Priscilla has been a good mother to Anna, and will be to Colin. But I will do it for her sake, too. On the off chance that you may prove worthy of *her* love." She turned away. "I will use Denovich's horse."

He caught her arm. "Sonia. It is not quite as simple as you think. If you go back to that man, to those people, you are going to be identified with the Reds. When this war is over, you may find yourself in serious trouble. Even I may not be able to save you."

Sonia smiled. "What makes you suppose you are going to win?"

"We have all the officers, all the expertise. We are professional soldiers. They are a rabble. How can we not win?"

"And your cause?"

"Well . . . rescuing the Tsar from his captivity in Siberia, and restoring him to the throne."

"I think the men against whom you are fighting, to whom I am going, have a greater cause than that: the possession of Russia for themselves."

"And you can believe that they will rule it for the people? My God, you have seen their atrocities for yourself. You have suffered for them."

345

"Are you going to hang the people in the village? They were once *your* people."

"I am going to hang them because they have turned against me, against the rule of law."

"The rule of law, Prince Alexei, is what the man in power considers to be the law. You happen to be in power here, now, so your decision is the law. But I doubt you will always be in power. Then someone else may make the law. I agree, it will probably be bad law, but at least I can play my part in alleviating the worst of it. As for you, Alexei, when next we meet, I may not be able to save *you*. Remember that."

Priscilla watched her friend walk the horse out of the village and on to the road to Poltava.

"Where can she be going?" she asked.

"Mount up!" Alexei shouted at his men. Then he turned to his wife. "She is going to her destiny. I think we should now hurry to ours."